A Time to Rejoice

ANNA JACOBS

A Time to Rejoice

HODDER &
STOUGHTON

First published in Great Britain in 2016 by Hodder & Stoughton
An Hachette UK company

1

Copyright © Anna Jacobs 2016

A CIP catalogue record for this title is available from the British Library

Hardback ISBN 978 1 444 78778 8
Trade Paperback ISBN 978 1 444 78777 1
eBook ISBN 978 1 444 78776 4

Typeset in Plantin Light by Palimpsest Book Production Limited,
Falkirk, Stirlingshire

Printed and bound by Clays Ltd, St Ives plc

Hodder & Stoughton policy is to use papers that are natural,
renewable and recyclable products and made from wood grown in sustainable
forests. The logging and manufacturing processes are expected to conform
to the environmental regulations of the country of origin.

Hodder & Stoughton Ltd
Carmelite House
50 Victoria Embankment
London EC4Y 0DZ

www.hodder.co.uk

*In loving memory of our dear friend
Rosalind Anne Merefield, who passed away
in September 2015 and who is sorely missed.*

I

In Hertfordshire, Francis Brady put down his spade and wiped the sweat from his brow with the back of his forearm. His heart lifted when he saw his wife approaching. Diana looked so pretty with her curly brown hair tied back with a red scarf. She'd walked across the village to see him, so maybe she'd got over their quarrel.

He watched her pick her way across the rubble where his family's garage and house had once stood. A stray bomb had scored a direct hit last year, the only one to land in the village, probably being dumped as the plane flew back to Germany. The bomb had destroyed everything and killed his parents instantly.

Diana scowled at him and his heart sank. She couldn't have come because she'd changed her mind about helping him, then.

He waited for her to speak and when she didn't, he tried to coax her. 'If you'd just pick up these bricks as I dig them out of the rubble and stack them over there, I could finish work more quickly, then we could—'

She set her hands on her hips. 'Why do you insist on doing this, Francis? You've been slaving away for days now, coming home filthy, with your hands all rough. And for what? To make a few measly shillings.'

'Pounds, not shillings, and I've made far more than I'd

expected, actually. Why do you ask when you know perfectly well why I want to make the extra money?'

'But there's no point to it! I met my father as I came through the village and he said again that you could sell this plot of land as it is. *You* aren't going to build anything on it, after all, so there's no *need* for you to clear the rubble. You've had a good offer already and my father says you can easily push the price up a bit.'

'I'll sell the land when I'm good and ready, *and* I'll get a much higher price for it than has been offered by your father's friend. But first I'm going to finish salvaging anything that's sellable. Whole bricks make nearly as much money as new ones since the war ended, because of the scarcity of building materials, and so do pieces of decent milled timber, even the short ones that have had one end blown off.'

She let out an exaggerated sigh. 'It's not worth the extra trouble and even if it was, I don't intend to ruin *my* hands by working like a navvy.'

He looked at her without a word. Two years previously he had fallen in love with Diana on sight and she with him. They'd got married after a few weeks, like many other couples in the war years, but he hadn't realised how hard she'd be to live with, how much time and money it took to maintain her immaculate appearance . . . or how unused she was to hard work. No, he definitely hadn't expected that.

He tried to speak patiently, though he was only repeating what he'd already said a dozen times. 'It *is* worth the trouble, Diana. You have to make the most of every single penny when you're starting up a new business.'

'*You* aren't a businessman! You're a mechanic. You'd be taking a huge risk and you might lose everything.'

There she went again, being scornful about his background. This usually happened after she'd been with her damned father. 'Being a mechanic doesn't mean I'm stupid, Diana.'

'Then be sensible. My father knows someone who'll give you a job, with the chance to become chief mechanic when the old one retires. That way you won't have to work such long hours. And once you've sold your parents' land, we'll have enough money to buy a decent house without borrowing anything.'

He looked at her in shock. 'We've already got a nice house.'

She went pink. 'Ah. Well. I didn't make a fuss because of the war, but our present house is rather small and . . . well, ordinary. I couldn't think of starting a family till we've got somewhere better to live and bring up our children.'

Francis could hear his own voice grow suddenly harsher and didn't care. 'How many times do I have to tell you that I don't *want* to work for anyone else, especially one of your father's friends. That man treats his staff badly, which is why he has trouble keeping anyone for long.'

He looked round with pride at what he'd accomplished. 'I'm getting to the end of the salvage work now. Come on, Diana. Lend me a hand. You don't need to damage your hands. I've got some working gloves you can put on.'

She took a step backwards, shaking her head vigorously. 'No! I wasn't brought up to do rough work and if you cared about me, you wouldn't even ask. Besides, it looks like rain.'

He looked up at the sky. 'Maybe a light shower. A bit of rain won't hurt you.'

'It'll make a mess of my hair. I said no and I meant it. Oh, there's no talking sense to you!' She stormed off down the street.

He saw the envelope sticking out of her coat pocket and yelled after her, 'Don't forget to post my letter!' She'd walked right past the post box on the way here. Why hadn't she popped the letter in then?

She didn't answer, but he saw her finger the corner of the envelope, so he knew she'd heard him.

Feeling depressed about their quarrels, which seemed to be getting steadily worse, he continued to sort through the rubble. Thieves had stolen the first pile of bricks he'd retrieved, so he slept here in his car whenever the builder couldn't collect the day's piles of salvage at teatime.

Diana hated him doing that, too. But he had to protect his property because there were looters everywhere since the war.

It disgusted him. He'd put his life on the line to defend his country and now the war was over, some people were ready to steal from him. Well, he wasn't going to let thieves make off with the fruits of his hard work. The building company he and his friends were going to set up in Rivenshaw was his big chance to make something of himself. He needed money to invest in it, wanted to be a partner, not an employee.

He took a breather and glanced round, remembering what it had once looked like, with the garage right next to the house and the vegetable garden on the other side. He'd grown up here, enjoying a very happy childhood. He'd only known Diana by sight in those days, because she came from the posh side of the village and went away to boarding school for most of the year.

When his parents were first married, they'd started up a bicycle repair business in a wooden shed and had sold petrol in big square cans. Each can had held two gallons, if he remembered correctly. Too heavy for a little boy to lift when he desperately wanted to help, but they'd found him other jobs and he'd been proud to do them well. *He* had never stood by and watched others work.

His parents had saved their money and bought this piece of land when he was about ten. He remembered them standing hugging one another next to the tumbledown old cottage, their eyes full of dreams.

After that, his father had started repairing motor cars as

well as bicycles. They'd installed one of the new petrol pumps, too, instead of selling cans of petrol. And they'd all lived in the cottage, happy to be together, doing the place up bit by bit. He doubted his mother had ever worried about breaking her nails.

Francis had picked up a lot of his father's mechanical skills even before he was old enough to do an apprenticeship with a qualified motor mechanic. He'd intended to go into the family business and had planned to sell cars later on. Ordinary cars for ordinary families.

Then the war had intervened and he'd been called up. He'd managed to get posted to work on maintaining equipment and had joined the Royal Corps of Electrical and Mechanical Engineers after it was formed in October 1942. He'd learned so much about modern electrical equipment in the army.

He was down to the foundation of what had been his home now. Tears welled in his eyes and he brushed them away with his sleeve. His parents should be here with him, enjoying the fruits of their hard work. He still missed them, turned round to ask his dad something or saw a woman selling flowers in the street and thought of buying a bunch for his mum.

He could never take money for granted, as Diana did. Her father was a solicitor like his father before him, so the Scammells were comfortably off. They hadn't approved of their daughter's marriage, even though Francis had been promoted to captain by that time.

Her father had even offered him money not to marry her, claiming they were too different to make a go of it, but Francis and Diana were both over twenty-one, so could do as they pleased. He'd never told her about that offer because she idolised her father. In the end, Mr Scammell had come round and insisted on arranging the wedding, so that it wouldn't shame the family. What a waste of money that had been!

But perhaps Mr Scammell had been right, after all. Perhaps Francis and Diana weren't suited.

One of the other chaps involved, Mayne Esher, owned a run-down old manor house and several acres of land in Rivenshaw, a small Lancashire town. The house had been requisitioned during the war, but had been returned to the family a month before the war in Europe ended. It was obvious by then that the Allies were going to win, so the government had started shedding its wartime acquisitions and gearing up for peace.

Sadly, Mayne didn't have enough money to restore Esherwood and live there. Like many other places, it had been carelessly damaged by its wartime occupants. But it was large enough to be converted into several luxury flats, perhaps even as many as twelve, which could then be sold at a profit. After that, the Esher Building Company would build houses on the rest of the land and sell those.

Francis was getting rather worried, though, because he'd written to Mayne after VE Day and again after VJ Day, when the war finally ended in the Far East, and he hadn't heard back. That puzzled him and he still didn't know if they were on track to start their business.

No, of course the project would still be a goer. He'd trust these particular friends with his life.

He'd asked Diana to find out if the Eshers were on the phone, and she'd discovered that the Rivenshaw telephone exchange had been badly damaged by bombs and was still being repaired.

That wouldn't have stopped Mayne getting in touch, so perhaps he had a family crisis or something had gone wrong at Esherwood. It wasn't going to be easy for anyone, authorities or citizens, to adjust to peace.

If Francis hadn't been so busy, he'd have nipped up to Lancashire to find out what was going on and why his letters hadn't been answered. But if he left the block unattended, it'd be looted.

Perhaps their building company wouldn't get off the ground. In that case Francis would start up in business for himself, though that'd have to be in a much smaller way. He was determined not to work for anyone else. He'd had enough of being ordered around during the war, thank you very much, more than enough.

Nor was he going to live near the Scammells. His marriage would have no chance with them interfering.

Besides, what Diana conveniently ignored in all this was the reason he'd managed to get demobbed early: the fact that he was going to work in the building industry. As long as he did that, he could stay out of the army. If he worked at any other job, they'd call him back to serve out the rest of his time till it was his turn to be demobbed, which was calculated by age and the months served in uniform.

Her father might be able to fix that, as Diana claimed, but Francis didn't want to start his civilian life by cheating and he very much wanted to go into business with his friends to build decent homes for people.

More than two million homes had been destroyed in German air raids during the war, so the construction of new dwellings was one of the biggest priorities for the recently-elected Labour government, and rightly so, Francis felt.

He was lucky to have his own home. There was such a shortage of accommodation that people were squatting in abandoned government camps and buildings.

Mr Scammell regularly waxed eloquent about how shameful this squatting was, but didn't have any suggestions to make about how people who'd fought for their country could find somewhere to live. It was all right for him in his big, comfortable house, but people were tired of squeezing into small houses belonging to relatives.

And of course, other homes and buildings had been damaged and would need repairing, some in a major way. Maybe he and his friends could pick up that sort of work, too. Scammell was wrong. There was a lot of money to be made in the building industry.

Just as important to Francis, it'd all be worthwhile. He'd be creating, not destroying.

He came out of his reverie as the builder turned up, earlier than expected, and they began to load his truck.

Once he'd been paid for today's salvage, Francis decided to go home straight away and take Diana out to the cinema. Surely that'd cheer her up?

When he saw his mother-in-law's small Austin Seven saloon parked outside his house, Francis slowed down with a sigh. Christine Scammell was always polite to him, he couldn't fault her on her manners, but somehow he never felt quite at ease with her.

He opened the front door and went into the hall just as the two women started laughing. They didn't hear him and he was about to call out, but heard his own name spoken and couldn't resist listening.

'Do you want your father to try yet again to talk sense into Francis, Diana dear?'

'No, Mummy. It'd do no good. He's got his mind absolutely set on us going up to live in Lancashire. I let him talk about it during the war, because it seemed to give him comfort, but I thought he'd see sense after he left the Army and got used to living in Medworth again.'

There was a silence, then, '*You* haven't changed your mind, though. You don't want to move, do you?'

'Of course I don't. You and Daddy are here. All my friends

too. I'd know no one up there. Anyway, I don't want to live in one of those ugly industrial towns. I've seen them on the Pathé News at the cinema – they're all smoky and full of common people living in rows of nasty little terraced houses.'

'We'll have to think of some way to change your husband's mind.'

'I'm working on that, wearing him down gradually. You'll see. I won't let Francis do this to me. I just won't.'

'Good. Let me know if I can help in any way. I'd miss you terribly, darling. Your brother's wife is so hostile to us, it's as if we only have one child now. Have you heard from William lately?'

'I'm afraid not.'

In the hall Francis gasped in shock. He knew very well that Diana had received a letter from her brother yesterday. She hadn't shared its contents with him, except to say that William was fine. There must be something in the letter she couldn't tell her mother about. What had shocked him most was how easily she'd lied to her.

Did she lie to him as easily? Surely not?

There was the sound of someone pushing a chair back and Mrs Scammell said, 'Now, I really must go, Diana darling. I'll see you tomorrow afternoon.'

Francis tiptoed into the kitchen and stayed out of sight until his mother-in-law had driven away.

When Diana brought the tray of tea things into the kitchen, she stopped dead at the sight of him. 'I didn't hear you come back.'

'No. You and your darling Mummy were too busy trying to think of ways to stop me doing what I want with my life. Doing what *we* had planned till you suddenly changed your mind.'

She slammed the tray down on the table, setting the china tinkling. 'Because it's not what I want!'

'No. You've made that plain enough. You won't even give Rivenshaw a try. But it's not you who has to earn the money, is it, Diana? Not you who'd have to work year after year in a job you disliked.'

He hesitated, then said it, because dammit, they were only going over the same old ground. And she *had* encouraged him while they were living away from her parents' influence, had seemed nearly as excited as him about that sort of future.

'We're getting nowhere, Diana. I'm ready to sell this house now. When I do, perhaps you should go and live with your parents for a while and I'll move up north on my own. You can take time then to decide whether you want to join me or not. It's up to you.'

She looked shocked. 'Francis, no!'

'What alternative is there? I've got a wonderful chance to make something of myself and to make a far better future for us. I'm *not* going to turn it down.'

They stared at one another, then her expression hardened. 'I thought we'd agreed to sell the house later, when you're more sure of what you're doing?'

'No. We didn't agree to anything. You decided that.'

'Because it makes sense. You might need to come back here if things don't work out in this Rivenshaw place.'

'I definitely won't be coming back to live in the village, whatever happens. I couldn't find the sort of work I need here. I'm not just a motor mechanic now. I've learned so much more during the war. If our building company doesn't eventuate, I'll start up something of my own and for that, I'll need to be in a town.'

'Daddy says—'

'Stop trotting out what your father says. It's what you and I say that matters.'

'I happen to agree with him.'

'You always do. It's about time you started thinking for yourself. And you might occasionally listen to what I tell you. I'll say it one last time: if my friends and I start a building company, it will *not* fail. The four of us are like brothers, and our skills fit together perfectly for such work.'

'Skills! What does a motor mechanic know about building houses or running businesses?'

He was shocked by the way she was sneering at him. He'd known her parents looked down on him for working with his hands, but she hadn't seemed to feel like that when they married. She'd changed so much since she'd come back to live here during the past few months.

He shouldn't have bought this damned house, but let her stay with her parents. Only, Mr Scammell had heard about the house and Francis had realised it would be an excellent investment.

Diana let out a huff of anger and began to put the cups on the draining board, rattling them about and making a lot of noise.

He reached out to stop her. 'No, let's finish this discussion once and for all.'

'It'd be better to let our emotions cool down, Francis. We shouldn't do anything till we can come to an agreement.'

'I heard what you said to your mother. How many times do I have to tell you I won't change my mind, whatever you say or do. As for this house, it's gone up in value, so I'll get a nice sum of money back, even after I've paid off the bank mortgage. I want as much money as I can scrape together to invest in Esher and Company.'

'But this is my home too. And *I* don't want to sell it.'

'You just said the house is too small. How come you suddenly don't want to sell it?'

'It is too small, but I want to live near my parents.' She burst into tears and dabbed delicately at her eyes.

She was waiting for him to put his arms round her, he knew, and he didn't like to see her cry, so he usually stopped arguing at this stage. But too much was at stake: the rest of his working life. He had to make a stand.

He left her weeping and went into the hall to hang up his jacket. He couldn't help noticing that the sobs stopped abruptly once he left the kitchen.

As he hooked his jacket into place, he saw the corner of his envelope still protruding from her coat pocket and called, 'You didn't post my letter.'

She came hurrying out to join him, looking guilty. 'Sorry. I'll just nip down to the post box now. I, um, have a letter of my own to send as well.'

'I'll come with you.'

'No need. You're tired and dirty. You need a bath and a change of clothes. You know I don't like the neighbours seeing you looking like a working man.'

'I am a working man, a very hard-working man.'

'You know what I mean.' She snatched her coat and backed away towards the front door, making a shooing motion with her hand. 'Go up and get your bath.'

But she'd looked so guilty, he'd have known she was up to something, even without overhearing what she'd said to her mother. After a moment's hesitation, he followed her down the street, taking care not to get too close. But she didn't look back.

When she got to the post box, she stood staring at it, holding the letter in front of her in both hands.

What the hell was she waiting for?

She moved at last, but didn't push the envelope into the slot. He watched in shock as she tore the letter up and shoved the pieces into a nearby dustbin. And she didn't have a letter of her own to post, either.

He nipped round the corner and pressed closely against

an overgrown hedge, mostly hidden by its foliage, waiting for her to pass.

A terrible suspicion was making him feel literally sick. She couldn't have . . . No, surely not? But what if she had done this before? That would explain why he hadn't heard from his friends.

2

Francis didn't go straight home, couldn't face Diana yet. He had to get his own anger under control first because you didn't make good decisions when you were seething with rage.

He walked round the village for a while, trying in vain to calm down. In the end he went into the pub for half a pint of beer. He waved to some fellows he knew but didn't join them, choosing instead to sit out in the garden on one of the rough wooden benches, even though the evening was rather chilly and the bench was damp from a recent shower.

After the years of blackout, it still felt strange to have lights on out of doors or to leave curtains open at windows after dark.

Everything in his life felt strange today.

He took a slurp of beer without really tasting it. Diana must not only have been throwing his letters away, but intercepting anything that came from Mayne and the others.

None of his friends would leave a letter from him unanswered and they had his address, so they'd be wondering what had happened to him. He thumped one fist on the rough wooden table. How *could* she do that to him? How could she?

After a while, he felt a few raindrops on his face and hands. Muttering in annoyance, he raised his glass to finish the beer, then realised it was already empty. Rain began falling steadily, so he stood up. Time to go home and confront Diana. That couldn't be avoided any longer.

She was waiting for him in the front room, which she always called the sitting room.

He'd hardly hung up his coat on the hallstand when she started.

'Where on earth did you go to, Francis? You knew I'd have your tea ready. And look at you. You're wet through.'

'That's because it's raining.'

'I did notice that. But why have you been out in it? *And* you haven't had your bath yet. *Don't sit down!* You'll dirty my upholstery.'

'*Our* upholstery, surely?' Annoyed by this barrage of sharp comments, he sat in the chair opposite her and spoke before she could say anything else. 'I was having a think. I followed you to the post box, you see.'

Her mouth fell open and her expression suddenly became apprehensive. She looked like a schoolgirl now, not a married woman. She acted like one too quite often.

'I saw you tear up my letter, Diana. Did you do that to the others I wrote to Mayne as well?'

She avoided his eyes, fiddling with the edge of a cushion.

'Well? Aren't you even going to answer me? Did you throw all my letters away?'

'Yes, I did.'

'And what about letters from my friends? Did they write to me?'

'Yes.'

She had lost her schoolgirl air and suddenly looked so like her mother he was startled . . . and repelled.

'We'll talk about it later, Francis. The water's hot for your bath, and you haven't had your dinner.'

'I'd rather talk about it now.'

She grasped the chair arms as if she needed to cling to something.

'It's against the law, you know.'

She looked at him in puzzlement. 'What is?'

'You can be prosecuted for tampering with the King's post.'

'Who's going to know, so what does that matter?'

'I know. Don't I matter?'

'Of course you do.'

'How long did you think you could fool me for?'

'Long enough for your friends to find another partner to replace you, I hoped. Or for you to see sense.'

'You were very determined to stop me going to Lancashire, weren't you?'

She shrugged.

'Well, you've failed. I'm even more determined to go now.'

'Please, Francis, don't do that to me.'

'It's not just about you, Diana. I spent over a year planning the new business with my friends. You knew exactly what I intended to do because I talked to you about it whenever I came home on leave. Why didn't you speak out then?'

'I thought it was just . . . dreams. To get you through the war.'

'Well, you're right in one sense. Planning what we'd do when peace came did help get all four of us though the last year of the war. It was a beacon of hope. Because we were planning how best to kill people in that special unit. None of us enjoyed killing.'

'You have to kill enemies.'

'Enemy civilians as well? Women and children and old people?'

She shrugged.

'We weren't *dreaming*, we were finding something constructive to do with the rest of our lives.'

'You can be constructive here, where we both grew up.'

'No, I can't. I want to build houses. I'm really keen to do that. I want to take care of the electrical side of things in our company. Electricity is going to become even more important as they start designing equipment for peacetime homes, which will have washing machines, refrigerators and who knows what else?'

As usual, she ignored what he was trying to tell her. 'If you insist on moving to Rivenshaw, you can't care about me. Did you ever really love me?'

He tried to say he had, but he couldn't lie, because he was no longer sure whether it had been love or infatuation. The best he could manage was, 'I thought I did at the time. And I believe it was the same for you. When you were called up for war work under the National Service Act, you'd never been away from home before. You were lonely. We both were.'

She nodded.

'When we met at that dance, we recognised one another from the village, though we'd never actually spoken before. And for all our differences, we had some good times together.'

Her expression softened still further. 'Yes, we did. You're a wonderful dancer.'

Dancing. Parties. Social life. That was what she seemed to care about most. 'Well, if it was love we felt, it wasn't the sort to build our whole lives on, apparently, nor the sort where you work *together* to create a home and family.'

'How can you say that? Of course it was love. It was! I'd not have defied my parents otherwise.'

He watched her put up one shaking hand to cover her mouth and allow tears to spill over it. He'd seen her do this a few times during the past two years. It was a very effective trick, making her look pitiful. Her father usually fell for it and gave her what she wanted, but she'd tried it on Francis one time too many.

'That pretty little show of tears falling won't convince me. Stop play acting and behave like a grown-up, for heaven's sake.' He wanted the full truth between them now and in the future.

If they had a future.

She let her hand drop, staring at him indignantly, the tears stopping immediately. 'How dare you speak to me like that?' She bounced to her feet.

'*Sit down!*' He hadn't meant to use his parade ground voice, but it burst from him and she dropped back into her chair, shrinking from him as if she expected him to hit her.

'You managed to get out of war work after we married. You seem to get out of doing anything you don't want, especially anything that involves hard physical work. Well, grow used to the idea, Diana: I'm going to sell this house and join my friends in Lancashire.'

'It's my house too. I should have a say in what we do with it.'

'How much of it is yours? The furniture and silver your family gave us? You're welcome to keep every stick of that. I put my life savings into buying this house. You said you didn't have any money saved. But that was another of your lies, wasn't it?'

He paused to stare at her and saw the guilty look on her face as she realised what he was going to say. 'I found out later that you had a substantial legacy from your grandmother. If you'd put some of that into the house, we'd have saved paying so much interest.'

'Daddy said the family money shouldn't be touched and he'd keep it safe for me. He understands finance and you don't.'

'He would say that. But I'm glad now that you did that, because since *I* paid the deposit and made all the payments on the mortgage, I think I have a right to take any profit I get from the house sale, don't you?' Thank goodness he'd followed his instincts and not done what her father urged. If he'd put the house in both their names, he'd be losing a good part of his nest egg when he sold.

She was crying for real now, sobbing and scrubbing her eyes without worrying about how she looked.

He tried to speak more gently. 'If you want to mend our marriage, Diana, you can still come with me to Rivenshaw. I'd really like to give that a try.'

She looked at him doubtfully.

'But only if you're prepared to *work* beside me. It's not going to be enough to take care of the lighter housework and look decorative. I won't have the money to pay for a charlady for quite a while, or to buy luxuries.'

'You need a female navvy, you do, Francis Brady. Well, I'll never be that. Never, never!' She ran from the room and clattered up the stairs, weeping loudly.

He followed her out into the hall. As he put one foot on the stairs, he heard the bedroom door slam and the bolt on the inside of it snick shut. What the hell did she think he was going to do? Attack her?

That was the last thing he'd ever do to anyone, man or woman. He had hated the mindless violence of the war, hated it with a passion. Oh, he'd done his bit and followed orders, praying that the men giving them knew what they were about. But he'd never been sure. No, never quite sure. And that had lain heavily on his conscience, giving him a lot of sleepless nights.

He went back into the sitting room, but didn't stay. This was *her* room, frilly and fussy. He preferred the kitchen.

He sat down at the table, feeling desperately sad. He should have guessed that Diana would cling to her cosy life here. He'd seen how unhappy she'd been when she had to work away from home, even though she'd been in the office not on the factory floor, thanks to Daddy's influence. And she'd been happy to return here when Francis was seconded to the special unit, even though they'd be separated.

She seemed to be putting her parents before him, so where were the two of them heading now? *Divorce?* He hated the thought of that.

He'd read that the divorce rate in Britain was rising rapidly and he wasn't surprised. A lot of people had rushed into marriage in recent years. It had been like a fever running through young men and women during the war years, an affirmation of life in the midst of death.

The physical attraction had certainly been there between him and Diana. He smiled wryly. Oh, yes. They were very good in bed. Mummy and Daddy didn't know everything about their daughter. But bed play wasn't a secure enough foundation for building a life together.

He supposed what Diana needed in peace time was a man from her own background, one who got on well with Mummy and Daddy, and could pay for a big house with a maid. Such a man would fit nicely into the same social set as she'd grown up with.

Oh, why was he agonising over all this again? *Let it go, Francis,* he told himself. *Let it damned well go. You've done your best to keep the marriage together . . . and you've failed.*

At least, it felt as though he'd failed.

Feeling hungry, he went into the tiny dining room. No eating at the kitchen table for Diana! Everything was beautifully set out, but it was still only bread with the merest scrape of butter from their meagre ration, a slice of ham so thin it was almost transparent arranged in a twist and one tomato shared between the two of them. Not an adequate meal for a hard-working chap.

He made the food on his plate into a sandwich, gobbled it down in four bites, then went into the kitchen and cut two more thick slices of bread. Pity the fire wasn't lit or he'd have toasted it. Dry bread wasn't very appetising.

He looked in the cupboards for something to put on it and saw the latest jar of jam from Diana's parents. They bought a lot of things on the black market and kept their daughter supplied with extras. She saved them for special occasions, doling them out to him like rewards to a child.

Feeling in a contrary mood, he opened the jar, spread jam thickly on one slice of bread and clapped the other on top of it. He ate the resultant sandwich with relish, licking every last smear of sweetness off his fingers and the plate. You missed sweet things when they were so strictly rationed.

He finished off with a pint mug of tea, ignoring the delicate china cups and saucers and getting his old tin mug down from the back of the top shelf, where he'd hidden it when Diana tried to throw it away. He made the tea strong and drank it right down to the soggy brown tealeaves at the bottom, then washed the mug and hid it again.

There was still no sign of Diana, no sounds from their bedroom.

He made a quick trip upstairs to change into the warmer working clothes kept in the spare bedroom in case they contaminated milady's pretty frocks. He dragged the quilt off the bed while he was at it. Might as well keep warm tonight.

He thumped on the door of the front bedroom.

'Go away!'

'I'm going out again. I need to keep watch over my salvage.' Some wood had been revealed that would be easy for looters to dig out.

Diana didn't answer, but when he went out to his van, he saw her pale face pressed against their bedroom window. He only used the van when he had to, because of petrol shortages, but tonight he'd be sleeping in it.

He parked and looked sadly at the ruins of his old home, murmuring, 'I'm not going to waste your money, Dad. I'll make you and Mum proud of me.'

He often talked to his parents when he was on his own here. It felt as if they were still lingering nearby. Well, he didn't have anyone else to talk freely to now in Medworth. His best friend from school had been killed early in the war, poor lad, and two others he'd been quite close to hadn't been demobbed yet.

As he strolled to and fro along the front boundary of his land, he watched the sun slide towards the horizon at the rear of it, then he got into the van and settled down to sleep. Fortunately it didn't take much to rouse him so if any thieves came sniffing round, he'd wake up.

His thoughts cut off abruptly as he saw something move in the shadows. 'Hoy! Who's there?'

A man ran out from behind a pile of useless rubbish, carrying something. Francis got out of the car and rushed after him, yelling, 'Stop, thief! Stop!'

The thief flung down what he'd been carrying and Francis nearly fell over the loot. He stopped and found several lengths of good quality wood. He'd noticed them sticking out at one side of the wreckage and planned to fish them out tomorrow.

He shouted, 'You dirty rotten thief!' at the top of his voice. The man might not hear him, but it felt good to hurl words after him.

An elderly woman came to the door of the next house. 'Everything all right, Mr Brady?'

'Yes, thanks, Mrs G. Just chasing away another thief.'

'I don't know what the world's coming to, I really don't. You even have to lock your front doors when you go out in the daytime these days.' She went inside again, still muttering to herself.

With a sigh he piled up the pieces of wood close to where

he was sleeping. They'd bring him a few shillings tomorrow. Good wood, that. And at least the thief had done the digging for him.

He got into his van again, leaning his head back against the worn leather upholstery. He didn't expect to sleep, but he could feel himself getting drowsy. It was a relief in a way to have things out in the open with Diana. Sad, but necessary.

Tomorrow morning he'd find out Mayne's father's phone number and ask him to pass on a message to his son that he was coming to visit soon.

Once this site was cleared, he'd make a quick trip north to see his partners. After that, all being well, he'd come home and make arrangements to sell this block of land and also his house in the village. If necessary, if he had to, he'd also start procedures to end his marriage.

Damn it all to hell! He had hoped for so much more from his marriage. But it seemed he and Diana were only good in bed, not at all good at living together.

In the morning he woke early with a crick in his neck. He watched the sun rise on the other side of the street, gilding the foliage in the nearby gardens and making the muted dawn colours gradually turn vivid once again.

He loved to listen to the morning chorus of bird calls and watch the dancing autumn leaves as the first of them let go of their hold on life and fluttered to the ground.

After allowing himself a few minutes gazing at the beauty around him, he took a deep breath. Time to get on with things.

3

After Mayne Esher and Judith got married, they took only one day off, joking that it was their honeymoon. But it was their first night together that they were looking forward to most.

They were gifted with a fine if cool winter's day, so went for a long tramp across the moors. At midday they stopped at a pub for a meal, enjoying some home-baked bread and sharp-tasting, crumbly Lancashire cheese made at a nearby farm, together with a beer and lemonade shandy each.

It was rare for them to have such privacy, since they were living at Mayne's family home with others who would be joining them in the building industry as part of the newly formed Esher and Company.

Judith's three teenage children waved them goodbye, then went to do their assigned chores. Mrs Needham, the cleaner, would keep an eye on them today, not that they needed it. They were good kids.

'They look happy, don't they?' Gillian said wistfully as they watched their mother and stepfather leave. 'I hope I meet someone as nice as Mayne when I grow up.'

'You've a few years of school before you think of boys in that way,' Kitty told her sharply.

'But don't you want to marry one day?'

Kitty shook her head. 'I don't think so. Mayne's lovely, but remember how horrible Dad was with all of us?'

'I hate him.'

'So do I.'

Their father had been more prone to deal out blows than kisses. Doug Cross was now in prison for bigamy and his children from his unlawful marriage were having to live with the stigma of being bastards.

'Who'd marry you two anyway?' Ben scoffed, and laughed as his sisters chased him round the big kitchen, threatening to tickle him to death.

The following day, even Judith stayed in bed longer than usual, chatting quietly with her new husband.

Mayne smiled and gave her a final lingering kiss before they got up and went down to join the family for breakfast.

He offered her his arm as they left the room. 'Back to work.'

'Yes, but it was lovely yesterday.' She cuddled against him for a moment or two, then forced herself to move away and speak more briskly. 'I'll come and help you when I've checked what we've got left in the pantry. Kitty and Gillian can do the shopping today.'

She sighed. 'Not that there will be much for them to buy. Food is still as limited as ever. I know we have to help starving people in Europe, but fancy having the rations cut again after we've won the war. Everyone is so weary of shortages and rationing and Ben is always hungry.'

'The rationing will be over one day.'

'Not as soon as we'd hoped, eh? Oh well. No use moaning about it. That won't change anything.'

When she went upstairs to join Mayne after breakfast, Judith stood watching him for a moment or two before making her presence known. When no one was around, he could look rather sad, poor love, and no wonder. Esherwood was in a terrible condition after being requisitioned by the War Office for the duration of the war.

There were problems wherever you turned. No maintenance had been done on the property, so the roof leaked in places, and the occupiers had done a fair bit of unnecessary damage to the interior. But at least no one had burned down Esherwood by being careless with cigarettes or driven motor bikes up the eighteenth century stairs and ruined them as had happened in other stately homes.

In theory Mayne would be able to claim compensation for the damage, but the amount was limited so what he'd receive wouldn't cover the costs of repairs.

And even if they somehow managed to set the house to rights, the annual running costs were now beyond their means. He'd drawn up estimates and shown them to her, because she was just as good at figures as he was. She'd been amazed at how much these huge old houses cost to run. People like her, who'd grown up in small terraced houses, thought the Eshers were rich, but it was all relative, as she was finding out.

It was like Mr Micawber's famous recipe for happiness, which she'd read once and been most struck by. She tried to remember Dickens' exact words. It went something like: annual income twenty pounds, annual expenditure nineteen pounds, nineteen shillings and sixpence, result happiness. Annual income twenty pounds, annual expenditure twenty pounds, no shillings and sixpence, result misery.

The only thing Mayne could do was save the house itself from demolition by turning it into flats and selling them, then use the remaining few acres of land to build houses for sale. She knew how sad that made him, how much he loved his home.

Esherwood was a most amazing house and Judith had

already fallen in love with it, could understand why it made him so sad to lose it.

In preparation for this, they'd been clearing out the rooms, sorting out the contents and deciding what to sell and how to get the most money for it. Everyday household items like crockery were in short supply still and even mismatched or chipped oddments were snapped up at the markets.

At least the more valuable family treasures hidden in the two secret rooms had been mainly untouched, apart from those pilfered and sold by Mayne's mother as her mind gradually deteriorated. Old age could be so cruel.

But it was no use standing here daydreaming. She had work to do. 'One wife reporting for duty,' she said, giving her husband a mock salute. 'What's next?'

Just before tea, Mayne led the way into the corner bedroom on the second floor. 'This is the last room to clear.'

She stood in the doorway, studying it carefully. 'It's the worst of them all, absolutely crammed with furniture, as well as old rugs and whatever's in those boxes. I think they just shoved everything into these upper rooms when they set up the hospital here.'

'How about we leave it till tomorrow, Judith?' He pulled her close and gave her a hug. 'After all, we are newly-weds.'

'No, let's make a start on it this evening. If you remember, we promised the children they could go to the cinema tonight as a reward for all their hard work.'

He pulled her into his arms. 'I can think of better things for us to do with an evening on our own, Mrs Esher.'

She flushed slightly. 'That's . . . um, not possible for a few days. I started my monthly this afternoon.'

'Damn!'

'Look on the bright side. If we work hard, we'll have

finished clearing out all the rooms by the end of the evening. Won't that feel good?'

'It's amazing how you always manage to look on the bright side.'

'I've had a lot of practice.'

'I think you're wonderful to be like that after all you had to put up with from your first husband.'

'So-called husband. You're my first *real* husband.'

After tea, Mayne gave his step-children the cinema money and sent them off for the first show of the evening.

Judith led the way upstairs. 'Let's get those dust sheets off the bigger pieces of furniture first, love.' She started tugging and he joined her, piling the dusty drop sheets in the corridor outside, ready to send to the laundry.

Next they pulled out a jumble of smaller furniture, some of it badly damaged because it had been dumped any old how in the room.

'I know someone who can repair most of these,' she said.

'Is it worth it?'

'Definitely. Everyone's short of furniture these days.' It always surprised her how careless he could be with smaller amounts of money. 'Look after the pennies . . .'

He finished the saying with her, '. . . and the pounds will look after themselves.'

'Don't mock me. It's true. Oh, look at that, Mayne! There are two identical armchairs, not just the one over by the window. Here's one near the fireplace. It's as if someone always sat here alone, moving from one seat to the other according to the time of day and the season. Whose room was this? Do you know?'

'I have a vague memory of it being occupied by an elderly cousin who was short of money and had nowhere else to live. Now what was her name? Oh, yes. Mariah Jane Esher.

Her first name was spelled the American way and pronounced Mar-eye-ya. She always insisted on that. She died when I was about seven and, as far as I can remember, no one ever mentioned her again after the funeral.'

'Why not? Weren't your parents sad that she'd died?'

'She and my mother didn't get on and you know how absent-minded Father is when he's got his nose in his research books. Mariah wasn't even invited to eat with us most of the time, just on Sundays.'

'Poor old lady. She must have been very lonely.' Judith sat in one of the armchairs and leaned her head back. 'These are very comfortable, much nicer than the ones in the drawing room. I think we should keep them for ourselves.'

He looked at the chairs doubtfully. 'They're rather old-fashioned.'

'Yes. Antiques probably. I prefer them to the modern Utility furniture they've started to make. And anyway, we won't qualify for that till it comes off the ration. I read an article in a women's magazine about it. There were a lot of illustrations. The furniture was square and lumpy, with only four colours of upholstery, none of which I liked, and wooden arms to save on materials. The cloth had itty-bitty designs on it so that there wouldn't be much wastage when matching patterns. It looked as though it had little beetles crawling across it to me.'

He smiled as she wrinkled her nose eloquently. He'd already learned that his wife had a good eye for design, whether it be in the arrangement of furniture or the alteration of clothes to suit her trim figure. She was avid for knowledge, and was currently learning some of the finer points of dressmaking from her friend Helen. It wasn't only Judith's children who were intelligent.

They'd found trunks of old clothes in the attics and she'd recently spent some of her savings on a second-hand sewing machine so that she and her daughters could alter the garments as needed.

Mayne sat down in the other chair and tested it, leaning his head back and closing his eyes. 'You're right. It is comfortable. We'll definitely add these to our collection for the time when we have a proper home of our own.'

She dared say it. 'Or maybe we could keep one wing of the house for ourselves.'

His face went tight. 'I doubt it. Anyway, I'd rather move out completely than see it filled with strangers and altered beyond recognition.'

She stood up. 'Let's go through all the drawers. Oh, look! These are still full of her clothing, even her underwear. What old-fashioned styles! You'd think someone would have thrown them away.'

'Not my mother! She had maids most of her life and always managed to avoid doing jobs she didn't like.'

'Actually some of these are very pretty.' Judith held a long, lace-edged petticoat against herself and looked at her reflection in the dusty mirror of the massive dressing table. 'I think I'll have this for myself. It'll be good practice to alter a petticoat and I can put the lace on the bottom again after I shorten it.'

Knowing how poorly supplied she still was with clothes, he watched indulgently as she stroked the fine lace with one rough fingertip. He moved closer, waggling his eyebrows in a mock leer. 'I shall enjoy taking it off you, pretty lady.'

She pretended to slap him, but her mind was still on the clothing. 'What I can't use will have some value. Worn-out garments can be cut down for a child, you know, even if the material has rotted under the arms. Clothes rationing is still hitting people hard. I could sell all the things we don't need at the market. I bet they'd go quickly, too. I think I'll take a stall for a couple of Saturdays and—'

His voice was sharp. 'You don't need to do that. Sell the things you don't want to another stall holder.'

'We'll make twice as much money if I sell them myself.' She stared at him challengingly. 'I *like* buying and selling at the market, Mayne, and I'm good at it. Besides, I'll enjoy catching up with people I've known for years.'

'Suit yourself.' He didn't like the idea of his wife playing the huckster, but he didn't try to stop her. He wasn't like the children's father, forcing other people to do what he wanted.

A door banged downstairs and they heard voices. 'I think they're back,' she said, relieved to change the focus of their attention. 'We're up here!' she shouted down to them.

The three youngsters were full of excitement about the film, *Fanny by Gaslight*. They'd hardly ever had the money to go to the cinema in their old life, so were starting to catch up on films from previous years as well as seeing the newer ones. Mayne loved to see their enjoyment.

Gillian, the youngest, told them about the film, and how frightened she'd been for the heroine and her supposed father. That girl would make a good actress, Judith thought, the way she told stories so vividly; still, she didn't want her children going into chancy professions like acting.

When they'd finished talking about the film, Judith gestured to the pile of underclothes on the bed. 'Look at what I've found. Do either of you need petticoats?'

The two girls both claimed petticoats to alter, as well as other bits and pieces of clothing, laughing at the old-fashioned knee-length bloomers, which Judith put into the pile for selling.

Ben stood next to Mayne and whispered, 'Women! They're always fiddling about with clothes.'

'Let them enjoy it. Your mother and sisters haven't had much chance to do that in the past.'

He watched for a few minutes longer, then suddenly yawned and clapped his hands to get their attention. 'It's getting late. Come on, everyone. Let's have a cup of cocoa and go to bed. These things will still be here tomorrow.'

He might not be able to make love to his wife tonight, but he enjoyed holding her in his arms and chatting until she fell asleep, mid-sentence.

The following morning Mayne woke to a sunny autumn day and an empty space beside him in the bed. He squinted at the clock and smiled wryly. Seven o'clock. Still early by normal standards but Judith rarely slept past five and now the honeymoon was over, she was back to her old habits. She would probably have breakfast on the table for everyone by now, and a dozen other small tasks completed.

He didn't mind getting up early, but remembering last night he lay there for a few moments. He felt sad to have finished clearing out the rooms, because it brought him another step closer to losing his home.

It shouldn't have come to this. His father and mother had lost more of the family money than any of the previous generations. He still couldn't work out what they'd done with it all. Surely his father's research books hadn't cost many thousands of pounds? And why had Reginald sold the last cottage they had for renting out? What had he done with the money from that?

As far as he knew, his mother hadn't bought any valuable jewellery, only a few pretty smaller pieces. Even if she had bought other things, she wouldn't be able to tell him any details now, because she had developed senile dementia and was in a special hospital, going downhill rapidly.

Thank goodness he had more financial sense than his ancestors. He'd managed to increase the value of a small inheritance from a great aunt, even during the war years.

She'd said in her will that she was leaving everything to him because he was the only member of her family who wouldn't waste her money.

As he went down the back stairs to the kitchen, he heard Judith humming and the sound cheered him up. She had taken charge of the housekeeping for everyone living here and ran her kitchen and helpers with the skill of a general managing crack troops.

Mayne's partner Victor and his second wife Ros were away at the moment, also on sorting out duties. They were selecting what they wanted to keep from Victor's former home before putting it up for sale, and had taken Victor's eight-year-old daughter Betty with them. He was expecting them back soon.

The architect of their little group, Daniel, wasn't living here at the moment and they weren't quite sure when he'd be back. He was having difficulty shaking off the effects of the war, and was more upset by his recent divorce than he admitted. Well, what Englishman wouldn't be upset if his wife left him to marry a rich American?

Mayne could only hope his partner and friend would come back soon. They couldn't begin detailed designs for converting Esherwood into flats until Daniel had worked out some preliminary plans. Unfortunately, his uncle had died suddenly just as he was about to return to Rivenshaw, and he'd stayed on to help his aunt sort out her husband's affairs.

Ben's voice echoed up from the big entrance hall and Mayne couldn't help smiling. That boy had a fine pair of lungs. He hoped to adopt his wife's three children officially as soon as he could, because he loved them already.

Judith was almost thirty-three, a couple of years older than Mayne, but there was still time, he hoped, for her to give him a child or two. She said she carried babies easily and would like more children, now that she could afford to feed and clothe them without a struggle to make ends meet. They were both hoping Mother Nature would oblige them quickly.

Thinking of his wife made him get out of bed, perform his ablutions and hurry downstairs to join her. She didn't notice him come into the kitchen, so he put one finger to his lips to stop the children saying anything and tiptoed across to her.

As he smacked a big kiss on her soft rosy cheek, she let out a squeak of surprise, then gave him a hug and one of her glowing smiles.

He kept hold of her for a moment, touching a fingertip to the dark, wavy hair framing a face that was full of character. To him, her best feature was her sparkling green eyes.

They became aware that the children were watching them. They still weren't used to open displays of affection. Ben, who was on toasting duty, winked at Mayne and speared another slice of bread on the metal toasting fork before holding it in front of the flames.

Judith moved away from him, blushing slightly. 'Go and sit down, sleepyhead. The food's almost ready. I was about to send Gillian to wake you.'

He took his place at the head of the table. 'How are you all this morning?'

'Hungry,' said Ben.

'You're always hungry,' Kitty told her brother.

'I'm a growing boy. I'll soon be taller than you.'

She elevated her nose. 'Who cares?'

'I'm missing Betty,' Gillian said. 'I do hope her father and Ros bring her back in time for the start of school. I can't wait for Monday to come. I'm dying to go to grammar school.'

Her blissful sigh made everyone smile. She'd been anxious to win a fee-paying scholarship, as her older brother and sister had done. Mayne would have been happy to pay for her to go to the girls' grammar school as a private scholar, but it hadn't been necessary. Gillian was as intelligent as the rest of her family.

'How about we start clearing out the Army's old Nissen hut today?' he suggested as the meal ended.

Ben jumped to his feet. 'Yes, let's. I'm dying to see what's hidden inside it. Mum says you saw some tools and parts of other huts when you looked at the front part. They'll come in useful, won't they, Mayne?'

'Very.'

'There's the post!' Gillian ran off to bring in the letters from the huge entrance hall.

Ben cut another piece of bread and stuck it on the toasting fork. He saw his mother looking at him and said, 'Well, I'm still hungry.'

In Hertfordshire, Victor Travers and Ros woke early on the last day of August, ready to continue clearing out the house he'd lived in with his first wife.

He'd have preferred to have bought new furnishings and kept sad memories at bay, but in these times of scarcity you had to be frugal with possessions.

The newly-weds were staying at the house temporarily with his seven-year-old daughter, who was making fun of any problems they encountered. Edna, Betty's former nurse-maid, was coming in daily to help cook and clean, because she still hadn't found a job.

'I'll walk into the village and buy a newspaper while you get breakfast ready,' Victor told his wife. 'Some fresh air will do me good after all the dust we've stirred up.'

'Will you be all right?'

'I'm sure my former mother-in-law won't have me attacked publicly, if that's what you're worrying about. We haven't seen any sign of her since we got here. And after all, we did take out an injunction to stop her going near Betty.'

Ros grinned. 'We needn't have bothered with the injunction. Edna's sister is still working for them and she says Mr Fitkin checks every farthing that's spent in the house.'

'She won't like that. She isn't used to stinting herself in any way. I hope he clips every feather in her wings, and serve her jolly well right.'

He walked briskly along the main street to the village shop, bought his newspaper and complimented the owner on how much brighter the shop looked without the criss-cross strips of tape that had been stuck across the windows during the war years in case a bomb shattered the glass.

'We'll not be back to normal, Mr Travers, till we can get supplies of the items our customers want. How they expect us shopkeepers to make a living without anything to sell, I do not know.'

'It'll happen, but it takes time to change production from war to peace.'

'Well, it can't happen too quickly for me.'

As he came out of the shop, Victor nearly collided with George Fitkin. He would have nodded and moved on had the other man not spoken.

'I'm glad to run into you, Travers.'

'You are?'

'Yes.' Fitkin lowered his voice. 'First, let me assure you that there was no need for the injunction. I'll make sure Amelia doesn't do anything else foolish about her granddaughter.'

'You will?'

Fitkin gave one of his thin-lipped near smiles. 'Oh yes. I believe in being master in my own home and I have no desire whatsoever to bring up anyone else's children. My three by my first wife all married young and are off my hands, I'm happy to say.'

'Good. I'm delighted to hear that.'

When Victor would have walked on, Fitkin held out one hand to stop him. 'Have you got a minute, Travers? There's a business matter I'd like to raise with you.' He glanced towards a woman hovering nearby, pretending to look at the meagre display in the shop window, and lowered his voice. 'Perhaps we could go somewhere more private?'

Victor wasn't taking Fitkin to his home. 'We could walk down to the river and back, I suppose. It's a fine day.'

They set off together, drawing surprised stares from a man they passed and afterwards from a woman pegging out washing.

'What did you wish to discuss?' Victor prompted.

'Your house in the village. What do you intend to do with it?'

'Sell it. And don't try to stop me. The Galtons gave it to me and my first wife as a wedding present, so your wife has no claim on it now.'

Fitkin stopped moving to draw himself very upright, though the effect was spoiled because he was still a good six inches shorter than Victor. 'I'm well aware of that. I simply wished to make you an offer for it. It's a nice little house and I have a younger brother in need of a home.'

Victor almost allowed himself to chuckle at the irony of that, but a moment's reflection told him this might actually be the easiest way to sell the house. 'How much are you offering?'

'£1,000.'

'Not enough.'

'How much do you want, then? I'm not paying more than it's worth just because you're annoyed with Amelia.'

To say he was annoyed with his former mother-in-law was putting it mildly, but never mind that. 'I'm not taking a lower amount than is fair, Fitkin. How about £1,200?'

'That's a bit steep. How about £1,100?'

After some haggling, they settled at £1,150.

Victor had been expecting to get about a thousand pounds, so was delighted with this sale. 'As you're aware, my lawyer is Stuart Melford, who lives in Rivenshaw. I presume your lawyer can sort out the rest of the legal matters for the sale with him?'

'Yes, of course. Um, there's another thing, Travers. If you're selling any of the furniture, my brother was bombed out last year and lost nearly everything. He and his family have been in lodgings ever since. So maybe we could come to some arrangement about buying the furniture you don't want as well?'

Better and better, Victor thought gleefully. Let him pay through the nose for it, too. If he didn't, other people would.

'Come and walk round the house with my wife and she'll tell you what's for sale. Ros has a much clearer understanding than me of what furniture is worth these days. I know she has her eye on some pieces to take back to Rivenshaw with us, but there are quite a lot of items we don't want. Ten o'clock this morning suit you?'

'Yes, that will be fine. You, um, won't change your mind about selling the house?'

'Definitely not. But don't bring your wife with you to look round. It'd be too awkward.'

'I agree. I shan't even tell Amelia until the transaction is complete. I'll see you later then.'

They walked off in different directions.

Victor didn't envy Fitkin, who had made a marriage of convenience to an older woman who was not well liked by anyone who knew her.

When her husband entered the house, Ros greeted him with, 'What's happened now, Victor Travers? You're looking unbearably smug.'

'I've just sold the house and the new owner is coming round at ten o'clock to go through the furniture with you. He wants to buy anything we don't need. It's for his brother, who was bombed out.'

'Good heavens, that was quick work. You clever man. Who's the buyer?'

'Fitkin, of all people.'

She stared at him in surprise then burst out laughing. 'I'll make sure he pays top price for every piece of furniture, then.'

'I hoped you'd do that. Crockery too. Where's Betty? We'll have to tell her about Fitkin's visit or she'll think he's coming to get her.'

'I'll tell her. Ought we to take her to say goodbye to her grandmother, do you think?'

'After what that woman did, trying to kidnap my daughter after my first wife died? Definitely not. Still, Fitkin sounds to have got Amelia's measure and he assures me we'll have no more trouble with her. I believe him, too. He seems even more selfish and ruthless than she is.'

'And her money? I don't want to sound mercenary, but oughtn't some of it to come to Betty one day?'

Victor shrugged. 'I'm not going to make a fuss. The less I have to do with them the better after this house sale goes through. I'll provide for Betty.'

'Or better still, help her train for a good job so that she can provide for herself, whatever life throws at her. The world is changing for women, Victor.'

'Yes, of course. I have to start thinking in a more modern way about my daughter's future, don't I? It'll be very different from her poor mother's life.'

'I hope so. Women aren't going to be pushed back into the kitchen after this war, as they were after the Great War. And, anyway, modern inventions like the refrigerator and washing machine will make keeping house so much easier. Some of us got a taste for working outside the home during the war years.'

'It's a good thing we have work for you in our new business, then.'

'We'll need to talk about pay too. Judith and I were discussing that a few days ago. Just because we're wives of partners in the business doesn't mean we intend to work for free.'

He gave her a cracking hug. 'What have I got myself into, marrying you?'

As he followed this up with a passionate kiss, it was clear he didn't mind in the slightest her modern views on women's roles.

When he pulled away, Ros said. 'Actually, I think Betty is very clever. You only have to listen to her chatting to Kitty and Gillian to realise that. Kitty wants to go to university when she leaves school, and we should think about it for Betty, too. I always wished I could have got a proper education.'

He put one arm round her. 'You'd have done well at university, I'm sure. But at least you can use your brain in our business.'

'Maybe that's why the four of you get on so well – you're all very open-minded and modern in your attitude to life. Well, most of the time anyway.'

'Thank you for the compliment, I think.'

She gave him a misty-eyed smile. 'You're a wonderful man, Victor Travers.' She pulled him towards her and raised her face for a kiss.

They were interrupted by Betty's voice saying, 'Oh, no! You two are kissing *again*! I don't think I want to get married if you have to keep kissing each other like that.'

Which made them both laugh and pull her into a three-person hug.

★　★　★

The telephone rang in the office and Judith picked it up. 'Esher and Company.'

'Ah. At last.'

'Who's speaking, please?'

'Sorry. I'm just so relieved to have got the right number. It's Francis – Francis Brady. Could I please speak to Mayne?'

'Oh, my goodness, yes, of course. Hold on. I'll fetch him.' She ran into the kitchen where her husband was drinking yet another cup of tea. 'Your friend Francis is on the phone.'

'At last!' He dumped his cup so hastily he splashed tea in all directions and set off running towards the office.

Judith smiled as she wiped up the mess, thankful they'd decided life would be easier if they just used the wooden table top instead of fancy tablecloths which would cause too much extra work.

She went back to the office in time to hear Mayne say, 'Come any time. We've got plenty of spare bedrooms, though the house is still in chaos.' His voice went softer. 'And I'm sorry about your marriage, Francis.'

He put the phone down. 'His wife has been throwing his letters to us away and she destroyed the couple we sent to him as well, because she doesn't want to move up north.'

'What a rotten thing to do! I don't like the sound of her.'

'I doubt you'll have to deal with her, Judith. He thinks they're going to get a divorce.'

'Oh. That's sad.'

'Better a divorce than a lifetime of misery. You know what some of these wartime marriages are like. Totally unsuitable couples and how they thought they could live together after the war ended, no one can understand.'

'People might say that you and I aren't well suited,' she teased. 'An Esher of Esherwood and a woman from the back streets of Rivenshaw.'

'Don't talk about yourself like that! I couldn't find anyone who suited me more.'

'No, you're not a snob about my background, thank goodness.'

'I'm delighted that Francis is still on board with our building company. He's brilliant with machinery and electrical gadgets, can turn his hand to a lot of other things, too.' He took her hand. 'Come on! We said we'd start clearing out that Nissen hut today.'

'About time, too. I've been dying to see what's hidden away in the back. I wonder if anyone in the Army knows what it contains?'

'I shouldn't think so. The authorities transferred people here and there, and when a new group came in, there was sometimes no one left who knew exactly what the previous lot had been doing. And if you were moved about a lot, you soon forgot the details of the earlier ones. Things got a bit frantic towards the end, as well.'

'But we won the war.'

'Oh, yes, we certainly did that. Come along then, Mrs Esher. To work. We have a war over chaos to win here.'

4

The children had finished their daily job of washing up the breakfast things, so they went outside with Mayne and their mother, eager to see what was in the Nissen hut.

Jan Borkowski was waiting for them at the other side of the stable yard because he was going to help with any heavy lifting inside the hut. Jan was a displaced person who had married a local woman and settled in Britain. He had stopped acting as night watchman at Esherwood, and was now doing odd jobs around the place until the building company got going, when they would find more suitable employment for a man of his intelligence. Mayne was sure Jan would be an asset to the company.

'Thank you for coming, Jan.'

'I am happy to help. What you are doing is very interesting.' Jan still showed a slight trace of a Polish accent, especially when he was excited or angry, though he usually spoke English more correctly than most native speakers.

'Is Mrs Borkowski coming to join us today?' Gillian asked. 'If not I'll nip down and see her later. I want to ask her help with altering a dress Mum's found for me.'

'Helen will be here presently. She has gone down to the shops because someone told her there had been a delivery of tins of soup. She said to tell you she'd get some for you if she could, Judith.'

'Thank goodness for friends like you two! All this queuing drives me mad.' Judith heard Ben sigh and smiled as she saw his eyes go impatiently towards the Nissen hut. 'Now, let's get these doors open before my son bursts from curiosity.'

With a ceremonial flourish, Mayne undid the big padlock and dragged the creaky double doors as far back as they would go. 'They usually have single doors on these huts. They must have wanted this one for storage of large items from the start, to have put in two. I'm surprised they didn't concrete the floor properly, though.'

'They could have been in a hurry to use the hut or maybe they couldn't get enough cement,' Judith said. 'I suppose even the Army wasn't immune to the various shortages.'

They all went inside the corrugated iron hut, with its semi-circular roof that went right down to the ground at each side. The entrance was at the highest point and led to an open space about two yards square, surrounded by ceiling-high barriers.

For the most part, these were formed from planks piled on top of one another to form a solid wall, but on the right-hand side, the barrier was made up of the backs of various metal cabinets about six foot high, with boxes piled on top of them right to the ceiling.

'They weren't wasting space,' Mayne commented.

Jan ran his hand along the edge of a plank. 'This is good quality timber, properly milled.'

Mayne went to feel it. 'You're right. I hope it's all like that. I saw some boxes of tools last time when we took off the top few planks and peeped behind the barrier.'

'New tools are very hard to get, I think,' Jan said. 'They will be most useful.'

'Very useful indeed. So maybe we've fallen lucky. Let's get cracking. We'll need a ladder to get the top planks down and somewhere to store them that'll be safe from thieves. Well-seasoned timber is in short supply these days; I can't believe the Army has simply left all this behind.'

'Perhaps those who knew what was in here were killed,' Jan suggested.

'Who can tell? But I have the official letter the War Office sent when the Army Medical Corps moved out of Esherwood. It says we can keep anything we find here, because it'd be more trouble than it's worth for them to transport and dispose of second-hand items.'

'There's a ladder in the laundry. We can use that to get to the top of the barrier,' Judith said. 'Maybe we could store the planks in the laundry too, for the time being? You said the Army extended the laundry at the back to cater for hospital linen, but *we* aren't running a hospital, so we aren't going to be laundering hundreds of sheets and towels every week, are we? We don't need even half that laundry space. Our voices echo in there now, it's so big and bare because they took most of the laundering equipment with them.'

'I'll go and fetch the ladder.' Ben ran off before they could stop him.

'You have a fine boy there,' Jan told Judith quietly. 'I hope my child will be big and strong like him.'

'You and Helen are expecting a child?'

He beamed at her. 'Yes. I never thought to be so fortunate. Not only to find a wife like Helen, but to have children too. I have not had a family since I was seventeen years old at the beginning of the war.'

'You have friends now, as well.' She patted his shoulder, knowing what hardships he'd endured during the war. He'd left home at not much more than Kitty's age to avoid being conscripted by the Russians and taken to a work camp, where he'd probably have been worked to death. It had taken him years to make his way across war-torn Europe to England,

and heaven knew what dangers he'd had to face. It was a miracle he'd escaped capture.

He sometimes grew quiet and stared into the distance as if remembering. Judith had seen that same look on the face of her husband's business partner Daniel.

Jan put his hand over hers for a moment in a silent thank you for what she'd said, then moved forward to help Ben put the unwieldy wooden stepladder in place against the barrier.

Jan gestured to Mayne. 'Your property. You should be the first to see what's really behind these barriers.'

Mayne smiled and climbed the ladder. 'We've already peered over the top, but we couldn't see much except boxes and papers, so we put the planks back again to keep things safe. This time we'll clear a path right through the hut to the rear wall.'

By the time Helen arrived at Esherwood with some groceries over an hour later, the barrier was down to thigh level and Ben was begging to be allowed to clamber over it into the chaos of boxes and packages beyond.

'No, Ben!' Judith grabbed her son by the belt. 'We don't know what's underneath and you might break something valuable.'

With a huffy sound of disappointment, the lad helped Mayne carry some more planks through to the laundry while Judith paid Helen for the three cans of soup and other groceries she'd managed to buy, and put them away in the pantry.

'Cup of tea, everyone?' she called.

'Mum, not now. We're nearly through!' Ben protested. 'Don't you want to see what's in there?'

'I'll make the tea,' Helen said. 'I've no desire to clamber over planks and boxes.' She blushed. 'I can see from your expression that Jan's told you why. He's so excited about the baby. Well, I am, too.'

'Yes. Congratulations.'

Once they got a proper opening made, Mayne stood for a moment frowning at the jumble of piled-up cardboard boxes to the left. 'You'd think they'd have stored these more tidily. They must have been in a tearing hurry to leave. We'll go through them slowly and carefully.'

The first two boxes contained only files and papers, so they started a pile of those in the library, which was large enough to be used as a dumping ground for materials they'd cleared. Then there were several boxes of tools and screws, which were going down into the cellar, Mayne said, stroking one of the boxes gloatingly.

The next box contained small bundles wrapped in oddments of crumpled paper and newspaper. Mayne unwrapped one of them and found an ornament, turning it round in his hands and studying it, then holding it out to Judith. 'I recognise this! It used to stand on the mantelpiece in the drawing room. What on earth is it doing here?'

'Perhaps your mother placed them here for safety?'

'She can't have done. The Nissen hut was erected a couple of years after the Army moved into the big house and my parents weren't allowed back inside. I know she packed away the more valuable ornaments or took them down to the Dower House when they moved there, but from what my father's told me, she took such a huff about the house being requisitioned that she never came up here during the war, if she could help it. And by the end of the war, she was . . . not herself.'

'She might have done it without telling anyone,' Judith suggested. 'After all, she sneaked up to the house with your ex-fiancée to steal pieces of silver from the basement not long ago.'

'Yes. But they only had to walk down to the cellar to do that, and I'm sure it was at Caroline's prompting. I think someone connected with the Army must have found this ornament in the house and hidden it here.'

'A thief, you mean?' Judith asked.

He nodded, fumbling with a second small package and unwrapping it carefully. 'This one stood on the windowsill of the library. And I *know* it's valuable because my mother used to yell at me not to touch it if I went anywhere near.'

He pulled out a third china figurine. 'And this used to be in her bedroom. Someone has definitely been looting our ornaments. They had good taste, I must say. I was wondering where my mother had put them. I thought she'd taken them to the Dower House.'

'We shall need to ask Mr Woollard about them. He'll either know what they're worth or be able to find out. He's going to be a very useful person to have in the company.'

Mayne gave her a wry look. 'I've admitted I was wrong about him. He might have been a black market profiteer, but he wasn't a fence of stolen goods, as rumour said.'

Jan was frowning. 'The thieves may be intending to return for these now the war's over. Perhaps they even live in Rivenshaw.'

'I doubt it. Most of our lads went into one of the northern regiments. It was the Army Medical Corps who managed this place: different bunch of chaps entirely. And whoever these villains are, they'd better not come back for my family's possessions, because if I catch them, I'll make them sorry for what they did!'

He lifted another box on to the makeshift plank table Jan and Ben had set up just outside the door and went through its contents, looking angrier by the minute. 'All treasured family ornaments from Esherwood, the sort of thing passed down through the generations. My grandmother used to tell me about them and how they first came into the family.'

He picked up a small vase and looked at the maker's sign underneath. 'This isn't one of ours, though. It's Sèvres.' He unwrapped the next item and placed an identical vase next to the first. 'Look at these! Delicate, beautiful and very expensive. I wonder whose ancestors bought these. Or perhaps it was my mother who bought them for the family collections. She loved beautiful china and silver.'

He paused, frowning. 'She couldn't have done, surely?'

'Couldn't have done what, darling?' Judith asked.

'Spent huge amounts of the family money on more damned china. It's so . . . breakable. Only I haven't been able to work out why she and my father became so poor. My father inherited an adequate, if not generous income and he can't explain what happened to it, either. Well, he doesn't understand money. He would just have told Mother to buy what she wanted if she'd asked him.'

'It's strange, isn't it?' Judith said. 'I never had much money, but I always knew where every single penny went. Your family had a lot of money and it just . . . vanished, because they didn't manage it carefully. I'm glad you don't take after your parents, Mayne. I never again want to live with the uncertainty of not knowing how much money we have from one week to the next.'

'My family may have lost most of their money, but I'm careful with mine and I can promise we'll always have enough to live on. Now . . . I think we'll pack these up, then lock them somewhere in the house.'

'Maybe we need to search the Dower House as well. I don't suppose your father will mind.'

He laughed, but the sound had a bitter note to it. 'Or even notice. Yes, you're right. Put it on the list of things to do.'

'How about we put the ornaments we find here in that big cupboard in the cellar?' Judith suggested. 'It's empty and you have a key for it.'

'Good idea.'

'I'll carry the boxes to the cellar as you finish with them,' Jan said. 'It will be better if you continue to check the other boxes because you may recognise things and I won't. Don't worry. I'll be extremely careful.'

Somehow, the pleasure had gone out of the day and when Ben asked if he could investigate what was hidden beyond the piles of boxes, his mother shook her head. 'No, love. Let Mayne do that. We don't know what we'll find there.'

Mayne saw the lad's disappointment. 'You can help us move those pieces of corrugated iron once this part is clear.'

Ben brightened up. 'And I can fetch and carry for you. I'm pretty strong for my age.'

Judith looked at her husband. 'If these are thefts, do we need to call in the police?'

'What's the point? It could only have been someone from the Army who did this but we don't know who and I doubt we'll be able to find out. It wasn't just a convalescent hospital in the big house, but special combat training groups coming in and out. They bivouacked out in the grounds and went on small-scale manoeuvres in the countryside. That's why the end stable wall was destroyed. *Target practice.*' His voice was bitter.

Not wanting to leave things unguarded, Mayne refused to stop for a meal, and asked Judith to bring him a sandwich, which he ate with one hand while studying some more pieces from another box, this time small silver items, none of which he recognised but all of which were beautiful and looked to be of high quality.

Kitty helped him by making meticulous lists of the unknown property. After lunch, Gillian went upstairs with Helen to work out what alterations would be needed to give her a couple of new outfits to wear.

★　★　★

By mid-afternoon Mayne had cleared the second area inside the hut and had found ten boxes of items either stolen from his family or of mysterious provenance.

Once they'd listed the contents and numbered the boxes, Jan and Ben took them down to the cellar.

That done, they were faced with yet more barriers before they could get to the rear of the hut, this time made up of cupboards and chests of drawers, on the right side, and equally hard to penetrate piles of corrugated iron, on the left side, which looked like parts of another Nissen hut.

'We'll move the furniture first,' Mayne decided, thinking aloud. 'Some of it might be valuable.'

'It all has some value,' Judith reminded him, 'because people are crying out for furniture.'

They found the pieces heavy and awkward to move, because the ground – which they had expected to be hard, beaten earth like the front part – was surprisingly soft.

Mayne frowned down at the muddy mess their boots had churned up. 'There's something wrong here. The ground shouldn't be moist inside the hut because there's no sign of leaks from the roof. I'd better check the outside. Don't touch anything else till I get back, Ben.'

He came back a short time later scowling. 'A drainpipe has been damaged and looks like it's been pouring water into the space between this hut and the stables for some time, possibly even years. Couldn't they even repair what they damaged when they built this hut, damn them?'

Judith looked at him and said mockingly, '*There is a war on, you know.*'

The sound he made was more like a dog's snarl. 'If one more person says that, I'll be hard put not to thump them.'

She linked her arm in his for a moment's comfort. 'I got sick of those words, too. They were used as excuses for all sorts of things, including sheer laziness.'

'Well, I'll have to jerry-rig some sort of repair to the drain-pipe so that it drains as it should from now on. I'll get Jan to help me.' The two men went off, with Mayne still muttering to himself and Ben trailing behind them like an eager puppy.

It made Judith's eyes fill with tears to see how deep her son's need was for men's companionship: decent men, unlike his father. She hoped Doug would rot in prison for the rest of his life for what he'd done to them all!

About four o'clock, with the drainpipe temporarily fixed, Mayne finally agreed to take a proper break.

'I keep wondering whether we should report the stolen goods,' he said as he sat down at the kitchen table, easing his shoulders. 'Only it isn't something for the local police to deal with; it'd be a military matter. Well, I think it would. No, better if we let sleeping dogs lie.'

After studying Judith's expression, he added, 'This is important to us, of course it is, but the thefts won't be a priority with the military authorities, especially since we've got so many of our own stolen articles back again. And knowing how slowly the Army can move on non-combat matters, well, I worry that they might confiscate the items and keep them for years as evidence. To be fair, they've got a lot on their plate sorting out the occupation of the various countries involved in the war.'

'And the British government must not only look after their own country's return to peace, but work out how to help feed the many starving people they've liberated,' Jan said softly. 'It's been bad here, but it's been far worse in Europe, believe me. Many have died from starvation there, especially the children and the weak, because there was no attempt to share out the food fairly – well, not like here, where I think it was very well done.'

'I'm very proud of how our country coped,' Judith said quietly.

'You have every right to be,' Jan agreed. 'I'm happy to live here for the rest of my life.'

They were all silent for a moment or two.

Jan stood up. 'Come on, Ben. We can do a little more work before the light fails.'

Once they were alone, Judith said thoughtfully, 'Even if the thieves are alive, I'd be surprised if they dared come back and try to retrieve their loot now that you're back in residence.'

Mayne didn't seem to have heard what she said. He was stirring his tea round and round, not even noticing how it slopped into the saucer and splashed on to the table. 'I wish I felt sure I was doing the right thing,' he muttered.

She reached out and stopped him making a miniature whirlpool. 'How about we clear the whole hut out, see what we've got, and make a final decision on the next step then? If it's only these boxes of ornaments and silver that have been stolen, I'd vote not to pursue the matter. If there's more than that involved, then maybe we should contact someone in the Army. Or even perhaps ask Judge Peters' advice. He's a very wise man and has considerable influence with the authorities.'

'You're right.' He smacked one of his sudden kisses on her cheek. 'I'm glad I married an intelligent woman who sees situations clearly. I'll get back to work now.'

He found Ben and Jan had carried a chest of drawers to the front part of the hut.

'There are things in the drawers,' Ben said. 'We left them for you to look through.'

'Good thinking. Jan, are you all right to continue for a while longer? You and Ben can sort out the pieces of corrugated iron and I'll go through these drawers, then start on the metal office cupboards.'

'Yes, of course I can stay. I'm very interested in solving the puzzle we are uncovering.'

'Puzzle, yes. It's certainly that.'

'And now that I don't have to work at night, I can work longer hours for you in the daytime, whatever suits. Al and his friend are very capable of guarding your sleep.'

Judith felt there wasn't room for another worker in the hut, so stayed in the kitchen to chat to Helen. 'Thanks for helping with the meals and buying me some food. Why don't you and Jan stay and have tea with us? I'm making a stew, so we can easily feed two more.'

'Thanks, but if you don't mind, I've got washing on the line and I'm rather tired. You could feed Jan, though, and then he can continue to help Mayne. I need a rest. I'm feeling a bit queasy.' She gave a wry smile. 'I thought you had morning sickness when you were expecting, but I'm having teatime sickness. And I get very tired around now.'

Judith gave her a quick hug. 'Every woman is different. It's all worth it, though, whatever you have to go through. I wouldn't be without my three for anything on earth.'

She said goodbye to Helen then stood at the kitchen door for a few moments, enjoying the last of the afternoon sunshine. They had started the day with such high hopes, she thought, but the thefts had made it feel as though someone had left a dirty mark across their lives.

When she went back inside, she checked the pot of beef bones simmering gently on the stove in the big stock pan. Yes, they were ready. She needed to sieve the liquid, take all the shreds of meat off the bones, and remove some of the fat floating on the surface. There was some good marrow in the bigger bones, and she'd put that back into the stew. There wouldn't be much actual meat. There never was these days. But she had plenty of potatoes and carrots, and a couple of onions. And she'd throw in some pearl barley.

Yes, that'd do. A hearty filling meal always lifted people's spirits.

She worked quickly, left the stew simmering and went out to see whether there had been any more surprises.

Mayne was standing outside the Nissen hut, looking so grim her heart sank.

She hurried towards him. 'What's wrong now? More stolen pieces?'

'Much worse than that.' Mayne barred the way into the hut. 'No, don't go inside. You don't need to see it.'

After his phone call to Mayne, Francis worked doggedly on clearing the last of the piles of rubble on his block of land. He felt deeply upset at the thought of how Diana had tried to manipulate him, couldn't get it out of his mind. If you couldn't trust your spouse, it wasn't a good marriage.

When he turned round and saw her father coming towards him, the day suddenly took a turn for the worse. Leonard Scammell had only once bothered to come and see him here and that had been to try to pressure him into selling the block of land straight away to a family friend at a ridiculously low price.

He slammed the spade down into the pile of earth and minor rubble, waiting, one hand resting on the wooden handle.

Leonard stopped two or three paces away and looked round. 'You've worked hard.'

'Yes.'

'Was it worth it? How much did you make?'

If Leonard had been genuinely interested, Francis would have shared the information with him, but his father-in-law had never shown an interest before. He was just prying, trying to find out how much money the younger man had made.

'I made far more than I'd expected.' He waited.

So did Leonard.

Francis picked up the spade and began scraping the last

of the rubble away from what looked like another broken beam, to see if it was worth retrieving.

'Can we please talk without you doing that manual labour, Francis? This is important.'

'You weren't talking. I don't like wasting my time.'

'Then I'll come to the point. My poor daughter is very upset. You've apparently told her to get out of the house.'

'Not exactly. I've told her I'm going to sell it and offered her the choice of coming with me to Lancashire or going back home to live with you. It's entirely up to her which she chooses.'

'It's the same thing. You surely can't expect a girl raised in a family like ours to go and live in a slum *and* do her own scrubbing?'

Francis inserted the spade into the rubble again and tossed some more dirt to one side. He would rather have tossed it in Scammell's face. 'Diana isn't a girl; she's a married woman. And I've no intention of us living in a slum.'

'Oh? You have a house in Lancashire already?'

'I have accommodation available in Rivenshaw. In a minor stately home, actually.' Aha! That surprised Leonard.

'What do you mean by a stately home?'

'I mean Esherwood, the house my friend has inherited, which we're planning to turn into flats – good quality flats for families, not slums, please note.' He heard the sharp edge to his voice and paused to take a deep breath before continuing more quietly, 'We shall all four be living on the site at first, and then who knows where we'll go once we start making the necessary changes to the building.'

'Have you actually seen this Esherwood place?'

'Not yet. I'm going up to Rivenshaw to look around as soon as I've finished here.'

'So it could be very tumbledown, this . . . *stately home*?' His tone was scornful, as if he didn't believe Francis.

'I doubt it. The house was used as a convalescent hospital until a few months ago.'

'Oh. Well, even so, you're prepared to abandon my daughter and take her home away from here to live temporarily in a house about which you know nothing.'

'Not at all. I've almost finished here and I'm going to visit Mayne on my own for a few days to discuss our business plans and have a look round. Then I'm coming back here to pack up and sell my house. Diana was invited to come too.'

'Hmm.'

'Now, if you've finished prying into my affairs, I'll get on with my work.'

'I don't like your tone, Brady. It lacks respect.'

'I could say the same about yours,' Francis shot back, losing his patience.

'I haven't finished talking to you, but I would prefer you to come up to the house tonight for us to continue this conversation in comfort and privacy.'

'What, meet the enemy on his own territory?' Francis asked flippantly.

'I am *not* the enemy. I am simply looking after my daughter's interests.'

'And weren't you the enemy when you offered me money not to marry Diana? Is your wife not my enemy when she pours poison into her daughter's ears about me and tries to break up my marriage?'

Scammell looked at him indignantly. 'Christine doesn't do that.'

'I've heard her criticising me – and more than once. She was doing it only yesterday. I'll not put up with that in my own home, so you'd better warn your wife that if she does it again, I shall forbid her to come to the house. Frankly, it's clear to me that if Diana and I are to retrieve our marriage, it'll have to be somewhere other than here.'

The two men glared at one another for a moment, then Scammell snapped, 'There's no reasoning with you.'

'Not if by reasoning you mean persuading me to walk away from the best business opportunity I'm ever likely to have.'

'Well in that case, Diana will keep all the furniture, for a start.'

'Have you already persuaded her to leave me, then?'

'It seemed obvious that this might happen since *you* won't change your mind and *she* doesn't wish to move north.'

Fortunately the builder arrived just as Francis was about to lose control and say exactly what he thought about their interference in his marriage. 'Here's my client. Excuse me. Business calls.'

He finished helping Johnson load the truck with bricks and timber, then negotiated a price for a pile of smaller pieces of wood which the builder wanted to use as kindling in his own home, an unexpected bonus when every shilling counted.

As Francis accepted the money, the two men studied the site and agreed that tomorrow would see the end of anything useful being turned up. They'd already checked out the scrubby land behind where the house and business had once stood.

Johnson lowered his voice. 'Just between you and me, Brady, you are still selling this place, aren't you?'

'I haven't put it up for sale yet, but yes, I intend to. Why?'

The builder chewed his thumb then said, 'I heard there was some problem with the title to the land and you might not own it.'

'Where the hell did you hear that?'

'In the pub. But I recognised the chap saying it. He's a clerk at Scammell's and he doesn't usually drink there with the hoi polloi. So I reckon someone's setting you up and trying to keep buyers away.' Johnson's eyes turned towards Scammell, who was still watching them. 'I thought you ought to know about it.'

'I'm grateful to you. Just to set the record straight, I inherited this place over a year ago and there is no problem whatsoever with the title. I own it outright. The only problem I've encountered has been that as soon as the ARP stopped keeping watch over the village at night, the looting began, as you know.'

'How about selling the land to me, then?'

'If you'll pay my price, I'd be very happy to sell it to you.'

'How much?'

'Five thousand pounds. There's quite a bit of land, and it's on two titles, actually.'

'I know. I've checked it. Perfect for my needs. I'll think about that price and get back to you.'

'Just one thing. I'd be grateful if you'd not discuss this with my wife or her family, or anyone else in the village, come to that.'

Johnson tapped the side of his nose. 'You don't need to worry. It suits me to keep it secret too. I don't want anyone outbidding me.'

Francis watched him drive away, then turned towards Scammell, who was still standing to one side, watching him. His father-in-law had no doubt counted the notes the builder had paid him.

Francis didn't speak to his father-in-law, but began to collect his tools, working quickly, wanting to get away.

After a few seconds, he heard Scammell walk off in the direction of his office.

Only then did Francis stop pretending to be busy. He went and sat in his van, and thumped his clenched fists on the steering wheel several times as he thought about the nasty tricks Scammell had several times played on him. But his anger gradually died down as he thought of the builder who seemed quite likely to buy the piece of land. He'd love to see Scammell's face if that came off.

What he couldn't understand was why Leonard and Christine Scammell were working so hard to break up his marriage when it was a done deed. The only way to undo it would be for him to get a divorce, which could take several years to finalise and would place a stigma on them both. For all any of them knew, Diana could be pregnant, and then what would happen?

He didn't think she was pregnant, because she'd have told him. But they hadn't been exactly careful, because they were still good together in bed, in spite of their quarrels.

When he got home, he called, 'I'm back.' But his words echoed through the house and when he went from room to room, there was no sign of his wife.

Diana didn't come home that night.

And Francis found that the thought of a divorce upset him far more than he'd expected. Oh, he was a fool! Diana had made it more than plain that she didn't want to move away from her parents. Why did he still want her?

The doors of the Nissen hut were closed now, and Mayne was standing in front of them, as if preventing entry.

'Mum! Don't try to go inside,' Ben called. He was sitting on an old bench to the right of the hut, with his sisters on either side of him. There was no sign of Jan.

Her son looked wan and upset, so Judith went across to him. 'What's wrong, love? Are you hurt?'

'No. But I was the one who found it.' He shuddered violently.

'What did you find?'

'A foot – poking out of the ground.'

'*What?*'

'It was when Mr Borkowski an' me dragged some of those pieces of corrugated iron away from the wall. The ground's all squishy there and the edge of the iron scraped a hole as we pulled it. When it caught in something, we saw a boot with a foot still in it. Ugh! Only it was bones, not a proper foot. And I was right next to it. I nearly touched it, Mum.' He gulped as if feeling sick.

She looked at Mayne for an explanation.

'Someone had buried a body in the hut, Judith, and they must have been in a hurry because they didn't bury it very deeply. The floor isn't concreted beyond the first couple of yards, as you know. Perhaps they hid the body soon after the hut was built, expecting it to be concreted over later.'

He shook his head as if annoyed at himself. 'The drain outside must have been overflowing and softening the ground for a good while – years I'd guess – because the ground was saturated a third of the way across the hut at that side. I swear to you, Judith, if I'd had the slightest suspicion something was wrong, I'd not have let the lad help.'

'You weren't to know.' She crouched by her son. 'Is that all you saw, love? The foot?'

'That and the bottom part of the leg. The bones were poking out of some mucky old trousers. It was horrible, Mum. I've never seen a dead person before.'

'It doesn't sound like you've seen much of this one, either,' she said crisply, standing up again.

She was aware of Mayne's surprise at her tone, but she'd found it did no good to sympathise with her children when they were facing difficulties. You had to be bracing and act as if they could cope. Which they usually did. She wasn't going to say 'Poor you!' to Ben or he'd continue to feel awful and dwell on the bad aspects of this experience.

She waited a moment then added quietly, 'Just think what the lads at school will say when you tell them you found a corpse. And you're all going back to school this coming week, so it'll be big news in town.'

Kitty gave her a quick smile as if she understood what her mother was doing.

Ben gaped at his mother, then began to look thoughtful. 'The other lads will be really jealous, won't they?'

'They certainly will, love. Absolutely green with jealousy. Now, go and wash your hands and face, then help the girls make us all a pot of tea. I need to talk to Mayne.'

When they'd gone, her husband said, 'You did that well.'

She shrugged. 'We've faced quite a few bad things together, my children and I. This isn't the first time and it won't be the last. Never mind that. What are we going to do about this, Mayne?'

'I've sent Jan for Sergeant Deemer. We have to report it to the authorities, can't just pretend we didn't find it. But what the hell is a rotting corpse doing buried under our Nissen hut?'

'Someone got killed by accident, I suppose, and those involved hid the body in the first place they could think of. Well, I hope it was an accident.'

'Could have been, I suppose.' He put his arm round her. 'Are you all right, darling?'

'Of course I am. I haven't even seen the body and if I had, well, it's only a person, isn't it? I've helped my neighbour, Mrs Needham, lay out dead people several times. I used to earn a few shillings doing that. I never told Doug about it, though, or he'd have taken the money from me.'

Mayne looked startled but she wasn't going to pretend about her past life. It had been hard going, and she'd done whatever she had to in order to put food on the table for her children. Her so-called husband had rarely provided enough for his family. Doug had preferred to spend his wages at the pub.

But she needn't have worried about Mayne's reaction. This wonderful new husband gave her a rib-cracking hug, chuckling softly and saying, 'That's my Judith: indomitable. That's what you are, love, indomitable.'

He was so different from other men she'd known, so kind and caring, yet strong too. She still marvelled that he'd fallen in love with her. She glanced over her shoulder to make sure no one was close then touched his cheek briefly. 'You're not bad yourself, Mayne Esher.'

'One day I'll teach you to hug me in public without thinking it over first,' he said in his deep, quiet voice. 'Ah, here comes the sergeant. And that looks like the new constable I heard Deemer had acquired.'

He turned to face the entire Rivenshaw police force – one elderly man, who had come out of retirement to serve the town during the war, and one fresh-faced fellow who looked too young to be a policeman and whose uniform was clearly brand new.

5

The following morning, Francis decided to carry on as usual. He'd finish today's salvage work – unless thieves had taken the rest of the useful stuff during the night – then with a bit of luck, he'd sell the land to the builder.

When that was settled, he'd insist on Diana discussing their future with him again, without her parents being present.

The first part of the day went well. There had been no looting and Johnson turned up at ten o'clock. 'Four thousand nine hundred pounds and you've got a sale.'

'It's yours.' Francis stuck out his hand and they shook. 'Did it make a difference knocking the price down?'

'It did to me. You asked a fair price for a piece of land like this, but I always like to pay a bit less than the asking price, on principle. Have I upset you?'

'No. You've pleased me. Someone else offered me much less for it – a friend of my father-in-law had been tipped off by him and was trying to take advantage. Selling the land means I can go and check out my next job in Lancashire.'

'They were talking about something else in the pub last night – what you're planning to do.'

'Oh? What were they saying?'

'That it's all a load of airy-fairy nonsense dreamed up by a few young soldiers with nothing better to do and no experience in building.'

'Scammell's clerk again?'

'No.'

'Who then?'

Johnson grinned. 'The clerk's brother. That Scammell thinks those he calls "the lower classes" are all stupid. Fancy sending someone who's well known as a layabout to spread nasty rumours about someone we've all seen working hard. I added a few words of my own to the mix. I told people you were a shrewd fellow who'd learned a lot during the war and you knew your electrics better than anyone I'd ever met.'

Francis was touched. 'Thanks for that.'

'You're welcome. I don't like to see people being slandered.' He grinned. 'And I might know someone who'd be interested in buying your house, if you still want to sell it. Well, it's my son-in-law, actually, but he's not been demobbed yet.'

'Oh?'

'Give me a few days to get in touch. You think what you want to sell it for and I'll help him decide what'd be a fair bargain. You'll let us have first refusal, eh? We won't keep you waiting long and we'll pay cash.'

'All right. I have to go up to Lancashire to sort out what's happening, so we'll get together once I come back.'

Johnson stuck out his hand and the two of them shook on the bargain.

Francis felt warmed by the builder's fatherly kindness, but that faded quickly as he walked back to face an empty house.

Why were the Scammells going to these lengths to blacken his name? They had already separated him and Diana. Why did they feel a need to destroy his reputation as well?

Well, they weren't going to succeed because he was known in the area and folk respected his family. He'd sold the land in spite of Scammell's slyness, and he'd sell the house too, if not to Johnson's relative, then to someone else.

It'd not be difficult to find a buyer. Returning servicemen were crying out for places to set up home.

But still, the thought of Scammell's vindictiveness nagged at him. Something didn't seem right about this whole business.

What was he missing?

Francis expected to go home to an empty house, but was surprised to find Diana waiting for him in the sitting room. She looked unhappy and uncertain, opening her mouth as if to speak then shutting it again.

'How about a cup of tea?' he asked to break the ice.

'Good idea.' She led the way into the kitchen.

When she set out two of the tiny china teacups, he said, 'I don't want to drink out of those,' and got down his tin mug. Seeing her disapproving look, he explained, 'a man who does hard physical work needs more than a thimbleful of tea to replace what he's sweated out.'

She shuddered. 'Do you have to be so vulgar?'

'We all sweat. Even you.'

'We don't all talk about it.'

When he got down his trusty old mug and put it next to the teapot, she wrinkled her nose in distaste but put one china cup away again. She added more tea leaves and hot water to the pot. After getting out some biscuits, she filled his mug, grimacing but making no further comment.

They sat down at the kitchen table and he waited for her to speak first. Given their recent differences, talking wasn't going to be easy, but he hoped they could find a way to bridge the gap between them.

In the end he had to break the silence. 'I'm glad you came back, Diana.'

'Are you? Father said he talked to you about this building project but you wouldn't change your mind.'

'Did either of you think I was likely to?'

'I hoped you might reconsider if he explained things to you, yes.'

A bark of scornful laughter escaped him. 'I don't need things explaining, Diana. I'm not stupid, though your parents always act as if everyone from the *lower classes* is automatically stupid. You do too sometimes when you're talking to me.'

'I don't!'

'You do, but we won't argue about that today. Go on. I've been wanting to talk things through. I was beginning to think all *you* wanted was to get away from me.'

She shook her head vigorously and her voice grew a little softer. 'No, Francis! I've never wanted that. But I haven't changed my mind about moving to Lancashire, either.'

'That's as may be, but I don't understand why you're refusing to come up north to see Rivenshaw before you make a final decision. It's quite a pretty little town, except for one industrial area, and all towns have those, even in the south.'

She frowned at him. 'What's the point in me going? I won't change my mind.'

'Then come anyway and we'll call the trip our final fling together.' He reached out to grasp her hand.

Tears filled her lovely eyes. 'Final,' she whispered. 'Oh, Francis! How did it come to this?'

He didn't try to answer that, because he didn't want to get into a quarrel about her parents' interference.

She sighed and let go of his hand. 'I blame it all on that horrible war. You'd never have met those men if you hadn't been in the Army.'

'And that would have been my loss. Those three have become my closest friends now. You'd like them too, I know you would. The war wasn't all bad, Diana. It brought you and me together, for one thing. We'd never have met socially without it, even though we grew up in the same village.'

Her voice was dull. 'Maybe that would have been easier.'

'*Easier*! Life isn't always easy and it's never predictable. You have to make the best of it as you go along. And whatever *you* decide, I at least will never regret our time together.'

'Oh, Francis!' She dabbed at her eyes with one of those ridiculously small, lace-edged handkerchiefs.

But she made no attempt to take the hand he'd stretched out to her again, so he drew it back and reached out with words instead. 'The war also gave me a wider view of the world, and I really appreciate that.'

'It changed you.'

'No one can live through the things I saw and did, and not change. I think the war changed most people, military and civilians. How could it not? Didn't it change you?'

Silence pooled between them, broken only by the gentle ticking of the kitchen clock as he waited in vain for her to respond.

'The war took things away from people, too,' he continued. 'My parents lost their lives right here in this village. And given what happened to them, I can't bear to see that piece of land every day, to remember how happy my childhood was living there, to know that I'll never see them again. Diana, I *need* to get away from here and make a new life somewhere else if I'm to be happy.'

'I can understand that. I can. But I still don't want to go so far away. Maybe, if you don't want to work in Mr Price's garage – and I must say, I don't like him either – you could get another job nearby. After all, mechanics are always in demand.'

He shook his head. How many times did he have to say it?

'*You* need to get away, Francis, but *I* need to be near my parents, because my brother hardly ever comes to visit them since he got married. Surely you can see that it's my duty as a daughter to be nearby?'

'What about your duty as a wife?'

She waited a few moments but didn't answer that question. Instead, she said in a coaxing voice, 'If you loved me, you'd do what I ask, when you know how much it means to me.'

It was the wrong thing to say to him. She'd been brought up to be selfish, he thought yet again. She put herself first every time in their relationship and expected him to put her first too. But he thought marriage should be a partnership, with each caring about the other's needs.

He'd expected Diana to grow up after they married. After all, she'd lived through a world war. But she didn't seem to have changed at all.

He did not, he realised bleakly, want to spend the rest of his life pandering to a spoiled brat.

Her parents might seem to put her first, but he'd noticed that it was only as long as she did what they expected. He could understand why her brother stayed away from them because the Scammells made no bones about not approving of William's wife. He hadn't been demobbed from the Army yet and was stationed in Norfolk. Francis would bet his brother-in-law never returned to Hertfordshire.

Taking a deep breath, Francis repeated what he'd said before, 'It's *because* I love you, darling, that I'm trying to do the best I can for our future. I want to be more than a mechanic.'

She stiffened. 'Don't you "darling" me. Best for *your* future, you mean. You don't even care what I want.'

'Of course I do. Look, I've just sold my parents' land, so that's the main step taken towards starting our new life. I'll have money to invest in the building company now and I'll be a partner. You see if I don't make you proud of me.'

'It was Daddy who got you the offer for the land.'

'I didn't sell it to your father's friend. I got nearly a thousand pounds more for it from someone else.'

She stared at him in surprise. 'But Daddy said—'

'Can we for once leave your damned father out of a discussion?'

'How dare you be so rude? Daddy only wants what's best for me.'

There she went again – saying *I* and *me*, not *us*. 'It's not best for me, though, to sell my land at a knock-down price.'

She elevated her nose and spoke more slowly. 'You simply don't understand business. You'd be making a useful contact by doing that.'

'No, I wouldn't. Your father would be doing a favour to a friend, and the favour would be returned to him one day, not to me.'

'Oh, there's no talking to you, Francis Brady! You won't even listen to those who know more about that sort of thing.'

He waved one hand. 'I'm listening to *you*, though I can't understand why you think you know better than I do. But carry on. Talk away.'

Instead she began to flip through the evening newspaper, still printed on the cheap wartime paper in a smudgy ink, still with only a few pages allowed.

Francis watched her pretend to read it and tried desperately to work out a way to make her understand. But even if he did this now, his father-in-law would no doubt undermine what he said and find some other way to come between them.

Scammell would be absolutely furious when he found out that the block of land had been sold to Johnson the builder, instead of to a friend of the family.

Francis wouldn't tell Diana what had been said in the pub to damage his reputation because it had failed to deter his buyer and was therefore unimportant. Anyway, she wouldn't believe him if he did suggest that her parents were responsible for those rumours.

He was looking forward to a more independent working life in the north, a chance to use his hard-won new skills, an opportunity to make decent money. It was sad though that it looked as if Diana would leave him. He longed for children, looked forward to being a father – a good one, he hoped – wanted to bring up sturdy youngsters who would be able to stand on their own feet as they faced the better world he'd fought for.

What sort of mother would Diana make, though, even if they did stay together?

He hadn't even considered that when he rushed into marriage, had been dazzled by her beauty and charm. His heart sank as he considered that aspect of her character now, really considered it.

Was she capable of letting go of her mother's apron strings and acting like a responsible mother herself? He thought not.

He'd heard that a lot of wartime marriages were breaking up. And yet, even now he didn't want his own to fall apart.

'Come with me to Rivenshaw, Diana,' he urged one last time. 'At least have a look at the town before you refuse to live there.'

'No! I won't move away from my parents. At least *they* love me, even if you don't!' She stood up, shoved her chair back so hard it fell over, then ran upstairs to their bedroom, sobbing like a child. Once again he heard the bolt on the inside of the door snick into place, locking him out.

As if he couldn't kick down that flimsy door!

As if he would ever do such a thing!

He not only felt angry with her, but stifled by the house that was so much a reflection of her mother's taste because even in setting up their home, Diana had been an obedient child, letting her mother guide her in choosing second-hand furniture.

He'd been excluded because he was away serving his country or he'd never have bought this stuff. Looking round with loathing at the fussy décor, he went out into the hall, grabbed his overcoat and slammed the front door behind him as he left. There was nothing like a walk in the fresh air for clearing your head.

Outside everything was peaceful, with dusk shading delicately into night. Now that the blackout was no longer in place, the streets in the centre of the village were punctuated by pools of light, and it lifted his heart just to see them. The air smelled faintly of bonfires, burning leaves, moist rich earth and the last of the summer's flowers – clean country smells.

He drew in one deep breath after another.

He hoped that by the time he got back to the house, Diana would have gone home to Mummy and Daddy, as she seemed set on doing. He was tired of being patient with her, tired of the Scammells, deep down weary after his weeks of hard, physical labour and equally hard disagreements.

Time to move on.

But . . . he'd miss her, for all her faults. And not just in his bed.

When Francis's silhouette had faded into the distance, Diana left her post at the window and went downstairs, weeping more quietly now.

She rang her mother. 'You were right and I was wrong, Mummy. He won't see sense. Can I—' She had to swallow hard before she could force the words out. 'Can I come back to live at home?'

'Yes, of course, darling. What's happened now? I can tell you're crying. Has he hit you?'

She stared at the phone in shock. 'No, of course not. He'd never do that.'

'Men of his class often do.'

'Well, Francis wouldn't. But he'll never change his mind about Lancashire, so . . .' She couldn't speak for crying and her mother made soothing noises into the telephone.

When she'd pulled herself together, Diana said, 'I'm going to pack my suitcases now. Will you come and pick me up in the car?'

'Yes, of course we will. Oh, darling, I'm so sorry. I hate to see you unhappy. But it's for the best. You should never have married a man like that. Don't worry. We'll get you free of him.'

She put down the phone, her mother's last words echoing in her head. *Free of him!* Was that possible? Francis was so much more vibrant than any other man she'd ever met. How could she ever forget him? How could she ever go with another man?

But how could she leave her parents? Her father had told her that her mother wasn't as well as she tried to make out and the doctor had said they mustn't upset her.

Tears sliding down her cheeks, Diana continued packing.

When her parents arrived to pick her up, Diana was sitting on the stairs with the front door open and her bulging suitcases were ready in the hall.

Her father bustled in, carrying a couple of empty shopping bags. He blew her a kiss then made straight for the dining room.

Diana stood up, looking at her mother. 'What's Daddy doing?'

'Getting the silver. We don't want that man to sell it. He's hungry for every penny he can lay his hands on, but he's not getting them from our family silver.'

'Francis would never take my things.' She walked into the dining room. 'Daddy, there's no need for this.'

'I think there is, dear. I've watched him haggling for pennies. These pieces would fetch a lot more than pennies if he sold them.'

'Well, he'll have no need to haggle for every penny now. He's sold the land.'

He froze, staring at her. '*What?* Are you sure?'

'Yes, of course I'm sure. Francis wouldn't lie to me.'

'Who has he sold it to?'

'I don't know. He didn't say.'

'What about this house, Diana? Has he sold it as well?'

'Not that I know of. No, he'd have told me.'

'I know two or three people who're looking for a house. I may suggest they get in touch with him.'

'Daddy, don't!'

He looked at her in puzzlement. 'Don't what?'

'Pull my life to pieces so *quickly.*'

'You said you were coming back to live at home. Are you or are you not leaving him?'

'I . . . suppose I am. But I'm not certain it's permanent.' She moved forward and tried to pull the silver coffee set out of the bag, but her father prevented her.

Her mother came and put an arm round her, guiding her back into the hall. 'No one will stop you coming back here, if that's what you really want.'

'I don't know what I want.'

'Well, then, let your father guide you. He knows what's best. We'll go and wait for him in the car, shall we, dear?'

Beyond tears now, feeling numb and distant, Diana allowed herself to be led outside. But the sounds followed her, metallic clinking sounds as her father continued to go through the silverware in the tiny dining room and fill the two shopping bags with the best pieces.

She felt so guilty about doing that to Francis. It was wrong. But she couldn't go against her father, she never had been able to.

When Francis got home, he saw at once that the dining room was in a mess and quickly realised the silver was missing. Had they been burgled?

He went running up the stairs, worried that someone had broken into the house and attacked Diana. Though that was the sort of crime you heard about in big cities not peaceful villages in Hertfordshire.

The bedroom was also in chaos and most of his wife's clothing was missing from the wardrobe and drawers. Burglars might take the silver but he doubted they'd take her clothes.

He plumped down on the bed. She really had left him now.

Anger began to replace the hurt. What had she thought he'd do? Sell her family's silver?

With a sigh, he got up off the bed and went downstairs. He stood in the dining room looking for the one piece that was from his side. That too was gone. They'd even taken the little silver bonbon dish he'd bought for his mother one birthday. It was slightly dented, but the bomb hadn't destroyed it and he treasured it.

That was the final straw. He stormed out of the house and made his way across the village on foot. Five minutes later he slowed down when he reached the Scammells' large, detached residence.

His army training took over. *Reconnoitre before engaging enemy.*

He went quietly into the garden and across the edge of the lawn to the house. The curtains in the sitting room weren't drawn because, like so many others, the Scammells were enjoying not being hemmed in by blackout curtains.

Diana was sitting on a sofa next to her mother. She looked as elegant as ever, though pale. It annoyed him further that she'd taken the time to dress nicely on such a day.

But she wasn't taking his mother's dish.

He moved into the lighted patch and hammered on the French windows.

The three people in the room stared across at him in shock.

'Go away, Brady!' Mr Scammell shouted. 'If you try to make trouble, I'll call the police.'

'Good. Do that. I'll be able to tell them you've stolen something from me. We'll see what they do then.'

'What the hell do you mean? That silver was Diana's grandmother's.'

'All except one small dish that belonged to *my* mother. Couldn't you even leave me that?'

He saw from Diana's expression that she realised which dish he meant and understood what it meant to him.

She stood up. 'I'll deal with this, Daddy.'

'You most certainly will not.'

She ignored her father and turned back to window, calling loudly, 'I'll get you the dish, Francis. Come to the front door.'

He heard them arguing as he moved away, but in this at least he trusted her, so he walked slowly round to the front door.

It opened to show Diana with her father behind her holding a heavy walking stick as if he expected to be attacked.

She moved forward. 'I'm sorry, Francis. I told them we didn't need to remove the silver, that you wouldn't take anything that didn't belong to you, but Daddy insisted.' She held out the little dish. 'Here. I didn't realise. I . . . wasn't thinking clearly.'

Their hands met for a moment and he could smell her perfume. He stepped back with a curt, 'Thank you.'

As he walked away, he heard the door slam shut behind

him and voices start arguing behind it. But though he slowed down to look back, the door didn't open again.

What did you think, you fool? That she'd come after you?

It was a while before he realised that if she'd been telling the truth, she'd actually disagreed with her father. Wonders would never cease.

His life was changing so quickly, he felt as if he was walking on slippery black ice, invisible but still there to make you uncertain of your footing. Indeed, he seemed to be feeling his way through a chilly, alien world.

He'd grown used to being married, dammit, and for all her faults, used to being with Diana.

As soon as they were sure Fitkin really did want to buy the house and would also buy all the bits and pieces they were leaving, Victor and Ros worked even harder on clearing it out, with the help of their temporary maid. He also called in a removal man, who agreed to transport their goods and chattels up to Lancashire.

'Makes a change to take a long journey,' he said cheerfully. 'Are you ex-army?'

'Yes, I am. Moving to a new job.'

'Good. That'll make it easier to get the petrol. They've loosened up quite a bit for people in my trade, but they can still make it difficult to get enough for long journeys. You'd better start applying for extra petrol yourself.'

'Thanks for the tip. I'll do that.'

'I'm afraid you're going to miss the first day or two of school, darling,' he told his daughter.

Betty didn't complain or throw a tantrum as another child might. She was still too passive after her years of repression, he thought sadly.

'I know, Daddy. I'm sad about that, but we have to get our things, don't we? I've missed my toys and books.'

She looked round thoughtfully and added, 'Will we ever come back here, do you think?'

'I hope not.'

'I wish we could visit Mother's grave before we go.'

He felt guilty, because he should have thought of that. He'd ask Fitkin, who seemed able to manage his new wife better than anyone Victor had seen dealing with her.

He'd point out how bad it'd look if they continued to be kept away from Susan's grave in the Galton family mausoleum.

'I'll ask about that, darling. I'm sure they'll let us do it.'

She nodded. 'Good.'

They worked until nearly midnight on the Sunday, by which time they were exhausted.

'Why don't we make a little holiday of driving my car back to Rivenshaw, stopping off a couple of times,' he suggested to Ros as they were getting ready for bed.

'I think it'd be better to get there as quickly as we can and keep holidays for later. Betty is nervous about starting the new year at school, though she tries not to show it.'

'I suppose so. I forget sometimes about a child's inflexible schedule of school and holidays.' He stretched and got into bed. 'I'm not looking forward to tomorrow. I'll no doubt have to spend hours queuing and filling in forms to get the extra petrol.'

'It'll be nice to be back, though. I'm missing Judith, and I know Betty is missing the other children.'

But she was talking to herself because he'd fallen instantly asleep. She snuggled down beside him, letting herself follow his example.

6

When Sergeant Deemer arrived to investigate the dead body, he joined Mayne and Judith outside the Nissen hut. Jan went to occupy his favourite spot at the top of the stable stairs, observing them with the grave interest that was so much a part of his character.

The constable stood to one side, stiffly at attention until the sergeant said absent-mindedly, 'Relax, lad. We're not on parade.' He winked at Mayne. 'This is Jimmy Waide. It's his first posting. Farrow's left the force. Got an offer of a job with a bright future working for his uncle. And a good thing too – he'll make a much better shop assistant than policeman.'

Mayne had been expecting Farrow to leave the police force. Men who didn't get on with Deemer usually did, one way or another. And if the sergeant didn't approve of someone, then as far as Mayne was concerned, there was something wrong with that person. The elderly officer was one of the shrewdest judges of human nature you could ever hope to meet.

'Mind if I check that it is a body, Mr Esher?'

'Not at all. I'll show you.' Mayne had seen enough death during the war not to be squeamish about bodies. He picked up the big torch and led the way inside the shadowy Nissen hut. 'They didn't bother to run electricity in here, I'm afraid, and we can't remove the wood nailed over the window frames until we can get hold of some panes of glass. Civilians still have to join a waiting list to buy that sort of thing.'

The sergeant removed his own torch from where it was attached to his belt and beckoned to his constable. 'Don't let anyone follow us inside.'

'Yessir. I mean, no sir.'

Deemer stopped just inside the door to stare around then followed Mayne along the space cleared through the middle of the hut. 'Waide is still at the eager puppy stage, but he's a trier. I like to see that in a young 'un.'

Mayne held up one hand to stop his companion. 'It gets a bit muddy from here on, so watch how you go.' He stepped to the left, off the central path, playing his torch over the dug-up area and then shining it steadily on the grisly find.

Deemer crouched down to examine the foot, holding his torch close to it and poking at the cloth covering the lower leg bone with the tip of a pencil. With a grunt at the effort it cost his ageing body, he stood up again. 'You're right. It is a body. Not that I doubted you. We'll let someone else dig it up, though.'

'Can't be more than a few years old. This hut was only erected in late 1941 – or was it early 1942? Looks like he's wearing the remains of an Army uniform to me. Whoever buried him didn't even wrap him up.'

'Hiding the body in a hurry, I'd guess.'

'What do you plan to do, Sergeant?'

'Pass the responsibility for the investigation up the line. I'd better get in touch with Halkett and leave it up to him to decide. Our temporary Area Commander would have a fit if I did anything without his say-so. I expect he'll get in touch with the Army and let them deal with it, given the circumstances. Well, that's what ought to be done, anyway.'

As they began to walk back towards the door, Deemer stopped for a moment to say in a low voice, 'Between you and me, Esher, the sooner the new fellow takes over as our Area Commander the better, as far as I'm concerned. Well, I hope it'll be for the better. I'm pretty sure they won't give the job to Halkett, even if he is filling in temporarily. He's famous for putting people's backs up.'

'Any idea who's in the running for the job?'

'No. But I did hear they'd already chosen somebody and a little bird told me Judge Peters was on the selection panel, so there's a good chance they'll appoint someone with a bit of sense in his top storey.' Deemer tapped his forehead to emphasise that last phrase, then started moving again, speaking normally now. 'We'd better keep everyone out of this hut until further notice.'

'Unfortunately, yes. But it's very inconvenient.' Mayne took the key out of his pocket, shot the bolts on the inside of one door and locked the other door to it. 'There. I hope they won't take too long dealing with this. We want to classify the rest of the hut's contents. It's just about the last place that needs clearing out.'

'What did you do with the things you removed from the hut?'

'Put them into the laundry for safe storage.' He didn't mention the stolen articles or the tools. He might or might not do that later.

'Make sure no one fiddles with them. You never know what *they* will consider important when they're investigating.'

'It's mostly planks, a few boxes and the odd piece of furniture. I doubt such items will tell the investigators much.'

Deemer shrugged and looked towards Jan, still sitting patiently at the top of the steps. 'Is your chap keeping watch tonight?'

'Jan? No. He's working days now. But Al will be patrolling the grounds. He alternates nights with a friend of his.'

'Well, as long as I have your word that no one will go into

the hut and young Al can keep an eye on it, I won't station someone here overnight. It's a sad look-out when you have to pay people to protect your grounds in Rivenshaw; it is that. It'd not have been necessary before the war.'

He turned to the constable. 'Waide, there's a dead body in there.'

The young man gaped at him in shock, then looked excited.

'I'll have to station you here for the rest of the day. No one to go in or out of the hut, not even Mr Esher. You can go home once the night watchman arrives, but you're to come back as soon as it's light.'

'Yessir.'

That same night, while Al was patrolling the grounds of Esherwood, he heard someone crashing through the bushes in one of the uncultivated parts further away from the big house. Mr Esher said this area would probably be used for building houses on, so it wasn't worth tidying it up. Let the birds and little creatures enjoy it until then.

The intruder was making no attempt to keep quiet, which thieves usually did, so Al waited to see what he was after.

The movements stopped and silence fell. After waiting a moment or two, Al pushed his way quietly through the bushes to see what was going on.

An old chap was sitting on a fallen tree trunk, only his outline and bald head visible in the dimness of a cloudy night. That chunk of wood must have come from a very large tree and Al made a mental note to suggest that Mr Esher haul it back to the stable yard to chop up for firewood before someone else took it.

The intruder seemed to be staring blindly into space, so Al moved forward. 'What are you doing here?'

'Eh? What? Oh, it's you, young Needham.'

Al took another step forward and shone a torch towards

the man's face. 'Mr Rennie. What the hell are you doing here at this time of night?'

'Just sitting thinking, lad. Since our son was killed, I've been having trouble sleeping. If I potter about in the house, I disturb Nellie and, anyway, I feel stifled sometimes indoors, so I thought I'd come out for a walk. I just need to sit quietly where no one will pester me and ask if I'm all right. Of course I'm not all right!'

He sighed wearily. 'I didn't want to trample round the allotments on Parson's Mead looking for somewhere to sit, because they're still getting in the last of their crops and I might have damaged something. So I slipped into the grounds of the big house through that little back path. I know I'm trespassing, but I haven't hurt anything. I thought it'd be nice and quiet here. Peaceful like. And it is.'

'I'm sorry about your son, Mr Rennie.'

'Yes, well, there you are. That's war for you. And we did beat Hitler. It's a comfort, at least, that our Mike didn't die in vain.' His voice thickened and he had to pause to pull himself together. 'I, um, heard you were working as night watchman here.'

'For the time being; Mr Esher's got another job lined up for me later.'

'Good boss, is he?'

'Very good.'

After a moment or two's silence, Mr Rennie asked, 'You going to turn me out, lad?'

'Nah. But I'll tell my friend who keeps watch sometimes that you come here, and to leave you alone. Maybe in return you'll help us watch out for thieves. Yell out or go to the house if you see anyone acting suspiciously.'

Mr Rennie's face brightened. 'I'll be glad to have some-thing useful to do. Lost me job, I did, when the factory stopped war production. It isn't easy to get another one when you're over sixty, not with all the younger men getting demobbed. Tell you what, I'll bring my football rattle in case someone comes. It's a nice loud one.'

'Good idea. How's Mrs Rennie coping?'

'She's fretting, of course she is. She's missing her voluntary war work, too. Doesn't know what to do with herself. And to cap it all, the landlord's raising the rent. He says he can get twice what we pay for the house because people are crying out for somewhere to live and if we can't pay it, we'll have to leave. We've been in that house for over thirty years and never missed paying the rent, not once. But this chap's not like his father. Only cares about money, this one does.'

After a pause, he added sadly, 'We haven't got anywhere else to go and you know what it's like finding somewhere to live these days. We'll end up in the workhouse or whatever they call it nowadays, that's what.'

As Al looked at the old man, an idea popped into his mind. He didn't say anything. He'd have to see Judith first, but he thought she'd like his suggestion.

And the more he thought about it after he left Mr Rennie in peace, the better he liked the idea.

When he went to report to his employers at the end of his night's work, Al waved to the young policeman, already standing guard over the hut in the grey dawn light, then went into the kitchen where Judith handed him his usual cup of tea.

Between mouthfuls, he told her and Mayne about Mr Rennie.

'I reckon you could employ him as a night watchman, Mr Esher.'

'He may not find somewhere to live that's close enough to walk here.'

'Ah. Well, I had another idea about that. Have you found anyone to go in and help your father yet?'

'We thought we had, but she worked for a week then decided she couldn't put up with his absent-mindedness and sloppy ways.'

'When you first came back, didn't you live in a house-keeper's room there?'

Both of them stared at him with comprehension dawning in their eyes.

'It's a small flat actually,' Mayne said. 'Self-contained. If you're suggesting offering it to the Rennies in return for looking after my father and keeping an eye on the place at night, I think it's an excellent idea.'

'That's exactly what I was going to suggest.'

'They're not too old for that?'

'No. Mr Rennie is in his early sixties and Mrs Rennie in her late fifties, or thereabouts. They're both good for their age, or they were till Mike got killed. Losing their only son knocked the stuffing out of them.'

'If Rennie takes the night watchman's job, it'll free you up to do other things, Al,' Judith said. 'You're wasted doing those duties.'

He grinned at her. 'I'll be glad to move on to something else, I must admit. It's a bit hard sleeping in the daytime, too noisy. I think things are settling down now. Word's got round that a careful watch is kept here and you've moved most of the useful stuff closer to the house anyway. Oh, and before I forget, it'd be worth you sawing up that fallen tree, Mr Esher, and hauling the pieces across to the stables. Lot of firewood in that and it's already dried out.'

'Another good idea. How about you do that for us, and take some of the wood to your mother as payment, say about twenty per cent?'

'Happy to. Well, I am if you've got a good saw. We haven't got one big enough.'

'Jan will know if we have. That fellow never forgets anything.

Oh, and there are some tools down in the stables at the Dower House, as well. We'll need to go through those. Maybe we can do that while the authorities are sorting out what to do with the dead body.'

When Al had gone home, Judith took off her apron. 'I'd like to settle this straight away, Mayne. Your father's making a mess at the Dower House and he's not eating properly, even when I leave food for him. People talk about absent-minded professors, but we've actually got one and he isn't easy to look after!'

'Do what you think best.'

She turned to her daughter. 'Kitty love, will you take over getting breakfast and see that the others clear up properly? Mayne, I'll go and see your father straight away and check out the flat while I'm there. It probably needs a good clean-out.'

'You're not doing that sort of work,' Mayne said firmly.

Their eyes met and after a moment she shrugged, knowing he didn't want his wife doing menial jobs like scrubbing. She certainly preferred working with her brain, but that didn't mean she wasn't prepared to do anything and everything that was needed. 'Oh, all right. Mrs Rennie would probably give it a going-over herself even if I did clean it out first. She's known for being house proud.'

'What shall we pay them?'

'I'll ask her what'd be a fair wage.'

Judith finished her cup of tea, grimacing as she caught a couple of stray tealeaves in her mouth. She wiped them off her tongue then tossed the dregs down the sink and turned to Mayne. 'Will your father be up by now?'

'Yes. He's an early riser these days. Whether he'll have bothered to get himself any breakfast is another matter. On second thoughts, I'll walk down to the Dower House with you. It'll be easier for me to boss him about. I can't do much about the contents of the Nissen hut till they sort out what to do with the body. I hope they don't delay things too long.'

They left by the front door, it being the shortest way to the main drive and the Dower House, which was situated near the front gates.

'We'll get Mrs Rennie to deal with your father's ration books.' Judith strode out next to her husband, taking deep breaths of the chilly morning air.

'You seem very sure she'll take the job.'

'It's a good opportunity for people of their age, given that housing is included.'

Mayne's father didn't answer the door, though Mayne knocked twice, so they went inside, finding Reginald, as expected, upstairs in his study. He was reading a book, scribbling notes now and then, and didn't even notice them coming into the room. Mayne had to go and tap his shoulder to get his attention.

'What? Oh, it's you, son. Was I expecting you? Is it time to go and visit your mother in hospital?'

'No, Dad. We're waiting for word from her doctor about when we should go. We've come because Judith and I have something to suggest about getting you another housekeeper, this time one who'll stay. Come down and have some breakfast while I explain.'

His father's eyes went back to the book. 'Can't it wait? I'm just checking the Tudor records of . . .'

Mayne knew how impossible it was to keep his father's attention when he was in the middle of some important (to him) but obscure (to everyone else) research. 'Well, give me five minutes and have a cup of tea and some bread and jam at the same time, then I'll let you come back to your work. I promise this is good news.'

Downstairs, Mayne explained their proposal, and Mr
Esher immediately said, 'Good idea. Will you arrange that
for me? I need to get on with—'

'Not till you've eaten something,' Judith said firmly, barring
his way out of the kitchen.

He sighed as she folded her arms and stayed where she
was, then looked down at his stomach in mild surprise. 'Now
you come to mention it, I am a bit hungry.'

He wolfed down the bread and jam she set before him,
putting extra cold water into the cup of tea to cool it, so
that he could gulp it down quickly.

'Now, if you don't mind, I'm just in the middle of . . .'
He went back up the stairs without even a thank you.

Judith cleared up quickly, muttering, 'I'm itching to give
that study of his a good clean out. It smells musty.'

'Dad would kill you if you even tried. Let's check the
housekeeper's flat instead.' He opened a door to one side of
the kitchen.

She walked round the living area, opening every drawer or
cupboard before nodding. 'Small kitchen, but adequate – Mrs
Rennie can cover the table with a piece of oilcloth to do her
cooking preparations.'

Finally she examined the small bedroom and the bathroom just off it, bouncing on the bed and turning the taps
on and off. 'This will do just fine. In fact, they'll think
they're in paradise with an indoor lavatory and plumbed-
in bath instead of having to fill and empty a tin bath in
front of the fire. I think I should go and see them straight
away.'

'Is there that much of a hurry? We were going to—'

'The Rennies will be worrying, love. Once I offer them
the job, they'll want to come and check this place out straight
away so that they can give notice on their house. They won't
want to pay more rent than they have to.'

'Do you want me to come with you?'

'No. Nellie Rennie will be more comfortable discussing the details with me. And anyway, you have to be at Esherwood for the police.'

'Damn. So I do. What a nuisance that body is!'

'And we still haven't decided what to tell the police about the goods stolen from your family.' She hesitated. 'If you want my advice, you'll show whoever comes to investigate a couple of boxes of ornaments and hide the rest. Don't even mention the tools. Then if they confiscate what you show them, you'll still be able to carry on working once the body's dug out. You might have to wait years to get your stuff back again if you turn it in.'

'I don't like lying.'

'Neither do I. But I know when it's wise to keep information to myself. Some officials think they rule the world.'

'I'll consider it.'

She watched him walk away, thinking what a wonderful man he was. Then she realised she was wasting time and hurried away down the side of Parson's Mead and into town to speak to the Rennies. She was looking forward to doing this.

When Nellie opened the door of the small terraced house, she'd obviously been crying, so Judith put an arm round her. 'I've got a bit of good news for you, Nellie love.'

'That'll make a nice change.' She fumbled for a handkerchief, couldn't find one and wiped her eyes on her pinafore. 'Come in and tell me your news. Like a cup of tea?'

'I've just had one, thanks. Did Mr Rennie get home safely last night?'

'Yes. He's upstairs sleeping. He told me it'd be all right for him to go to Esherwood when he wants to walk about at night. He always did like being out of doors, my Steve did. How's life in the big house, Judith – or should I call you Mrs Esher now?'

'My name's still Judith to my old friends and neighbours. And to answer your question, I love living at Esherwood but it's going to take a lot of work to get the house straight again. The Army didn't look after it.'

'Listen, something's cropped up and I think you and Mr Rennie can help us.' She began to explain.

When she'd finished, Nellie burst into tears again.

'What's wrong? It was only a suggestion. I won't be upset if you don't want to do it.'

This time it was a tea towel that acted as a handkerchief. Judith patted the older woman's back and waited for an explanation.

The tears quickly dried up. 'I've been at my wits' end about what to do. I didn't tell Steve, but the rent man said last time he came that if we couldn't pay double rent then we had four weeks to get out. But if we left sooner, we could have our last week rent-free. Nasty man, he's grown into. I used to know him when he was a lad with his bum hanging out of his breeches.'

Judith couldn't help chuckling. 'You know what my dad always said about nasty people? *I hope their rabbits die and . . .*'

Nellie joined in the second line of a well-known pretend curse in the terraces, '. . . *they can't sell the hutches.* As if people keep rabbits when we don't even have back yards round here.'

'Well, jokes take the sting out of the bad things people do, I always think.'

'Yes. I'd forgotten that silly saying till you reminded me.'

Now that Nellie was calmer, Judith went back to the serious business of the day. 'Anyway, you'll want to come and see the flat at the Dower House before you decide, I'm sure. It's not very big, but it's got its own bathroom and indoor lav.'

Nellie stared at her as if she was promising a visit to paradise. '*Indoor lav! Plumbed in bath!* Oh, my. Just let me wash my face and put my coat and hat on. I'll be with you in two ticks.'

Judith noted with amusement that Nellie donned her best coat and her chapel hat, a squashy felt shape with a rather battered silk flower over one ear that she'd been wearing on Sundays since Judith was a girl.

At the Dower House, Nellie walked round the flat, shaking her head as if she couldn't believe what she was seeing. 'It's perfect,' she said at last.

'Good. You'll take the job, then?'

'Of course I will.'

'We can leave the crockery and other things if you'd like them, Nellie; otherwise you can clear out what you don't want and we'll sell it at the market. Oh, and bring your own furniture too.'

The older woman sat down in the nearest armchair. 'Ah. That's a comfy one. Can we keep some of this furniture? The springs have gone on our armchairs and our bed sags. And we could do with some new crockery. We've had no way of replacing any that got broken during the war, and I don't like using chipped cups. My Steve can be a bit clumsy.' She stopped and gave Judith a worried look. 'This stuff isn't valuable, is it?'

'No, just everyday things.'

'That's all right, then. And I can sell the rest for you without bothering about markets. I've a nephew who's just got married and he's having trouble getting all the bits and pieces you need when you're setting up home for the first time. Any bits and pieces of furniture too, if you want.'

'Good. You do that. You'll know what a fair price is. You can take ten per cent of the money you get from selling them for your trouble, and use the rest to buy Mr Esher's food till the money runs out. And talking of my dear father-in-law, you'd better come and meet him.'

She stopped at the foot of the stairs. 'Let's get one thing straight first. You don't have to take any nonsense from him. He hasn't a clue about running a house and he's so absent-minded he forgets to eat. He needs a very bossy housekeeper to make him notice when it's mealtime.'

Nellie nodded and followed her up the stairs, looking round with great interest. 'Big house, isn't it?'

'I'm hoping you'll go through it for me gradually and tidy it up a bit.'

'I shall enjoy that.'

When they came down after a very brief interview with Mr Esher, leaving him to his books, Judith asked, 'Well? Still want to come here now you've met him?'

'He doesn't seem nasty.'

'He isn't. In fact, he's quite kind – if he notices someone needs help, which he doesn't always. But I meant what I said about you being firm with him. You have to boss him about when it comes to eating and stuff like that, not the other way round.'

'All right. How soon can we move in?'

'As soon as you like.'

'I'll be back later to scrub out the flat, then, and we'll move in tomorrow.'

'Could you make Mr Esher something for tea while you're here today? *And* see he eats it. There are a few bits and pieces in the pantry. It'll be easier to make the same thing for all three of you from now on. I promise he hardly notices what he eats, till he gets really hungry – then he'll eat anything he can lay his hands on, whether he has a right to it or not. Perhaps Mayne should have a lock put on the pantry door.'

'If you think so. My Steve knows better than to take any food without asking, given the rationing. I do hope the Ministry of Food won't tighten up our rations again. I know people are starving in Europe, but we're not doing too well here, either, after six years of shortages. Some people are quite run down.'

Judith put ten shillings on the table. 'That'll cover Mr Esher's food for the next day or two. You may need to buy some staples like flour as well. Let me know when you need more. Or if you sell anything, let me know how much for and use that money.'

Nellie picked the ten-shilling note up. 'This will last more than a day or two if I have the spending of it. I can't abide waste.'

'Right then. You're in charge here from now on. Here are the house keys.'

As they moved towards the front door, Nellie gave her a sudden convulsive hug. 'You always were a good lass. Thanks for thinking of me and Steve.'

'It's Al Needham who thought of it first. And it's not a pretend job; we really do need your help.'

'I'll thank Al too when I see him. But *you* had to agree to it or we'd not be moving in. I can't abide people who go up in the world and forget the folk they used to know. You're not one of those.'

Words failed her, so she hugged Judith again, then bustled out, brushing her forearm across her eyes once she was far enough away to hope her new employer couldn't see that she was weeping for happiness again.

It felt so good to help people, Judith thought, as she strolled back to the big house, eager to see what Mayne wanted to do next.

If she had any say about it, they'd fetch in Mr Woollard and make a start on the valuations.

She was still trying to understand the whole picture. Mayne seemed rich to her, but when it came to running the big house, he considered himself short of money.

7

Francis didn't even take the time to phone Mayne the next morning to let him know he was coming to Rivenshaw. All he could think of was leaving the village and getting away from the Scammells.

The previous night, he had immobilised his van by taking out the rotor arm and hiding it, because you could never be too careful, then he'd locked the van in the garage before going upstairs to pack. It hurt to see the empty spaces where Diana's clothes had hung.

It was nearly one o'clock before he went to bed, but tired as he was, he only slept fitfully.

In the morning he woke before his alarm clock. It was a relief to walk through the quiet village without encountering anyone he knew. He was at the station in plenty of time to catch the early milk train to London.

Even though it was a Sunday, Euston station was fairly busy and there were some trains running to the north. How travel had changed from pre-war times when the world seemed to shut down to observe the Lord's Day!

He bought his ticket and didn't have long to wait for the express train to Manchester. It was quite crowded but he was lucky enough to get a window seat. As the train got under way, he made no attempt to chat with his fellow passengers, just stared out of the window and let his thoughts drift where they would.

He couldn't stop thinking about Diana leaving him. Was she upset about it too, or were Mummy and Daddy consoling her?

The journey seemed to go on for ever and he let himself close his eyes, just for a minute or two. He woke with a start when someone touched his arm.

'We've arrived in Manchester.'

He realised the train was standing in a big station and people were pouring off it, hurrying past his compartment towards the ticket collector.

The elderly woman standing beside him smiled. 'Will you be all right?'

'Yes. Thanks for letting me know we'd arrived.'

'Well, I hope you sort out whatever's upsetting you, dear. You've looked sad for the whole journey.' She got stiffly out of the compartment and followed the last few passengers towards the barrier.

Francis took down his suitcase and hurried after them, getting directions from the ticket collector to the platform where the slower local train left for various smaller towns, including Rivenshaw.

Not having been to Lancashire before, he studied the scenery as the train chugged out of the city. The suburbs of Manchester seemed to go on for a long way. The better suburbs had the usual rows of semi-detached and detached houses with well-tended gardens. In poorer areas, parallel rows of small terraced houses clustered around factories, like chickens round mother hens. Most factory chimneys weren't letting out smoke on a Sunday, but one or two had a thin thread of it twisting into the sky.

Was Diana right? Would Rivenshaw look as ugly as the industrial areas did?

The city gave way gradually to farmland, which seemed

to act as a frame for a series of industrial towns. These were smaller than Manchester, but still dominated by those tall mill chimneys. Then there were occasional villages, separated from one another by a patchwork of farms and overlooked by stretches of rolling moorland, something he'd only seen before in photos or cinema newsreels.

The moors were more impressive than he'd expected and he felt soothed by their gentle folds and curves, which were pierced here and there by narrow river valleys.

Diana and her parents were wrong about Lancashire being unremittingly ugly. It was extremely beautiful in parts. He'd enjoy going for long tramps across those uplands, he was sure. Diana used to like going for walks too.

He felt angry all over again that she had made no attempt to find out what this part of the country was really like before dismissing it as a place to live.

And when you got married you didn't put your parents before your spouse. You should— Why the hell was he still thinking of her? She had probably put him out of her mind the minute she left their house.

The train slowed down and he saw a sign saying RIVENSHAW. Jumping to his feet, he yanked his suitcase down from the luggage net above his head, muttering, 'At last!'

He waited impatiently behind two women and a small child to hand over his ticket to the only official in sight, then strode out of the station, eager to see what he hoped would be his new home.

Mayne had described the town centre so well, it seemed familiar. The station filled most of one side of the big square, and it had a simple but elegant façade overlooking the open area. Shops and commercial buildings lined the other three sides of the square. There was only one bombsite to be seen and even that had been tidied up.

The war must have been easier on the people here. He

could still remember the devastation in London, with whole streets destroyed. Heartbreaking, that had been.

There was one pub to the right, not large but apparently well cared for. Of course, it was closed today or he'd have been tempted to treat himself to half a pint of beer, because he was thirsty after travelling.

The centre of the square was paved with what Mayne called setts: flat, oblong paving stones about a foot long and half that in width, easier to walk on than lumpy round cobblestones. The setts looked good, matching the rows of grey stone buildings that framed the open area.

Streets led out of the square at the two corners opposite the station and he caught a glimpse of shops on one of them.

Noticing a taxi parked nearby, Francis waved the man across, feeling too weary to carry a heavy suitcase, even if he had known where to go.

'Do you know a house called Esherwood?' he asked the driver.

'Yes, of course. Everyone knows it.'

'Oh, good. Can you take me there, please?'

'Happy to. Come far, have you, sir?'

'From the south.' Francis didn't elaborate, didn't want to chat to a stranger, wanted desperately to be among friends again. Mayne's new wife had sounded very pleasant on the phone, but he hoped the four men would have time together occasionally without the women.

They had felt like brothers when they worked at Bletchley Park. He wasn't allowed to talk about his work there, but he'd never forget the place and the quiet purposeful workers, men and women, using their brains to help end the war.

The taxi driver slowed down as they approached a curving drive that led to a large house at the top of a slope. 'People usually go round to the back door these days, sir.'

'Then we'll do that, too.' Francis studied Esherwood as they drove slowly round it on a narrow gravelled track that needed levelling and resurfacing. The house was pretty but looked in need of care, like many buildings since the war. It was four storeys high, if you included the attics, and more imposing than he'd expected. Perhaps that was because Mayne had never put on airs about his privileged background, so Francis hadn't expected this.

As the taxi drew up, a lad poked his head out of the back door, vanishing immediately with a shout of, 'Someone's come in a taxi.'

On the other side of the yard a young policeman was standing, as if on guard.

'Hello, Jim lad!' the driver called.

The policeman looked quickly to either side, then hurried across the yard. 'Do you think you could call me constable when I'm on duty, Mr Willis? If you don't mind.'

'Yes, of course. I should have thought of that myself.'

'Thanks ever so much.' He hurried back to his post.

'Eh, I knew that lad when he were nobbut a babby,' the taxi driver muttered. 'He's lucky to have missed the fighting. Only just eighteen, he is.'

Then Mayne came to the door and Francis broke off mid-sentence and stumbled out of the taxi. He gave his friend a quick slap on the back and shook hands, holding on for a moment or two. He wished men hugged each other. He could have done with a hug or two at this moment.

'Here's your case, sir.'

Francis turned to pay the driver, then found that Mayne had picked up the case and was waiting to take him inside.

'You should have phoned, then we'd have got a room ready for you.'

'I'm sorry. I had a few problems to sort out. I left in a hurry. I'll tell you about it all later.'

Mayne studied his friend's face for a moment, then squeezed his shoulder and nodded, before leading the way into the kitchen.

'I can't tell you how glad I am to be here,' Francis confessed as he followed. 'You're sure it's all right to descend on you like this?'

'Of course it is. I'm delighted to see you. Now, this is my wife, Judith, and these are her children.' He grinned at the youngsters. 'But I'm adopting them and then they'd better watch out.'

The trio grinned back at him, in no way abashed by this pretend threat.

'Are you hungry, Francis?' Judith asked. 'I can make you a snack, and there's some tea left in the pot. It'll be a couple of hours before we have our evening meal. We've been busy getting my three terrors ready for school, which starts tomorrow.'

'A cup of tea would be wonderful, Mrs Esher. I'm thirsty but not hungry.'

'Call me Judith!'

'Judith,' he repeated obediently, liking the no-nonsense look of her. *She* wouldn't worry if her hair got blown by the wind, he was sure.

He drank the mug of tea quickly, relishing its warmth.

'I could squeeze a bit more out of the pot,' Judith offered.

'Yes, please.'

She filled his mug, then turned to her children. 'Go and finish getting your schoolbags ready, you lot. I'll be up to check them later.'

The younger girl led the way out, giving a couple of little skips as if very happy. The boy went last, hands thrust into the pockets of his trousers, sighing audibly.

Judith turned back to Francis. 'Sorry to be a bit preoccupied, but my youngest starts at the grammar school tomorrow and she's driving me mad fussing.'

'Big step for her.'

'Yes, but Kitty's already at the school, so she'll keep an eye on her sister. Now, Mayne, why don't you and Francis go and choose a bedroom for him? Somewhere on the second floor would be best. You might have to carry up a bed, though, unless . . . why don't you put him into Cousin Mariah's room? If the bed seems reasonable, that is.'

'We'll check it out.'

'I'll come up and get you some sheets in a bit.'

'We're quite capable of making up a bed, love. The Army taught us men all sorts of useful skills.' He held up one hand. 'And I know where the sheets are kept, too. I helped you sort out the linen cupboard, remember.' He gave her a quick kiss on the cheek.

Francis watched them enviously. It was obvious how much they loved one another, how comfortable they were together.

The two men walked upstairs, stopping a couple of times on the way so that Mayne could point something out.

'What a shame to split this lovely old house into flats,' Francis said as they reached the first landing and looked down at the hall.

'Needs must.'

'Yes, of course. Where are Victor and Daniel?'

'Victor's down south, retrieving anything he wants to keep from the home he shared with his first wife; Daniel is with his family in Blackpool. An uncle died and he's been helping his aunt. He's not been very communicative, though. He's having a bit of trouble adjusting to civilian life, I think.'

He stopped at the end of a short corridor to throw open a door. 'An elderly cousin had this room. We've cleared out her personal things but there's still too much furniture in here for my taste.' He went to sit on the bed and bounce. 'Not bad. What do you think?'

Francis sat down briefly on the bed, then went over to the window. 'What a lovely view. I shall be comfortable here, I'm sure.' He turned to see Mayne looking at him thoughtfully.

'What's wrong, Francis? And don't tell me there isn't anything wrong. You look sad and worn, not yourself at all.'

It took a couple of deep breaths to get the words out. 'Diana has left me.'

'Oh, hell! I'm so sorry.'

'These things happen. It's only been a couple of days, so I'm still . . . you know, getting used to it.'

'Do you want to tell me what happened?'

'In brief: her parents. When we told them we were getting married, her father offered me a hundred pounds not to do it, then upped that to two hundred when I refused. I didn't tell Diana about that. She knew her parents weren't happy about us, but she insisted, so in the end we got married. They were very stiff at the wedding, and as Diana was getting ready, I heard her mother beg her to wait till after the war.'

After a pause, he added, 'Our marriage was the only thing she's ever defied her parents about. They still ran her life even after we were married.'

Mayne nodded and Francis took it as a sign to continue. 'Diana and I were happy together at first. Then I got posted to the special unit and couldn't always get away at weekends, so she started going home more often. She moved back in with them. I wasn't going to spend my leaves in their house, so when I got a chance to buy a house nearby, I did.'

He paused. 'I wish I hadn't. *They* chose our furniture and tried to control who we saw socially. And she let them run our lives and paid no attention to my wishes, or to the need to be careful with money. That upset me more and more.'

He closed his eyes and it was a few moments before he continued. 'Her mother detests me. You can always tell. Oh, she doesn't say that – it's all very subtle and civilised. Unfortunately Diana refuses to move away from Medworth. I wish to hell I'd never bought that house, except that it's gone up in value.'

Another short silence, then, 'Diana knew what we four were planning to do after the war and never said a word against it till the war ended. Then suddenly she started parroting her father's criticisms of my plans and *he* found me a job nearby – a rather menial job. But I'm not going to let them stop me being part of our building company. I still believe in what we're doing.'

'Some women are like that, cling to their families.'

'It's far worse than that, Mayne. Frankly, Diana hasn't really grown up. She's been spoiled all her life and thinks the world revolves round her.'

'What I most remember was how beautiful she was. Elegantly turned out, too.'

'She still is beautiful, but that comes at a high cost in time and money: and she absolutely hates to get her hands dirty or let her hair be blown about. Her mother's charwoman has been doing all the dirty work in our house. Heaven forbid Milady Diana should mop a floor. Oh, let's change the subject. It's done, over. Aren't we supposed to be making up this bed?'

'Yes. Let's get some sheets. Judith's got the bed linen sorted out by type. She's a ferociously efficient organiser, my lass is.'

As they started making up the bed Army style, Francis changed the subject firmly. He'd said enough to help Mayne understand, at least he hoped he had; now he had to look to the future. 'The good news is that I've sold my parents' land and probably our house, too, so I'll have money to invest – a bit more than I expected, actually, because I made quite a bit extra by salvaging the bombed buildings on my parents' land. Amazing what you can sell used bricks for these days.'

'Well done!'

As they finished up, Francis said, 'If it's all right with you, I'll stay here for a few days, to get some understanding of what we need to do and to get to know the town, then I'll go back, sell the house and pack up.'

'That's fine by me. Come and live here afterwards. There's plenty of storage for your furniture or whatever you want to bring. We got used to sharing quarters in the forces, so no one seems to mind living together for the time being. Victor's wife was in the Wrens, so she has a similar attitude. You'll like Ros, I'm sure. As for my Judith, she's wonderful, takes everything in her stride.'

'And Daniel? How's he coping with his divorce?'

'I don't think he and Ada were close, so he's not broken-hearted, if that's what you mean. But he's a bit miffed that she's run off with a Yank. He and his wife don't seem to be fighting about money and dividing their possessions, though, thank goodness. Well, they wouldn't need to, because she apparently hooked up with a rich guy.'

'I dare say Diana will find a rich fellow too next time round. Well, she will if her parents have anything to do with it. And they'll probably try to get every penny they can out of me.' Francis scowled at the thought.

Mayne tactfully didn't comment on this. 'I'd better warn you, Daniel can seem a bit sharp at times. He gets bad nightmares about the war. He never was the warrior type.'

'Who was? We had no choice but to fight.'

'We did our bit, as the saying goes. Now we can do things for ourselves. Daniel has some excellent ideas for transforming the house – and for the other houses that we'll build later. I think that'll be the saving of him. That or meeting another woman.'

'Do *you* ever get nightmares, Mayne?'

'Not very often. I'm not the sort and though I did see some fighting and I definitely didn't enjoy killing, I spent quite a while on behind-the-scenes work even before you joined the group. In that sense I had quite a good war, if there is such a thing. And since I met Judith, I've been happier than I ever hoped, even though I'm going to lose Esherwood. Oh, I'd better warn you about her situation . . .'
He explained about the bigamous marriage and Francis whistled softly in surprise.

Footsteps pounded up the stairs and Ben called, 'Where are you, Mayne? Mum says tea's nearly ready.'

'We'll talk again,' Mayne said quickly, turning to greet his stepson by ruffling the boy's hair affectionately.

Ben beamed at him, clearly fond of Mayne already. 'Hurry up! I'm *dying* of hunger.' He clattered down the stairs again.

'I've never seen Ben when he wasn't hungry. He's growing fast at the moment, going to be tall like his half-brothers from his father's real marriage, I should think.'

Francis nodded and followed his friend to join the others. He hoped he could hold himself together till bedtime. He felt wracked with sadness.

Exhaustion hit him suddenly as he was finishing his meal. He couldn't prevent a yawn, and another followed it quickly.

'Go to bed, Francis,' Judith said in her quiet firm voice. 'I think you're far beyond exhaustion and if you don't lie down soon, you'll probably fall down. And don't worry if you sleep late. I'll be too busy getting this trio off to school to be a good hostess.'

'I'll walk upstairs with you,' Mayne said.

'Did you give him a towel and show him the bathroom?' Judith asked.

'No. I forgot. Come on, sleepyhead. This is the bathroom

you should use and we'll grab a towel for you from the linen store.'

As they got to the door of Francis's room, Mayne hesitated, then gave him a quick hug, an unusual gesture for either of the men. 'Don't drive yourself crazy worrying, my dear chap. Things will get better slowly, one way or another.'

Francis nodded, closing the door and leaning against it for a moment, thankful to be alone. All he wanted now was to lie down and sleep for a thousand years. He felt as if he'd been on a long route march with a full pack.

On the Monday morning Victor went to pick up his newspaper in the village at the same time as usual, but there was no sign of Fitkin. As he paid the newsagent he asked casually, 'Will Mr Fitkin be coming in for his paper?'

'Oh yes, sir. Regular as clockwork, he is. He'll be here in about quarter of an hour.'

'Could you please give him this note?'

'Certainly, Mr Travers.'

Twenty minutes later someone rang the doorbell and Victor answered it. 'Ah good. Would you like to come in for a moment, Fitkin?'

'Not just now, thank you. Look, I got your note. When are you leaving?'

'Probably on Thursday morning, early.'

'Then I suggest you visit the mausoleum on Wednesday afternoon. As you so rightly say, it wouldn't look good to keep the child from visiting her mother's grave.'

'Mrs Gal— I mean Mrs Fitkin doesn't object?'

His caller shrugged. 'My wife won't get the chance to object because I shan't tell her till after you've gone.'

'I see. Well, thank you for your help.'

'The gate to the mausoleum will be open. The child is well?'

'Yes. Settling in nicely in the north.'

'Good. We'll leave the sale of this house in the lawyers' hands and please thank your wife for her co-operation about the contents of the house.' He put his hat back on and left.

What a cold fish that man is, Victor thought. He's got what he wanted from us by buying the house, but can hardly be bothered to give us the time of day from now on. Well, we've got what we wanted too. I shall be relieved when this place is off my hands.

He went back to tell Betty she could visit her mother's grave before they left and she nodded politely.

He glanced sideways at Ros, who shook her head slightly as if to tell him not to say anything more.

'We could pick some flowers on Wednesday to put on the grave,' she said. 'There are still a few in the garden.'

Betty nodded and moved her porridge around her bowl, making patterns in it with her spoon before pushing the bowl aside. 'May I leave the rest of this please? I'm not very hungry this morning.'

'Of course, darling,' Ros said. 'Give me five more minutes and I'll come up and help you finish clearing your room.'

They watched her walk out.

'Poor child,' Ros said. 'It's hard to lose your mother.'

'She's got you now and I think you're doing a wonderful job with her.'

Ros shrugged. 'Well, I've got you to share things with, so neither Betty nor I are on our own. I think we both appreciate that. Besides, that daughter of yours is easy to love. Now, hurry up. I want to get a lot done today.'

He nodded. 'So do I. I don't like living in the same village as that Fitkin fellow. I don't care if he is buying this house. I don't trust him an inch.'

8

Judith got the children off to school, standing at the front door to wave them goodbye. Then she went to find Mayne, who was supposed to be working in the office but instead was standing scowling out of the window at the stable yard. 'Poor love, you look so frustrated.'

'Every time I see that Nissen hut I feel angry that we can't continue clearing it.'

'Where's Jan?'

'I sent him to prepare the vegetable garden for winter and see if there's anything else we can salvage from it. He knows more about gardening than any of us. I don't want to leave the poor chap without an income while we wait for some official to solve the mystery of the dead body. I wish Daniel would come back. We could be starting on the design work. I was going to give him Jan as an assistant.'

'Good idea.'

'Any sign of Francis waking up?'

'No. I went up and listened outside his room, but everything was silent.'

He took her hand. 'Let's stroll round the ground floor rooms and study the objects we have stored there. We don't often get the house to ourselves for a planning session.'

They moved slowly from one big room to another across the front of the house, then into the smaller rooms to the rear. Inevitably they ended up in the library, where piles of goods had been roughly sorted into groups of similar items, some valuable, some not.

She decided to take the bull by the horns. 'We need to get Mr Woollard working on valuations now. Even the rubbishy things in that pile will sell at the market, because people are so short of household goods.'

'I'd rather not bring him in till we've signed a contract of some sort with him, even if it's only a statement of intent,' Mayne said firmly.

'You don't think you're being a bit too suspicious?'

'Woollard's a very clever man and I *think* I can trust him, but not to the same extent as I trust my other partners. When you've been through the war together, it forms a bond and the only thing that comes close to it is marriage to someone you love.' He was going to kiss her, but just then they heard the sound of footsteps on the uncarpeted wooden stairs leading down to the entrance hall.

'Bad timing. Sounds as if Francis has woken up.'

Judith smoothed her hair. 'I'd better get him some food.'

In the hall they found their guest staring round.

'It's a beautiful house, or it could be, but they didn't take care how they ran in electricity, did they? I could have done it better standing on my head, and kept most of the wiring out of sight. The man who taught me in the Army would have had the fellows who did this sort of thing up on a charge for shoddy work.'

'Well, you'll be involved in sorting out the wiring for the flats, so you can make a better job of the refit.'

'Did you sleep well?' Judith asked.

'I didn't stir. I was exhausted. I hope I made sense last night.'

'Of course you did. You must be hungry. I'm the quartermaster for the time being, so if you'll let me have your ration books I can use them as necessary while you're staying here.'

He ran one hand through his hair. 'Oh, hell! I forgot about them. I think Diana still has them. Or else she's left them somewhere in the house. Perhaps I can find somewhere to eat out for my main meals – is there a British Restaurant in town? And I could buy unrationed food for the other meals. I'm not fussy about what I eat.'

'We'll manage somehow. At least bread isn't rationed. I'll send you off into town with Jan to see what they can find for you at the grocer's.'

'I'll have a wander round Rivenshaw while I'm out, if you don't mind. If this town is going to be my home, I need to get my bearings.'

Mayne had followed them to the kitchen and chatted to Francis while he ate.

When Francis left with Jan, Judith waited, but to her annoyance her husband didn't mention going to see Woollard.

He looked up suddenly and seemed to read her mind. 'I'm waiting for the sergeant to contact us before I do anything at all today. I may be needed here.'

Unfortunately that made sense, but she could have screamed with frustration. She wanted to get on, do something about the organised chaos in which they were living, put some of their plans into operation, make a real start.

The only thing she wasn't worrying about was how her children were getting on. Apart from the fact that she trusted them, she knew the two oldest enjoyed school, and she was sure Gillian would soon settle in at the girls' grammar school and make friends. Well, she would know a few of the girls from junior school already.

Judith looked at the clock and sighed. It seemed that keeping people waiting was a game played in peace as well as in war. She ought to be used to it by now.

★　★　★

Sergeant Deemer didn't turn up until the middle of the morning. He waved a greeting to his constable and knocked on the kitchen door.

Judith let him in and suggested he sit down at the big table while she fetched Mayne from the office. She wasn't going to be left out of this but she needed to get on with preparations for their midday meal. She had a cabbage and was shredding some to make a salad, together with slices of tomato and a little grated onion. Those who wanted could sprinkle vinegar on it to give it a lift, and Jan had found her some mint. If he found more mint than they needed to use, she'd hang it up in the huge, nearly empty pantry, and let it dry for use in the winter.

Knowing how the sergeant loved his cups of tea, she made a pot, listening to the two men as she did so.

'Well, Sergeant?' Mayne prompted. 'When can we remove that corpse from the Nissen hut and get on with our business?'

'I'm not sure, so don't hold your breath while you wait. Halkett nearly threw a fit when I told him what you'd found. He gave me some contradictory orders, then changed his mind and told me to do nothing till he got back to me.'

Deemer took a sip of tea and sighed in appreciation. 'You always make a nice cuppa, Mrs Esher . . . When Halkett phoned back, he said someone had better guard the scene of the crime. I asked him who would do that, with only me and the new lad available to police the town. After some humming and hawing, he said to hire someone, just for the daytime.'

Another sip of tea, then, 'Any of your lads free to help, Mayne? How about Jan? He's a shrewd one.'

'He's gone into town on an errand, but we need to find work for him till we can get on with clearing the hut, so if you want to employ him for a few days, I'm sure he'll agree. You can ask him when he gets back. How long do you think this investigation will take once they get started? A couple of days?'

Deemer gave him a frustrated look. 'Who knows how long it'll take? Them in charge don't tell me anything!' He heaved himself to his feet. 'Look, I'll just speak to my lad out there, then try to catch Jan on my way back into town. Thanks for the tea, Mrs Esher.'

Mayne was tapping his fingers on the table, a sure sign that he was contemplating doing something he found unpleasant. 'I think I'll have to ask my old friends from the special unit whether they can give someone in the Army a nudge about the body.'

'It'd be a big help if they could speed things up, but are you sure they'll want to help you now you're a civilian?' Judith asked.

'Um, yes. Very sure. We were and still are . . . close. That's where I met the other three.'

She gave him a thoughtful glance. 'Are you ever going to tell me exactly what you were doing during the last year of the war?'

'It comes under the Official Secrets Act I'm afraid, darling, so I doubt I'll ever be able to say anything. Some of it was quite boring stuff, but it made a difference. I'll go and make that phone call now, get it over with.'

When he came back, he said only, 'My friend is looking into it for us. He doesn't want them investigating my background.' After a pause, he added, 'I wonder why the poor chap was murdered.'

'We're not even sure it was a murder.'

'How can it be anything else with the body buried like that?'

'Let's get on with something else. Why don't we bring Mr Woollard in to start on the valuations?'

Mayne hesitated, then shrugged. 'I suppose so. I'll go and see him.'

'How about I go with you? Mrs Needham is coming in another half hour to clean the kitchen and I'll only be in her way. It's a bit annoying you not wanting me to scrub my own floor. I'm not used to watching others clear up my family's mess.'

'Bear with me about this, love. I like to keep these soft.' He took her hands and raised each in turn to his lips. 'In fact, whatever comes of our building venture, I shall always make sure we have enough money to save you doing the heavy, dirty work. You've had more than your share of that, I feel.'

She'd always insisted on a clean house, however poor they were, so had been glad to get down on her knees and scrub, but she and Mayne would never see that sort of work in quite the same way. What must it have been like to be brought up without ever going hungry, or having to scrimp and save to keep yourself and your children decently clad?

She still hadn't got used to her new life, still marvelled that there was always food of some sort in the pantry and that nearly all the washing was sent out to a laundry, where the clothes were ironed as well.

All that and a husband she adored! What had she done to deserve such luck?

Diana slept badly in her old bed at her parents' house. She didn't like single beds any more, she found, because it felt as if she was going to roll out of it if she tossed around too much. And she missed Francis's warm body next to hers, the way he reached out automatically to hold her hand as he began to wake up, the wonderful way he made love. There had never been a problem about that side of their marriage.

She heard her parents chatting in their bedroom as they got up, but her mother didn't come to wake her, so she stayed in bed. She didn't want to face them, didn't want to face anyone yet.

'Let the girl sleep,' her father said in what he thought was a low voice but which carried clearly to Diana's bedroom. She was beginning to wonder if he was going deaf because he always spoke a bit too loudly.

'I'm not letting her lie in bed all morning,' her mother said. 'She needs to be kept busy or she'll only mope.'

'We need to start smartening up the way she dresses before she goes out and about. You can keep an eye on her to make sure she behaves well in public too. She is, after all, a Scammell. We don't want her getting emotional all over the place and making a fool of herself in front of people. That wouldn't reflect well on the family.'

'Well, her marriage has broken up. She's bound to be upset.'

'Let her do her crying in private, then. *I* think she should be rejoicing at getting rid of the fellow. I certainly am. And I'll make sure her next husband is our own sort.'

'Yes. So you keep saying, Leonard. But don't forget there is going to be a shortage of eligible men for this generation of young women.'

'The family name still means something. There are still men who will find it useful to have a connection with me.'

Her mother's voice became fainter as they went into the kitchen, so Diana didn't hear her response. She got up and went to eavesdrop from the landing, as she had so many times before.

'You can't force young people to marry to order these days, Leonard.'

'Oh, can't I? You wait and see.'

Diana let out an indignant huff of air.

There was silence then her mother said, 'You do think we did the right thing about Francis, don't you?'

'Of course we did.'

'I feel guilty sometimes. After all, the man did seem to

love her. And she loved him. Perhaps we shouldn't have interfered.'

'She had no business loving a man of his sort. We couldn't let her spend her whole life tied to the fellow, so we did what we had to. Imagine if they'd produced children! What sort of babies would *he* have fathered? I thank God we got her away from him before she became pregnant.'

He gave that disgusted, throaty sound that always annoyed Diana because it sounded to her as if he was about to cough up some phlegm. His words annoyed her, too. What did he mean? *Got her away from him. Did what we had to.* What had they done?

'Hurry up with breakfast, Christine. You've got the rest of the day to worry about your daughter and fuss over her. I don't want to be late for the office.'

Diana didn't dare try to eavesdrop when they went into the breakfast room, which looked up the stairs towards her bedroom, so she closed her door quietly and lay down again.

But her father's words kept echoing in her mind. *Got her away from him.* Had they really done that on purpose? Francis had been saying for a while that her parents were deliberately coming between the two of them and she hadn't believed him.

She didn't hear anything clearly till her father started putting on his coat and hat in order to leave for the office.

His voice floated up from the hall. 'Mind you keep her occupied today. Don't let her dwell on things.'

The front door banged shut behind him and her mother went back to the breakfast room, where she always had another cup of tea after she'd 'got him away'. Her peaceful moment, she called it.

Diana couldn't stop thinking about what they'd said. Surely her parents hadn't deliberately set out to break up her marriage? No, it was Francis's fault for making such unfair plans, for not taking her needs into consideration.

She snuggled down, still feeling tired. She didn't feel at all refreshed by her night's sleep. Perhaps it was all the arguing with Francis that had upset her.

Maybe if she got a little more sleep she'd be able to think more clearly about her future.

What woke Diana fully was the smell of toast. She'd been coming to the surface gradually, stretching and yawning. Now, her stomach was rumbling and she was suddenly hungry.

She heard footsteps on the stairs and the bedroom door opened. 'I heard you moving about so I could tell you were awake, darling.' Her mother set a tray down beside the bed.

Diana looked at the bedside alarm clock, the one that had stood by her bed ever since she learned to tell the time. Francis had hated it, said it had an annoying tick, but it had felt like an old friend to her. She gasped when it sank in that it was eleven o'clock.

'How can it be that late?' She eased herself up into a sitting position. 'Tea and toast in bed. What a luxury! Thank you so much, Mummy.'

'Just one piece of toast. We don't want to spoil our luncheon. And I shan't do this every morning, just today to welcome you back home.' She kissed the air above her daughter's cheek.

Mummy never touches you when she kisses, Diana thought. She doesn't even touch Daddy if she can help it. She once told me it didn't do to encourage men to behave like animals. She watched her mother step back from the bed.

'We'll have an early lunch then drop in to see my friend Pauline.'

'Oh, Mummy, no! She's the biggest gossip in the neighbourhood. If we tell her why I'm living at home again, it'll be all over the village that I've left Francis.'

'Exactly what we want to happen, surely? Dear Pauline can spread the word for us.'

'Please don't tell anyone yet, Mummy. I need to get used to it myself.'

'Stiffen your spine, my girl, and get on with your life. *He* isn't worth a single tear.'

The toast suddenly tasted of cardboard and the tea lost its fragrance. 'I married Francis because I loved him. It'll take a long time for me to get over him.'

'Rubbish. You married him because you were lonely and away from us. And I daresay it seemed a romantic thing to do, given that it was wartime. The marriage hasn't lasted long, has it? I told you it wouldn't because he isn't our sort of person, but would you listen? No.'

The marriage had lasted two years, Diana thought. Well, nearly two years. But when her mother got that expression on her face it was best not to argue. 'I still don't want to tell your friend Pauline.'

Her mother sat down at the dressing table, fiddling with Diana's makeup. She eyed her daughter in the mirror. 'Perhaps it'd be better if I called to see her on my own. You can take the rest of the day to smarten yourself up. Go into the village and get your hair done.'

That made Diana realise she didn't have much money left from her housekeeping, and had no way of getting more. 'I'll, um, do my hair myself. I've got quite good at that.'

'Because *he* kept you short of money. Well, there's no need to worry about money from now on. We'll give you an allowance again. And you can put your shampoo and set on my account at the hairdresser's. You won't really need much money while you're with us, but you should have something in your purse. Your father will see that you get money out of *him* when you get your divorce.'

'I don't want to take Francis's money.'

'It never hurts to have something behind you.'

'I've got something behind me: my grandmother's legacy.'

'Well, it's only fair that you get your share of the money from the house. Your father was only talking about it this morning over breakfast.'

'I didn't put anything into the house.'

'Thank goodness your father stopped you doing that.'

Diana didn't argue, but she didn't want to take the money Francis had worked so hard for. It seemed unfair.

She did need money of her own, though. She'd better draw some out of the bank. And she supposed she'd have to find a job, only her parents would have a fit if she even tried to do that. Besides, she wasn't very good at office work. She'd proved that during the war, making mistakes, putting entries into the wrong columns, making blots in the precious ledgers.

Oh, why was life so difficult? If you didn't marry a man with money, you were helpless. She hadn't done well in her studies, so she couldn't go to teacher training college, as a couple of her former workmates were planning to do.

She was useless for anything except being a wife, and only the wife of a wealthy man at that.

She realised her mother was waiting for her to finish eating, so picked up the tray and held it out. 'I'm n-not hungry. I'm too upset.' She tried not to cry, but didn't manage to hold back the tears.

'Diana, this won't do. You really must pull yourself together.'

When she'd calmed down a bit, her mother cleared her throat, looking embarrassed. 'Um . . . your father said I should ask this for legal reasons. *That man* didn't beat you or ill-treat you in any way, did he?'

'*He* has a name: Francis. Why will you never use it?'

'Because I don't think of him by name. Who cares what he's called anyway, now you've left him? Did he?'

'What?'

'Beat you.'

'Of course not. Francis would never hurt anyone and he loved me. I loved him, too. Can't you understand that I'm upset, Mother? My marriage has broken up.'

She buried her face in the sheets and started sobbing as she realised that she hadn't wanted it to. Only it had all seemed to happen of its own accord.

The thought crept into her mind: or someone had manipulated the situation.

'I'll leave you to cry it all out,' her mother said hurriedly. 'But this is not to happen again.'

As the bedroom door closed behind her, Diana continued to weep.

She felt utterly lost. What was she going to do with the rest of her life? She wasn't marrying someone to suit her father, not after experiencing true love.

Was Francis missing her? Did he care?

By the time her mother went out to the shops, as regular in her habits as ever, Diana was dressed.

As soon as she'd seen her mother turn the corner of the street, she slipped out of the house the back way, and returned to her own home.

Perhaps Francis would be there. Perhaps they could still find some way to compromise about the future.

But the house was empty.

She went upstairs to find the bed unmade and rumpled. Some of his clothes were gone from the wardrobe and that ratty old suitcase was no longer on top of the wardrobe in the spare bedroom.

He'd left already. He must have gone north to his friends.

He didn't care about her at all.

She was beyond tears now. Numb, that was the best way to describe how she felt.

When she got home, her mother was back from the shops.

'Surely you didn't go out looking such a mess, Diana? Really, what were you thinking of?'

'I needed a walk to clear my head.'

'You've been back to that nasty little house, haven't you? Honestly, Diana, you are a fool. Do you want to be an object of pity in our circle?'

'I don't care. I don't care about anything.' She burst into tears and ran upstairs.

Her mother didn't follow.

When her father got home, he and her mother spent a long time talking, but they closed the sitting room door and Diana couldn't hear what they were saying.

She heard her mother go into the kitchen, probably to prepare dinner. She tidied her hair, ready to join them, hungry now.

But the dinner gong didn't ring and no one called up to her that the meal was ready. What was she supposed to do? Just walk down as if nothing had happened?

In the end she did nothing but lie on the bed and stare into space, feeling hard done to.

No one loved her. She wished she were dead.

9

Mr Woollard's house was a comfortable, detached residence with immaculate gardens. No shortage of money here, Judith thought. Well, let him use his money-making skills on Esher and Company now. And she'd help him.

Woollard's niece, Stephanie, who had travelled to Rivenshaw from the south on the same train as Daniel, opened the front door. She was pretty and you'd have thought he'd have shown an interest in her, but he hadn't. And Stephanie didn't encourage men's attentions in that way, either. She had a sad expression sometimes.

Daniel had said he thought Steph must have lost someone she loved in the war, which would account for how cool and distant she seemed whenever you spoke to her – pleasant enough but not encouraging anyone to get close. Grief took people in so many different ways.

'Mr and Mrs Esher, how nice to see you. Do come in.'

'We wanted to see your uncle on business. Or is he at his office?'

'No, he mostly works at home in the mornings nowadays. Please take a seat in the hall and I'll see if he's free.'

A door opened to the rear of the hall and Ray Woollard came out to greet them before his niece could fetch him. 'I thought I recognised the voices. Come in, come in. We'll sit in my office if that's all right with you. Steph love, you'll join us?'

'Yes, uncle.'

He patted her shoulder and beamed at his visitors. 'Steph's taken a job as my assistant and she's doing well. Never forgets a thing. This way.'

His office was a large room looking out over the back garden, with some comfortable chairs grouped in the bay window. Their host didn't waste time on polite preliminaries. As soon as they'd sat down, he said, 'Well, then? What can I do for you?'

'We wondered if you'd like to start the serious valuing of my assets. After all, we've signed a preliminary agreement now, so we know where we all stand.'

Mayne's voice was a little cooler than usual, Judith noticed, but though Woollard's eyes narrowed slightly as if he too had sensed that, to her relief he continued to speak calmly and affably.

'I heard you'd had a nasty surprise at the big house. Rum business, that, burying a dead body so carelessly. Who's dealing with it, police or Army?'

'I don't know. They're still deciding. Which is preventing us from clearing out the Nissen hut . . . hence our visit today.'

'They'll take forever. You're right to make new plans. And I'm looking forward to doing the valuations. I haven't enough other work to keep me busy just now.'

'When can you start?'

'Tomorrow. Steph and I will be there at about ten o'clock, if that suits.'

'It suits me very well.' Mayne stood up. 'We won't waste any more of your time.'

'Let me introduce you to my wife on the way out. She'd be helping with the valuations if she were well. But she's a lot better than she was, thanks to this new medicine they're using. Penicillin, they're calling it – silly sort of name. Cost me a fortune to get some, but it was worth it.'

'They've been using it on troops for a while.'

'Yes. It's a real wonder drug, so I've still got my Edna, thank goodness.'

Judith liked the fond way he spoke about his wife. It made him rise in her estimation.

As they were walking home, they met Francis, who appeared down in the dumps until he noticed them approaching, then forced an unconvincing smile.

'Had a good look round Rivenshaw, old chap?' Mayne asked.

'Yes. I wanted to get to know the town and also – don't take this the wrong way – I needed some time to myself. This thing with Diana has only recently blown up in my face and I'm still trying to get used to it all. I don't *feel* single, you see.'

'You don't have to apologise. I'm not your commanding officer now,' Mayne said gently. 'You should take all the time you need.'

Judith thought it wise to change the subject. 'What do you think of Rivenshaw, Francis?'

'I like it. It's a nice little town. My wife had completely the wrong idea about it, well, about the north generally. Beyond the railway station I found some three-storey terraced houses with a row of windows on the top storey. Stone built. They look solid and comfortable, as if they're *right* for this area.'

'Weavers' cottages. When people did the weaving on hand-looms at home, they needed the extra windows in the top floor to catch as much light as possible. Those are some of the earliest buildings in town.'

'Those rooms must be lovely and bright. It'd be nice to have a house with lots of windows everywhere.'

'It'd let in the cold in winter,' Judith said thoughtfully. 'But I must say, I don't like dark houses. And you could put up thick curtains to keep the warmth in. How did you and Jan get on at the shops?'

'We were able to get quite a few things that weren't rationed, so I won't be taking your food. The butcher let me have some liver. Diana thinks it's common and never buys it but I love liver and onions for my evening meal.'

'So do I. I wonder if Deemer caught up with Jan. The Area Commander wants someone to keep watch on the Nissen hut, so they're going to offer Jan a temporary job doing that till they figure out who should investigate the murder.'

'In other words, they don't mind how long they keep us waiting for access to the hut,' Francis said. 'Typical! At the unit we had to think up all sorts of tricks to push things through what we called the paper walls.'

There was a shout behind them. 'Mum! Mu-um!'

Gillian came running up, followed more sedately by her sister. 'Mum, I had a lovely day at school. There are so many people to talk to, so much to learn, and I made lots of new friends.'

'I'm sure you did. I'm looking forward to hearing all about it,' Judith said. 'But we'd better get a move on, so wait to tell me till we get back. I can listen as I prepare tea. I could do with a cook to take over once everyone is in residence again. It's not my favourite job and people who enjoy it do it better than me, I'm sure.'

She saw Mayne look at her sharply and said to him, 'No! You're not hiring a cook till we know where we stand financially. We'll just muddle along till then and anyone who complains can take over the cooking.'

He rolled his eyes. 'You wouldn't want me to take over, I promise you. I can manage cups of tea, or toast and boiled eggs, but that's about it. I'll take charge of the washing-up brigade.'

'I'll hold you to that.'

'I'm going to learn how to cook at school,' Gillian said. 'We have cookery lessons for half the year and sewing for the other half.'

'You won't enjoy cooking,' Kitty said. 'Miss Lowery is so strict, you hardly dare breathe in her classes. Mum, I have to write about the oldest thing we have in our home. What would that be?'

'Heavens, I don't know. We'll ask Mr Woollard tomorrow. He's coming to start valuing all the bits and pieces.'

'I like Mr Woollard,' Gillian said. 'He's got such twinkly, smiling eyes.'

'We have a little wooden figure that father always told us was medieval,' Mayne said as they started walking. 'I'd guess that's one of the oldest things, Gillian. It's such a lumpy little thing, crudely carved and yet somehow, you can see the real person it was based on. Well, I always think you can.'

The following morning, just before Woollard was due to arrive, Mayne received a phone call from his former commanding officer.

'Let's make this brief, Esher. There's all hell on here about what the Russians are doing. I wish you hadn't dug that body up just now, but we owe you a favour or two, so I'll see what I can do to help. Can't tempt you back to work for us, can I?'

'Sorry. I'm trying to save the family home from falling to pieces – and set up a building business.'

'Yes, you said you would. Your being there is good for your family, but bad for the unit. Anyway, what I rang to say was that two men from the Military Police will be arriving at Rivenshaw any day now. May I remind you not to talk to them about what you were doing while you were working here.'

'I know that, but what if they feel they're in a special position and are entitled to know something?'

'Refer them to Peter. You know how to get in touch with him. I've spoken to a friend of mine and he'll make sure the military police do what they have to as quickly as possible. We can't ignore a murder, so they have to be allowed to investigate, and— Just a tick.'

His voice became muffled, so he must have put his hand across the phone. 'Yes, yes, I'm coming!' His voice grew louder again. 'All right, Esher?'

'Yes. I do understand the need for secrecy about exactly what I was doing.'

'Yes. Of course you do. We all signed the Official Secrets Act, after all. Tell these MPs you were attached to the Foreign Office if they pester you.'

The call cut off abruptly and Mayne sighed. The people still working at the unit wanted to continue in obscurity, because they felt another sort of war was brewing, one perhaps without direct fighting, but which would need behind-the-scenes people even more than the war that had just finished.

The destruction that atomic bombs could cause had got his former colleagues very jittery about relations with other major world powers. And rightly so . . .

Mayne heard footsteps, realised that Woollard had arrived and went out to show him the piles of goods in the library. Steph was with her uncle, carrying a clipboard with a pad and pencil, looking neat and efficient.

In the library, Woollard walked round the various piles. 'You've got lots of small stuff. What about the paintings and bigger items? You weren't happy with the other chap's valuations, if I remember rightly.'

'No, I wasn't. I'm no expert but surely they must be worth more than *he* offered.'

'Of course they are. The sharks are out now the war's over, trying to snap things up cheaply. Where are you keeping them?'

'In the attic.'

'Dry up there, is it?'

'Yes.'

'Then we'll leave them there for the time being and concentrate on clearing these things out, if that's all right with you. Small pieces would be very tempting to burglars, who could just sneak into the house and filch a few items without it even showing, because I bet *you* don't know exactly what you've got here.'

'No, I don't. Not yet.' He hesitated, then confided, 'Just between you and me, my former fiancée had been doing exactly that with the smaller silver items for a while, with my mother's unwitting help.'

'I don't like that young woman, can't stand females who think their looks entitle them to do what they want. I remember hearing her threaten you that time in the street.' He made a disgusted noise. 'Anyway, enough about her. How's your father coping without your mother? Is he keeping the things they've got at the Dower House safe?'

'He's fine now we've got the Rennies in to help him, and Mrs Rennie will keep an eye on all the items there. I bet she knows by heart what's there within the month. She's not a stupid woman, not at all.'

'People speak well of them both. You seem to have a gift for finding people to do jobs, or finding jobs to suit people, Esher.'

'That's what they told me in the Army. It was one of the

things I did, find the right people for . . . special jobs. They still occasionally ask my advice.'

Mayne broke off and changed the subject. It was all too easy to tell Woollard things. He'd have to watch that. 'Anyway, Dad just wants to be left alone with his books. When the publisher gets access to more paper, they're going to publish a couple of his books, one of them for use in schools.'

'It was very sad how publication of books was slowed in the war because of lack of paper,' Stephanie said. 'As an avid reader I really regretted that.'

'Everything seemed to be rationed – except fresh air!' Woollard frowned. 'There isn't much money in writing schoolbooks, considering how hard your father works.'

'No, but Dad loves what he does and it pleases him to share his knowledge. We don't want British children growing up without knowing our country's history, do we? Now, which pile do you want to start with?'

'The ones you think are cheap. Do you have any old tables you can bring in to put the goods we've priced on?'

'No tables, but how about iron bedsteads with mattresses on them? We have quite a few of those left over from the Army's occupation of Esherwood. We're intending to sell them.'

'Let me sell them for you. I'll get far more money than you would.'

'What'll you charge us for doing that?' Mayne asked.

Woollard shook his head. 'Nothing. I'm part of the company now so I want it to do well.'

When the younger man didn't respond to this, Woollard grinned at him. 'Mayne lad, I really am on your side. More than anything I needed another interest. I'm not short of money, so I won't be looking to cheat you. Now . . .'

He didn't wait for an answer, but started walking slowly round the pile of cheaper goods. After a couple of circuits he removed three items from it and handed them to Judith. 'Put those pieces of crockery on your market stall, Mrs Esher. They'll fetch a few shillings and that's all they're worth.'

Mayne brought in the beds and watched for a while, feeling useless. In the end, he said, 'Is it all right if I leave you to it, Woollard? Call me if you need anything. I don't seem to have much to contribute. I don't even recognise most of the stuff on this pile. There are a lot of other jobs I need to get on top of.'

'You go, lad. Me and the two ladies will deal with these.'

As Mayne neared his office, the phone began to ring. He rushed inside and grabbed the phone. 'Esher and Company.'

'Daniel here.'

Mayne perched on the corner of the desk. 'Thank goodness! We were getting worried about you.'

'Sorry. I should have rung sooner, but it's been chaos since my uncle died. My aunt is normally a capable woman but at the moment she's lost without him and there's so much to sort out. I know I'm not pulling my weight in the building company, but she's like a second mother to me, so I can't leave her like this. She doesn't live close to anyone else in the family and you know how hard it is to get enough petrol to drive to and fro. Well, it's impossible.'

'We understand. It must be difficult for you. And in any case, there's been a development that's slowing things down this end as well.' He explained about the corpse.

'Ugh. Glad you're there to deal with it. I've seen enough corpses to last me a lifetime.'

After a short silence, he went on, 'I'm not totally wasting my time, though. I'm working on the preliminary designs for the flats and figuring out some minor improvements to the prefabs the Council wants to erect at the back. It's getting hold of proper paper for my architectural drawings that's the problem. You haven't got any paper you could send me, have you? Even if it's not proper draft paper, it'd help. I need some big sheets, if possible.'

'I think our new partner could supply that.'

'New partner?'

'Woollard.'

'Oh. You did let him into the business, then. I said you should.'

'Yes. Reluctantly. He's taking a five per cent share and working on valuing and the supply of materials. He's here at the moment, actually, going through my ancestral porcelain and silver – what's left of it. He certainly seems to know his stuff, and he can obtain things that aren't in the shops.'

'Sounds a useful fellow to have on board.'

'I'll ask him about paper. Give me some sizes and tell me where to send it to. And give me your phone number, too.'

Daniel rattled off the necessary details. 'I'd better go. I'm taking my aunt to the bank today, to sort out their money. She's very nervous, never had to deal with financial matters before.'

As Mayne put the phone down, he sighed. They'd got used to delays and shortages during the war years, but if the government wanted houses building quickly, they were going to have to get relevant materials produced for builders, and that included paper for the architectural drawings. He got up and went to find Woollard.

His partner looked pleased at the request. 'Told you I'd be useful. Give me Daniel's address and, when I go home for lunch, I'll tell my secretary to send him some bits and pieces from our stores to be going on with. After that, she'll find your friend some proper supplies. Well, if anyone can, she can.'

'Thanks.' Mayne looked at him ruefully. 'I think I've been a bit touchy with you.'

'Happen you don't think much of us war profiteers. But without some of the smaller comforts I got for them, people would have struggled.'

'Judith did mention knicker elastic.'

Woollard chuckled. 'I couldn't get enough of that. Hairpins were very popular, too, and combs. Now, let me get on with this valuing till lunchtime. I'll see your friend gets some paper by first post tomorrow.'

'I think he'd welcome a few pencils and rubbers as well and . . . you know, anything relevant that you can get hold of.'

'Yes. I know.' He hesitated. 'There might be a couple of pieces of china here that I'd like to buy for myself. Would that upset you? I'll pay a fair price, I promise you.'

'It's going to upset me whoever buys certain items, if they're objects I care about, but most of them mean nothing to me. They were just . . . always there. If I can, I'm going to save one or two of my favourites for my children. If I ever have any.'

Woollard laughed outright. 'The way you and Judith look at one another, you'll have more than one child. After all, she's proved she can have them and you're a healthy-looking chap. She's a good mother, too. I like her three. The younger lass is going to be a real heartbreaker. I can see her going into films.'

'Gillian?'

'Yes. You watch her tell a story. She can light a room up.'

Which gave Mayne something else to think about.

Daniel put the phone down with an involuntary mutter of frustration. He was itching to get on with detailed planning for the conversion of Esherwood into flats. But though he had approximate measurements for the old house and a rough floor plan, ready to show the other partners, he didn't have the detailed measurements and drawings he would need to draw up specific plans.

Most important of all, they hadn't been able to have specialist surveys done of the structure, so that he would know which areas were suitable for load bearing and which internal walls could be adjusted or removed. Oh, he could guess and would be pretty accurate, too, but you didn't undertake major jobs by guesswork. Well, he didn't and he never would.

What's more he wanted to be there for the survey, to make sure it was done properly. He didn't know the local surveyors yet.

The trouble was, now that he'd been to Esherwood, he wasn't looking forward to tearing the old house to pieces and putting it back together again. It would feel like desecration. He knew how much the idea of doing it hurt Mayne and he sympathised with his friend's dilemma.

But if you didn't have the money to maintain an old house – and such places absolutely gobbled up money – it was either turn it into several dwellings and sell or lease them, or else knock the house down and sell the land. He'd heard of the latter happening, families razing their ancient manors and selling the land, or even selling off the contents and simply abandoning the empty buildings to rot and crumble.

At the moment, until he could go back to Esherwood, he'd carry on designing the single dwellings they would one day erect in its grounds. Even with tight government restrictions on building, he was sure he could provide people with comfortable homes to live in.

He smiled. You weren't allowed to build big houses these days, however much money you had, and that was upsetting some people. But he could design houses that would be easy to add on to later, couldn't he?

Before he could go back to Rivenshaw, he had to sort out what his aunt was going to do. While he was staying with her, she'd insisted on providing the food, as a thank you for helping her. However, he was getting worried because it was obvious she was being extremely economical, especially with herself. He'd had to insist she took a fair share of the meat and other proteins.

He had to wonder whether she'd been left with as much money as the family had expected.

Still, his uncle did own this house. Daniel had checked that with her. It was too large for a woman on her own so she'd probably move out of it, but they could take their time about that. No need to rush things.

He'd made an appointment for the two of them to see the bank manager, but this couldn't be done till the following week because the manager had been ill. Daniel knew Auntie Beryl was dreading this meeting.

He turned his thoughts back to building, because there was nothing more he could do to help her till after they'd seen the bank manager.

Perhaps their company could build some modified prefabs to make a quick start? He remembered seeing an exhibition of prefabs in London in July at the *Daily Herald* Post-War Homes Exhibition. They might not look pretty from outside but they were sheer luxury inside to people who'd grown up without indoor lavatories and plumbed-in bathrooms.

At the exhibition, he'd listened to women talking about what they were seeing and what seemed to appeal to them most was the kitchens. They loved the fitted and built-in cupboards. To have a refrigerator seemed an unattainable luxury to most of them, but the planners had been far-sighted enough to provide them in all the prefab kitchens he'd seen.

He smiled wryly as he remembered one young woman he'd overheard agreeing with her companion that the kitchens were wonderful. She'd added that any two-bedroom house with a waterproof roof over it would make her very happy for now, because she was sick and tired of squeezing herself, her husband and two small children into one bedroom at her mother's house.

Daniel wanted to give people homes they could love, not just any old set of walls covered by a roof and—

A sound interrupted his thoughts and he listened intently. Was that . . .? Yes it was. His aunt was weeping again. The two of them made a fine matched pair, each alone in the world. His uncle had died, leaving his aunt to manage on her own, and Daniel's wife had walked out on him and divorced him very rapidly in an American court in somewhere called Las Vegas.

Because of the war, his moods were uneven and he still had nightmares. Maybe if he could put his skills to work, he could dream of houses, instead of spiralling down into nightmares of bombs and bodies.

After dinner, Francis turned to Mayne and Judith. 'Could I have a word with you two about the business, please? I do want to play my part.'

'If you need to take more time before you start doing anything . . .'

'Thanks, but no. I have to go back in a few days to sort out the house and the rest of my possessions, but while I'm here, I'm better keeping myself occupied. I've been thinking how best to contribute at this stage, and I've come to the conclusion that one of the main preliminary tasks will be to understand the electrics in this house. *All* the electrics and how they fit together.'

He frowned. 'Frankly, the place is in a right old mess and some of the wiring is downright dangerous. There are connections cobbled together, overloading of circuits – though that's probably less of a problem now that the house isn't being used as a hospital and needing so much electricity. But still . . . I do believe in keeping things safe.'

'That sounds to be an excellent idea. Quite frankly, I don't have any idea of the details of what they did, and by now, I doubt anyone else does, either. They kept the family out once they requisitioned it, but different groups moved in and out. Anyway, I was away in the Army most of the time.'

'Good. I'll work on that. But I'll need some paper to make charts. I really can't hold a whole house like this in my memory, nor should I even try.'

Judith said at once, 'See Mr Woollard. If anyone can get hold of paper, it's him.'

'Yes, of course. It's going to be useful having our own Mr Fix-it, don't you think?' Francis said with a smile.

Mayne shrugged. 'I'm getting used to bending the rules, though I don't like it. I'll ask him if you like.'

'I'd rather do it myself so that I can tell him exactly what I need.'

'All right. I'll leave it up to you.'

Francis nodded. He felt pleased at the thought of having something constructive to do. He was dreading going back to Medworth, kept wondering if Diana was stripping their house of its contents.

Or more likely, whether her damned parents were supervising that.

10

The following morning Woollard and his niece were at the big house at ten o'clock, ready to continue valuing the piles of oddments.

'Just one thing before you start,' Mayne said. 'Francis here needs some supplies, similar to Daniel's actually.'

Francis explained the situation and Woollard nodded. 'I'll telephone my secretary and she'll get you started. You can walk into town and pick the things up from her. If there are other things you need, she'll see if she can find them for you. I can see that our tame architect won't be the only one making plans.'

He grinned at Mayne, who was frowning, and held up one hand as if to stop him commenting. 'I should be able to get more supplies of that type legally, given the need for homes to be built. *Some* people have to benefit from the various government restrictions and regulations, and why not us?'

Judith chuckled and Mayne was betrayed into a reluctant smile.

'If you have time, Brady, I'd welcome your advice on a few things at home,' Woollard went on. 'The electrics seem to have been cobbled together in my house, as well as here.'

'Happy to help you, sir.'

'Call me Ray. I'm getting a bit tired of being Mr Woollard.

Makes me feel old. And yes, I know I'm getting on a bit, but I don't usually *feel* it.'

'Ray it is,' Francis agreed. 'Tell me where your office is and I'll go and see what your secretary has. After that, I'll pop into your home and check the electrics. If there's not too much wrong, I can make a start on getting to know this house later. Mayne, if you have any idea, even for parts of the house, you can tell me what they changed during the war. Though I daresay I'll notice most of it. They did some slapdash work and the original electrics are showing their age.'

Mayne took Woollard – no, he must remember to call him Ray – to the office to use the phone, then left him to continue valuing the bric-a-brac in the library.

He allowed himself a few moments outside to get a breath of fresh air, and asked the young constable if anyone had been in touch with the Rivenshaw police.

'I don't think so, sir. At least, the sergeant didn't say anything to me.'

'Damn them! Why are they keeping us waiting like this? How many men does it take to dig up a few bones?'

When he went back into the house, Mayne heard someone hurrying across the big entrance hall and turned to see who it was.

Steph stopped as she caught sight of him. 'Ah, there you are! Can you come and see something please, Mr Esher?'

'Is something wrong?'

She gave him one of her half-smiles. 'Wait and see.'

He followed her into the library where her uncle was standing beaming at a group of battered and dusty pottery figurines that had turned up in one of the bedroom cupboards. Mayne had wanted to throw them away but Judith had assured him they'd still be worth a few shillings from women hungry for ornaments, and had insisted on them being put with the other low-value items.

'We've found your first real prizes,' Woollard said and gestured to the figurines.

Mayne wondered for a moment whether the older man was trying to trick him. 'Those ghastly things? They're all chipped.'

'You'd be chipped if you were two hundred years old. These Staffordshire figurines are very popular with collectors, war or no war, and these spaniels and lions are very good examples of early figures.'

'They don't even look like spaniels, even less like lions.'

'They're not to my taste, I must admit, but nonetheless these are quite valuable.'

Mayne walked over to study them more closely, but they looked even worse when you got near them and he noticed the brown earthenware showing through the glaze here and there at the chipped parts. 'How can they possibly be valuable?'

'Because people have strange tastes, and because these are early pieces. Pratt ware, I think they're called. Trust me. They'll bring in a good few pounds.'

'Never!' He rolled his eyes.

'They will. We must find somewhere safe to keep the more valuable items. With a house this big, it's hard to make sure everything is locked up carefully and, anyway, those locks on your French windows are clumsy old things. I could pick them myself in seconds. Be sure to put the bolts on as well at night.'

'Oh. Yes. I will. I'll tell everyone.'

'Can you find me a safe room and bring a chappie in to put a heavy locking door on it?'

Mayne thought quickly about the rooms on the ground floor. 'How about the butler's pantry? It's got a silverware store, though minus the silverware at the moment.'

'Show me.'

Woollard examined the room with its rows of shelves and the inner store room with its extra-heavy door for the most valuable items. 'Perfect. Small windows, too: not easy for a grown person to get through. We'll put those figures here and I'm sure I'll find plenty of other valuable pieces to join them.'

'If you think it's necessary. I can't see there being enough valuable pieces to fill this room, but we have to put the ones you do find somewhere, I suppose.'

'You'll see. Now about selling things, if you take my advice, you'll not flood the market. I don't sell antiques but I know people who do and who will treat us fairly. I'll just hint to them about what I've got and say I may be able to find other stuff. They'll come running. They know I won't waste their time on rubbish.'

'Do you know that much about antiques? I thought you dealt in, well, more minor everyday stuff during the war.'

'Everyone has a hobby and I love old things. Also, I found I had a knack for putting people in touch with one another. "Ask Woollard" they used to say, and I usually knew someone or knew someone to ask for help finding someone. I've got a very good memory for names, if I say so myself. I never forget a name, either of a person or of an object.'

'Well, we're in your hands completely in this area.'

'I'll see you right, lad, don't worry. Remember, it's my company too.' He clapped the younger man on the shoulders in what might previously have seemed an over-familiar gesture, except that somehow he was turning into an ally and today that gesture seemed . . . well, genuinely friendly.

Mayne offered a confidence of his own. 'Wait till Judith finds out about those figurines. If she hadn't stopped me, I'd have chucked them all in the dustbin.'

Woollard's smile slipped and he shuddered. 'Promise me

never, ever to do that without consulting me, however ugly or battered an item is.'

Mayne spread his hands in a helpless gesture. 'I promise.'

His companion let out his breath audibly, and from the corner of the library Steph allowed herself a quick smile.

Francis sorted out Ray Woollard's electrical problems, which were minor to a man of his experience, then after his midday meal he went to look at the main collection of fuse boxes at Esherwood.

There were several on a wall near the kitchen. The trouble was, there were fuse boxes elsewhere, too, presumably installed during the various changes made to the building. They seemed to have been planted randomly in the nearest spot.

He opened the boxes and winced at what lay inside. Sloppy work, that. After some consideration, he decided he couldn't do much about the situation until he moved to Esherwood permanently. For the time being he'd go round the house, putting together the jigsaw puzzle of additions and extensions.

He'd also tighten a few connections here and there, and make sure things were relatively safe. He could *not* leave them loose like that. What had these people been thinking of?

He spent the afternoon in the attics, because less had been done up there and he thought he'd get an understanding of that floor most easily. Which would be a start.

After an hour's work, he came to a cable that hooked out of the bottom of a cupboard, seeming to come from nowhere that he could tell. It twisted along for a foot or so then went into the floor again, perhaps to avoid a joist or heavy beam. What the hell was it connecting?

He didn't have a clue. It didn't seem to belong to any of the other wiring groups up here.

He went to perch on an old travelling trunk that happened to have a ray of autumn sunshine warming it, trying to think through what he'd found so far. But however he considered it, he couldn't connect that cable to anything he'd found in the attics. And he was usually good at picturing things.

What sort of lunatics had set up this electrical system? Francis wondered. They hadn't been properly trained engineers, that was sure. The sergeants in charge of that area in his regiment would have had his guts for garters if he'd done such dangerous and shoddy work.

His stomach growled and realising he was hungry, he left the puzzle for the time being and went downstairs to see what was available.

Judith looked up as he came into the kitchen. 'Ah, Francis. I was hoping you'd turn up. Look, if you can go and buy your midday meals from the British Restaurant in town from tomorrow onwards, I can manage to give you a decent tea most nights. It's only a ten-minute walk away.'

'My pleasure.' He could do with a bit of exercise after all the crouching and poking around in awkward corners and he didn't want to inconvenience Judith more than he had to. 'Just give me directions.'

'You'd better wash your face before we have our tea.' She grinned. 'You've been playing around in dusty corners, I can tell.'

He smiled too when he went to look in the little mirror on the wall and a filthy face peered back at him, with a cobweb strand decorating its forehead. 'All part of the job.'

How stupid of him not to have thought of ration books when he was packing. He remembered that Diana had kept them in the kitchen drawer. Well, he hoped that's where they were still. He didn't want to have to confront the Scammells in their lair again.

'Go and find somewhere to sit until I call everyone for tea,' she said.

As he turned away, she called, 'Just a minute! I nearly

forgot to tell you. Mr Woollard's secretary sent some stuff over for you. I put it in the sitting room, because I wasn't sure where you were going to be working.'

'What do you mean by stuff?'

'Paper and pencils – you told him you needed some. Apparently you and Daniel have very similar needs. Good thing Woollard's around, isn't it?'

But she was talking to herself. Francis had rushed off to find out what had been sent. It seemed like a treasure trove: several pencils, a rubber, two big rulers, paper large and small, in quantities it had been impossible for civilians to obtain during the later years of the war.

'Oh, well done!' he muttered. He looked up to see Judith standing in the doorway. 'Where shall I set up office? In my bedroom?'

'No need for that. Use one of the rooms in the nursery suite on the second floor. There are several small ones, which would be very suitable as offices, and not as hard to heat in winter.

'OK.' Beaming, Francis carried the first load carefully up the stairs. Now he could really start work. How good that felt!

Someone knocked on the front door and Daniel went to answer it. To his delight the postman was there, holding out a cardboard roll and a neat parcel the size of two big books. The latter was wrapped in brown paper and tied with string, finished off by a blob of red sealing wax impressed with a large W.

He opened the cardboard roll eagerly, letting out a yell of triumph when he found it contained some large sheets of paper. A note said *More to follow, Woollard*.

He turned to the parcel and had to stop himself from tearing it open. If he took care, the wrapping paper could be used again, even if only for rough preliminary sketches. And Auntie Beryl would go mad if he cut a piece of string, so he scraped off the blob of hardened sealing wax and began to fiddle about with the knot.

Even as he was thinking of her, she came downstairs, eyes reddened, hair untidy. 'Did the postman bring something nice, dear?'

'Some large sheets of paper. See! And I'm hoping this parcel will contain more paper in smaller sizes.'

She came across and nudged his hand away from the knot. 'Let me do that. My fingers are much more nimble than yours, with all the sewing and mending I do.'

While she was rolling up the string into a small bundle, securing it then putting it into her sideboard drawer, Daniel opened the parcel. More paper and other treasures too: pencils, two rubbers – he'd be careful with those, because they were as rare as hens' teeth these days – pens, a few paperclips and even two bottles of black ink, carefully wrapped in cotton wool. But the biggest treasure of all was a brand new slide rule, of very good quality, perfect for an architect's needs.

How had Woollard known he'd need that? Daniel's own slide rule was still packed away somewhere in his share of the marital goods. He was sure Ada wouldn't have taken it or thrown it away. He trusted her to have divided their possessions fairly.

His aunt pounced on the cotton wool, with a 'Just what I need!' and moved the bottles of ink carefully to the centre of the table top. 'Dear me, Daniel, take more care where you put things. We don't want these bottles to fall off and smash. And what is that thing you're holding?'

'Hmm? Oh, sorry. It's a special type of ruler for calculating with. I use it for working out the mathematical details of big designs. Oh, it's so wonderful to have proper supplies! Look at all these pencils! I've had to buy most of my own on the black market during the war. Now, I need to find a piece of board to make myself a drawing slope. I can make do with a small one for the time being.'

She turned pink. 'I, um, happen to have a slope. If you think it'd be suitable, you're welcome to borrow it.'

'If you don't mind me asking, why would you have a drawing slope?'

'I took up painting before the war. I didn't tell people, though. I like to paint flowers. I wasn't able to go on with it during the war because I couldn't get new paints once mine ran out. But I didn't give away my slope.'

'You didn't tell me you were an artist.'

'I'm not really. I just . . . dabble. But Egan liked the paintings.'

'Show me the slope.'

On the way up the stairs he paused to stare at a painting of three roses on the landing. He'd admired it but not looked at the painter's signature. Now he did. Hers: Beryl O'Brien.

She flushed and made shooing motions with her hands.

'It's lovely,' he said.

'It's just an amateur water colour.'

'It's still lovely. You're good.'

She flushed bright red and hurried up the stairs. But she absolutely refused to show him the rest of her paintings, and when he saw the tears gather in her eyes and the way her lips trembled, he didn't press her.

By dinnertime he was set up to work on her dining table, even if it was only for a few days. They agreed to eat their meals in the kitchen, so that he didn't have to clear his work away and he sat down with a happy sigh to enjoy doing what he loved best.

He noticed that helping him had taken his aunt's mind off her loss a little, but once that need was satisfied, she became quiet and withdrawn again. And she didn't mention seeing the bank manager next week, let alone discuss what they needed to find out from him.

That afternoon he was going to look at some prefabs the local council was erecting and he decided to invite his aunt to go with him. They were within easy walking distance. He'd tell her he needed a woman's point of view, and the trip would take her out of herself for a while. Well, he hoped it would.

Only time could dull the pain of her loss. She had been very happily married to his father's brother and Uncle Egan had seemed happy with her.

After they'd looked at the prefabs, they came home and he decided to make rough sketches of any ideas he'd gained.

But as he headed for the dining room, he saw in the mirror that his aunt was looking sad again. How could he go back to Rivenshaw and leave her like this? No other family member lived close enough to visit her every day. He had to do something to help her. She had always been his favourite aunt, even though she wasn't a blood relative.

Only, he had a job waiting for him in Rivenshaw, had already spent too long away. Where did one obligation end and another begin?

Diana developed a severe head cold, which her mother blamed on her associating with slum dwellers. She ignored these snide comments and kept to her bed for a couple of days. She had to, she felt so awful. But as the worst of the feverish stage passed, it suited her to have time to think, so she pretended to be still feeling weak.

Unfortunately, her mother was growing increasingly short-tempered with her.

And even more unfortunately, she couldn't work out what to do with herself now.

'I'm not doing it on purpose, Mummy,' she croaked. 'I can't help it if—'

As a sneeze interrupted their conversation, her mother took a quick step back towards the bedroom door, a handkerchief to her mouth. 'I know you're not doing it on purpose, but you won't get better lying in a stuffy bedroom. You could at least manage a short stroll. Some fresh air will help clear your head a little, blow the germs away. Just try it.'

Rather than argue, Diana did as suggested.

It felt good to be out of the house, away from their watchful eyes, even though she felt too weak to do more than stroll along slowly. She no longer dared weep because her mother noticed her reddened eyes and scolded her. But she wanted to weep. Oh, how she wanted to!

She had no idea what Francis was doing or if he'd ever return.

She had even less idea what she would say to him when they met again. If only her head wasn't so full of the cold, she might be able to think straight.

As she strolled listlessly along the main street of the village, she saw one of her mother's friends in the distance. She couldn't face talking to her and being asked humiliating questions, so turned hastily down a side street. She didn't want to see or speak to anyone.

After a few moments she realised she'd wandered into the poorest part of the village. She didn't know it well, because she hadn't been here since she was a child of seven, when she'd been soundly spanked for going there and bringing home who-knew-what germs.

Feeling suddenly dizzy, she stopped and leaned against a wall.

'Are you all right, dear?'

Diana tried to open her eyes and everything went black. When she recovered consciousness she found she was lying on a rag rug inside someone's house. Two small children were sitting on a similar but smaller rug to one side of the fireplace, staring at her, and a young woman was crouched beside her.

'There. You're coming to again. How do you feel?'

Across the room a young man was slumped in a chair, the only person not staring at her. He was staring at the floor, rocking slightly and mumbling to himself.

Diana looked at him nervously because he seemed so strange.

'Terry won't hurt you,' the young woman said. 'It's because he doesn't like hurting people that he's in such a state. Unless you tell him to do something, he just sits there all day. Half the night, too. That's how they sent him back to me from the sodding war.' Her voice was bitter.

Diana struggled to sit up and the stranger helped her.

'I didn't know what to do with you when you fainted. Couldn't leave you lying in the street, though, could I? Someone would have stolen your handbag. So I asked my neighbour to help carry you inside.'

'Thank you so much.'

'It can't be hunger that made you faint if you can afford such pretty clothes.' She reached out to stroke Diana's blouse with rough, reddened fingers. 'Lovely, that material is.'

'I'm really grateful for your help.'

'That's all right. Do you feel you can stand up now? Only I have to get on.'

'Can you . . . give me another minute or two? I've had flu, or a cold and I still feel a bit dizzy.'

'Is there someone I can send for to help you home? Though you'll have to give the lad a penny to do it because I haven't a farthing to spare.'

Diana shook her head. 'I don't want to go back yet. They'll just scold me.'

'Who are they?'

'My parents.'

The stranger's eyes went to Diana's left hand. 'Lost your husband, have you?'

'You might say that. He's left me.' Then the tears came and Diana sobbed her heart out in the arms of a complete stranger.

After a while she pulled herself together. 'I'm sorry.'

'Best get it out of you. I cried a lot when my Terry came home like that. It helped ease the pain a bit, but it didn't feed the children.'

'Will he get better?'

'They don't know.'

'How do you manage?'

'They give him a bit of a pension and I do what work I can.'

'That must be hard.'

'Yeah. But my cousin slips me a shilling or two sometimes and people give me food if they can spare it, so we manage.' She stood up. 'Well, if you're feeling better, I'll get on.'

Diana surprised herself by asking, 'Can I come again?'

'Why would you do that? I don't have time to chat.'

'You made time to comfort me. I might be able to bring you some food and . . . you're the first person who's both-ered to listen to me. Really listen. What are you called?'

'Annie.'

'I'm Diana Brady.'

'Yes, I know. You used to live in that big house on posh street, didn't you?'

Diana could feel herself flushing. 'I'm back there again.'

'With your parents? I'd run away to sea rather than go back to live with mine.'

'It's a bit difficult, I must admit. I didn't expect them to treat me like a child.'

'Parents always do. They never see that you've grown up.'
Annie shrugged. 'Look, if you want to come round, I'll not
turn you away. And any food you can bring will help them.'
Her jerk of the head took in not only the children but the
young man with the agonised expression alternating with
sadness on his thin face.

As she walked home, Diana marvelled at how strong her
rescuer seemed, especially given how much she had to cope
with. Her mother always said the poor brought bad things
on themselves by their careless ways, but she couldn't see
what Annie had done to bring such a disaster on the small
family.

When she got home, her mother took one look at her face
and shrieked, 'Surely you've not been crying in public? Have
you no pride?'

'Not much now, mother. Actually, I fainted and a kind
lady took me in till I felt well enough to walk back.'

'Where was that?'

'Waterside Brow.'

Her mother's expression showed utter disgust. 'What on
earth were you doing in that part of the village?'

'I wasn't thinking where I was going. I just . . . found
myself there and felt dizzy. I didn't have any money on me,
so I couldn't give the poor woman something for her trouble.
I think I ought to, don't you? She has a husband who can't
work because he was injured in the war and two small children.'

'Certainly you should give her something, if she deserves
it, if she isn't feckless. We'll go there tomorrow and—'

'I'd rather do it myself, if you don't mind. I don't have
any money but if you have any food to spare . . . and maybe
you could lend me a shilling?'

'I'll see what I can put together. It's about time you started
thinking about others, not just yourself.'

'Yes, Mummy. I'll try to do that.'

To her surprise, Diana suddenly wished she was back in the small house with Annie. She'd felt more comfortable with a stranger than she did with her own mother. How was that possible?

It was one thing, she decided, to see her mother, but quite another to live with her again. She'd made a mistake coming here. She knew that now.

II

Victor walked slowly round the house, glad that Ros had left him to do this final check on his own. They'd worked themselves to a standstill each night to get the sorting and packing finished and now he needed to say farewell to more than his old home, to his first marriage as well. It'd not be fair to load Ros with his memories of Susan, so he would mainly speak of his first wife to Betty from now on.

But he'd give the past a little of his time now, give it a decent farewell. Like him, a lot of people all over the country would be packing up to move house. Some had already put the past in its place; others would still be doing so.

People had been bombed out and had to move in with relatives. Or their homes had been taken away from them, like Mayne's. In the forces, they'd lived cheek by jowl; civilians had squeezed together wherever they could. Like Susan, wives with husbands serving in the armed forces had often gone back to live near parents or had moved back in with them. He'd heard of people occupying garages even, leaving the car standing in the drive, because it was useless for lack of petrol.

Now, dispossessed people would do anything to have a home of their own again. On every side, he sensed that longing, heard people talk about where they'd like to live, what they'd do in a home of their own. There was such a need for all aspects of life to start moving again – real peacetime life. But people had to have somewhere to live and he thought he and his friends could contribute to that.

It wouldn't happen overnight, couldn't possibly, everyone realised that. The British people had been superhumanly patient for the past six years, comforting themselves by sayings like, 'There is a war on, you know.'

In such a total war effort, everything had been focused on arming the dragons of war – and filling the stomachs of those at home who catered for the war's needs. Now many factories would need completely refitting in order to produce peacetime goods and that took time, even if you could get the raw materials.

People were waiting more or less patiently for the fruits of peace, and though they might grumble, most of them were deep down glad the war was over. He smiled involuntarily at the mere thought.

He wondered how many of its promises the new Labour government would carry out, like free universal health care. The ability to see a doctor without worrying about the cost of the consultation would make a huge difference to poorer people.

He stood in the bedroom he and Susan had shared. Even money and the best medical care hadn't been able to save his young wife, though. He'd made her happy, he felt. Yes, he was pretty sure he had. But the war had cut that happiness short as he went to serve in the armed forces. And then her parents had taken over her life again bit by bit, damn them. And they hadn't made her happy.

He wouldn't do that to Betty, or to any other children he fathered. He didn't intend to dictate every step his offspring took, whether they were girls or boys. He wanted them to fly high and free, get a good education, find jobs that meant something, enjoy their lives.

He smiled. Ah, he was just like everyone else, dreaming of better times, wanting more for their children than they had had themselves. And why not? People had earned the right to dream and hope.

This final trip to his former home had gone well, far better than he'd expected, thanks to Fitkin keeping Susan's mother under control and buying the house off him. In the new post-war world, Victor was beginning to realise, you never knew when an enemy would stop being an enemy, as Fitkin had.

He'd heard that some German and Italian prisoners-of-war who'd been working on the land were marrying local women and settling in Britain. Others were staying to work here and being welcomed for their expertise in various areas.

You couldn't have a true peace unless you let go of your animosity. Though he could never forgive Hitler. Never. It was a good thing that evil man was dead. How had maniacs like him and Mussolini become leaders in the first place? That still baffled Victor and many others with him.

Well, he couldn't solve the world's problems, just (he hoped) his own. Tomorrow he would take Betty to lay flowers on her mother's grave, then, the morning after, they'd leave for Rivenshaw in his car and never return.

He was looking forward to putting his energies into rebuilding. That was a job well worth doing.

Thank goodness for Mayne Esher and his clear-sighted vision of future possibilities and needs. They hadn't invited anyone else in their unit to join their small group, only the four of them.

The future would bring great changes, he was sure.

And that was enough thinking. Time for him to act. He needed to do a few final jobs about the house, so that it was left in a good condition.

Raising one hand in salute aimed in the direction of the

village cemetery, he said a silent farewell to Susan and went down to join Ros and his daughter.

They were his future. What a lucky man he was.

Once Victor and Betty got back from paying their respects at his first wife's grave, he looked at Ros, who had a slightly anxious expression, and offered her a solemn promise: 'It'll just be us from now on, my love – you, me and Betty. I've laid Susan to rest.'

'I know that. But you and Betty won't forget her, nor should you. That doesn't upset me as long as you can love me too.'

'You know I do.' He changed the subject. 'Look, we've finished in the house and I don't want to linger here. Let's pack the car tonight and leave at first light.'

He turned as his daughter joined them. 'What do you say, young lady? Do you want to get up really early tomorrow and head north?'

'Yes please, Daddy.' She grew thoughtful. 'Do you think Mother will know I put flowers on her grave?'

'I'm sure she will. I think love can cross any barrier.'

The little girl nodded acceptance and went to stand next to Ros, who automatically put an arm round her shoulders. After a moment, Betty glanced hesitantly sideways and then gave in to the temptation to lean against the sturdy figure and put an arm round Ros's waist. She got a quick hug from her stepmother as she did so.

'Grandmother said it was vulgar to cuddle people,' she confided. 'But I like doing it.'

'That was because no one ever cuddled *her*.' Victor went across and put his arms round both his women. 'I like doing it too.'

Ros gave him a glowing smile, cuddled them for a moment or two then said briskly, 'Right. As soon as you've phoned the removal men to tell them they can start as early as they like tomorrow, we'll start loading the car. Edna will be able to tell them what things to take. We should give her a bonus, you know, she's been so helpful.'

She kept up a gentle flow of conversation with her step-daughter, as they all moved to and fro carrying things from the house to the Wolseley Ten, a sturdy vehicle that Victor had had no difficulty resurrecting after its years of storage during the war.

He patted it as they placed the final box into the back next to where Betty would sit. 'She's a hard-working creature, this old car. I'm looking forward to having her around again.'

'I've never had a car of my own,' Ros said, 'though I learned to drive in the Wrens. Will you let me drive yours occasionally?'

He grinned at her. 'As soon as we can get petrol regularly, I'll insist you drive her often. I can't afford a chauffeur, so will have to make do with you.'

She gave him a mock slap and they both laughed.

Then he said quietly, 'We'll share everything, I hope, everything we can. I don't ever want our marriage to turn polite and distant, or for us to lead separate lives.'

She threaded her arm in his and leaned her head against his shoulder for a moment. 'Neither do I, my darling.'

The following morning, they all got up early, ate some bread and jam quickly, and left the village.

Not one of them looked back.

Diana collected the food her mother had grudgingly got together for Annie, put it in her shopping basket and took the shilling doled out for her rescuer as well. She made her way to Waterside Brow, ignoring the rather hostile looks people in this district gave her. She felt a bit nervous but no one attempted to accost her to ask for money.

Annie opened the door, looking frazzled and tired. 'Oh, it's you.'

Diana suddenly felt shy. 'I, um, brought you a present as a thank you for helping me.'

'Hmm. I suppose you'd better come in then, if you're going to play Mrs Bountiful.'

Which wasn't exactly a welcome. But Diana could see why Annie wasn't wasting time on politeness. Terry was lying down on a nest of blankets on the big rug, not seeming to notice what was going on round him, and breathing heavily, as if he too had a cold . . . or worse. One of the children was crying softly to itself.

'What happened to your husband?'

'I don't know. He sleeps down here because he's too heavy for me to get upstairs safely. He was like this when I came down to get breakfast for him and the children.'

'What did the doctor say?'

'Terry hasn't seen one yet. I don't have money to pay doctors, so I had to send my neighbour to the charity doctor. Whoever is on duty comes when they've time, not when you say you need them.'

'Oh dear.'

'Excuse me asking, but what did you bring? The kids are hungry and I didn't have time to do any shopping.'

'A loaf and part of a jar of jam. There are some potatoes as well.' Suddenly the food looked what it was. Old stale bread, the jam you got on the ration, which was either red or yellow but apart from that, of unknown origin, and potatoes that were starting to sprout. 'My mother put this together. I'm sorry. I didn't realise it was so . . . meagre.'

'It'll still fill their bellies. Beggars can't be choosers.'

'And I thought . . . this might help out a bit.' She pushed a shilling into her companion's hand.

Annie looked as if she'd eaten something sour, but took

the coin. 'Thanks. I'm sorry, but I have to get on and—'

There was a knock on the door and it opened straight away, without so much as a by your leave. Dr Lorden, whom Diana's parents knew socially, came in. He noticed her and nodded politely, then looked at Annie impatiently.

'Well, what's wrong?'

'You can *see* what's wrong if you'd look at your patient instead of your friend. My husband's not moving, not talking. He was like that when I got up this morning.'

The doctor looked angry at her tone but did at least go over to Terry and give him a cursory examination. He straightened up again, shaking his head. 'I don't like the looks of this. He'll have to go into hospital.'

'Not the infirmary!' Annie pleaded.

Even Diana knew why. 'I'm sure Dr Lorden will ask for a place for him in the cottage hospital. After all, he was injured serving his country. I'm taking an interest in this case, doctor, trying to help Annie. Is there anything you want me to do?'

'Find better food for them all then they won't get ill as often.' He pulled out a pad. 'I'll ask for a place in the cottage hospital, but I can't guarantee anything. They'll send an ambulance for him when they can fit him in. Get his things ready, Mrs, um, Digby.'

He left the house then with nothing more than a nod to Diana and no instructions for caring for the poor man.

'Well, how rude he is to his patients!' Diana said. 'He's always been very polite when I've met him.'

Annie let out a scornful laugh. 'Ah. I bet he's never rude to people of his own sort.'

'Well, no.'

'He's always rude to poor people who depend on his charity, but at least he does treat a few of us. Anyway, thanks for what you said. It's the best chance my Terry has, going into the cottage hospital. If he went into that infirmary, he'd never come out again. Have you ever been inside it?'

'Um, no.'

Annie's shudder was eloquent. 'It stinks like a privvy in some areas.'

'Can I help in any other way? Not that I'm sure what to do. I've never helped anyone like this before.'

The other woman's thin face softened. 'No, love. You still look a bit pale. You should go home and have a good rest. I appreciate what you've done for us today. You can consider me more than paid back for helping you yesterday.'

It must be awful to depend on charity like that, Diana thought as she walked home. By the time she got there she was dizzy.

Her mother took one look at her and sent her to bed, not even asking how things had gone.

Diana had a sleep then lay dreading a long, boring evening. She'd already read the books in her bedroom, but if she went down to find other reading material, or asked her mother to do so, she'd be told that if she was well enough to read, she was well enough to get up for dinner.

She could have joined them for the evening but if she did that, she'd not be able to eavesdrop. She was still worrying about various things she'd overheard. What else were they planning to do to her and her husband?

Francis didn't deserve any unkind treatment and as for taking money from the sale of his house, Diana would refuse to do that, at least. The trouble was, she'd heard her father boast before about getting money out of people and she worried that they would go after her husband's money, with or without her agreement.

She hadn't cared about other people before, not really; she found she did care now – about Francis, anyway.

And she definitely wasn't going to let her father choose

her next husband, as he had said to her mother. *Next husband?* She hadn't got rid of this one and still wasn't quite sure she wanted to divorce Francis.

She didn't feel sure about anything.

Only she knew how cunning her father could be about persuading people to do things his way. She'd never defied him before. Could she do it now?

She shuddered. She'd rather not try, thank you very much. Well, not openly anyway.

Mayne heard a vehicle draw up in front of the big house just as the children were clattering about, getting ready to leave for school. The engine had a growling sound, as if it was larger and more powerful than other vehicles. It reminded him of the cars full of bigwigs who had visited the special unit.

He changed direction immediately this thought sank in, hurrying across the hall to the doorway of the sitting room instead of going into his office. From here he could see outside at the front of the house without being seen. 'Aha! If that's not officialdom come to deal with the corpse, then I'm a Dutch uncle,' he muttered.

Someone thumped the front door knocker hard.

He didn't hurry to answer it and smiled when they used the knocker again almost immediately.

He opened the door to see a tall, grim-faced man. 'Can I help you?'

'Mr Esher?'

'Yes.'

'You reported a corpse, a soldier.'

'I did indeed. And you are?'

'From the military police.'

Mayne waited but no names were offered. 'If you'll drive round to the rear of the house, I'll show you the corpse, which is in a nearby Nissen hut. There's a police constable on duty outside and the local police have employed a night watchman, so no one has tampered with the body. I'll just get the key to the hut and meet you there.'

With an inclination of the head, the man ran lightly down the stone stairs.

Mayne cut through the house calling, 'Visitors to see the body. You kids get off to school and don't hang around gawping. You don't want to be late.'

'But I'm the one who found the body,' Ben protested. 'They'll want to question me.'

'Yes and the sight of it turned you sick,' Gillian said at once. 'Fat lot of good you'll be to them.'

Her brother glared at her. 'It'd turn anyone sick to see a dead body.'

'No quarrelling,' Judith said in her stern, no-nonsense voice. She turned to her husband. 'They might want to see Ben.'

'Yes. I suppose so. But the girls can go to school as usual. They weren't involved.'

'Aw. It's not fair if Ben has all the fun. Can't we wait and see what happens?' Gillian coaxed.

'No, you can't, Miss Nosey Parker.' Judith pretended to slap her bottom. 'Get off to school with you.'

'Come outside with me, Ben,' Mayne said. 'We'll check whether they need to see you. If not, you can still get to school on time.'

Outside Constable Waide was standing very upright, bright-eyed and eager to see everything he could. Mayne was hard put not to chuckle at how youthful the constable looked.

The two investigators, a captain and a lieutenant, were waiting. One was tapping his foot impatiently; the other was scowling. 'Ah, there you are, Esher! It took you long enough.'

'I didn't hang the key to the hut where anyone could snatch it and I brought Ben with me in case you wanted to see him.'

The spokesman relaxed a little, studying Ben. 'Is this the lad who found it?'

Mayne laid one hand on his stepson's shoulder. 'Yes. But he only saw the foot, because that's all that was uncovered. Most of it's still concealed. I didn't let anyone touch it.'

The man relaxed marginally. 'No. Good thinking. A quick interview with him should do it, but first, let's take a look at what you've uncovered so far. You can explain what exactly happened.'

Ben jerked and looked pleadingly at his stepfather. 'I'd rather wait out here, if you don't mind.'

The man in charge frowned.

'Unless you want to waste your time reviving him when he faints, that's a good idea,' Mayne said. 'It's quite obvious what happened: someone buried a corpse. If you need more details, you can interview Mr Borkowski, who was also there when it was found. Here. I'll unlock the door.'

'Is that the displaced person?'

'Yes. Jan arrived here after VE Day and married a local lass.'

'Why did he come to Rivenshaw?'

Mayne opened the door. 'Jan's family knew the Bretherton family slightly, which is how he met Helen. One of our older residents vouches for his family having visited Rivenshaw in the thirties.' It was a lie, but Miss Peters never minded lying in a good cause and they'd had to protect Jan against anti-Semitism as well as helping him stay.

'Ah. So he's not likely to have been involved in this crime.'

'Impossible, timewise. And he's not a criminal type anyway. He should be here soon. He works for me.'

'Who else is living at Esherwood?'

'One of my partners, Victor Travers. We were in the Army together.'

'Did he visit you often in the past?'

'Never came here until a couple of weeks ago.'

'Right.' The man allowed himself a wry smile as he turned back to Ben and saw how apprehensive he looked. 'You can stay here, lad.'

Mayne pulled out his torch and the two investigators did the same, following him along the pathway that had been cleared through the piles of stores down the centre of the semi-circular hut, the highest part.

He stopped and gestured, shining the torch downwards. 'There. Jan had the wit not to attempt to uncover any more of the body.'

'They didn't say we'd need shovels,' the second man complained.

'They were in a hurry to get it sorted out. As usual.'

The two of them were thawing out a little, Mayne felt. 'If you want someone to dig the body out for you, I can find a man. But you'll have to pay him. In fact, Borkowski would be a good chap to do it. He's clever and not likely to damage the evidence, and he's willing to turn his hand to anything.'

Mayne explained about Jan eluding capture by the Germans all through the war as he travelled across Europe, and saw they were impressed. He glanced at his wristwatch. 'He should be here soon.'

'Let's talk to the lad first and then perhaps he can get off to school. If the sight of that,' he indicated the foot, 'turns him woozy, we don't want him fainting on the evidence and smashing up the clues.'

Definitely military police, Mayne thought. *But not your average Joes.* He'd guess they hadn't relished the thought of this rather minor job.

They heard voices outside in the stable yard and the two visitors fell silent, looking questioningly at Mayne.

'Jan's arrived. I should think Ben is telling him about you.'

'Let's go and meet this fellow then. Perhaps you can supply him with a shovel. We'll cover his wages.'

'Fine by me.' Mayne led them outside and introduced Jan, then turned to Ben. 'Our visitors want to ask you a few questions, then you can go to school.'

'I'll need a note for my teacher or I'll be in trouble for being late.'

'Your mother can write you one.'

Ben gave an aggrieved sigh, which won a quick grin from the senior of the two visitors.

After a few questions, he said, 'I think that's all the young-ster can tell us.'

'Get off to school now!' Mayne gave Ben a friendly little push and turned to the men. 'Don't you think we should be given your names?'

'No. You can address me as Captain and my companion as Lieutenant. The powers that be want to keep this as quiet as possible: no names, no pack drill, literally. I can let you have a phone number if you wish to complain about that.'

'The only thing I'm likely to complain about is that this is preventing me from clearing out the hut.'

'Let's get on with it, then. We'll be as quick as we can, I promise you, because we have more important things to deal with.'

He waited a moment and, when Mayne didn't protest further, turned to Jan. 'Mr Borkowski, I gather you were with Ben when the foot was uncovered. Mr Esher has suggested you might do us the favour of uncovering the body . . . slowly and carefully. We'll pay you for your trouble, of course.'

Jan nodded. 'I'm happy to be of use. I've been wondering how he was killed and why he was put there.'

'You and a few other people.'

Four hours later the body was revealed to be wearing a private's uniform without any badges or identification. The material was torn where these had been ripped off. The face was no longer recognisable, but it was obvious that he'd been hit on the head with some violence, because the back and part of one side of the skull were smashed in.'

'Murder, then,' the captain said. 'Lieutenant, perhaps you and Mr Borkowski can check every inch of his clothing, while I have a chat to Mr Esher. All we can tell at the moment is that the victim was fair-haired and probably not more than about thirty.'

Jan stayed the lieutenant's hand for a moment. 'I don't think anyone will have given him a proper farewell.' He bent his head and murmured a quick prayer, not in English.

The lieutenant's nod showed approval of this gesture of respect and he bowed his head as well.

As the two men began to go through every pocket and, at Jan's suggestion, every seam too, the captain gestured to Mayne to accompany him and led the way out of the Nissen hut. 'Rum business, eh, Esher?'

'Definitely bizarre. What are you going to do about the body?'

'Have it properly examined, make a few inquiries and try to find out whether someone disappeared from this place when it was a hospital. I dare say they'll give it a proper burial when they've finished with it. What else can we do? There are more important things to deal with and that poor chap has been dead a good while. It'll go on record as an unsolved case.'

Once in the kitchen, Mayne made the universal offer of hospitality, 'Would you like a cup of tea?'

'Yes, please. We'll not offer the lieutenant a cuppa till he's finished, if you don't mind. He'll need to wash carefully.'

'There's a sink in the laundry that he and Jan can use.' He wondered what this chat was in aid of, but the captain had finished being garrulous and sat quietly in the kitchen while Mayne dealt with the refreshments.

When he had his cup of tea, the captain asked what exactly had been going on at Esherwood during the war.

Mayne explained about it being requisitioned and little being known to outsiders of its internal workings.

'Lots of groups moving in and out on the short training courses, eh?' the captain said with a frown.

'Apparently. You'll have your work cut out to find who killed him.'

'I can see that and I don't like leaving murder unpunished, I must admit, especially that of a serving soldier.'

It was two more hours before the lieutenant and Jan walked across the yard to the big car and unloaded a rough coffin from the boot.

'You came prepared,' Mayne said.

'In some ways.'

'I'll be glad to see that corpse gone. No one liked having it about.'

'There's some good equipment in that hut,' the captain said thoughtfully.

Mayne could guess where this was leading. 'And we have a formal letter from the War Office telling us we can keep everything we find at Esherwood.'

'Lucky you.'

'Not really. I'm still going to have to sell my home.'

'Ah. Difficult for you.'

As the captain got into the big car, he paused to say, 'You'll be hearing from someone – or your former commanding officer will – to let you know when you can continue going through the contents of the Nissen hut. You shouldn't have to wait too long.' He grinned. 'And do let us know if you find any more bodies.'

Mayne hoped the captain was right, that getting permission wouldn't take long. He knew the final remark had been meant as a joke, but he shuddered at the mere idea of finding more bodies and having to face further delays.

He turned to find Jan standing there watching and spread his hands in a helpless gesture. 'You heard that?'

'Yes.'

'So I'll continue working with Woollard on sorting out how to sell stuff, and I'll also be preparing the paperwork for the town council. Perhaps you could go through the stables and find out exactly which parts are safe to use, then clear up what you can in there? Maybe if we can find a room with a solid door, we can store some of the less valuable, larger objects there.'

'I'd not do that,' Jan said quietly. 'There's word in the town already that you've found valuable items here.'

'Who the hell found out about that?'

'I don't know. But when they asked me, I became the very stupid foreigner who didn't know anything.'

Mayne grinned. 'You'd not fool anyone with that.'

Jan looked at him in surprise.

'You're getting a reputation as a shrewd fellow.'

'Oh. That is good, I think.'

'Yes, very good. So we'd better continue to use the cellar as a store room. It makes it hard to prepare stuff for sale, though. Even our cellar isn't elastic.'

12

Diana grew increasingly unhappy about living with her parents, who were treating her more like a child than a married woman. She bitterly resented that. She was, after all, twenty-four years old and had been running her own home for nearly two years. Luckily, after her fainting spell, her mother had stopped nagging her to snap out of it, so she'd managed to stay out of their way most of the time and keep her annoyance to herself.

Why did Francis have this ridiculous urge to move up north? They could have been happy here if he'd only seen sense.

Only . . . could they? She was beginning to see her parents in a new light. They hadn't changed but she had. The way they spoke about Francis, the way they'd tried to come between her and her husband was very unfair. He hadn't been a bad husband in most ways. In fact life with him had been far more pleasant than her present life.

Was it possible she'd put herself in a worse situation by leaving him? Made a mistake?

No, of course she hadn't. She'd seen pictures of the industrial north. She wasn't going to live in such an ugly place. Or scrub floors and manage without a daily help. How dare he say she'd have to do that? She'd never scrubbed floors in her whole life and she wasn't going to start now. It was unfair of him even to ask it of her.

She couldn't continue pretending to have a debilitating cold, so she started getting up for a late breakfast with her mother after her father had gone to work. But she continued to go to bed early, pretending she was tired, not quite recovered.

Whenever she could, she eavesdropped because it was the only way to find out what was going on. She couldn't get her mother's words out of her mind. *'You do think we did the right thing about Francis, don't you?'*

She didn't dare ask what Mummy meant by that because it hadn't been said to her. Her parents hadn't done anything that she could work out apart from saying unkind things about him. They'd even helped to arrange the wedding. Without that help, she and Francis might have had to wait longer to marry.

And yet Mummy had said *'I feel guilty sometimes.'* About what?

One evening, her father came home from a Masonic meeting rather the worse for wear, as occasionally happened. His voice boomed up the stairwell and her mother shushed him, trying to persuade him to go into the living room.

'No, dammit. I'm hungry, Christine. Let's go into the kitchen and you can make me something to eat.' There was the sound of a hand lightly slapping flesh and he chortled. 'Then you can come upstairs and do your wifely duty.'

'Leonard, shush! She'll hear you.'

'The light's out in her bedroom. She'll be fast asleep by now. And I don't care if she does hear us. She knows what happens in bed. And *I* need my little wifey. Give me a cuddle, Christine. It's been a long time.'

'Not here!'

Astonished by her father's behaviour, Diana nudged her bedroom door open a little wider and crouched down near the bottom of the gap, so that she could catch glimpses of them through the banisters.

Her father was refusing to move from the hall. When her mother tried to push him towards the kitchen, he reached out and fumbled with her body, which made her mother jerk hastily away.

'*Not here, I said! You'll wake her up.*'

'Oh, all right. But it *is* about time we told her,' her father said abruptly.

'Not yet. I need to prepare her.'

'What's to prepare? She'll be glad to be rid of him so easily.'

'I'm beginning to wonder about that. I think she's still fond of him.'

'If she is, she'd better get un-fond again. The war's over and we don't have to mix with people of his sort. Life will gradually return to normal, thank goodness.'

'Give me a few days to prepare her, Leonard.'

Prepare me for what? Diana wondered, utterly baffled.

'I'll give you two days. No more. Then if you haven't told her, I will.'

There was the sound of cupboard doors being opened and the refrigerator too, then silence as her father ate.

Her father's voice rang out again. 'Ah, that's better! Now, let's go to bed. I'm hungry for other things as well tonight.'

'You always are when you've been drinking.'

'I'm a man. I need my woman.'

Her mother's sigh was followed by the sound of chairs being pushed back. Diana stood up, closed the door quietly and got back into bed. She pulled the pillow over her head as the noise of her parents' headboard banging rhythmically against the wall and her father's grunts and groans echoed across the upper storey.

It was disgusting. They were too old to do this.

But the sound of her parents' lovemaking made her even more aware of how much she was missing Francis in bed. Missing his casual kisses and cuddles, too. He was such a loving man. She'd never met anyone like him for displaying affection.

Oh why was life so difficult?

Her last thought as silence fell abruptly over the house and she drifted into sleep was to wonder yet again what it was her mother was going to tell her?

In Rivenshaw Francis was equally wakeful, missing Diana's warmth beside him in bed, wondering if she was missing him at all.

He'd made a good start here at Esherwood, he felt. The job would be interesting, though it'd be a big challenge to sort out the electrics. He knew he'd be happy working with his partners again. It was as if he and Mayne had never been apart.

He was getting to know Rivenshaw better and liked the small town and its friendly people very much. Maybe he'd have one final try at persuading Diana to come and look at the town. She owed him that and so he'd tell her.

He was nowhere near finished going through the electrics of the big house. It was so frustrating, with wires leading nowhere and other wires which were obviously still live vanishing suddenly under a floor or into a wall cavity. You couldn't hack the house apart to follow them, especially such an old and beautiful house.

As things stood, Esherwood was an electrician's worst nightmare and the first thing he'd do when he got back was install a few safety features, so that if necessary he could switch off the electricity to whole sections of the building. Well, he hoped he'd be able to work out enough of the patterns of wires to assign cut-outs to various areas.

Even if Mayne hadn't been planning to remodel the house, he'd have had to do something about the wiring. This tangle of botched jobs was just not acceptable and in some parts potentially dangerous.

When he got up on the Friday morning, Francis couldn't settle. If he'd been a fanciful man, he'd have said he had a feeling Diana was in trouble and needed his help. Could that be possible? If two people were close, could they sense each other's needs?

No, of course it wasn't possible. Apart from anything else, they weren't close now. But still . . . he had to go back sometime, so why not go now and find a way to see her? At the very worst he'd be able to check that she was all right.

He found Mayne in the kitchen chatting to Judith and Kitty, and felt a sudden spurt of envy at his friend's happy family life. This made his words come out more abruptly than he'd intended. 'I'm going back today. There are things to sort out, including that offer to buy the house. I shouldn't delay dealing with that any longer.'

Judith gave him a sympathetic look. 'If you can persuade Diana to come for a visit, Francis, I promise we'll make her welcome.'

'I know you will. I've tried to persuade her before, but in vain. I mean to have one last try, though.'

'If she won't come back with you, why don't you buy a train ticket and leave it with her, in case she changes her mind? That might tempt her to give it a try.'

He thought that over then nodded. 'Good idea.'

Was he being a fool? Expecting a miracle?

Who knew? He certainly didn't. But it was worth risking the price of a train ticket.

★ ★ ★

The journey from Rivenshaw to Hertfordshire seemed to take forever. Francis couldn't settle to reading the newspaper he'd bought, and several times he took out the ticket he'd purchased for Diana at the station in Manchester and stared at it.

Would it ever be used? He hoped so.

He arrived in the village after dark at this time of year, and it felt chilly with a light drizzle falling. He hoped he would be able to buy something to eat, and to his relief the village shop was still open. The owner greeted him warily, as if he'd done something wrong, and he wondered what the Scammells were saying about him now.

'Do you have my ration books?'

'No, sorry. Your wife prefers to keep them herself and bring them in when she needs coupons to buy something.'

That was his mother-in-law's habit, because Christine didn't trust anyone from what she considered to be the 'lower classes'. What a snob she was!

'I'll let you have something for tea and perhaps you could ask Mrs Brady to bring in your ration book to cover it?'

'Yes, of course.' Or he'd drop in himself once he got the ration book back and let them cut out whatever coupons they needed.

'Are you . . . back here to stay now, Mr Brady?'

'No, I'm just here for a quick visit; I'm not sure how long I'll be staying. I have a good job up north now, as partner in a building company, so I have to get back as soon as I can.'

The grocer gaped at him in surprise. '*You're a partner in the company?*'

'Yes. Why do you look surprised at that?'

The man flushed slightly and muttered something about, 'Must have misheard what Mrs Scammell said.'

'My wife's parents haven't taken an interest in what I'm

doing, so I doubt they understand the situation.' Francis slammed down the money for his bread and single slice of ham and marched out, burning with anger. Damn the Scammells! Still blackening his name.

Why?

On the way home he made a detour to call at Mr Johnson's house, ignoring the rain that was falling more heavily now. 'Sorry to disturb you so late, Mrs Johnson. Could I please have a quick word with your husband?'

'Of course. Do come in. You don't want to stand out there in the wet.'

Mr Johnson came bustling into the hall. 'You're back then.'

'Yes. I need to know if your son-in-law is still interested in buying my house. Because if so, I'd like to get moving on that.'

'He definitely is and has left it to me to negotiate.'

'I'll ask round about house prices, then. I'm not giving it away.'

'I've asked already. Look, I'll call round in the morning and we'll come to an agreement, eh? What time do you get up?'

'Seven o'clock, give or take.'

'I'll be there at eight.'

Francis set off for home, but somehow his steps led him to the Scammells' house and he stood by the gate, staring up at Diana's bedroom window. What looked like a bedside lamp was on, giving a faint glow, but he could see someone staring out of the window. On an impulse, he waved.

The window opened immediately and Diana leaned forward, waving back to him. The moon was just about full and he could see her quite clearly. He was about to go and knock on the front door, asking to speak to her, but when he opened the garden gate, she put one finger to her lips and he guessed immediately what she meant. He mustn't let her parents know he was back.

She made a sign he thought meant two minutes and then vanished. When she reappeared she had something white in her hands. He was hard put not to laugh when she sent a paper dart skimming through the air towards him. It landed in a bush, so he nipped into the garden and picked it up.

He could read the words quite clearly in the moonlight: 'Tomorrow afternoon at the house.' He nodded vigorously to show he'd understood. On an impulse he blew her a kiss before carrying on home.

It was cold inside the house and felt damp. He was soaked so went upstairs and changed into some old clothes. When he came back down, he switched on the little electric heater and sat close to its single bar to eat his bread and ham. There was still tea in the caddy, but he'd forgotten to buy any milk.

That reminded him. He opened the kitchen drawer but couldn't find his ration book. He opened all the drawers, but there was no sign of it. He'd have to ask Diana tomorrow afternoon.

Surely it was a good sign that she wanted to see him?

He slept better that night, buoyed by the first sign of hope.

In the afternoon of the day Francis left Rivenshaw, Victor arrived back, driving up to the big house with a triumphant toot of the horn.

Mayne came out of the kitchen, beaming at him, and the children rushed to welcome Betty, who vanished with them almost immediately.

'They missed her,' Judith said. 'She seems more like a younger cousin than someone who isn't related to them at all.'

'She missed them, too,' Ros said.

'I'll help you unload the car,' Mayne said.

Judith linked her arm in Ros's. 'You must be parched.

Let's leave the unloading to the men, while we figure out what to do to stretch out the meal tonight.'

'Just a minute. Victor visited the village butcher before we left and got some sausage meat, and there are some bits and pieces left.'

In the end they decided to spread out the sausage meat thinly and cover it with potato and carrot slices, fried with a little onion, as a topping for the 'pie', which could be browned in the oven.

Ros looked at it in amusement. 'The cook in the Wrens would have a fit at how little meat there is. We won't know ourselves once food comes off the ration, will we?'

'It can't happen too soon for me,' Judith said. 'I'm sick of trying to make a little go a long way.'

'We're all in the same boat, at least.'

'Except for those who're rich enough to buy black market goods.'

'Well, as I've never been rich enough for that, I don't miss it.' Ros took the cups into the scullery and washed them up while Ben set the table for tea, it being his turn.

She smiled as she went back into the kitchen. It felt good to be back, like coming home.

The following morning after a long negotiation, Francis agreed a price for the house with Johnson, who was going to pay cash. The two men walked into the village to the bank and the builder paid Francis a deposit, which he put straight into his own bank account.

It suddenly occurred to him that Diana would have very little money, unless her parents were subsidising her. If so, he'd give her some money and get more out for himself.

Then he went to buy some more food, before starting to clear his things out of the house. He soon realised he couldn't complete this task without Diana, who needed to decide which pieces of furniture she wanted to keep and which she wanted to dispose of, since they'd come mainly from her family. Ugly, old-fashioned things they were, too.

After the midday meal he heard a knock on the front door and hurried to answer it, hoping it was his wife.

It was a very large, muscular man whom he didn't recognise.

'I've brought a message for you,' the stranger said. 'Get out of town.' He drew back his fist to punch Francis in the face, but Francis had seen the hostility in his eyes and the clenched fist. He'd always had quick reactions and had experience of fighting from his boyhood in a rough part of the village, as well as in the Army. He ducked quickly back and tried to slam the door on the visitor. The man put a foot in the way and laughed, shoving it with his hand.

As Francis, much the lighter of the two men, struggled to keep him out, he wondered what the hell was going on. To his relief he saw someone walking past and yelled, 'Help! Help! I'm being attacked. Call the police.'

A face peered over the front hedge and a woman began to scream loudly, repeating his calls for help.

The attacker glared at Francis. 'Bloody coward. I'll be back, though, if you don't leave the village.' He scowled towards the street, where the woman was still standing, and ran off round the house to the rear.

'I'll be ready for you next time,' Francis yelled after him.

As the woman continued to scream for help, two more neighbours came running. They stopped to stare as the sound of breaking glass came from the rear of the house.

Francis hesitated, glancing towards the three women, one of whom was brandishing a rolling pin.

'Someone's gone to phone for the police,' she yelled. 'Don't go after him on your own, Mr Brady.'

'Thank you!' he yelled. He went into the house to make

sure the man hadn't broken in the back way, snatching up a walking stick for protection as he went.

There was broken glass all over the kitchen floor but the hole in the window wasn't large enough for anyone to have climbed through and fortunately the back door was still locked.

'What the hell was that about?' he muttered. But it didn't take him long to realise who had to have sent the man. There was only one person eager to get him out of the village: his father-in-law. But Francis was already arranging his move north so why was Scammell going to such lengths? It didn't make sense.

When the police arrived, Francis showed them the damage and told them what the man had threatened. The neighbour corroborated his story of a man attacking him and had over-heard the threat too.

'We'll tell the constable on the beat to keep an eye on your house, sir, but he's only one person when all's said and done. Best make sure your doors and windows are locked tonight, and watch your back when you're out and about tomorrow.'

'Yes. I shall.'

The policeman had only just left when Francis heard a sound at the back door. He ran towards it, but he could see through the kitchen window that it was Diana.

She stared at the broken glass. 'What happened? You're not hurt, are you?'

'No.' Once again he went over the incident.

'But who would threaten you like that?'

He stared at her, reluctant to accuse her father, and saw the moment when she guessed what he was thinking.

'No, Francis! Daddy would never do such a thing.'

'I didn't accuse him. You did.'

Dead silence. When it went on for too long, he said gently,
'Look, why don't you sit down and let me sweep up the
broken glass while the kettle boils?'

She nodded and sat down on the nearest chair, staring
down at her hands. Once she gave a little shake of the head,
as if to deny her thoughts.

When he put the cup of tea in front of her, she looked
up. 'What did you do to upset Daddy? He gets so angry
every time he speaks of you.'

'I married his precious daughter. I have an Irish surname,
even though there's no Irish in my family for the past two
generations. Some people don't like the Irish. Whatever the
reason, he doesn't think me good enough for you.'

'I don't agree with him.'

'Then why are you sending me away alone? Diana, you
ought at least to come and see Rivenshaw. It's quite a pretty
little town and I think you'd like it. You'd certainly like my
friends and their wives. And we'd be living in a big mansion,
not a mill worker's hovel, as your father keeps insisting. He's
got a very vivid imagination when it comes to twisting the
facts about me, I must say.'

'And if I didn't like it there, what would I do then? I don't
think my parents would have me back again once I left.'

'You can't mean that.'

'I do. They've changed so much. They're treating me more
like a prisoner than an adult. Actually I'm . . . well, a bit
frightened of Daddy these days.'

'Or maybe they always treated you like that and it's you
who has changed. Their little girl has grown up.'

'Maybe.'

She looked so downhearted, he took her hand. 'Do we
have to separate? I don't want to.'

'I don't know what to do.'

It was the best answer he'd had for a while and suddenly

he *knew* that if he pushed for an answer now, it'd be no, so he got out the railway ticket and held it out to her.

'On the way here I bought this. Take it and keep it safe. If you want to join me, your fare is paid and the ticket can be used any time during the next three months.'

She stared at the small piece of card but made no move to take it from him.

He continued to hold it out towards her not saying anything else, waiting.

At last she took the ticket and put it in her handbag.

'I got some money out too. In case you were short. It's in the bedroom. I'll give it to you before you leave.'

'I am short. Thank you. You always were kind.'

He let out his breath in a whoosh. That was surely a hopeful sign? 'Diana, I forgot to take my ration books with me. Do you know where they are?'

'Our ration books are in my bedroom drawer at my parents' house.'

'I need mine.'

'I'll get them for you, bring them here tomorrow.'

'Thank you. Um, will you be able to get away if you want to come to Rivenshaw?'

Another silence, then, 'I think so.'

'And if you can't get away?'

'Of course I'll be able to leave if I want.'

'Right then, I'll be here. One more thing: I've sold this house and for a good profit. We said you'd have the furniture and you can remove anything else you want to keep; I'll take my things away too and clear the house.'

'What shall I do with the furniture?'

'Ask your parents. I'm sure they'll tell you exactly what to do.' He nearly said 'damned parents' but managed to stop himself in time. This conversation was like treading on the thinnest of ice.

She looked round and tears welled in her eyes. 'I'll have nowhere to go if the house is sold.'

'You can always come to Esherwood. There's plenty of room for you there. Judith said to tell you you'd be made very welcome.'

'Oh, the perfect Judith!' Diana said scornfully. 'From the way you talk about her, *she* always says the right thing.'

'She's an admirable woman who has had a hard life and still carried on. You've never even met her and yet you're insulting her.'

And they were off again, quarrelling. In the end Diana ran out of the house by the back door and left him wondering if he'd ruined everything.

He hoped not. Oh, he did hope not.

Only then did he remember the money he'd been going to give her. Oh well, he'd do that the next day.

13

By the time she got back to her parents' house, Diana was regretting her hasty departure. Her mother looked out of the kitchen towards the hall as she came in.

'There you are. Where have you been?'

'For a walk. Getting some fresh air. You told me to.'

'Well, in future, let me know when you're going out and tell me where you're going. Look, Diana . . . we have to talk.'

'Could we talk later, please? I feel exhausted now. I need a nap.' Before her mother could refuse, she ran up the stairs.

In her bedroom she stood still for a moment with her back pressed against the closed door, wondering what to do with herself. Then she remembered the ration books, so went to look in her drawer.

They weren't there!

She stared down at the drawer. She'd put them there and she always knew where her things were. Just to be sure, however, she checked all the drawers.

There was no sign of the ration books, his or hers. And her clothes had been disturbed.

She went downstairs again. 'Have you been looking through my drawers, Mummy?'

'Yes, of course. How else would I know what clothes you need now you're back among civilised people?'

'Our ration books are missing.'

'I have yours safe but I burned his.'

'*What?* Why did you do that, Mummy?'

'Because you're not with him now, you're with us.'

'But he'll still need the ration books. I was going to post them off to him.'

'Well, he can just get himself new ones. Serve him right for marrying out of his class.'

Her mother's face had turned pink and Diana guessed this had been her father's idea. He could be a bit . . . well, more than a bit nasty when someone upset him. Not with his own family, of course, but with outsiders.

'I don't like you going through my things, Mummy. Please don't do it again.'

'Of course I will. Your father likes to know everything that goes on in his house. He's relying on me for that.'

The two of them stared at one another.

'I see.' Diana turned round and walked slowly back up the stairs. This situation was getting rapidly worse. She felt suddenly glad of the train ticket Francis had given her. She might not have more than a few shillings in her purse, but she had a means of getting away. It was a comfort to know that.

Where could she hide the ticket, though, if her mother was going to search her room regularly? After a few minutes' thought she opened her handbag and slid the ticket into the place where the lining was torn. She'd been meaning to mend it for ages, had been feeling guilty about that slackness, but was glad now that she hadn't sewn up the seam. It was only a small gap and it might be hard to get the ticket out again, but when she slipped the little piece of card in, it didn't show against the bottom panel of the handbag unless you knew it was there.

She spent the rest of the afternoon going through her things and deciding what she might take with her if she had to get away quickly. She wasn't stupid enough to move those things into one place, but she knew exactly where they were and what she'd need.

She continued to feel very angry about them searching her room. That was no way to treat someone you were supposed to love. It showed a complete lack of respect for her. Only, what had she done to make anyone respect her? She hadn't even been very good at her wartime job.

Francis had once told her she was a spoiled brat. Maybe . . . just maybe, there was some truth in that.

Her father came home from work soon after her encounter with her mother, banging the front door shut, a sure sign that something had upset him.

Now what? Diana opened her bedroom door the merest crack and tried to listen to what her parents were saying. But her father was speaking in a low voice and all she heard her mother say was, 'I told you not to do that.'

Whatever it was had upset them both. This was turning into a nightmare, like one of those awful dreams where you couldn't find your way out of a maze.

She was glad she was going to speak to Francis again tomorrow. She'd have to apologise to him about the ration books. How embarrassing!

And she might, she just might decide to go back to Rivenshaw with him and at least have a look at the place.

She wasn't completely sure of that. How could you be sure of anything when your whole life had been turned upside-down? The war years had been easy compared to this.

After Diana had left the house in a huff, Francis thought hard about how to protect himself – and the house – that night. He had a feeling he'd be attacked again. It was the need to keep the house safe that gave him the idea of who to ask for help.

He slipped out through the back door and pushed through the neighbour's hedge, then kept to the back lanes as he made his way round to Johnson's house.

'Sorry to disturb you again, Mrs Johnson. Something's cropped up and it's urgent.'

'I hope you've not changed your mind about selling the house!'

'No. But it *is* to do with the house.'

She took him through to the sitting room and he explained what had happened.

Johnson gaped at him. 'Bloody hell! Has Scammell run mad?'

'I'm beginning to think so. Only I don't know how to protect the house if he sets those thugs on to damage it.'

'Well, I do.' He heaved himself up from his chair. 'I'm going out, Mavis. I don't know when I'll be back. Might not even come home till morning. I have to look after that house. We don't want our daughter to miss out on it, do we?'

'We certainly don't. I'm looking forward to having her living nearby.'

'What are you going to do?' Francis asked as Johnson led the way down the road.

'Hire some watchmen. No one's going to damage one of *my* family's houses. You did the right thing to come to me, young fellow. But if I were you, I'd leave the village at once. Don't give that slimy, lying devil a chance to accuse you of something that would make the police lock you away.'

He saw Francis's shock at that and said grimly, 'He's been known to do it before, yes, and get away with it, him being a lawyer. I'll stay with you while you go through the rest of your things and pack what you're taking now. Then you can leave it to me to clear the house for you and send your stuff on.'

'That's a bit drastic, don't you think?'

'Yes. But a necessary precaution when Scammell's after you.'

With two burly men standing guard outside and chasing intruders away from the back a couple of times, Francis sorted and packed. Johnson wrote a document for them both to sign. It handed over management of the house until the sale to Johnson or his nominees.

The watchmen were brought in to witness their signatures.

It was four o'clock in the morning before Francis finished, then Johnson drove him through the dark streets to the station, stopping on the way to rouse another man, with whom he conferred for several minutes. The man nipped back inside his house, then came to join them in the car a couple of minutes later.

'Nolan's coming with you in case we need another witness as to when you left the village and what you did in London,' Johnson said grimly.

He made sure the ticket officer would remember them by dropping his wallet and kicking it under the counter, so that the man had to get down off his high stool to pick it up and hand it back.

'Simple but effective, annoying someone. He'll remember us,' he told Francis grimly. 'Now, if anyone asks, Nolan just happens to be going up to London by the same train as yourself. He'll get in the same compartment and be able to prove you got there safely and that you took the next Manchester train.'

'This all seems . . . a bit excessive,' Francis said.

'That so-called man of the law has a dozen nasty tricks up his sleeve when someone upsets him. He doesn't dare touch me, though, because I have some very good legal connections as well *and* I'm in the Masons. Bear with me, lad. I know what I'm doing. I want that house of yours for my son-in-law – and you want to be free of Scammell. We'll do what it takes to satisfy us both.'

'I didn't get the chance to say goodbye to Diana.'

'That's the least of your worries. I'll ask my wife to speak to her if she sees her at the shops.'

The following morning over their late breakfast together, Diana's mother said, 'Don't go out today, dear. There have been some louts causing trouble in the village and your father's worried about your safety.'

'Surely the police will have caught them by now?'

'I don't know. But your father said to stay in the house.'

'I'll just go down to the paper shop first and buy a magazine. I'll be careful, I promise you. But I've got nothing to read.'

Her mother didn't say anything, but she didn't look happy about that.

Diana finished her breakfast and ran upstairs to get her coat. The bedroom door banged shut suddenly and when she tried to open it, she realised it was locked. That couldn't have happened by accident.

'Mummy!' she yelled. 'Mummy, open this door.'

But there was no answer.

She went to look out of the window to see if there was anyone she could call out to for help, but when a neighbour walked past who was on good terms with her mother, she felt too embarrassed to yell for help.

She stood by the window for a long time, worrying what Francis would say when she didn't turn up.

All day long she was kept in the bedroom, without food or drink.

At first she was angry and planned to leave for the north straight away. Then she realised that her father would take offence if she spoke to him in anything but a gentle tone of voice. And who knew what he'd do then?

She'd just have to laugh off the incident and assure them that if she'd realised how worried they were about her going out, of course she'd have stayed in.

Her only hope was that Francis would come again tonight and she could throw down a note about his ration book. But she wouldn't write it until she was sure he was there. If her father found a note to her husband in her bedroom, he'd throw a fit.

In the middle of the afternoon, he came home from the office early and tramped heavily up the stairs. She could always recognise his footsteps. By that time Diana was feeling parched with thirst and weary of all this.

The key turned in the lock of her bedroom door and it opened.

'Oh good. You're all right. I was worried about you,' he said.

The liar! she thought but spoke in a semi-joking tone. 'Honestly, Daddy. There was no need to lock me in.'

'Your mother thought it was better to be safe than sorry.'

Trust him to blame someone else. 'Can I come down and get something to eat and drink now?'

'Yes, of course. And then your mother and I have something to tell you, something very important indeed.

So he wasn't waiting for Mummy to prepare the way. Diana braced herself to hear something unpleasant. She didn't know why she was so sure it would be unpleasant, but she was.

Diana sat in an armchair while her parents sat side by side on the sofa, facing her. She felt as if she was in court, about to be sentenced by a very stern judge. Her father said nothing, but she knew from years of experience that he often did that to make her feel more apprehensive so that she blurted things out.

Today, his trick wasn't going to work, she vowed. She was going to make him start the conversation and she wasn't going to break down in floods of tears, either, whatever he said. She would dig her fingernails into the palms of her hands till it hurt to remind herself of that – one of her other little tricks.

'We have something to tell you,' he began at last, 'about your marriage.'

'Oh?'

'You are not actually married.'

That puzzled her. 'Of course I am. You arranged the wedding yourself and you were both there when it took place.'

'I, um, didn't do the paperwork properly. And I must confess that it was on purpose because I *knew* such a marriage couldn't last. I also know from experience how hard it can be to get a divorce and how long it takes to finalise one and free the people to remarry. Several years! You'd be thirty before we could get you married again.'

He fell silent for a moment, contemplating his own astuteness with a smug smile. 'I was right. Oh, yes. As a result, we can easily prove to the authorities that you're not and never have been married to that *electrician*.' It might have been a dirty word from the way he said it.

She stared at him numbly, his words echoing in her mind. *Not actually married. Not actually married.*

It didn't seem possible. She felt married and she knew Francis did too. Not even her father could have been so cruel, surely? She turned to look at her mother, but her mother was staring down at her clasped hands, avoiding her daughter's gaze.

He was waiting for an answer. She had to say something. She couldn't think what and eventually, after what seemed a very long time, she faltered, 'I . . . don't know what to say or do.'

'I'm glad of that because I can tell you. *You* don't need to say or do anything. In fact, I forbid you to take a single step from now on without my guidance. Do you understand, Diana?'

That was easy to answer. She could say the right words in her sleep, probably did. 'Yes, Daddy.'

'We will get you free of *that man* but it will have to be done carefully, so that people don't realise the mistake was made on purpose. You have to understand that if we don't do this, your reputation will be blackened and you will not be an acceptable wife to another, more suitable, professional man.'

It was out before she could stop herself. 'I don't want to get married again.'

'Oh, but you *need* to get married to make up for this mistake, and it must be to a man acceptable to your family this time. Make no mistake about that. And you will not be marrying against my wishes.'

Like her mother, she stared down at her lap, but he didn't let his prey go easily.

'Look at me when I'm speaking to you, Diana.'

She braced herself, dug in her fingernails and raised her head, summoning up the glassy-eyed expression she'd used at school when she got into trouble, an expression she'd practised in front of a mirror till she could do it perfectly every time. She could feel the muscles of her face settle into the usual pattern, thank goodness.

'From today onwards you will not leave this house on your own or speak to anyone else unless your mother is present. Least said soonest mended is to be your watchword. In fact, you will be guided by your mother and me in every single thing you say or do.'

'Yes, Daddy.'

'Be very sure you mean that. You don't sound convincing to me.'

'I'm still . . . shocked, Daddy. I can't seem to think straight.'

'I will do your thinking for you from now on until we have you safely married to a strong and suitable husband, who will then guide your behaviour. An older man would be best, I think.'

She judged it safest to nod and stay glassy eyed. She wondered if her fingernails were drawing blood.

'Let me make it clear that if you disobey me in any way, I'll have you drugged and locked away in a private hospital I know of until you can be brought to your senses.'

He never made threats he couldn't carry out. She swallowed hard, trying not to give in to her fears. But oh, she had never felt as terrified and alone in her whole life! She'd never felt the full extent of his ruthlessness herself but she didn't doubt he'd do as he'd threatened, even to his own daughter.

And yet, in that moment something changed inside her. The small seed of rebellion took root and began to grow rapidly. She felt it. She might not be married to Francis, but she was definitely not going to marry a man like her father, a despot who hid his cruelty from other people and seemed to the rest of the world to be a normal, caring man looking after his family. It was as if she was seeing him clearly for the first time in her life.

She had no idea how she was going to escape. But she would find a way.

And yet, at the thought of how hard it would be to win free of him, a great tide of despair rolled across her and she felt the room spinning round her. She didn't try to stop herself falling, heard her mother cry out, but didn't attempt to open her eyes. She preferred to huddle in the concealing darkness where she couldn't see his face and he couldn't see hers.

She didn't want him to see that she intended to escape from him. But somehow she'd do that. Whatever it cost.

She heard her mother's voice as if from a great distance. 'That's enough, Leonard. You've made your point. She's quite terrified.'

'Good. And you had better keep an eye on her during the daytime.'

'Don't I always do what you tell me to, Leonard?'

'Usually, yes.'

Diana allowed herself a small sigh, then a groan. She let her mother help her to her feet and escort her up to her bedroom. Her father didn't say anything and she didn't look in his direction.

She would never forget the way he'd treated her tonight. If Francis rejected her and she had to emigrate to the colonies under an assumed name to escape her father, she would.

He had gone too far this time.

14

In Lancashire Daniel had been fretting for a few days. He was making sketches of individual dwellings that could be prefabricated, and had thought of some good details. But he was itching to get back to his main work of planning the conversion of Esherwood into flats.

The day for the visit to the bank arrived at last and he escorted his aunt into the nearby town. She looked so terrified he tried to cheer her up, but her expression only lightened briefly. She might have been going into an arena to face some hungry lions.

As they entered what he considered to be a pretentious building with its heavily marbled foyer, she clutched his arm even more tightly and he patted her hand. 'It'll be all right, really it will.'

'I just don't understand money. I never have. I'm bound to say something stupid.'

'They won't shoot you at dawn if you do. And I'm here to help you.'

But she was not to be teased out of the doldrums.

They were shown into the manager's office and he greeted them crisply, not wasting much time on pleasantries or condolences. Bank managers were usually more affable than this with good clients. What did this attitude mean? Daniel wondered.

'Now, let's get straight down to business. Do you have any idea of the state of your husband's finances, Mrs Brady?'

'I'm afraid I don't understand money matters at all. Egan always saw to that sort of thing.'

'I see. Well, I'm sorry to say that I have bad news for you.'

She gasped and pressed one hand across her throat in a protective gesture. Daniel reached out to hold her other hand and they waited for an explanation.

'Your husband's account was overdrawn when he died. The war had hit his business very badly, I'm afraid. If he'd been able to continue working, I'm sure he'd have traded his way out of the problem, because he'd never had any financial difficulties before. Sadly, the war has been harder on some business people than others. As it is . . . well, there will be no more money coming in and the bank still needs to have the overdraft repaid.'

'How much overdrawn was he?' Daniel asked.

'Over two hundred pounds, I'm afraid, and there may be one or two other small debts, money owing to his suppliers. You'll have to close down his place of work.' He looked at Mrs Brady and waited for a response of some sort, before explaining, 'The money will have to be paid from his estate so unless you have any money of your own, I'm afraid you'll have to sell your house to clear the debt.'

She turned to her nephew, her face white with shock. 'Oh, Daniel, how do I even start to pay that much money back? I only have a few pounds left. And how am I going to live with no more money coming in? I was counting on selling the house and buying a smaller place for myself, something I could manage, a flat, maybe.'

The manager didn't bother to soften the blow. 'If you can't pay and don't know how to deal with this, the bank may have to foreclose on the house and do it for you.'

'I'll guarantee the debt,' Daniel said at once. He knew it'd be better if they sold the house themselves rather than letting the bank get rid of it at a knock-down price because they were only concerned with getting their money back and not with obtaining a good price so that she'd have something left afterwards.

'Can you do that, Mr O'Brien?' the manager asked.

'I have several thousand pounds in my bank. You can easily check that with them.'

'Ah. Right. That will be fine, then. I feel bound to warn you that you may be even more out of pocket if the house doesn't sell for a decent amount. Perhaps you'd better leave the selling to us.'

The old devil! Daniel thought. He probably had a relative needing a house. Everyone was scrambling for accommodation these days, helping their friends and relatives jump in ahead of the queues. 'Thank you, but no. I doubt there will be much difficulty in selling any house in these troubled times and my aunt's home is in a very nice condition, even now. No, we'll deal with the sale privately. And I'll close down my uncle's office as well.'

'As long as your bank assures us that you are able to stand guarantor for the debt.'

'Oh, it will, don't worry. In fact, I think I'll pay off the debt straight away, then you can stop charging interest on the loan.' He felt in his inside pocket. 'I have my cheque book here. Perhaps you can tell me precisely how much is owed?'

It was more than he'd expected and would have to come from the money he was putting into the business, but he could easily afford that much. Even if it had been a larger amount, he couldn't have left her in trouble. He looked across at the smug face behind the desk. He hadn't taken to this bank manager at all, didn't trust him. It was a good thing he was there to protect his aunt.

'Why don't you sit in the foyer and leave me to pay the bill, Auntie, then I'll take you home.'

She nodded, looking dreadfully anxious, her face chalk white.

When she'd gone, Daniel looked at the manager. 'I'd be obliged if you'd hurry up with that total. My aunt isn't feeling well.'

The look the man gave him wasn't promising, so he added, 'It wouldn't look good if people heard that the bank had been harassing a poor widow, with her husband only just buried.'

'We have no intention of harassing your aunt. I was merely offering to help and I could still—'

'She has a nephew to help her, thank you anyway. Will you kindly furnish me with the exact amount that's owing, and with interest only calculated until today, if you please.'

His aunt linked her arm in his as they left the bank. 'You shouldn't have done that, Daniel, paid for me. I know you need all your money for your new business.'

'I can spare enough to make your life easier, Auntie Beryl. I won't see you in trouble.'

'But what am I going to do after the house is sold?'

He looked at her gentle, bewildered face, with its uneven dusting of beige powder on the nose. She'd never survive on her own and she was only a relative to his family by marriage, so they wouldn't offer any major help.

'Do you have any close relatives of your own left, Auntie?'

'No. My cousin died during the war and I don't know where his children have moved to, because they lived in London and were bombed out.'

'Then it's a good thing you've got me. Why don't you come and live in Rivenshaw, keep house for me?'

'I can't impose on you like that.'

'It's no imposition. I remember how kind you were to me

when I was a lad. I won't ever let you go short of a home, Auntie Beryl.'

She began sobbing loudly and he pulled her quickly round a corner into a side alley. Great fat tears were rolling down her cheeks and he held her till she'd wept herself to a standstill.

When she stopped, he said gently, 'I'll have to ring Mayne and tell him what's going on, make sure it's all right to take you with me. I'm sure it will be, but it's only polite to ask. In the meantime, you should go round the house, seeing if you can make it look its best for people who might buy it. You'll also need to consider what furniture to take with you. Can you manage that?'

'Oh, yes. I'm good at dealing with household matters; it's just managing money that makes me freeze in terror. I was never any good at sums, even as a child.'

As they turned into her street, she said thoughtfully, 'Every other person I talk to seems to have a relative trying to find a house to live in, and they're buying or selling second-hand furniture, too, so I should think we'll sell it quickly and then get rid of what I don't want. But oh dear, I shall be sad to leave my home.'

'Of course you will. But some things can't be avoided, Auntie Beryl.'

'I know. I'll leave you to make your phone call now, dear. You'll tell me if there are any problems?'

'There won't be. But I'll speak to you again after I've rung Mayne. We'll put the house up for sale in the local newspaper this week, eh? I'm sure we'll sell it quickly, and for a better price than the bank would bother to get. There's a desperate housing crisis in Britain, you know. You'll see.'

When Francis returned to Rivenshaw, he was happy to see Victor, Ros and little Betty again. Over the evening meal, he explained to everyone exactly what had happened.

Mayne looked at him in astonishment. 'I can't believe someone can get away with that sort of thing in this day and age.'

'The war has made it difficult to maintain law and order,' Ros said grimly. 'Look how my stepfather cheated me out of my money. Look at the murder we've had on our own doorstep, one they don't expect to solve.'

They sighed but nodded agreement as Francis continued his tale. 'Anyway, I believed what Johnson told me. He's a sane, level-headed man in his late fifties, well respected in the county. He's known for straight talking, even when the truth is unpalatable. He wouldn't have lied to me or even exaggerated about Scammell, I'm sure.'

After another pause, he added, 'The problem is, what do I do about Diana? I left a message for her at the house on the dressing table, but how am I to know whether my message got through?'

'You could phone Johnson and ask.'

'Yes. Unsatisfactory just to speak on a crackly phone line, given how important this is, but it's all I can think of. I shan't do that till tomorrow. I might suggest his wife tries to find a way to approach Diana. At the shops, perhaps.'

Francis realised he was staring blindly at the wall so pulled himself together. 'Take my mind off my own problems, old chap. Tell me what's been going on here while I've been down south. Has anyone discovered the identity of the corpse? Have you heard from Daniel? Have the preliminary plans gone through council yet?'

'Whoa! Give me time to answer one question at a time. Even Victor doesn't know everything yet, because we haven't been able to bring each other up to date on every detail. Basically, the main thing we've been able to do here is let Woollard loose on the valuations, and I must say he's turned up some valuable items. It looks like I'm going to do better out of the remaining contents of the house than I'd expected. Sadly, they still won't make enough money to save my home.'

'Every bit helps. And the contents of the Nissen hut?'

'We're still waiting for permission to go through the things in there. Sometimes I feel as if I'm doing nothing but wait for things to happen, and that it's been going on for years.'

'There was a lot of waiting around in the Army. It used to drive me mad.'

'Yes, well. If you want specifics about the hut, the only news is that the corpse has been taken away and they'll let us know when we can get on with clearing the place. Until then, we're to stay out of it in case someone wants to examine the scene of the crime again.'

Victor shook his head in amazement. 'Good heavens! I can't leave you alone for a minute, without you getting into trouble. Did the MPs say how long they expected it to take?'

'Of course not. And I have to admit it won't be easy for them to wrap up the case. There was absolutely no identification on that poor sod. Someone had gone through his pockets and clothing very carefully.'

'Our other news is that we heard from Daniel today.' Mayne explained about their friend's aunt. 'The poor old thing is quite helpless about money, and if she has to sell the house to pay off the bank, she may not have enough left to live on after she's bought a smaller place.'

'There are a lot of women in that situation,' Francis said. 'At least Diana can handle money, not that her father was lavish in providing it. She might have spent more on herself than I wished, but she always knew where every penny had gone.' He sighed and added as if thinking aloud, 'And she did always look beautiful.'

'We're going to let Daniel bring his aunt here,' Mayne said. 'At least until he finds her a house. She's thinking of taking in lodgers to make a bit of money. She was younger than her husband, so she's only in her fifties.'

'Good heavens, you are going to have a houseful, Mayne. How are we going to remodel Esherwood if we have so many people to accommodate?'

'I don't know. But it has to be done. Maybe we can put some of them into the Dower House later. Mrs Rennie is a very capable housekeeper and there are several empty bedrooms. As long as no one stops him doing his research, I doubt my father will mind who's living there with him.' Mayne grinned and added, 'He probably won't even notice them most of the time.'

'What about the preliminary building plans?' Victor asked.

'Bogged down in red tape at the council.'

'What the hell's wrong with them? We followed their instructions to the letter.'

'They're quibbling about all sorts of details, won't even give us permission in principle.'

They were all three silent as they contemplated that.

'I bet someone doesn't want it to go through,' Francis said. 'Can you ask around, find out who? You may have to buy him off.'

Mayne scowled. 'Over my dead body. I didn't fight for a country where people have to pay bribes to get things done.'

'We've had this discussion before. You're too optimistic about people. Many of them go onto the local town council to further their own business aims. If you want them to further yours, you'll have to find a way to make it worth their while.'

Victor shook his head warningly at Francis, who took the hint and let it go at that.

Mayne changed the subject. 'What about your side of things, Francis? Can you get on with anything here while you're waiting to hear how Diana is?'

'There's a lot needs doing just to make the electrics of this place safe, what with old-fashioned systems of wiring topped by haphazard additions. How the Army could have let so many electrical incompetents loose on one house, I don't know.'

'Because they didn't care about Esherwood and were stretched to their limits to find anyone with the necessary skills. But I care very much, so I'd be grateful if you'd do what you can to make it safe.'

'I will. But I may have to dash away if Diana needs me.'

Mayne was called away to answer the phone again, and Victor said in a low voice, 'I'll speak to Woollard about the town council. Between his local knowledge and my legal skills, I think we'll manage to expedite matters. You know what it's like with town councils. Even if it's not self-interest, they think people are there to follow the rules, rather than the rules having been set up to help people.'

He smiled. 'Even so, it's good to be back here permanently. I really like Rivenshaw. I'm sorry about your troubles, though, Francis. I hope your wife will get away from her father. He sounds to be a dreadful bully.'

Diana didn't go downstairs the next morning until her father had left for work. She stood in the kitchen doorway, uncertain how to deal with her mother.

'You might as well come in. You didn't have anything to eat last night, so you must have a good breakfast.'

'Did you know what Daddy had done about our wedding?'

'Not till later.'

'I feel awful. It means I've been living in sin.'

Her mother let out a short mirthless laugh. 'Just like the woman who married that Mayne Esher. Francis was always talking about them, admiring her, for heaven's sake. Why couldn't you have attracted a man like Esher, a man of property and of the right social class? It'd have been a perfect match.'

'He's older than me and I don't think he's very attractive, actually. I didn't meet him till after I was married to Francis.'

'Well, we'll have to look for someone like him. He's from a good county family, and even if he has to sell that house of his, he'll be able to keep his wife in comfort. That's the most important thing to a woman. You'll come to understand that once you have children.'

'Is that why you married Daddy?'

'Of course it is. If a woman has any sense, she marries with her head, not on a whim.'

'But I love Francis.' She hastily amended that to, 'Loved him, I mean.'

'I wouldn't advise you to repeat that to your father. Not if you want any say in who you marry next time.'

Just let them try to force her to marry an old man, she thought, allowing the glassy-eyed expression to take over. Listening to her mother, she forced down some breakfast.

'We'll go shopping this morning, Diana dear. We must show everyone how happy you are to be rid of Francis. And don't you *dare* say anything to the contrary or look anything but content with your new life.'

'No, Mummy.'

She managed to do as her mother had ordered as they stopped and chatted to a few people, but it was a huge effort.

Only once did she let her guard slip, and that was when they met Mrs Johnson in the haberdasher's.

Was it her imagination or was the woman looking at her questioningly? Diana took another quick glance at Mrs Johnson and when her mother took some embroidery silk over to the window to match a colour, Diana risked mouthing the words, 'Help me get away!'

Mrs Johnson nodded and soon after she left the shop.

'That woman has let herself go,' Christine told her daughter on the way home.

'Which woman?'

'Mrs Johnson. The builder's wife.'

'Ah. I thought she looked familiar, but I couldn't place her.' Another lie. She was building a pyramid of lies.

At home, Diana was told to vacuum the living room and dust all the ornaments carefully. Each hour of the day from then on was filled with such tasks.

She felt like screaming herself hoarse at the frustration of it all and the day seemed to go on for ever.

When at last she went up to her bedroom, she opened the window and stared out. No way of getting down from here unless she was desperate enough to tie sheets together. But they'd hear her if she tried that, she was sure. And anyway, she was afraid of heights.

She was afraid of all sorts of thing at the moment – most of all, afraid of her father.

There had been no phone call from Diana or about her, and Francis couldn't sleep for worrying.

The following morning, two days after his escape from the village, Judith came to find him. 'Your Mr Johnson is on the phone and—'

She didn't get the chance to finish her sentence because Francis had set off running towards the office. 'He still loves her, faults and all,' she muttered. 'I wonder what she's really like when push comes to shove.'

Francis picked up the phone. 'Brady here.'

'Johnson. My wife saw your Diana in the shops with her mother. The two of them were putting on a show for the ladies of the village, she thinks, because Mrs Scammell was only buying a skein of embroidery silk. Your wife looks pale and her eyes were a bit swollen. She mouthed the words

"Help me get away". At least, that's what my wife thinks she said and she's quite good at lip reading.'

'I'll come back straight away and get her.'

'You'll do no such thing. Leave it to me and my lads – and my wife, who is enjoying the conspiracy and has worked out a way of getting a note to your Diana. We didn't want to do anything until we'd confirmed that you really do want her back.'

'Yes. Well, I do if she wants to come. I know Diana can be selfish and a bit silly, but she can also be fun and she's very loving. She seems hungry to be loved. If this incident makes her grow up a little, it'll not have been in vain.'

He was answered by a chuckle. 'No one learns the import-ant lessons of life the easy way, lad. Let's hope this helps your wife get to grips with what the world is really like. 'Now, just let me check that I've got the right address for you . . . Right. Got it. Very well. I'll phone you tomorrow and let you know how our little plan goes.'

'Wait!'

'Can't. Someone's just come in.' He changed tone and said into the phone, 'Goodbye for now, Mrs Pargeter. I'll come and give you an estimate for that other job tomorrow.'

The line went dead.

Francis sat with the phone receiver in his hand, hearing it buzzing, on and on. He felt frozen. It ought to be him helping his wife to escape. He'd let Diana down.

No, they'd let each other down. They would have to do better from now on, both of them, or they'd never set their marriage to rights.

And he wanted that. Even after all that had happened.

15

Mavis Johnson made her preparations then sent her maid to keep watch on the lawyer's house and let her know when Mrs Scammell and her daughter went out shopping.

Even the better-off ladies of the village had learned to queue nearly every day in order to get their share of what was available on ration, because maids never got as much from the shopkeepers. And if you saw a long queue these days, you joined it, even when you didn't know what it was for. Some items might not be rationed, but that didn't mean they were easily available.

If fate was kind, Christine Scammell and her daughter would go to the grocer's. Mavis felt the task would be easier to accomplish there than at the greengrocer's.

The maid came running back to the house, out of breath. 'They've gone out, Mum, and they were carrying baskets, so I bet they've gone to the grocer's like you wanted.'

'Right.' Mavis set off, glad her house was close to the village centre. She slowed down just before she got to the grocer's shop and sauntered inside. Sure enough, Mrs Scammell was there, haranguing the unfortunate man about the poor choice of food available and demanding more than her share.

Selfish old madam, that Mrs Scammell was. She deserved taking down a peg or two and Mavis intended to do just that. She was determined to get near the younger woman and have a private word with her. Poor lass, she looked pale and unhappy.

Then an idea of how to do it popped into Mavis's mind, as it often did at a time of need. Such a good idea, too. Ooh, it'd give her a lot of pleasure to do it this way.

She moved along the shelves, fingering items, surreptitiously loosening the top of a jar of honey as she studied the label, then putting it back right on the very edge of the shelf. She turned away with a regretful sigh. 'Not enough points left for that.'

Fate was on her side. Her prey had come closer.

Mavis waited till no one was looking her way and let out a shriek. 'A mouse!' Whirling round as if afraid, she made sure her arm made contact with the jar of honey and knocked it off the shelf right on to Mrs Scammell's face and shoulders. She'd always had a good aim with a ball and her eye didn't let her down now.

The shriek her victim let out was even louder than the one Mavis had produced at the pretended mouse sighting. The jar hit Mrs Scammell squarely on the side of the forehead and the loosened lid came off. A sticky stream of honey followed it, covering the side of the victim's face.

It surprised even Mavis how far that honey spread and the result was far better than she'd hoped, better than a comedy show at the cinema, too. The honey lodged in Mrs Scammell's hair, trickled down her face and neck and continued on its merry way.

Screaming loudly, Mrs Scammell tried to wipe it away. But it was good runny honey, bottled and sold by a farmer's wife who belonged to the local Women's Institute co-operative. It clung to Mrs Scammell's fingers, hair and collar, and the more she rubbed at it with her handkerchief, the further it spread.

The other women in the shop snorted and gulped, trying not to laugh out loud, because no one wanted to offend the Scammells. But Christine wasn't popular with the village women.

Even the woman's own daughter was gulping back laughter.

Mavis stepped forward. 'Oh, my goodness, I'm so sorry. And there wasn't even a mouse. It was just a bit of paper that looked like one. I've always hated mice.' She paused to admire her handiwork. 'I'm mortified, that's what I am. Absolutely mortified.'

'You did it on purpose.'

'No, I didn't. I'd never waste good honey like that.'

The grocer, who had been standing behind the counter in frozen horror, pushed his way through the women. 'My dear lady. What a terrible thing to happen. Come through to the back room and my wife will sponge it off.'

He tried to look sternly at Mavis, but when she winked at him, he was nearly betrayed into laughter. 'Come this way.' He hurried Mrs Scammell through the group of women.

Diana stayed where she was.

Mavis pretended to wipe a few blobs of honey off her companion's face, whispering, 'Do you want to get away from your parents?'

'Yes, but they lock me in my bedroom at night and I could never slide down sheets. I just couldn't do it.'

'Could you climb out of the window if we brought a ladder?'

'Yes.'

'Which bedroom are you in?'

'The one on the left as you look at the house. My parents sleep round the back, where it's quieter. They don't go to bed till about midnight, though.'

'We'll come and get you about one o'clock then. Your husband rang mine and he—'

The grocer was back. 'Mrs Brady. Your mother wants your help.'

Diana sighed and turned to follow him without another word.

'Don't forget to tell your mother how sorry I am!' Mavis called after her.

When Diana was out of sight, Mavis looked at the other customers. A couple of women mimed clapping their hands and she pretended not to see them applauding her, but she did allow herself one quick smile. Then she pasted a regretful look on her face and said loudly, 'I'm so upset about that accident.'

'I'm upset at the waste of good honey,' someone said in a disguised, high-pitched voice.

The grocer came back, throwing an angry look back over his shoulder in the direction Mrs Scammell had taken. 'Who's next?'

'Before you serve anyone, I want you to know that I'll pay for the honey,' Mavis said. 'I don't want you to be out of pocket. But I'll take what's left in the jar, if you don't mind. Waste not, want not.'

The grocer's wife came bustling in as he was wrapping up the jar. She held a scrap of paper in her hand with a list on it. 'I'll just sort out Mrs Scammell's shopping then let her out the back way, George.'

By that time it was Mavis's turn to be served. 'Do give Mrs Scammell my apologies.'

'Best not rake it up again, dear. If I were you, I'd get my shopping and go straight home. You could write her a civil little apology, though.' She lowered her voice. 'She'll probably tear it up, but at least you'll know you did the right thing by her.'

'I'll do that and get my husband to drop it off at their house tonight after he comes home from work.'

Once she'd left the shop, Mavis couldn't help chuckling softly as she hurried home. Once she was inside her house, she let out peal after peal of laughter, and then laughed some more as she kept remembering details of the scene.

The maid, who'd been with her too long to stand on ceremony, came running and Mavis described what had happened.

'Oh, I do wish I'd been there.'

'I'm glad I did it. You should have seen madam's hair. She'll have to go to the hairdresser and get it washed and set again.'

They both kept chuckling as they shared a pot of tea. It had been wonderful to do that to such a snob.

When her husband came home, Mavis described it all over again and he had tears of laughter rolling down his cheeks.

When they'd calmed down, she said, 'You can take my letter of apology round to their house tonight and it'll give you a chance to study the place and see how you can rescue that poor sad lass later on. You will help her, won't you? After all, her husband's kept his word to us about selling the house.'

'Of course I will.' He raised her hand to his lips. 'You are the queen of wives, my love!'

'Get on with you!'

'I mean it. I've never stopped being glad I married a clever woman like you. That lass will never be as happy as we are. How can she, raised by parents like them?'

Mavis raised her hand to caress his cheek. 'I think you and I make a very good team, George.'

Diana was setting the table for dinner, while her father and mother had a glass of sherry together in the living room. Her mother had washed and set her hair herself, not wanting anyone to see her like that on the way to the hairdresser's. She had forbidden Diana to mention the incident ever again.

They hadn't invited her to have a drink with them. They did a lot of low-voiced talking together.

She felt on edge. Would Mrs Johnson and her husband really manage to rescue her? Did she dare hope? And how would she get away from the village afterwards?

Someone knocked on the front door.

'I'll get it,' her father called.

She heard him open the door and Mr Johnson's voice.

'My wife has sent a written apology. She's mortified about the accident.'

'My wife wants nothing to do with her or her apologies . . . though I admit it's the right thing to do, at least, send an apology, I mean.'

'The thing is, Mavis is terrified of mice, always has been. Silly, really, when they're such tiny creatures.'

'Yes, well, I'll give Christine the letter and we'll call the incident closed.'

'Thank you. If there are any dry cleaning costs, I'm happy to pay them.'

Her father's voice grew marginally less harsh. 'That's very generous of you, but no need.'

'I just need a clean handkerchief,' Diana said. 'I'll nip up to my bedroom. Won't be a minute.'

As she ran up the stairs, her father went back into the living room. Soon there were the sounds of a short, sharp disagreement.

'Be reasonable, Christine. Mrs Johnson has no possible reason to wish you ill.'

'She did it on purpose, I tell you, and this letter of apology is only worth throwing on the fire.'

Her father's aggrieved sigh could be heard from the landing.

Diana went into her bedroom and stood by the window, hoping Mr Johnson would see her. He turned at the gate and studied the house briefly, giving a little nod, which she took to be a signal to her.

Taking a handkerchief, she went slowly back down the stairs to face another tedious evening.

Diana went up to bed before her parents, as usual. She put her nightdress on over her clothes and set her flat lace-up walking shoes ready by the side of the bed. Listening carefully in case they came up early, she gathered the things she'd planned to take into a bundle and for lack of anything else, put them into a clean pillowcase, which she stuffed under the bed.

She was too het up to sleep, but had to lie down and act as usual. The hours till midnight seemed to crawl by and all she could think of was what might go wrong.

At long last she could see from where she'd left her bedroom curtains slightly open that the light from the living room had been switched off, leaving the front garden in darkness. There was the sound of footsteps on the stairs.

Her mother peeped in to check on Diana, which was usual now, then closed the bedroom door. Though she spoke quietly as she went along the landing, every word carried in the still night air. 'She's fast asleep, Leonard. She's taking a while to recover fully. That was a very bad cold.'

Diana made a mental note to be extra careful about making a noise. While her parents were still moving to and fro from the bathroom, getting ready for bed, she opened her bedroom window. It made for a chilly room, but the sound of her opening it was masked by her parents performing their usual ablutions, so wouldn't give her away later on.

She had to be very careful indeed or her father would

carry out his threat to lock her away. She shivered at the mere thought.

If there was the slightest chance of getting away, she was going to take it. Surely Francis would have her back?

Then she remembered with a dull leaden feeling in her stomach what her father had said. She wasn't married to Francis, had no right to expect his help. What would he say when he found out it was all a lie?

Only somehow, she kept hoping Francis would still want her. Why else had he given her the train ticket? Even if he didn't want her now, he was a kind man and he'd help her get far away from her father, she knew he would. She loved that about him.

She had put her wedding ring on again for this escape. Her father had told her to 'take that damned thing off' and she'd hidden it in her purse. It had felt strange to be without it.

She kept touching the ring to give herself courage.

Time passed slowly, then she heard something outside, the faintest of sounds, and slid carefully from the bed to look out of the window. Two men were carrying a ladder into the garden. The way they moved suggested they were young, so it couldn't be Mr Johnson. Well, whoever it was, there was only one reason for them to be here.

She stripped off her nightdress, stuffed it into the pillow case and put on her coat and shoes.

By the time someone climbed up to the window, she was ready.

The man put one finger to his lips and she nodded. When she passed the bulging pillowcase to him, he dropped it to the other man and moved down a couple of rungs.

With his help she got her feet on the ladder and was about to move down it when the bedroom door opened and her mother peeped in.

For a moment the two women looked at one another across the room and Diana wobbled on the ladder. She managed not to scream and looked pleadingly at her mother.

The bedroom door closed again.

'What was that sound?' he asked quietly.

'My mother,' she whispered. 'She'll tell my father and they'll be coming after me.'

'We'd better hurry, then.'

She scrambled down the ladder more quickly than she'd ever have believed possible, all the time expecting lights to go on and someone to start yelling inside the house.

But nothing happened.

'Come on.' The man who'd helped her down picked up her pillowcase and tugged at her hand. 'Quickly! But move quietly. We don't want them to hear where we've gone.'

The other man had already picked up the ladder and started towards the gate.

They followed him.

Diana ran as fast as she could, at every step expecting to hear shouts from the house. But she didn't.

'What's going on back there?' the man muttered. 'I thought they'd have come after us by now.'

'I don't know.'

Was it possible her mother was letting her get away? Did she not agree with what her husband was doing? It was the only explanation and it surprised Diana.

Once they were further down the street, her companion said, 'Now we can really run and never mind whether we make a noise or not.'

The man with the ladder had vanished in another direction.

'Where are we going?'

'Save your breath for running.'

★   ★   ★

Daniel painted a FOR SALE sign and then he and his aunt set to work to make sure everything looked perfect.

Unfortunately that meant he had to put his house plans and other things away, except for a few bits and pieces that could be shoved into a drawer at the drop of a hat.

When they thought it was ready, he put the sign up outside his aunt's house.

They walked round the house together doing a final check. But as he'd expected, everything was in beautiful order. Well, she had always been a superb housewife, so it had just been a question of getting her best ornaments out from the cellar, where they'd been stored for safety during the war.

There was a knock on the door and he let his aunt answer it, thinking it'd be one of her friends calling.

She came rushing into the dining room where he was working. 'Daniel, someone wants to buy the house.'

'*What?* Auntie Beryl, you must be mistaken. We haven't even shown anyone round yet.'

'No, I'm not mistaken. They said "buy" and I said "Don't you want to look round first?" and they said they wanted the house whatever it looked like.'

'I'll come and see them.'

A man and woman were standing outside, looking at the small front garden. He was pointing something out to her.

'Can I help you?' Daniel asked.

'Yes. We want to buy the house,' the man said, chin jutting aggressively. 'We don't care what it's like, but if I don't get away from living with my mother-in-law, I'll strangle her. And my wife's expecting a child, so we're even more desperate. Every house we've gone after was sold before we got there. This time we saw you putting up the sign, so we knocked on your door straight away.'

Daniel heard a gasp behind him. 'Um, congratulations, then. You're the first to look round and if you meet our price it's yours. Why don't you come in and see what you're trying to buy?' He opened the door wider and gestured.

They came in and stood in the little oak-panelled hall. It was old-fashioned in style, but in good condition, but they didn't seem disposed to linger to check anything.

'You lead the way, Auntie,' Daniel suggested. 'Tell them about your house.'

He turned back to the strangers. 'My uncle died recently and my aunt is coming to live with me.'

'You must be sad to leave your home,' the young woman said sympathetically.

He saw his aunt relax a little.

'Yes, I am. But if someone nice buys it, I won't feel as bad.'

'Did your children grow up here?'

His aunt shook her head. 'We were never fortunate enough to have any, though Daniel, my nephew, has been like a son to me.'

'That's nice.'

'Well, this is the living room . . .'

It took them half an hour to go round the house, then Daniel took over again. 'We're asking eight hundred pounds for the house. It's a good solid one, with four bedrooms.'

'Oh, Brian, that's all our money. What about furniture?'

'I don't care if I have to sleep on the floor,' he said. 'We'll take it. We have the money from an inheritance so we don't even have to apply for a mortgage.' He gave his wife a quick hug. 'If we own the house outright, I'm sure the bank will lend us the money to buy some furniture, darling.'

Daniel turned to his aunt, and raised one eyebrow. She nodded.

'Very well. Sold.' Then he laughed. 'We don't even know one another's names.'

After an introduction, his aunt said, 'Come and have a

cup of tea. My husband always said business discussions needed lubricating.' Her voice wobbled for a moment then she regained control of her emotions and led the way into the kitchen.

'My aunt will be selling some of her furniture,' Daniel said as they sat down.

'We'll buy it,' Mr Rokeby said.

Again, Daniel was startled. 'Without knowing what it is?'

'As I said, I'm a desperate man. Look, you couldn't let us have a bedroom in the meantime, could you? Take us in as lodgers, I mean? We'll pay. I have to get out of there.'

Mrs Rokeby sighed. 'Mummy's a bit fussy about having things done her way.'

'A bit?'

'All right, very fussy indeed. She's made our lives miserable. She doesn't want us to leave, especially now that I'm expecting, but if we're to stay on good terms with her, we have to.'

Her voice became wistful. 'I've never had a home of my own before. We got married in '43, you see, and Tom was away so much, I stayed on with my parents. We used to meet near where he was stationed most of the time, so he never had to deal with Mum's fussing for more than a day or two before.'

'You could take the back two bedrooms,' Auntie Beryl said. 'But I'd have to charge you ten shillings a week and you must provide and prepare your own food. Only . . . won't your mother be upset?'

'Not as upset as I'll be if I have to stay. Done!' Mr Rokeby hugged his wife, then hugged Auntie Beryl for good measure and shook Daniel's hand vigorously. 'Let me be plain. We won't be bothering you, because we shall want to spend our evenings together. We've missed too much time already.'

'This is all dependent on you proving to me that you have

the money,' Daniel put in, feeling as if the situation was galloping away from his control.

Mr Rokeby beamed at him. 'I can do that this very afternoon, and I can pay fifty pounds deposit here and now, but I can't get hold of the rest of the money for about a month. Will that be all right?'

'It'll take that long for our solicitors to deal with the legal side of things. Who is your solicitor, by the way?'

'Anyone who'll have me. Come to the bank now and I'll prove I've got the money. Then we'll go back and pack our things.' He smacked another kiss on his wife's cheek.

Daniel went with them to the door and said, 'Just a minute. I forgot to tell my aunt something.'

He ran back into the kitchen and looked at her. 'Happy about this?'

'Yes, dear. They're such a nice couple. If I have to sell, I'd prefer to do it to someone like that.'

'He's a bit impatient.'

'My Egan was always impatient when he wanted something, too.' She smiled mistily. 'I haven't forgotten and I hope I never will forget what it's like to be young and in love.'

Daniel forced a smile and went to re-join the purchasers. He'd thought he'd been in love with Ada, and look what happened to that.

It'd take a lot to make him court a woman again, by hell it would! Falling in love made you stupid.

16

Diana stumbled along a side street, panting, wondering where they were going but she did her best to keep up. She kept looking over her shoulder, fearing pursuit, but it didn't come. Her mother mustn't have given her away. One day she'd say thank you for that.

If she ever saw them again that is.

It was a while before she realised they'd passed the turn-off to the Johnsons' house, and were getting to the edge of the village.

The man guiding her stopped for a moment. 'It's all right to speak from now on as long as you keep your voice low.'

'Where are we going?'

'There's a smallholder who takes his milk to the railway station. He's not fond of your father and is going to put you on the early train with his milk.' He fumbled in his pocket and shoved an envelope into her hand. 'Mr Johnson said to give you this.'

When she opened it she found ten pounds in one pound and ten shilling notes, and sighed with relief. 'I shouldn't take it, but just in case . . . Tell him I'll pay him back every penny as soon as I can.'

'Mr J would have come himself, but he has to live in the village so he's going to pretend to be ill during the night, then his maid will be able to tell everyone he never left the house.'

'Oh. I see. He seems to have thought of everything.' She looked uncertainly at her companion.

He grinned as if he could guess what she was thinking. 'Don't look so frightened. I'm quite safe. I've worked for Mr J for years. He's a good boss. And your father isn't. He's made a lot of enemies in the village.'

'I'm beginning to realise why people stay away from him. He'll come after me, though.'

'You'll be long gone and he'll have to find you first. No one will remember seeing you, because you'll be catching the train at the next village. Once you get to Rivenshaw, your husband will be able to look after you. Mr Johnson thinks well of *him*, says he's a clever fellow.'

She nodded, feeling cold in the chilly night air, in spite of her warm coat. Now that she was away from the comfortable house, it was sinking in that she'd burned her bridges. Upsetting her father was a terrifying thought.

Equally terrifying was the worry about what Francis would say when she told him their marriage wasn't legal. Would he still want her?

She shivered.

'You're getting cold, Mrs Brady. Let's start moving again. We've got a bit of a walk yet.'

It seemed strange to walk through the dark countryside with a man she'd never met before, a man who hadn't told her his name, even. One of her shoes was rubbing her heel and this was the only pair she had with her. You couldn't fit much into a pillowcase, especially when you had to carry it down a ladder.

She was tired and thirsty. Would they ever get there? Or would they just go on walking for ever through the moonlit darkness?

'Here we are, love.'

Diana stumbled to a halt and stared round. They were standing outside what looked like a small farm. 'This isn't a railway station.'

'Of course it isn't. You're going to the station with the farmer on his cart. You'll pretend to be his niece, Penny, going home after a visit. Don't forget to call him Uncle Derek and kiss him goodbye at the station.'

As her guide knocked on the door, Diana's heart began thudding. Would she be safe here?

The woman who answered the door looked as sleepy as Diana felt. 'We expected you sooner.'

'She's not a fast walker.'

'My husband's nearly ready to go. Come in, missus. You can have a glass of fresh milk and warm yourself by the fire for a few minutes.' She turned and vanished inside.

Diana's rescuer thrust the pillow case into her hand. 'Good luck.'

'Thank you for helping me.'

With a final nod he was gone, just like that.

'Shut that door,' the woman called.

She did and went inside, following the warm draught to a big kitchen at the end of the hall.

'Are you hungry?'

'A bit.'

A glass of frothy milk was poured and thrust into her hand. 'Here. That'll hold you for a while. And I've made you some sandwiches. You'll be travelling for a long time. Do you want to use the privvy before you go?'

'Yes, please.'

She wrinkled her nose in disgust at having to use an earth closet on the edge of the back yard. After she came back inside, the woman asked, 'Is that all your luggage?'

'Yes.'

'You're going to be cold.'

'I think I packed a scarf.' She tipped out the contents and looked through them, horrified at how little there was. 'No. I must have left it behind.'

Her hostess walked across to some pegs near the outer door and pulled a grey knitted scarf off the layers of outer clothes hung there. 'Take this. We've got a few scarves. This one is old, but warm.'

'Thank you. You're very kind.'

'We're poor sorts of creatures if we don't help one another. And your father had it coming to him.'

Diana had only just finished drinking the milk when the farmer came for her.

He led the way outside, took her pillow case and tossed it into the back of the cart, which looked dirty. 'You come and sit next to me.'

Diana was so weary he had to give her a boost to get her up on the seat beside him. He clicked his tongue and his horse set off.

'Takes us about fifteen minutes to get to the station.'

'Right. Thank you.'

'Did he tell you to call me Uncle Derek? You're supposed to be my niece Penny and I don't want anyone finding out differently. Wrap that scarf round your neck and keep away from the lamp on the station platform. If you stay in the shadows, no one will know any different. You're a bit like our Penny, but she's bigger built.'

After that, he didn't talk.

The horse's breath steamed slightly in the early morning chill. It stopped outside a little country station without being told and the farmer got down, making no attempt to help Diana.

'Hurry up, Penny. We haven't got all morning. Get your

bag from the back of the cart, while I deal with the milk churns.' He added more quietly, 'As soon as the train comes in, get on it and stay away from the window.'

When he pointed to a bench, she sat on it, waiting as the slow minutes ticked by. She felt as if she was in a nightmare, one where she travelled on and on without ever reaching her destination. And she'd only just begun her journey.

She wished suddenly that dawn would break. She'd feel better once it was light, she was sure.

Five minutes later a train chugged into the station and the farmer jerked his thumb towards it, yelling, 'Bye, Penny. Give your mother my love.'

She found an empty carriage and got on the train, huddling in the corner out of sight as instructed.

A man came out of the small station building to help the farmer load his milk churns on the train quickly and put the empty ones that had been unloaded on the cart. No one looked at the passenger compartments.

A whistle blew and the train set off, rattling along slowly, gathering speed, leaving everything she knew behind.

She was free now . . . and utterly terrified. She had felt a bit like this when called up to work during the war, but this was far worse because when she got there she had to tell Francis they weren't married. If she didn't do that, her father would.

What would Francis say?

The night Diana escaped from her parents' house, someone hit Al on the head from behind as he strolled round the gardens, keeping watch.

He came to and found himself well and truly trussed up, with his hands tied behind his back and his feet tied too. There was no way he could find to get out of his bonds, or even get the gag out of his mouth to call for help.

He lay there, feeling furious at himself for being so slack. And yet, he'd thought he was being careful. The person who'd hit him had chosen his place of ambush very well, must have moved swiftly as well as silently, and knew what he was doing when he tied someone up.

What the hell was going on?

He rolled to and fro, trying to find something to rub the piece of rope against.

It was sheer luck that old Mr Rennie went out walking that night, as he sometimes did, and found Al by the simple act of tripping over him and falling flat on his face.

He had the wit to roll away from the man's body. 'Eh, what's going on? What are you doing here?'

Al tried to speak but could only make grunting sounds.

Mr Rennie looked more closely. 'Is that you, Al lad?' He pulled out his penknife and carefully slit the gag. 'What happened?'

'I don't know. Someone hit me over the head and knocked me out. When I came to my senses, I woke up tied like this. Can you get me free quickly? I have to warn Mayne. Good thing Victor and Francis are there too.'

'You'll have to hold still, because they tied you tightly.'

'I noticed, damn them to high hell.'

As the bonds fell away from his wrists, Al groaned and had to wait a minute or two to move properly, as feeling started to come back to his hands and arms.

The rope round his ankles was strong and it took Mr Rennie, with his small penknife, precious time to saw through it.

When Al could move properly, he whispered to the old man. 'Go home, Steve. This isn't something for a man your age to get involved in. These people know what they're doing.'

'I can tag along behind you and trip anyone who tries to run away,' Mr Rennie said hopefully.

'No. Not at your age. I'll wake Mayne and Francis, and we'll catch the devils. First I have to find out where they are.'

'There was a light near that Nissen hut. I thought it was someone keeping watch, so I kept out of sight as I walked past. I don't like to disturb you people when I go walking about in the middle of the night. I never saw anything at the front, so they must have come into the grounds the back way.'

'Thanks. Now get yourself back home.'

Steve Rennie watched him go, but disobeyed orders and followed him. He was a countryman and could move quietly when he had to, making even less noise than a small animal creeping through the bushes. By now he knew every inch of the grounds, so he followed a narrow, little-used path he knew of, heading towards the big house.

As he walked he kept his eyes open and soon found himself a knobbly branch lying on the ground among a pile of wood ready to be taken to the house. He hefted it in his hand, nodding approval.

They weren't going to keep him out of this. He wasn't so old that he couldn't play his part in defending the place he now considered his home. Whoever this was, Steve was on the side of the Eshers, who'd been so kind to him and his wife.

Al used his key to enter the big house by the library, first making sure there wasn't anyone around on that side of the house. He locked the door carefully behind him and moved quietly through the house.

He gave two double knocks on Mayne's bedroom door and waited.

There was a faint sound from inside the bedroom and the door opened a crack as Mayne checked who it was.

'Intruders,' Al said succinctly. 'Don't know what they're

after, but they knocked me out and tied me up good and tight. If Mr Rennie hadn't come by, I'd still be lying there. What do you suppose they're after?'

'It might be something to do with the corpse, or perhaps an organised robbery on a bigger than usual scale. Let me put some clothes on and we'll investigate. Francis is sleeping two doors down. Can you go and wake him? I'll get Victor.'

'I'm coming too,' Judith whispered from behind her husband.

'No, you're not.'

'Yes I am, Mayne. I'll stay to the rear, but you may need me and I'm not just a helpless flower, you know that. I'll waken Ben on my way. He's nearly as big as you are now and strong with it. I'll bring my rolling pin. I've used that before to defend myself with.'

He sighed. 'Very well. But please . . . don't get involved unless you have to.'

'I might say the same to you.'

'Have you got a gun, Mayne?' Al asked. 'I don't think these people are amateurs.'

'Yes, I have.' He patted his pocket.

By that time, Francis and Victor had joined them.

'Got a gun?' Mayne asked them.

'No. And I don't want to hold one ever again.' Francis shuddered.

'Mine's locked away,' Victor said quietly. 'I need to get a licence for it.'

'Well, with a house this big, I bought one legally and got it licensed when I was demobbed.' With the help of the people in the special unit to speed matters up. Just in case they needed his help about something.

'Let's see if we can spot the intruders.'

The four men went to look out of one of the rear bedroom windows that overlooked the Nissen hut.

'Dammit, they've got the door of the hut open and left one man on guard,' Mayne muttered.

'How the hell did they manage to open it?' Al asked.

'They might have had a key,' Mayne said slowly. 'They might . . . know about our corpse . . . and the valuables they left there. I should have changed the padlock and kept another man on watch as well. These people must know the police decided it wasn't worth guarding the hut any longer.'

'Well, let's go down and see if we can find who they are,' Al said.

They crept through the dark house, hearing footsteps behind them. Mayne stopped and warned Judith and her son to stay back. 'We'll go out through the library, to make sure of taking them by surprise.'

'Just give me a chance and I'll surprise the sods,' Al muttered, rubbing the back of his head, which had a large and painful lump on it.

'You'll get your chance.'

When they crept round the corner via one of the many shrubberies, they saw that the man on duty outside the hut was holding a gun.

'Damnation!' Mayne gestured to them to get back.

Round the corner he said tersely, 'I'm not risking someone getting shot. Judith, take Ben back into the house. The situation is too dangerous for any of us to challenge them. I'm prepared to risk my life in the service of my country, but I'm not risking a bullet to catch burglars. If this one has a gun, they probably all do.'

Judith did as he'd ordered, knowing it'd be foolish to stay and wanting to keep her son safe.

Mayne looked behind them and sighed as he saw a dark silhouette. He nudged Victor and whispered, 'Tell him to go home.'

Victor walked across to where the old man was standing in the shadows and did as he asked.

'If they're carrying guns, they're bad 'uns,' Mr Rennie said. 'I can't fight a gun. I hope you catch 'em.'

They watched him walk off into the shadows without making a noise.

'I bet he was a bit of a lad in his day,' Francis said softly. 'You can usually tell. He's not enjoying feeling old and useless now. Well, who would?'

'I'd guess he was enjoying himself tonight in a strange sort of way. Now, if we could get rid of that fellow on guard,' Al said slowly, 'we could lock the others in the hut.'

But even as he spoke there was activity in the stable yard and when they peeped round the corner, they saw three men dressed in dark clothing with their faces blackened, moving away from the hut in the direction of the drive. They were walking jerkily, like men who were angry.

'Didn't find what they were looking for, do you think?' Mayne wondered aloud.

'Could be,' Francis said.

'I wish we could have got one of them,' Al said wistfully. 'I'd like to pay someone back for walloping me like that.'

'We're going to have to bring the authorities back in on this. I'll phone my friends in the special unit as well. Those men looked like . . . well, soldiers on duty.'

He went inside the house, moving swiftly to the telephone in the office, keeping his voice low as he reported to the night duty officer what had just happened.

When he re-joined the others, he said, 'They're getting in touch with the Army. There's a crack-down on looters at the moment apparently.'

'And on murderers too, I hope. I don't want criminals feeling free to attack and rob us.' Judith's voice was sharp with anxiety.

'As soon as it's light, we'll check whether those fellows moved or damaged anything inside the hut. We'll stay here on watch until dawn. I'm not risking them coming back again with reinforcements. How about a cup of cocoa, love?'

She flourished one hand towards the gas cooker where a kettle was just coming to the boil. 'I anticipated you.'

'What a swizz that they got away!' Ben muttered.

'They won't do if they come back again,' Mayne said grimly. 'And we'll make a better job of keeping them out of the hut from now on.'

Even though it wasn't yet fully light, they went into the hut with their torches and checked what they could. Near the front, boxes of tools had been slashed open but the tools were still there. The ground had been disturbed where the corpse had lain.

'Well, they knew about the dead chap anyway,' Mayne said grimly. '*And* about the valuables that had been stashed in those boxes.'

'Just a minute, come and look at this.' Francis pointed to the ground a short distance away. 'Is it my imagination or has the ground over here been dug up and then tamped down again as well.

They all studied the patch of ground. 'It definitely has. It's darker than the ground elsewhere, so that must be the damp soil from underneath.'

'But why did they dig up this part? Surely there isn't another corpse buried?'

'I think we'd better leave it to the Army wallahs to investigate that. Murder is a bit beyond our jurisdiction.'

As they walked back into the house, Mayne said quietly, 'If the Army doesn't catch them, though, we're going to have to do something about these men ourselves. We can't have them thinking they can loot and murder at will.'

The same two officers drove up to the house that morning around ten o'clock, but this time there were two soldiers in the back seat as well.

One of the soldiers jumped out and opened the car door for the captain, who went straight across to Mayne. 'Been having some more fun and games, eh?'

He gave them a quick summary of what had happened.

'That makes me much more eager to catch the buggers,' the captain said. 'I'd guess they had plans to follow through on whatever it was they were doing after the war. I've brought a digging squad this time. There has to be something we've missed if they were poking around beyond where the corpse lay.'

'Be my guest. Any chance of me observing?'

'We'd rather work alone and we'll be going slowly so as not to miss anything, so you'd find it boring anyway. Don't worry. We'll call you in straight away if we find something of interest.'

'I'll get on with the eternal paperwork, then,' Mayne said. 'The authorities say they want houses building but they don't make it easy to get the necessary permissions.'

'Red tape rules the country,' the captain said with feeling.

The phone rang just as Mayne was settling down. 'Esherwood.'

'Johnson here. Could I speak to Brady, please?'

Mayne poked his head into the corridor and yelled, 'Francis, you've got a phone call from your Mr Johnson.'

Francis came running into the office and grabbed the phone his friend was holding out. 'Brady here.'

'I thought you'd like to know. Your wife asked us to help her get away and we did. We put her on the early train to London. She'll probably arrive in Rivenshaw this evening some time, can't say when. The trains still aren't running on time.'

'Thank you. I'm grateful. Very grateful.'

'My pleasure. Just don't tell anyone it was me. I have to live in the same village as your dear father-in-law and I don't want a legal war on my hands. Give me a call tomorrow to let me know she's safe. This is my number. Got to go now.'

The line went dead and Francis sat smiling at it. He'd scribbled down the number on the nearest piece of paper, which happened to be a bill. He hoped Mayne wouldn't mind.

Diana had chosen him over her parents. That meant a lot to him. He was sure she'd be pleasantly surprised by Rivenshaw. It was going to be a very nice place for them to make a home in, even with the current troubles at Esherwood. Surely they'd sort out their differences if they both tried hard?

When he went to tell Mayne what had happened, his friend said quietly, 'I can tell you're happy. You've not smiled like that since you've been here.'

'I'm getting her back. I can't seem to fall out of love with her. With all her faults, she's still my Diana.'

The two officers sent one of their men to fetch Mayne a couple of hours later.

'Look what we found.' One of them flourished his hand towards a pile of dug-up earth.

Mayne stared in shock at the deep hole revealed by their digging. When he moved closer he saw stone stairs, slippery with muck, disappearing into the darkness below. 'How can the people who put up the hut not have seen this?'

'Well, obviously one of them did see it and covered it up again. The big question is, what's down there? Did you have any idea there was another cellar here? I presume it'll be a cellar behind that heavy door.'

'I had no idea at all. I've never heard my father talk about it either, and he's the expert on the house and the family history.'

'We have torches. Fancy having a look at what's there with me? Maybe you'll have a key to open that door stashed away somewhere.'

As Mayne moved forward eagerly, the captain held up one hand. 'I want your word that if I yell at you to get out, you will. It probably isn't booby-trapped, because that door is really old, but still, better safe than sorry.'

'Yes, of course.'

'Come on, then, Esher.' He led the way down the steps, moving slowly and carefully. The opening at the bottom was roughly square, about as wide as a man's spread arms, and the top of the cellar door only seemed to start about a yard and a half below ground level.

Mayne was puzzled. 'Why do you think they tried to hide this place?'

'Hidden treasure?'

'How can it be? I never heard any family stories about a hidden cellar and I played around the back yard all the time as a lad. Believe me there was nothing to show that this existed underneath the stables.'

They both stood still at the bottom of the steps and played their torches round the space that had been revealed. It went back about three yards and most of it hadn't been filled in. Some upright planks had obviously held back the piled-up earth.

The walls that had been uncovered were of rough stone and the main feature of this cave-like space was a heavy wooden door with huge iron hinges and a lock.

'I don't think I've ever seen a key big enough to fit that lock.' Mayne moved forward to try the door, but it was firmly locked and even when he shook the handle good and hard, he couldn't budge the door or even make it rattle. It was definitely meant to keep the wrong people out and it must have done that for centuries. It *felt* old, somehow.

Why hadn't he heard of this place? Other family secrets had been passed down the generations. Did his father know?

'We need to get a locksmith out to open it up,' the captain said. 'The soil our chaps dug out of the stair well wasn't firmly packed, so I reckon those men got this far last night. And this part hadn't been filled in at all. The muck was held back by that line of planks. There was a bit of spillage from the bottom of the stairs, but that's all.'

For once his face was lit up with interest as he turned to Mayne. 'This is something a bit different, eh? We'll need to find out what's behind that door, but of course, as long as there are no more corpses, anything we find is likely to belong to your family. We'll keep quiet about it for the moment, eh? Then we'll set a trap to tempt those sods back. I'm really going to enjoy this.'

He gestured towards the stairs with one hand. 'Let's go and tell your friends about it. I presume you can trust them to keep the secret?'

'I'd trust them with my life. We served together.'

'Ah, well, that forms a bond, doesn't it? I'll let 'em come down and have a look, then we'll leave it till a locksmith can be found.'

'Do you need to bring in your own locksmith?' Mayne asked. 'Because if not, I think one of my partners knows one.'

'Can he get the fellow here quickly?'

'Oh, I'm sure he can. But Woollard is our antiques expert, so it'd be a good idea to let him join us when we open up the door. I'll go and see my father later and ask him if he's heard anything about this place.'

17

Mayne walked down to the Dower House in the late afternoon. For once his father wasn't shut up in his study, but was sitting in the kitchen chatting to the Rennies. It was good to see how comfortable they looked together. Judith's housekeeping arrangement was working out well.

He chatted for a moment or two then asked to speak to his father alone to deal with some family business.

'I'll go and finish off that bedroom,' Mrs Rennie said at once. 'I'm working through the unused rooms one by one, Mr Esher, setting them in order. I'm enjoying myself.'

'That's good.' He turned to his father. 'We'll go into the living room, shall we?'

'Yes. Has something cropped up? I hope it isn't bad news. I hope it won't take the Rennies away. Mrs Rennie is an excellent cook. I've not eaten so well in years. She even makes wartime rations into tasty meals.'

'No, it's not bad news. At least I don't think it is.'

When they were seated Mayne explained about the secret cellar.

His father gaped at him. 'It really exists?'

'You knew about it?'

'I knew about the legend, but when I checked through the family diaries, I found that my great-grandfather had investigated and dismissed it as just a tale.'

'What legend?'

'About the English Civil War. There was a different house here then and family tales of the eighteenth century said that the house was captured by the Roundheads and burned to the ground. The lady ancestor leading the defence is supposed to have hidden the family silver and other valuables, and though people hunted high and low, no one ever found them.' He stood up, his eyes glittering with excitement. 'Show me.'

'Not till tomorrow. We've locked it up safely for the night and we're going to have men keeping guard over it. Someone else is after the supposed treasure. Remember the corpse? We think it's all connected.'

'Oh. Pity. But I can make a start on checking the family diaries tonight. Well, if I can find them all again. It's been a while since I looked at them and then we had to move them down here when the Army requisitioned the big house. I shouldn't have taken my great-grandfather's word for it being a myth. I don't know how accurate a researcher he was. I should have found the sources he mentioned and drawn my own conclusions.'

Muttering to himself, not even saying goodbye to his son, Reginald left the room and hurried up the stairs.

Mayne went to find Mrs Rennie. 'I'm afraid you'll find my father even more absent-minded than usual. I've given him some family history to think about and investigate. If you could make sure he bothers to eat, I'd be grateful.'

She smiled. 'Bless him. He's easy enough to manage once you get to know him better. Likes my cooking, he does. Do you have time to look at the bedroom I've finished cleaning up?'

Mayne spent ten more minutes at the Dower House admiring her progress, told her she was a treasure and left her beaming. He smiled too as he walked back along the drive to the big house. It was good to make people happy.

He intended to tell the others what was going on tonight. He wasn't keeping information from the group, and he even trusted the children to keep their mouths shut about family secrets. Anyway, Judith's three were going to be adopted into his family and Betty was still too quiet and restrained for a child of her age.

He stopped to gaze at the old house and allow himself one quick sigh. He was going to miss living here.

No, he mustn't think about that, just had to get on with things, he told himself firmly as he set off again.

At least he could save the building, unlike his ancestors, who'd seen the first family house razed to the ground and then had to flee into exile. That must have been agonising.

Diana nearly fell asleep on the train to London, and she did fall asleep on the train heading north to Manchester. That wasn't a bad thing, because it was a slow train and it would take hours to get there.

People got in and out at the various stations and she half woke up, checking the name of the station and then letting herself slide back into sleep again when it wasn't anywhere near Manchester.

Somewhere past Birmingham, she woke up fully and had to ask a kind-faced old lady to mind her seat while she went to the lavatory. But when she came back, her place had been taken by a soldier with a heavily bandaged foot.

'I'm sorry, dear, but I think the young man's need for a seat is greater than yours, don't you? You're young enough to stand for a while and you may get a seat later on.'

Everyone in the compartment nodded agreement and the soldier apologised for taking her seat. Well of course she'd give up her seat to an injured soldier, but she was still very tired.

She took her pillow case down from the overhead luggage

net and went to stand in the corridor, clutching it to her chest. There were a lot of other unfortunates standing too, but she was annoyed when first one young man then another tried to flirt with her. She wasn't interested in them, didn't care whether they thought she was pretty or not. And surely they could see that she was wearing a wedding ring?

She hung on grimly, rocking to and fro as the train jolted over the rails.

At Manchester, feeling dizzy with tiredness, she had to rush to the ladies before she did anything else. She wished she had seen to that on the train but the lavatory there had had a queue of people to use it and she had decided to wait.

When she got back to the platform where trains to that part of Lancashire left, it was to find she'd only just missed a train that stopped at Rivenshaw and the next slow train wouldn't be for over an hour. She couldn't help it; she burst into tears.

No one came to ask her what was wrong, let alone offer to help, and in the end she stopped sobbing, found a bench and dried her eyes. *Don't be such a baby!* she told herself. *You're managing, aren't you?*

Within a few minutes of sitting down, however, she began to feel drowsy again, so got up and went to look for refreshments. A cup of tea might help keep her awake. It was late afternoon by now and all she'd had since last night was a glass of milk and a couple of stale cheese sandwiches wrapped in an old paper bag.

She bought a cup of dark, stewed tea and a bun that looked days old. After forcing it down and drinking the worst tea she'd ever tasted out of sheer thirst, she walked up and down her platform till the train arrived.

As it set off, a woman with a small child asked, 'Are you all right, dear? You don't look well?'

'I didn't get any sleep last night and I'm terrified of falling asleep now and missing my stop. I'd better stand up in the corridor, I think. It's much harder to fall asleep standing up. It's only an hour or so to Rivenshaw, I was told.'

She half-expected the woman to tell her to stay and offer to wake her up when they reached Rivenshaw, but the child began to cry just then and no offer was forthcoming as the mother rushed the child to the lavatory.

Sighing, Diana picked up her pillowcase, which was now extremely grubby, and went to stand in the corridor. She leaned her aching head against the window, because it was cool and soothing.

A ticket collector came along and stopped to punch her ticket. 'There are plenty of seats, love.'

'I know. But if I sit down, I'll fall asleep and I daren't miss my stop.'

'Been to a party, have you?' But he didn't wait for an answer, just lumbered on along the corridor.

When the train began to slow down and she saw the sign saying RIVENSHAW, she felt so surprised to have actually arrived, she froze for a moment, then had to rush to get a door open in time.

She stumbled as she was getting down on to the platform and would have fallen but luckily another passenger caught her by the arm. He was quite old and looked affluent, so she didn't feel afraid of speaking to him.

'Thank you very much. So clumsy of me.'

'You look exhausted, lass. Anyone meeting you?'

'No. They don't know I'm coming. Is there a taxi?'

He looked across the square. 'Yes. But it's just been taken by someone else.'

By the meagre light of three street lamps she saw a vehicle with a TAXI sign on its roof drive off. She could feel tears trickle down her cheeks, in spite of her resolution not to cry again when things went wrong.

He looked at her shrewdly. 'Been travelling for long?'

'All last n-night and all today.'

'Where are you going?'

'Esherwood.'

'Oh? Know the family, do you?'

'Yes. Or at least my husband does. He's staying there.'

'Ah. What's his name?'

'Francis Brady.'

'He seems like a nice chap.'

'You know him?'

'I'm starting to. I'm a minor partner in their enterprise now.' He held out his hand. 'Raymond Woollard at your service, Mrs Brady. My niece said she'd leave my car parked here for me because we weren't sure which train I'd be taking back. Yes, there it is! Allow me to give you a lift to Esherwood.'

'I . . . don't know you.'

'Easily remedied.' He beckoned to the porter. 'Tell the lady who I am, Joe.'

'Mr Woollard.'

'And you'd better assure her I'm respectable while you're at it.'

The porter looked at him indulgently. 'You will have your little joke, Mr Woollard.'

Her rescuer cocked one eyebrow at Diana. 'Satisfied now? I really am one of the partners, I promise you.'

'Yes. Sorry to be so mistrustful. I'd be very grateful for a lift. I'm exhausted.'

And she was starting to feel highly apprehensive about how Francis would greet her, even before he heard her news. What if he didn't want her back?

Someone was shaking her and Diana tried to push them away. The person chuckled and that annoyed her, so she dragged herself out of sleep to tell them to leave her alone.

That was when she saw Francis bending down at the open car door, with Mayne standing behind him.

She realised to her horror that she was half-lying against Mr Woollard. How he'd driven the car with her leaning on him, she couldn't think. She could feel her cheeks getting hot as she sat upright and let Francis help her out of the car.

She did manage to gather her wits together enough to thank her rescuer before getting out.

He called after them. 'You've left your pillowcase.'

'I'll see to that.' Judith went to collect it from the floor in front of the passenger seat. It was grubby and its contents made it look all knobbly.

Francis put an arm round Diana and she leaned against him thankfully. 'Thank you for bringing her from the station, Ray.'

'You're welcome. She looked ready to drop with exhaustion, poor lass, hardly seemed to know what she was doing. Shut the car door and I'll be off. You two love-birds will want some time alone. I've got good news for you all, but I'll save that for tomorrow.'

'Don't go yet, Ray!' Mayne said. 'I've something else to tell you about.'

Diana looked sideways at her husband, feeling suddenly at ease with him. No one had looked at her so fondly since she moved in with her parents. 'I was very stupid, Francis,' she whispered.

He looked at her solemnly. 'Were you? Why?'

'Going back to my parents instead of staying in my own home.' She shivered at the memory. 'They'd been nagging me to do it, but it was wrong – and they were horrid to me. My father has changed so much. He's a bully.'

'Or perhaps you've changed and you're seeing him more clearly.'

'Oh. Yes. I think you're right.'

'Well, I won't let them take you away from me again, not unless you want to go. Welcome to Rivenshaw, Diana. Look, Judith's waiting for us in the doorway. Let's go inside, eh?'

As she moved, everything felt to be slipping and sliding around her and she clung to him. 'I feel . . . dizzy.'

He picked her up and carried her into the house.

She loved how strong he was and let her head fall against his chest. 'I did it, though. I got away from my father. Your Mr Johnson helped and—' A yawn prevented her finishing what she was saying. 'Oh, I'm so tired.'

She heard Francis chuckle but couldn't keep her eyes open. It was important to make sure he understood one thing, though. 'I missed you.'

'Well, now you've got me back again.'

He planted a quick kiss on the end of her nose.

'Mmm. Nice.' As he put her down on a bed, she sighed happily, snuggling down. 'I'll just close my eyes for a minute . . .'

Judith whispered, 'I've brought her luggage.'

'Thanks.' He stared at the pillow case in shock. 'Is that all?'

'Yes. Not much to start a new life with, is it? She must have been very eager to come to you.'

That thought made him feel more hopeful: Diana of all people to run away with hardly any clothes.

The two men watched Francis carry Diana into the house and Judith follow them, then Mayne said, 'There's been another discovery underneath the Nissen hut, Ray. Beyond where the corpse was unearthed, the intruders found a buried entrance to what looks like a hidden cellar.'

'Well, there's a turn-up for the books.'

'Goodness only knows how long it's been concealed or what's inside, because it's got a very heavy door which is locked tight. I couldn't get the door even to rattle when I shook it. The door looks very old, heavy dark oak.'

Woollard brightened. 'I knew it'd be interesting working with you chaps.'

'Could you get your locksmith friend to come here tomorrow morning first thing, do you think? And ask him not to say anything about where he's going or why? The military police want to keep quiet about the discovery for the moment.'

'Oh, he'll come running. He'll be fascinated by the tale of a secret cellar. And if he says he won't tell anyone, I trust him not to. What does your father say about it? There must be family stories about such a secret.'

'I'd never heard of it because he never mentioned it. It's not in the family diaries or archives that I've seen, but I haven't read them all. He says his great-grandfather looked into the legend and dismissed it as untrue. Dad took his word for it and didn't investigate further, but clearly, the ancestor was wrong. Dad's now got his head buried in the family diaries and I doubt we'll get a word of sense out of him till he's done some more research. If there's anything to be discovered, he'll find it, believe me.'

'I'll get my locksmith to come round early tomorrow and meet you all here. I want to see this door of yours. I can leave my niece in charge of the office.'

Mayne couldn't help smiling as he watched Woollard drive away. He'd not trusted the man at first, but now he was starting not only to rely on him, but to like him.

It was strange how things turned out sometimes.

Francis stared down at his wife. Diana was fast asleep and looked so exhausted he hadn't the heart to wake her up.

Judith said, 'I doubt she'll stir till morning. Shall I see if there's a nightdress in here?'

'Thanks.'

She tipped the contents of the grubby pillowcase on to the other side of the double bed. 'Is this all she was able to bring with her? We'll have to help her find some more clothes.'

'Isn't there a clothing exchange in Rivenshaw?'

'Yes. It's still operating. Well, it'll be ages before manufacturers can produce enough clothes to prevent the need for rationing them, I should think. There might be some old clothes in the attics that fit her. Does she sew?'

'Yes. She's very good at it, actually. Well, women have had to be during the war years, haven't they?'

Judith let out a scornful sniff. '*Make do and mend* is a literal description of how we've kept our families clothed during the past few years. And turning the sheets sides to middle when they wear thin. That's a very boring job when you don't have a sewing machine, as I didn't. As for my Ben, his clothes seem to need mending every week. He's at the clumsy stage, drat him.'

She moved towards the door. 'I'll leave you to put her to bed. I'm glad she's come to you, Francis.'

'So am I.'

When she'd gone he looked down at his wife, beautiful even in sleep, and then studied the small pile of clothes. How would she cope with so few things to wear? How she looked seemed to be very important to her, too important perhaps.

Indeed, he kept wondering how she would adapt to living here among a group of people. They could only wait and see. She'd have to fit in, whatever it took, because if she'd had to escape from her father, he doubted Scammell would take her back again.

Just let him try!

He moved the pile of clothes from his side of the bed to the top of a chest of drawers and switched on an electric lamp so that she wouldn't wake up alone in the dark. He wasn't worried about leaving her, because he'd rarely seen anyone so hard asleep.

As he went downstairs to chat to the others, who were sitting in the kitchen after a later than usual evening meal, he decided he'd ask Judith to be tolerant with Diana, though not too slack. No one would have the time to spoil her here.

He greeted the others with, 'My dear wife is sleeping so soundly I couldn't wake her up.'

'Best leave her to it,' Judith said. 'We were talking about that hidden cellar.'

'What do you think will be inside it?'

And they were off, speculating happily, even the children being allowed to offer suggestions.

'Well, we'll no doubt find out what's in there in the morning when the locksmith opens it up,' Judith said at last. 'Look at the time. Get off to bed now, you four. Betty, how on earth have you stayed awake so long?'

'I wanted to see what was happening, so I kept quiet.'

'I'm not tired at all and we don't have school tomorrow,' Ben protested, but was betrayed by a sudden yawn.

His mother laughed and gave him a push towards the door. 'Get to bed!' She went as far as the doorway to make sure he followed his sisters upstairs.

She turned to Mayne who had joined her in the hall. 'Life is never dull here, is it? Do you ever regret filling your home with people?'

He pulled her to him. 'No. Especially not with you in my arms.'

She dug an elbow in his ribs. 'Stop that. The others are just inside the kitchen.'

'A man is allowed to kiss his wife. In fact, it's his duty to do it.' He proved how very dutiful he was.

★ ★ ★

Francis watched through the half-open door as Judith and Mayne kissed one another passionately. He felt envious. Would he and Diana ever be so comfortable with one another again, given their recent troubles?

After a while, he left everyone getting ready for bed and went out for a breath of fresh air, standing in the stable yard in the intermittent moonlight of a cloudy and breezy evening.

He smiled at the thought that Diana had come to him! She really had. Their situation wouldn't be easy to resolve. Nothing about Diana was ever easy or straightforward. But she was here; she'd chosen him. They had a chance of making a life together now.

Across the yard, one of Al's friends was on duty guarding the Nissen hut. Francis raised one hand in greeting, wondering where exactly the other guard was. Mayne had stationed one man in plain sight but kept the other hidden in the shrubbery, to make sure no one took the first guard by surprise.

'Think those two will be enough to keep whatever it is safe till tomorrow?' Mayne murmured from behind him.

'If they're friends of Al's, they won't be fools. A lot of the lads came back from the war more capable than they went into it. And these guys can always yell for help. We'd hear them.'

'I'm keeping my gun handy.' After a moment or two Mayne added quietly, 'I'm glad Diana came back to you.'

'Yes. I feel there's hope now for our marriage.' Francis smiled ruefully. 'I've loved her since she became a grown-up young lady after she left school. And even when she was a child, I used to look at her in the street and think how pretty she was. She was my dream princess. I never expected to be able to marry her.'

'She is lovely, even with that bruised, exhausted look round her eyes. Good luck!' Mayne clapped his friend on the shoulder and went back to his own wife, who'd gone to bed. Victor and Ros had already gone upstairs.

Francis stayed outside for a while, feeling better than he had in weeks, then he went back inside and locked up.

When he climbed into bed next to Diana she didn't stir and he didn't try to wake her. A few minutes later she turned over and, still without waking, cuddled close, as she usually did.

It had always seemed to him that she couldn't get enough affection and he'd understood that better when he saw her with her parents. None of the three touched the others in public and he doubted they did in private, either. Diana said her father sometimes claimed his marital rights and her mother got a look of disgust on her face, as if it wasn't something she enjoyed.

Thank goodness Diana didn't find the bed play disgusting. For him it was a wonderful expression of their love for one another.

He felt so happy to have his wife back, so very, very happy.

18

The military police turned up at nine o'clock prompt, all four of them again. Judith called along the office corridor to let Mayne know and he went out to greet them.

Ros and Victor had gone into town shopping for the household.

Shortly afterwards, Mayne's father turned up. His clothes were rather crumpled and surely the same ones he'd been wearing yesterday. Had he even been to bed? Mayne wondered.

'Did you find anything out, Dad?'

'No. But I've got quite a few books to work through yet, so it may take time. My great-grandfather's sources are only casually mentioned. He wasn't nearly as good a researcher as I'd thought. But I was younger when I looked at his work, not as well versed in proper research methods as I am now. I'm starting this by going through the early diaries because the cellar must have been concealed before the first house was razed. Well, why else would they go to all that trouble?'

He grimaced. 'The thing is, my books have got into a bit of a mess, and I'm having trouble finding all the ones I need.'

'Keep on looking,' Mayne said cheerfully. He wasn't going to waste his time on his father's books and papers, because no one understood the filing system – if there even was one. He was much more interested in the cellar itself, if it was a cellar, but he had to keep reminding himself that it might not contain anything of value. Well, his ancestors had not been noted for their ability to accumulate wealth, just occasionally marry it.

What did upset him was that the military police had made a mess of the inside of the Nissen hut, just piling the soil any old where. He was going to ask the captain if his men could take the piles of soil outside and dump them out of people's way.

Excitement was humming through him. They might manage to open the cellar door today and then they'd know what lay inside. Perhaps soon he'd be able to get on with his main task in life. Perhaps.

The group of men stood around in silence for a few more moments, then the captain consulted his wrist watch. 'That friend of yours did say he'd get the locksmith here by nine o'clock, didn't he?'

'Yes, but it's only a few minutes past the hour.'

'I prefer people to be on time.'

It was ten more minutes before they heard a car approaching, by which time the captain was tight-lipped.

That was the trouble with regular army fellows. They thought the whole world kept to as strict a time schedule as they did. 'You're getting a free service from this locksmith,' Mayne murmured. 'Don't annoy him.'

His companion let out an aggrieved sigh. 'You're right. But if you knew how many things there are that need sorting out back at headquarters. No offence, but I was surprised they even assigned me to this case. It's quite a minor one by the standards of the section where I work. Oh well, here we go, at least.'

The locksmith greeted Mayne cheerfully, waited to be introduced to the captain and lieutenant, then shook hands with Mayne's father as if they were old friends. 'Fascinating stuff, eh, Reginald?'

'Could be.'

The two new arrivals followed the others down into the small antechamber outside the supposed cellar. Mayne's father came down last, took a quick look round, then bolted back up the steps.

'He gets claustrophobia in small spaces like this, especially if they're underground,' Mayne explained. 'He's OK in our big cellars, as long as the lights are on, but he won't go into caves, if he can help it. He wouldn't go into the air raid shelter in the garden of the Dower House during the war, either.'

Everyone fell silent as the locksmith started examining the keyhole. He examined it and stepped back, frowning. Taking a torch out of his bag of tricks, he shone it into and around the aperture, which was larger than usual and seemed to have a complicated set of tumblers, parts of which were just visible inside.

After a while the man stood back and beamed at them. 'It's a puzzle lock. Very rare. This is so exciting. I never thought I'd be the person to find a new one, and such a big one, too.'

'What the hell's a puzzle lock?' the captain demanded.

'One which needs a complex series of steps to open it, not just a quick turn of a key. People have been making this sort of thing since the Middle Ages, perhaps earlier, though they were usually on strong boxes, not doors.'

'The point is, we need to get it open as quickly as possible,' the captain said.

'If we try to force it, metal barriers will fall into place inside or behind the door – I can't tell which from here – and it'll be very hard indeed to open. You'd have to chop and saw your way in, and sawing through steel bars can take a long time. It'd be best if you found the key to the door and the instructions for using it, and even then you should probably let me open the door for you.'

'Damnation!' Mayne felt just as annoyed about the delays as the captain, perhaps even more. He thumped his clenched fist against the solid oak door.

The others looked disappointed, too. In fact, the locksmith was the only cheerful person there.

'I'm surprised they could construct locks so complex in those days. Are you sure?' Mayne asked.

'Oh, puzzle locks go back a long way in history, believe me. And our early locksmiths weren't fools.'

'There's a family legend about it which my father didn't bother to tell me about till now, because he was sure it wasn't true. There's supposed to be a hidden cellar somewhere which apparently dates from the Civil War. This may be it. The Roundheads burned the original house to the ground because the Eshers supported the King, but the family are supposed to have hidden their valuables carefully in a secret cellar before this happened.'

'The door certainly looks old enough to fit those dates,' the captain said. 'But I'm not sure about this puzzle lock idea.'

'It wasn't common to have one like this,' the locksmith agreed. 'As I said before, most of them are on strong boxes. It must have cost a lot of money to have one specially built into a door. Your ancestors must have been planning well ahead, expecting the King to be defeated.'

After a pause, he went on, 'There have been a few exceptional locksmiths throughout history who made particularly fine puzzle locks. It took a long time to do each one, because they had to produce each part of the door and apparatus specially.'

He studied the door again and said thoughtfully, 'There was one particular locksmith in the north of England during that era, who was known to make these locks. This is probably one of his. Well, who else could have done it? I wonder . . .'

He bent to look at the bottom right-hand corner of the door, shining his torch down on it. 'Aha! It *is* his. He always left a tiny cross carved into the bottom of the door itself.'

One by one they bent down to inspect the tiny carving, which none of them would even have noticed without it being pointed out.

'He called himself Crosskey and no one knew his real identity, because he was afraid of being kidnapped and forced to work for people with bad intentions. Those who wanted his services used to let it be known and he would contact them to find out why, but only if he thought they were decent people. He wouldn't work for moneylenders, for instance.'

'How do you know all this?' Woollard asked.

'I've always been interested in the history of my trade.'

There was a pregnant silence, then the captain said, 'Well, it's clear we can't get inside this cellar for the moment. And if we can't, neither could the murderers. If there *is* a cellar behind that door. As I said, I reserve judgement on that.'

'Oh, there will be something valuable behind it,' the locksmith assured them. 'It would have been far too expensive to do it for no reason. I have no doubt about that.' He studied the door again and then turned round on the spot to study the small antechamber.

'You can see that this whole area hasn't been touched for a long time, so it won't be easy to get into the cellar.' He fixed the captain with a stern eye. 'I'm calling it a cellar *pro tem* for lack of a better term.'

'Well, since those present-day rogues won't know we can't get into it, I think we can use its existence to trap them. I'll have to work out a plan.'

Woollard pressed a five pound note into the locksmith's hand. 'We'll let you know when you're next needed, lad. Well done.'

'This has made my day, my whole year in fact.' The locksmith didn't offer to return the money, however.

He paused partway up the stairs with a final reminder. 'Call me when you find the key, Mr Esher. Do not, whatever you do, try to force open the door. I can probably tell you which type of sequence it uses by the key's appearance, but the exact details may be difficult. You should try to find the code which guides the use of the key, if it still exists. They usually wrote them down somewhere and kept that information in a secure place.'

'Don't say a word about it to anyone,' the captain warned.

'Of course not. Well, not until it's all over and you give me permission, then I'm sure you won't mind me writing an article for the locksmiths' journal. You'll get people wanting to come and see it, I should think, Mr Esher. It's a rare treasure.'

When he'd left, Mayne shot an aggrieved glance at the door. 'Pity it isn't evening yet. I could do with a stiff whisky. You think you know your own house and then something like this turns up.'

'Have you any idea where the key might be?' the captain asked.

'None at all. I can't remember ever seeing any keys big enough to fit that lock. I'll set my father on to it. If anyone can find the key and code, it's him. Let's go up and tell him. He'll probably be waiting outside.'

When they got out of the Nissen hut, there was no sign of Reginald Esher but Victor was waiting to see how they'd got on.

'I didn't join you because there didn't seem to be enough room down there,' he said cheerfully.

Mayne wasn't smiling. 'It was quite claustrophobic. My father left in a hurry. He hates small underground spaces. I suppose he's gone back to his books. I'll go and see him later.'

He scowled and exclaimed, 'Hang the time of day! It's nearly lunchtime. Let's have a whisky anyway. I've been saving a bottle for a special occasion and if finding a hidden cellar isn't special, I don't know what is.'

He looked at his companions in an unspoken offer of a drink. They all nodded agreement.

The lieutenant exchanged glances with the captain and went across to the car, whispering something to the two soldiers, who brightened up. He slipped some coins into one's hand and they didn't waste time driving out of the grounds.

'I told them they could spend an hour at the pub and I bought them a half pint each,' he said when he re-joined the others. 'Seems only fair. After all, they did the digging and they've been kept hanging around.'

Francis moved away from the group. 'You lot go ahead and get your drinks. I want to check on Diana. She ought to be waking up soon.'

Victor and Mayne exchanged smiles.

The two soldiers found a small pub in a side street, because the one on the town square looked too posh for ordinary soldiers.

'Half a pint, Jim?' the older one asked.

'The officers won't know whether we have a half or a full pint.'

They both grinned and Jim turned to the barman, waiting patiently for their order. 'Two pints of best, please. If you haven't run out.'

'No. We've just tapped a new barrel. Very nice it is too. I'll bring it across to you. I don't like to hurry my beer.'

They went across to a table and sat down.

'What do you think of that Esherwood place?' Jim asked.

'Must have been nice before the war. Bit run down now.'

'Too much digging involved in this job for my taste. I

thought I'd left digging behind when I joined the military police.'

'Well, we've finished that now.'

'You hope.'

The barman arrived with the beer. 'Couldn't help over-hearing, lads. Are you stationed at the big house? Only we thought the Army had moved out.'

'It has. We're just doing a little job there.' He lifted his pint to his mouth and waited, not drinking till the barman had gone back behind the counter.

'Nosey bugger, that one,' Jim said in a low voice.

And indeed, it seemed as if the barman had nothing else to do, because apart from one trip into the back room, he stood behind the bar polishing glasses. Though he didn't stare at them, they could tell from the way he was holding his head that he was trying to hear what they were saying.

A couple of minutes later another man came in and asked for a pint, chatting in a low voice to the barman. With a nod towards them, he took his beer to the window seat, which was much closer to them.

Although he had a newspaper and opened it to read, something about him said he too was listening to them.

The two soldiers exchanged quick glances and began talking about today's football matches and what it'd be like when sport got back to normal and there weren't so many scratch matches.

When they left the pub and got into the car, Jim saw the man who'd been drinking come out and watch where they went.

'What the hell was going on there?' he asked his companion.

'I don't know, but we should mention it to the lieutenant. There's something not quite right about the fellows in that pub, if you ask me.'

★   ★   ★

Francis tiptoed into the bedroom and sure enough, Diana was staring drowsily round.

'Hello, sleepyhead,' he said softly. 'Want directions to the bathroom?'

'Yes, please.' She got up and hurried after him along the corridor. He pointed out the bathroom and left her to it.

When she came back, he didn't know whether to hold out his arms or not, and she didn't walk across to him but stared, looking nervous.

'What's the matter, darling? What has your father been doing to you?'

'Can I tell you tonight, when we're alone? There's such a lot to talk about and I can't think straight when I'm ravenously hungry. I hardly had anything to eat yesterday.'

'Get dressed and I'll escort you to the kitchen. You can meet the others. Judith can always find food, whatever the time of day. Did you bring our ration books?'

Her face crumpled. 'My mother burned yours.'

'*What?* Why would she do that?'

'Sheer spite. They both seem to hate you and I can't understand why. You don't deserve it, not at all. It made me so angry.'

'Well, it's nice to have you on my side again and I can always get another ration book. That isn't the end of the world.'

'They kept my ration book from me, too.'

'Spite again?'

'Part of keeping me tied to them, I suppose. Look, there are some other things I have to tell you that are far more important than ration books, but I'd rather do that tonight, when we won't be disturbed.'

'All right, darling. Whatever you say.'

'Darling,' she echoed. 'Oh, I've missed you calling me that,

Francis.' She broke off for a moment, then said in a different tone of voice, 'Let me get dressed and we'll go and get a cup of tea. I'm parched.'

She emptied the pillow case on the bed, muttering, 'I'm going to look such a mess. I could only bring what I could carry down the ladder.'

He looked at her in surprise. 'Down the ladder?'

'I had to climb out of my bedroom window because my parents had locked me in. Your Mr Johnson provided men and a ladder.' She sniffed hard but didn't burst into tears as he expected. 'My father threatened to have me drugged and locked away in a mental home if I disobeyed him.'

'Dear heavens, has the man run mad? I knew he could be nasty when someone upset him, but to threaten his own daughter with something like that beggars belief.'

'He frightened me, he looked so furious.'

She went to study herself in the only mirror in the room. Trust her to know where that was, he thought.

'Well, I'll just have to go down looking a mess, because I don't want to faint on you.' As if to back up what she was saying, her stomach gurgled.

She put on the navy blue trousers she'd been wearing yesterday and found a clean if crumpled white blouse in her pillowcase, then dragged on yesterday's cardigan. When she'd brushed her hair and tied it back, she went across to the mirror again, grimaced and spread her hands wide. 'I don't think I've ever looked such a mess.'

'You always look beautiful to me.'

Tears came into her eyes. 'I don't deserve you, Francis.'

'Well, you've got me. We're well and truly married and— What's the matter, darling?'

'I'll tell you tonight. Come on. Feed me before I faint on you.'

She led the way out, moving so quickly it felt as if she

was running away from whatever it was she had to reveal to him.

To distract her, he took her down the main staircase rather than using the back stairs, knowing she'd love the entrance hall.

Sure enough, she stopped on the landing and then again partway down to gaze around. 'It's a beautiful house, or it could be. A lot of things look shabby because of the war. Well, the whole country is shabby.'

'Mayne loves his home.'

'I didn't realise the house was so big. It's quite old, isn't it, and beautiful? Well, it will be beautiful when it's brought up to scratch. Why did they pull out the panelling over there? They did it very clumsily.'

'Some of the people stationed here did it when they were short of firewood, I believe. A big house like this gets very cold in winter.'

'No! They just prised it off the wall and burned it?'

''Fraid so. And they played darts in another area, so the panelling there is full of little holes. They weren't at all careful with the poor old house.'

He took her hand and drew it through his arm, leading her to the back of the hall and into the servants' quarters. He stopped in the kitchen doorway to announce, 'The sleeper has arisen.'

He saw Diana flush and glance quickly round. When she encountered only smiles of welcome, he could feel her relaxing a little.

'I'm glad to be here. Thank you for letting me stay, Mayne and Judith. Nice to meet you, Ros and Victor.'

She'd always had exquisite manners, Francis thought proudly. 'The poor girl is ravenously hungry, Judith.'

'Sit down and I'll get you some food. I made potato scones yesterday and hid the second batch from my son, who is a stomach on wheels. You can start with a couple of those. I'm not the world's best cook, but they're edible at least and we can spare a scrape of butter and jam. I'll warm them up for you. And we have some apples from our own orchard. They're not very pretty, because no one's been looking after the trees, but they taste delicious. It's wonderful to be able to go out and pick them as needed.'

There was so much to tell Diana about Esherwood that they didn't stop talking the whole time she was eating, and afterwards too.

Francis took pity on her after a while, because he could see by the increasingly glassy look in her eyes that she'd been overloaded with information. 'I'd like to take my lovely wife out for a stroll round the grounds now. Or if you need some more shopping, Judith, we could go into town.'

'Victor and Ros got it this morning, but you could leave your ration books at the grocer's.'

'Ah.' After a quick glance at Diana, he decided to tell the truth. 'Her mother burned mine and they've still got hers, so they'll probably burn that, too. They're . . . um, not exactly in favour of us being together. We'll go and apply for temporary ration sheets and new permanent books while we're in town. Won't life be easy when people don't have to count coupons all the time?'

'And when we don't have to queue for everything,' Ros said with deep feeling. 'I'm sick and tired of queuing.'

'And when we can buy any type of food we want,' Judith added. 'I'm sick of trying to make something out of nothing.'

Francis and Diana walked into town, enjoying the mild sunshine. They didn't say much but they held hands. They called in at the police station, where they had to sign up for temporary ration books and put in a claim for new ones.

The sergeant in charge looked at them sternly. 'What exactly happened to the old ones, sir, madam?'

'My in-laws burned mine, I'm told. I left it behind when I came up to Rivenshaw.'

'And my parents kept mine.' Diana sounded nervous. 'They didn't want me to move away, but of course I came to be with my husband.'

'We could fine them for maliciously damaging government property,' he said with a frown.

'Oh, please don't,' she begged. 'The situation between us is bad enough as it is.'

'Families, eh? There are a lot of chaps trying to adjust to living with their families now they've been demobbed. But you'll be all right at the big house, Mrs Brady. Nice place, plenty of room and pleasant people to deal with, all of them.'

A man poked his head round the police station door. 'All right if I bring in the children's orange juice, Sarge?'

'Not if there's a broken bottle in the box. It's amazing how much mess one broken bottle can make.' He saw Diana looking puzzled and said, 'They keep the supplies of orange juice in the back room here because they've nowhere at the clinic to store them safely. There were a few thefts before we arranged this.'

'Oh, goodness. Fancy stealing from children.'

'Some folk will steal anything they can lay their hands on, believe me.' He smiled at her. 'Now, your ration books should come here within four days, Mrs Brady, and those temporary sheets of coupons will see you through the first week.'

Francis took her for a walk round the town centre and it was much more attractive than she'd expected. She'd been too tired to notice anything the night before when she arrived, didn't really remember what the big square was like.

'I know we're going to be happy here,' he said as they made their way to the grocer's shop and joined the queue.

'I hope so.'

But she still had to tell him what her father had done. She was dreading that.

When Francis suggested they should go to bed early, since she was looking tired, Diana nodded. But she felt sick with apprehension as they walked up the stairs.

She sat on the bed. 'No, stay where you are, Francis, so that I can see your face when I tell you.'

'OK.' He leaned against the wall by the door, looking worried.

'And please, please don't get angry with me. I didn't know what my father had done, truly I didn't.'

'Look, I promise I won't get angry with you, but I can't promise the same about your father. Now, stop beating round the bush and tell me straight out what he's done that's upsetting you so much.'

She took a deep breath. 'When he arranged our wedding, he made sure it wasn't done properly so that we weren't legally married. He said he knew our marriage wouldn't last and decided it'd be easier to do that than get me a divorce later. And he—' She broke off at the fury on Francis's face, not daring to say another word or even move till he said something to her.

It seemed a long time before he did anything. She waited, stomach churning, then he moved – but not towards her, across to the window. He stood with his back to her, staring out at the starlit sky, but she could see that his hands were clenched into tight fists by the side of his body.

After a minute or two, he turned to look at her, then shook his head and went back to staring out again. 'Is that why you left their home and came here?'

'Partly.'

'What were the other reasons?'

'I missed you. I didn't want to end our marriage.'

'It took you long enough to discover that.'

'No, it didn't. I realised it almost as soon as I'd left you, but I didn't know what to do to get you back. And you left the village. I knew the name of this house and that the town was Rivenshaw, but you didn't give me an address to write to.'

'Surely I did?'

'No, you didn't. You stayed away and I had hardly any money, so I couldn't come chasing after you. And when you did come back, you didn't stay long. You vanished one night. My father was furious about that, too. If you hadn't given me that train ticket, I don't know what I'd have done.'

'I was warned by someone I trust that your father was planning to have me arrested on some trumped-up charge.'

It was her turn to be silent, then she bowed her head. 'It was probably true, knowing my father.'

'But you could still have written to me. Esherwood is well known in this town.'

'How was I to know that? And how was I to get a reply while I was living with them? Anyway, they went through my bedroom drawers and took away things like writing paper and envelopes. I wouldn't have dared write, even if they hadn't done that. I'd have been terrified of the letter getting into my father's hands. Once I left my bedroom in the mornings, my mother stayed with me every single minute of the day.'

'I find all that hard to believe. They've always spoiled you, not ill-treated you.'

'Because I did as they wished. You've never actually lived with my father so you don't understand what it's like. Even I hadn't noticed how tightly he controls every detail of what his family does, until I went back and saw it all with new eyes.'

'I'm amazed he ever let you leave home during the war.'

'He was furious that he couldn't stop me being called up to do war work.' She sighed, remembering how excited she'd been to get away and yet how bewildering it had been at first, having to make her own decisions.

'Francis, till I moved away, I thought it was normal for a head of the household to be like that. But the other women I worked with talked about their families, and their men weren't so . . . so domineering. Then I met you, and you weren't like that either. You were kind and thoughtful.'

'Your father acts as if he owns you and your mother. I can't treat people like that.'

'I know. And that meant a lot to me, though I didn't show my appreciation well enough. At first I felt almost drunk on freedom, and then you got transferred and my father pulled some strings so that I had to go back to the village.'

'I thought you wanted to.'

'I didn't want to be alone, but I was so glad when you bought us a house. I liked having my own place to live.'

Francis fell silent. He felt sick at the sneaky tricks played on him by the Scammells, and he couldn't help wondering whether his wife – no, she wasn't his wife, it seemed – had inherited any of those characteristics from her parents. He turned to study her.

She was huddled on the bed, her arms clasped round herself as if for comfort, and she looked young and lost, nothing like her sneering, supercilious parents, thank goodness.

'It's been like living in a nightmare lately.'

Her voice was so low, he had to strain to hear what she was saying. One thing surprised him. 'You used to cry when things went wrong, Diana. Why aren't you sobbing now?'

'I cried a lot at first when we were separated. It didn't do much good, though.'

He felt like crying now, whether it did any good or not.

If she wasn't his wife, where did that leave them? He saw her watching him anxiously, her face pale. He tried to explain why he wasn't saying much. 'I'm having trouble coming to terms with it all, Diana. I need time to think. Are you *sure* we're not married?'

'My father said we weren't. He said it with relish, as if he'd done something clever. I suppose we can check, but I don't think he was lying.'

'You keep calling him "my father" not "Daddy". Is there a reason for the change?'

'I'm not a child and the word Daddy seems childish. Also, I don't feel friendly towards him any more. I don't think I ever shall again. He shouldn't have interfered in our marriage. That was so wrong. I don't want to be free of you, Francis. I don't.'

He thought she was telling the truth but he didn't know how he felt about spending his life with *that man's* daughter. And he didn't know if the changes he sensed in her were permanent. 'I'll have to think about this before I can decide what to do.'

'The things I said and did before—' She broke off then continued in a rush, 'My parents told me how to make you toe the line. I didn't want to get rid of you, I just wanted to stay in the village where I knew people, so I did as they suggested. They said I'd be lonely, that I wouldn't fit in here. I was frightened of that. I was lonely at first when I started doing war work, you see, and I didn't fit in till I met you. Then you went away and it was lonely again.'

'Tell me what you want to do about our situation – what *you* want, not your parents.'

She stared at him with sheer terror on her face now. 'I want us to stay together, of course I do. I thought we could just, you know, get married somewhere quietly. Properly married this time.'

'But you left me.'

'My mother said you were besotted with me and that it would make you come back to stay. I felt desperate not to lose you.'

'Your mother was wrong. As I told you several times, I didn't enjoy living in the village after my parents died. There were too many memories, and the sight of the bare land where their garage had been upset me every time I saw it. But I loved you, so I bought the house while the war was on, because you needed someone to turn to while I was away.'

'You were away a lot and you never said what you were doing.'

'I wasn't allowed to. I'm still not allowed to tell anyone. I've signed the Official Secrets Act. I could get put in prison for revealing what we were doing.'

'Goodness. It must have been very important work. I didn't realise.'

'The project was important, but I was only one of many working there.'

After a moment, he continued, 'I'm not sure you'll be able to settle in with me here even if we do get married properly. No, I'm not at all sure of that. Quite frankly, you've been spoiled and you aren't used to working hard. Everyone here is prepared to do whatever it takes for our company to succeed. I've never met such hard workers.'

'I don't know what else I can say or do to convince you, but I will try very hard, Francis, I promise.'

'Good. And I think we should carry on as normal for the time being, not tell anyone.'

'Pretend we're still married, you mean?'

'Yes. For your own sake, you should see how you fit in here before we do anything to rectify matters. They're decent people and this is the sort of life I want to lead from now on: working with others, enjoying their company, not being suspicious of the whole world. Can you try it?'

'Yes. Oh, yes, I want to very much.'

He sat down on a chair, still keeping away from her, because if he sat on the bed with her and touched her, they'd end up making love. They had no problems in that area, thank goodness. It was one of the things that gave him hope for their future together. 'I don't want to tell the others, not yet anyway. Only, I'm not sharing a bed with you. The last thing we want is for you to get pregnant and you know what we're like in bed.'

She blushed and stared down at her own tightly clasped hands.

'I'll bring in another bed, say I'm sleeping badly and disturbing you.'

'Please don't do that.'

He ignored her whispered plea. 'I have to. I can't rush into a decision, Diana. This is too important. Our whole lives depend on what we do now.'

'But—' She broke off.

'What?'

'Nothing.'

'I shall think about it and you must too. Decide what you really want. In the meantime, can you muck in and help around the house, like the other women do?'

'Yes. Even if I have to mop floors.'

That made him smile briefly. Trust her to worry about that. 'I don't think you'll need to do any mopping. A cleaning lady comes in for the rough work. Mayne insists on that. He doesn't want Judith scrubbing floors, either. But we're valuing goods from the house, and there are ornaments and antique bits and pieces to wash or dust carefully. I'm sure you could do that.'

'I think I'd like that. I'll do whatever you say, Francis. Really I will.'

'Because you're afraid to be on your own if we don't stay together?'

'No. Whether you believe me or not, because I want us to be together. I'll do it because I love you.'

He nearly gave in and cuddled her then, but managed to restrain himself. This had to be done carefully. 'Give me time, Diana. Give *us* time as a couple, time without anyone interfering between us.'

She nodded, but looked sad.

He went to get one of the spare mattresses from the pile at the end of the landing and some bedding from the huge linen cupboard, then slept on that makeshift bed. It was hard and narrow, and he slept badly. And wished desperately that he was sleeping with her.

He thought Diana was awake quite a bit during the night but he didn't speak to her. Couldn't think what to say.

This was the last thing he'd expected from her return. He'd been so happy to see her, sure she'd come back to him in every way. The more fool he! The Scammells' machinations were still coming between them. Would he ever be free of them?

It still upset him that she had left him once. He wanted a wife who'd stick to him through thick and thin, have children, make love and laughter together over the years. As his parents had done.

But he still wanted that wife to be his lovely Diana. Could she change enough for their marriage to work?

19

Neither Daniel nor his aunt felt like going to church, but as it was fine, if chilly, he did go out for a brisk walk. When he came back, he found his aunt sitting in the kitchen looking sad. She hadn't even heard him come in and jumped in shock when he spoke.

'Something wrong?'

'What? Oh, just the thought of leaving. I've lived in this house for over thirty years. Still, it's going to a nice young couple. I do take comfort from that. They're moving in this afternoon as lodgers.' She smiled. 'That young man is very eager to get away from his mother-in-law.'

'Some people are difficult to live with.' Daniel waggled one finger at her in mock severity. 'But no giving these lodgers any of your meat or cheese rations. I know how generous you can be, because you've tried to feed me more than my share several times.'

She patted his cheek. 'I have to learn to be very careful from now on, don't I? I have to make my money spin out. I've been thinking about that as well. I shall be earning a little from taking in lodgers. Do you know, I've never had to earn money before. Egan took care of all that and I was quite young when we married, not very experienced at anything.'

'I can help you with money, Auntie. The trick is to work out what amount of money you've got each week, allocate it to each expense and try to break even or, if you can, save a few pennies.'

'I'll do my best. I'm not an extravagant person and I have managed my housekeeping for years. I'm sorry you've had to pay off Egan's debts though, Francis dear, especially as it's taken some of the money you were saving to invest in your building company. He never said a word to me about there being money trouble. I wish he had. I could have been much more frugal about what I bought.'

'He loved you, wanted to protect you. Anyway, I'll get my money back when your house sale goes through. You should have enough left to buy a little house and something to spare. And I can afford to make you a small allowance.' He didn't intend to let his aunt go short.

'I don't want to take your money. I'm sure I can manage to look after lodgers. It'll be company, too. I've been a bit lonely since Egan died.'

'Well, we'll see.'

She gave him one of her stubborn looks. 'We will indeed see. I'm only in my fifties, not ready for the scrap heap yet. There will be something I can do to earn money, but I very much want a house of my own, even if it's very small. I don't want to *be* a lodger myself.'

'We'll make sure you aren't, then.'

'Thank you. Now, you told me it was going to take weeks to sort out the legalities of the house sale and I know you need to get back.'

'We might leave your lodgers here and both take off for Rivenshaw. You're not going to be feeding them, after all. What do you think? Mayne says we can stay at the big house.'

'That's very kind of him, but I'd rather wait, if you don't mind. Now that I've taken in lodgers, I don't like to leave my furniture and personal possessions in someone else's charge. Anyway, I have to clear the house out, don't I? Get rid of Egan's things, sell some of the furniture.'

He saw her lips wobble and how she pressed them together and took a deep breath before continuing. 'I'll help you with that. You've been putting it off because it'll be painful, haven't you?'

She nodded. 'But I've already cleared out the rooms I'm giving to my lodgers, one for their bedroom, the other bedroom to use as a sitting room. You could help me decide about the furniture then go back and leave me to see to the smaller things. We'll know by then what my lodgers are like.'

'I'm staying.'

She ignored that. 'You have your work to do, dear. And you need to find me a home. I trust you to do that. Only, will you write and tell me how much of the furniture we can fit into it? Then I shall sell the rest. Some of it's antique and though it's not hugely valuable, it's good quality and will bring in some worthwhile money, I think. See, I'm beginning to think more practically already.'

'Clever Auntie!' He patted her mockingly on the head and made her smile.

'If you still want us to live together, that'd be lovely. But you may meet a nice girl and get married. I wouldn't get in the way of that. I could help with your children later, though. I love children.'

He held out his hands, palms towards her in a stop this sign. 'That's the last thing I'm thinking about at the moment, re-marrying. I've only just got rid of Ada.'

'I never thought she was right for you. You needed someone gentler, because you're a gentle sort of person, however much you try to hide that. I do hope you can find us somewhere to live in Rivenshaw, though. It isn't easy these days, with all the houses that got destroyed by bombs. Look how that couple jumped in to buy this place.'

He put on a mock Irish accent. 'Well, me old darlin', I'll be after stayin' here with you. We'll go through this house together, so we will, and I'll be helping you sell things.'

'You don't do a very good Irish accent, for all your Irish blood. Are you sure you can stay?'

'Yes.' He saw her sag in relief and knew he'd taken the right decision. She was putting a brave front on it, but she was having to do so many things she had never done before.

He was relieved that she was coping better than he'd expected, but she still needed him.

When Daniel rang Mayne that evening to tell him that he couldn't come back yet and explained why, his friend seemed not to care as much as he'd expected, and indeed, Mayne sounded rather depressed.

'Something's up. Tell me.' Daniel listened to the tale of the corpse, the military police and the secret cellar in amazement. 'To think I'm missing all the fun.'

'Some might call it fun. I think we're going to have more trouble at Esherwood before this is all settled and we can get on with things. If these fellows have committed murder once, it must have been because they thought there was something valuable behind that door. Though they'd also dumped boxes of valuables from the house in the Nissen hut.'

'I hate looters.'

'So do I. The thing is, if they're local, it'll be easy for them to keep an eye on Esherwood and make a sudden raid if we show any weakness. I don't think they'll hesitate to kill again, because if they're captured they'll be sentenced to death and hanged. They'll have nothing to lose.'

He sighed. 'We taught all sorts of men to fight and kill, so it's not surprising that some of them will use those skills for the wrong purpose now that the war is over.'

'Surely they won't come back with you in residence?'

'They've come back once already, and it was a well-planned operation.'

'Damn!'

'They've probably been making plans for a while, just as we four did. I've heard a few men say they'd risked their lives for a miserably low wage, so they deserved what they could get afterwards. And they didn't care what they had to do to get it.'

'Not at the special unit, surely!' Daniel protested.

'No. The people there were as fine a bunch as you could ever meet, both the men and the women. Pity we all had to sign the Official Secrets Act. The country will never know what's owed to the SOE and its various units for the way they planned the final stages and pulled the wool over the Nazis' eyes about where we were going to land.'

'If things are so chancy, do you need me to be there to help protect the big house?'

'No. We've got several people helping guard Esherwood now. Victor's back to stay, Francis is here and I think he'll be staying now his wife's joined him. The military wallahs are going to set a trap for the murderers, so with a bit of luck they'll pounce and our troubles will be over. But just in case, I've pulled out my trusty old gun.'

Daniel's voice grew harsh. 'Who'd think you'd need to carry a gun in England now the war's over?'

'I did. Violence doesn't evaporate overnight. Quite a few chaps made sure they had a gun of their own for afterwards, legally or illegally. Those who went to France and Germany found it easy to buy them on the side. Mine's legal.'

'I didn't do that. I hate guns. I never want to touch one again.'

Mayne knew that – not that Daniel hadn't done what was necessary during the war, but since it ended, he'd been struggling to find peace in himself because of what he'd seen and done.

'Francis feels the same as you, but I want to be able to protect myself and my family. Victor has a gun tucked away, too. Anyway, that's beside the point. As a result of finding the corpse and fiddling around with filling in forms for the council, the building work isn't going to get started as quickly at Esherwood as we'd hoped, so you don't need to worry about rushing back. Stay and help your aunt, and bring her with you when you come back. She can stay here till she finds somewhere of her own.'

'Are you sure?'

'Yes. We've plenty of room.'

'Thanks.'

'Mind you, it wouldn't hurt to have some designs worked out for when we do build houses on that useless land at the rear. You could be working on that. We'll need house plans sooner or later, maybe even for our own houses after we move out of the big house, though the government limitations on the size of houses that can be built will stop us doing anything more than smallish places.'

'And we could put up some prefabs quite quickly,' Daniel said. 'I bet the council won't hold you up on that. For the proper houses, I can do designs where more rooms can be added once it's permitted. It'd be interesting to work out.'

'Good idea. I'll leave that to you.'

Daniel was thoughtful as he put down the phone. In one sense he was glad to keep his gentle aunt away from the possible violence at Esherwood; in another, he wanted to be there, to help his friends, because all their future plans were based on the Esher Building Company.

He was still having nightmares, though. His aunt said he cried out in his sleep sometimes.

Would the marks of war ever leave him?

Early next morning Mayne walked round the house, feeling restless. He ended up helping Judith. Her children were cleaning their bedrooms and didn't usually help with the cooking. They took care of the clearing up.

She sighed as she put a huge blackened saucepan on the stove. 'I'm going to cook another stew for tea. I know you're all sick of them – well, I am too – but at least I can leave this pan on top of the stove to simmer while I get on with cleaning the items that have been valued. Pity Ray wanted to go to church today. I'd rather have continued working. I want to get this job over, so that we have a better idea of where we stand financially.'

She began to rinse the bones for stock under the tap.

'Has anyone complained about your cooking?' he asked idly.

She chuckled. 'Of course not. No one else wants to take over the job. The children just eat what's put in front of them because they've never had much choice. Ros and Victor help where they can, but she's been altering clothes for Betty, who's having a growth spell.'

She poured some water over the bones in the saucepan. 'As for Francis, he's like the kids: eats what you put in front of him and says thank you with that lovely smile of his. He's still sad underneath it, isn't he? I wonder . . . do you think he's certain about his marriage? She doesn't look all that happy, either.'

'I don't think those two should have got married in the first place. They're from such different backgrounds socially.'

'So are we and yet we seem to get on all right.'

'Ah, but you're a very special woman.'

'Maybe there's more to Diana than meets the eye, as well. Don't be too quick to judge her.'

He plonked a quick kiss on her cheek. 'Never mind her. How about I help you with the cooking and washing the ornaments today? I'm at a bit of a loose end, waiting for those damned military police to come back tomorrow. I can't seem to settle to anything. Anyway, you must be sick to death of peeling potatoes. I learned to peel them and chop vegetables when I was first in the Army – mountains of them every day – so let me take that chore off your hands for once.'

'Lovely. I accept.' She immediately dumped several pounds of potatoes in front of him.

'Are we feeding an army?' he joked.

'Our group is certainly growing bigger. Now, wash the dried earth off them first then they won't make such a mess.' She got out an old enamel washing-up bowl for him to put the peel into.

'It's good that we can throw the peelings into the pig bin,' she went on. 'I always feel guilty not eating the skin, as the Ministry of Food wants people to do. It's all right when you cook a potato in its jacket, but I don't like bits of potato skin floating around stews. Still, that farmer will take any food scraps we can give him to boil up for his pigs.'

As her husband started to prove his expertise, she began to cut up the meat, not that there was much meat, only about an ounce per person, as well as what she could pick off the bones after they were cooked. But at least the bones plus a few Oxo cubes would give them a tasty stock as basis for the stew, and they'd been able to buy onions most of the time recently, unlike during the war.

When she'd finished dealing with the meat, she added it to the bone mixture and began to clear the table. She picked up the heel of bread remaining from the morning's two break-fast loaves and grimaced at it. 'The children are complaining about the British loaf and I have trouble cutting thin enough slices to make the sandwiches because it crumbles. I do wish the government hadn't ordered that bread can't be sold till it's a day old. Such a stupid rule!'

'They think people will eat less that way, because fresh bread tastes so much nicer.'

'Well, it wouldn't hurt to let people have something that tastes nice. Not that the taste of the bread worries my Ben. And Betty has a good appetite, too.'

Mayne put his arms round her to stop her moving away. 'Is it getting you down, supervising the catering and everything else?'

'A bit,' she admitted. 'I've never had to cook for a lot of people before and cooking isn't my favourite job.'

He pulled her close, kissed her and then stood cuddling her for a long, quiet moment.

'You'd think I'd be glad to have enough to eat every day,' she murmured, 'but I have to admit that I enjoy organising the office far more than running a big house and doing the menial chores. Now that I've had a taste of working with my brain, I'm spoiled as a housewife.'

'Perhaps Diana will be able to take some of the cooking off your shoulders.'

She gave him an incredulous look. 'Did you see her soft, white hands? I doubt she's done any dirty chores in her life.'

'Well, she'll have to muck in here. I'm sure Francis will make sure she does.'

When Diana woke up, she couldn't think where she was for a moment or two, then it all came rushing back to her.

She looked towards the mattress where Francis had spent the night and saw that he was still asleep. It was rare for him to sleep so late but she'd heard him tossing and turning in the darkness. Well, she'd found it hard to get to sleep, too, and had kept waking up to worry about her future.

He opened his eyes suddenly, looked across at her and

smiled. Then he remembered what she'd told him. She could tell the exact moment that happened, because the smile faded and a scowl took its place.

He picked up his wrist watch from the floor beside his mattress and looked at it. 'We're a bit late getting up.'

'Will they mind?'

'No, of course not. They trust me to pull my weight.'

'I'll try not to be a burden.'

'That'd be good. Come on. I'll wait for you and we'll go down to breakfast together.' This time his smile was genuine. 'You go to the bathroom first. You always take a lot longer than me to get ready in the mornings.'

'Thank you.'

'For what?'

'Understanding that I'm nervous of going down on my own.'

'That's all right. You're bound to feel strange at first.'

'And it won't take me long to get ready. I couldn't bring many clothes, so I'll have to wear my trousers and the same blouse again. I must see if there's a clothing exchange. Oh, dear! I never thought I'd be wearing second-hand clothes!'

As soon as the words left her mouth, she wished she hadn't said that, but he didn't comment. Indeed he seemed to think carefully about everything he said to her. After last night's revelations, they sounded like two polite strangers talking to one another.

When they were ready, she had to ask, 'Did you . . . um, come to any decision last night? About us. I know you didn't sleep well. I didn't either.'

'Only what I said before: I don't want to tell the others what's wrong and I want time to think about it.'

'Would they throw me out if they knew we weren't married? I-I've nowhere else to go and not much money.'

He looked at her in shock. 'Of course they wouldn't throw

you out. Neither would I. We're not like your father. Anyway, Judith will understand your position better than most. She's had a difficult life.'

'You can see how much she and Mayne love one another,' Diana said wistfully. 'People are more likely to be kind to someone they've known for years, but they don't know me at all. I feel such an outsider. And Victor and Ros seem to be just as loving as Mayne and Judith.'

'You'll settle in if you give it a chance. Friendships aren't made overnight. You'll soon feel at ease with them all, I'm sure. But they'll expect you to pull your weight.'

She knew he was warning her about something important and she vowed not to let him down. 'I'll try to help with the dirty work, but I don't know how to do some jobs.'

Francis knew that promise was a big thing for her. Even as she spoke, she glanced down regretfully at her soft pink hands and that amused him. She hadn't changed completely, no one could. Her vanity was an integral part of her, probably because she'd always been recognised as a beauty. Her obsession with her appearance might irritate him sometimes but he felt proud when people admired his lovely wife.

She looked so forlorn he gave in to the temptation to pull her towards him for a quick hug. Only it wasn't all that quick. She clutched him tightly and once again he heard her gulping as she fought back tears.

Well, he'd been fighting tears in bed last night because his whole world seemed to have crumbled around him. What's more, he was quite sure the Scammells would still try to stop him and Diana staying together. What a mess this was! Damn them. They didn't care who they trampled on, even their own daughter, as long as they maintained their elevated social position. People like them had had to accept different ways of doing things during the war. Did they think things would return to what they had been? He was quite sure they wouldn't.

But he intended to do things properly this time with Diana. No rushing blindly into a re-marriage. They must both be certain being together was what they wanted for the rest of their lives.

When Diana and Francis went downstairs they found everyone else had eaten and gone about their business. She'd expected disapproving glances, but got only welcoming smiles from Judith and Mayne, who were cooking together, chatting quietly.

Francis got their food ready, which apparently everyone did for themselves. He showed her where things were kept and she nodded. She'd have no trouble remembering such details. Keeping things tidy and in their place was one thing she was good at, because it had been drilled into her from earliest childhood that her father wouldn't tolerate a messy house.

She stole a glance at Mayne, who was helping Judith chop vegetables for a stew. It seemed amazing to see a man doing such things, and even enjoying them.

Once they'd finished eating, Francis collected their plates and took them into the scullery, leaving Diana to follow with the teacups. Well, she didn't need nudging to clear the dirty things away, thank you very much.

'We'll wash up the breakfast things, shall we, Judith?' he called.

'That'd be lovely. The kids are doing their bedrooms.' She turned to Diana. 'I insist on a good turn-out on Sundays.'

After Francis had shown Diana where to find things, she gave him a little push. 'This is one job I can do on my own. Leave it to me. What will you be working on this morning? Or are you taking time off because it's a Sunday?'

'No. I need to make this house safer electrically.'

'Shall I come and find you when I've finished? Perhaps I can help you.'

'I doubt it. It needs a specialist eye. It's a bigger job than I'd expected, trying to work out how the various electrical systems were put in, because they were done piecemeal. I have to make a diagram showing where all the wires run and where the systems are linked. That means clambering all over the place.'

'Do be careful!'

'I will. The trouble is they set up and then extended the hospital a couple of times, so the wiring was done so haphazardly. It's a wonder the place hasn't burned down! I've found several places where the wires get hot if you try to plug anything in.'

He shuddered at that, then lowered his voice. 'When you've finished in here, it'd be better to ask Judith what you can do to help her.'

'Fine. I have understood that we all muck in. You've said it several times and I'm not absolutely stupid.'

'Only where your parents are concerned.'

She breathed deeply and didn't answer back and after a moment he went out without another word.

After washing the dishes carefully, she dried them and stacked them on a table, not sure where they were stored because they were such a mixture of types of crockery. Gathering her courage together, she went into the kitchen to find Judith. Mayne wasn't there any longer and it looked as if the stew had been started. There were bowls of vegetables waiting to be added later.

'It must be hard work cooking for so many.'

'It is. And tedious.'

'I'm not a very good cook, and I've never cooked for a lot of people, so if I can help in any way, it'd be better if you told me straight out what needs doing rather than expecting me to guess.'

'All right.'

'I washed and dried the breakfast dishes but I don't know where they go, so I couldn't put them away.'

Judith gave the stew a quick stir, put a lid on the pan and wiped her hands on a towel. She went into the scullery to see several neat piles of dishes on the scrubbed wooden table. 'It's still a bit impromptu. I keep meaning to organise the crockery in here. When we moved back in after the Army left, the place was in chaos so we just gathered things together as we found them and dumped them where they were needed.'

'I could organise how the crockery is stored if you like. I enjoy doing things like that. I'll . . . do my best with the other jobs, but please be patient with me at first.'

Judith studied her for so long, Diana was beginning to wonder if she had a smut on her nose, and what her companion said surprised her.

'You shouldn't be nervous of me, Diana, or of anyone here. We work as a team. Like the Three Musketeers: all for one, one for all. As long as you're doing your best to share the various jobs, no one will take umbrage if you get something wrong.'

Judith couldn't help noticing Diana's crumpled blouse. 'There's something we probably need to do before you sort out the scullery. I carried your pillow case up when you arrived and I couldn't help noticing that you hadn't been able to bring many clothes with you.'

'I had to pack in a hurry and climb down a ladder with my bag of clothes. And it was night.'

'That must have been scary.'

'It was.' She shuddered at the memory of how afraid she'd felt of her father catching her.

'Well, there are a lot of big trunks in the attic with old clothes stored in them. I don't think the Eshers ever threw anything away. Some clothes are made of lovely materials and hardly worn; some are worn out and you have to wonder why they bothered to keep them. We're gathering them together for rags when we find them. How about I take you up and show you the trunks? You may find some things you can use. Francis said you were good at sewing. I've just got time before I do a job in the office for Mayne.'

'That'd be wonderful. I was feeling a bit desperate about what to wear. I don't usually wear trousers all the time, but I only have one skirt with me.'

'You look good in trousers. You'd probably look good in anything, though. I'm jealous.'

But her smile said she was teasing and Diana relaxed a bit more.

'Come on. I'll show you that part of the attic and leave you to go through the trunks on your own. Just take what you need for now, then you can get more things later.'

Was there a hidden warning in that not to be greedy? Diana wondered. Or didn't they expect her to stay very long?

She forgot about everything else when Judith started opening trunks. Some of the clothes were absolutely gorgeous.

'You seem to know about clothes. Was Francis right about you and sewing?' Judith asked. 'You'll need to alter most things.'

'I'm pretty good with a needle, if I say so myself. I enjoy sewing.'

'I hate it, though I've been trying to learn to do it better. We usually have to ask our friend Helen to help us fit things when we get clothes from here. Look, I've had a thought: there's always mending to be done and I could do with some help with clothes for myself and the kids. That'd be far more use than tidying the crockery. Kitty, my oldest, has slowed down in her growing, but Ben seems to be shooting up quickly. I'm for ever having to alter his clothes, or find him bigger ones.'

Her voice was full of pride and love. Diana envied the children having such a loving mother.

When she was on her own in the attic, she took her time, working carefully through the trunks and reorganising some of the clothes, so that the same things were together. She didn't think they'd mind and it was instinctive to her to set things in order.

She decided that she would ask Judith to check what she was taking before she did any alterations. Oh, but this was so interesting!

And Judith had been friendly. That meant more than the clothes, even.

If only Francis would still want to be married to her, she thought life might not be nearly as bad here as her parents had predicted.

Why hadn't she come here to see it before deciding? She had been so stupid!

A little later Diana turned round and saw Francis standing in the doorway, watching her.

'Find anything?'

'Yes. Judith's been very kind. She realised I'd need clothes quite quickly and brought me up here. And from now on I'm going to help her with the sewing and mending. She doesn't enjoy it and I like sewing.'

'That's good. She sent me up to tell you to take a break and come down for a cup of tea.'

Diana stood up. 'Ooh, yes. I'm a bit stiff after crouching over these trunks.'

'Well, at least we haven't put you off Esherwood so far,' he said as they walked down.

She didn't know whether he was teasing her or not, so made a non-committal noise.

He hadn't kissed her since she told him about their marriage. She wished he would.

She hoped her father would leave them alone from now on. Surely he wouldn't pursue her?

If he did, it'd be out of spite, and that thought was rather frightening.

20

On the Monday morning, the military police contingent returned to Esherwood. The two officers asked to speak to Mayne privately, but he insisted on Judith joining them. 'I don't have any secrets from my wife. She's a full partner in the business.'

'*Really?* Very well, then.'

But the captain clearly wasn't pleased to include her and he didn't address her directly. Probably not used to dealing with women as equals, Mayne decided.

Once they'd all sat down, the captain said, 'We intend to find the people who caused the trouble here and see that they pay the full penalty of the law.'

'I agree.'

'We can work out the details together but I'll start off by saying I feel very strongly that we should tempt them out into the open and then nab them.'

'How to do that is a bit of a stumbling block when we don't have a clue who they are,' Mayne pointed out.

'Exactly. So we must set baits to our trap. I suggest we let it be known in the town that we've managed to open the door to the secret cellar and have found some valuable antiques.'

Mayne felt this was all too vague. 'We haven't a clue who these people are. How can we get word out without arousing their suspicions that this is a trap? We can hardly announce it in the town square. After all, they already know how hard it is to open that locked door.'

'We may have had a bit of luck. My two men went out for a beer on Saturday lunchtime while we were enjoying your excellent whisky. They said the man running the pub was asking questions and later another man came in and sat near them. He seemed to be trying to eavesdrop on their conversation.'

'The public house in Market Square?'

'No, some smaller pub in a side street – The Black Horse, it was called.'

'Oh, that place. A lot of riff-raff drink there.'

'My chaps felt suspicious, especially when the second fellow came out to watch them get into the car.' He gave Mayne a smug look. 'We don't encourage stupid people to join the military police.'

'I was thinking about sending the two of them down to the pub again this lunchtime and telling them to speak rather more loudly than last time. They could talk about us finding some treasures in the cellar and handing them over to you, and pretend we've had word from headquarters that they've given up on identifying the corpse. This afternoon we four will drive away in style, as if our job is completed.'

Mayne was amazed. 'You think one of the gang is from The Black Horse in Rivenshaw?'

'Could be. The men there were certainly interested in what my chaps were saying. It's surely worth a try.'

'Well . . . I suppose so.'

'I can't see them trying to break into the hut and get to the cellar during daylight hours, so my men and I will return by that back road after dark. It'll be interesting to see who picks up the bait.'

If anyone, Mayne thought but he didn't say that. 'Is this sort of thing part of your remit?'

'Of course it is. The dead man was a soldier and it's our job to catch the person or persons who killed him. And they did it in wartime, too. That is unconscionable. We have powers of arrest for military crimes. Who else is there to do it? Let's face it, your local bobby is a good man but too old to be of much use in a fight.'

Mayne didn't think this idea had much chance of working because it depended too much on chance. And he didn't like his companion's slightly scornful attitude towards himself and his friends, as if he felt only the MPs could solve this crime.

'How about I talk about the supposed treasure as well when I go to the shop?' Judith suggested. 'I could be chatting to one of the other wives, Ros perhaps. Or Diana. Yes, Diana would be best. She's a newcomer and could be asking me questions. If the murderers really do live in Rivenshaw, then someone in their families will have to do their shopping locally, like everyone else. Once I mention the secret cellar and finding treasure, Mrs Wallis will talk about it to her customers. She's an inveterate gossip.'

'You think wives will know what these men are doing?' the captain asked doubtfully.

'It'd be a very dopey wife who didn't know her husband was up to something, whether he'd told her or she'd just noticed things, even if she didn't know exactly what it was. Wives see more than most men realise.'

The captain looked at her with slightly more respect. 'It's quite a good idea, actually. Spread the word, what?'

Mayne stifled his urge to criticise this plan. Apart from the fact that he didn't think it'd be that easy to find and trap the men, he didn't want Judith involved in anything dangerous. He'd have a talk to her later and put a stop to her playing any part in this.

No doubt Victor and Francis would feel the same about their wives.

But they'd all have to be on their guard to protect Esherwood and the people who lived there.

'I don't think the captain's plan is going to work,' Mayne said to his wife immediately they were alone.

Judith looked at him in surprise. 'Then why didn't you say something when we were discussing it with him? Or suggest doing something else?'

'If I learned one thing in the Army, it was that you can never tell MPs anything. They're always sure they know better than anyone else. The murderers may have given up and moved to the other end of the country after their last attempt, for all we know. This is a town, not a small village. It's like finding a needle in a haystack, trying to catch that gang.'

'Well, I'll feel better if I at least try. It's not like you to give up, Mayne.'

'I'm not giving up but I don't like you getting involved.'

'You invited me to join you to discuss it.'

'I wish I hadn't now.'

She shook her head. 'Well you did and I'm not in favour of giving up. I've told the captain I'll gossip in the shop about the treasures we've found and I'm not letting him down. If you're right, it won't matter one way or the other what I say in public; if these men are still around and we manage to catch them, I shall sleep more soundly at night for knowing they've been locked away.'

'And if you get involved, I shall sleep less soundly until they're caught, *if* they're caught, because I'll be worrying about you.'

'What can happen to me if I walk into town with Diana?' She got up and moved towards the door. 'I'll go and find her now and ask her to come with me to the shop.'

'Please don't.'

'Mayne, I'm not going to act like a protected doll. *I* think this is the right thing to do. I bet if I wasn't involved, you'd be trying a lot harder to catch them.'

He flung his arms wide and muttered under his breath about 'stubborn women' as he watched her walk away. He loved his wife, but had found out how stubborn she could be. Once she had an idea fixed in her mind, there was no changing her.

The trouble was, she was right. It was mainly her safety that was making him hesitate to fall in with the captain's plans.

And Francis would be worried about Diana's safety, he'd guess.

Judith found Diana sitting in the small breakfast parlour they rarely used, which had been someone's office during the hospital days. It looked bare and uncomfortable, but had good light, with a small table and chairs near the window. Diana had some sewing in her lap – the skirt from the attic that she was altering for herself – but she was staring into space, lost in thought, and didn't even notice that someone had come in.

'Are you all right?'

'What? Oh, it's you, Judith. I was just thinking about something.'

'Tell me to mind my own business, but is something wrong between you and Francis? You both look so sad.'

Diana hesitated, then nodded. 'There is a problem. But I can't talk about it. Francis wants us to . . . um, sort it out privately.'

'All right. But if you ever need a friendly ear, I'm available. I wouldn't even tell Mayne, if you didn't want me to.'

'You're so kind. Thank you. Did you want something?'

'Yes. Those MPs are going to set a trap for the murderers,

and I've agreed to do some careless talking in the shop. I thought you might like to help me. You could ask me questions since you're a newcomer and I could answer them. We could speak a little too loudly perhaps. What do you think?'

Diana put down her mending at once. 'I'm happy to help in any way possible. And I wouldn't mind a walk into town. I've been sewing for ages. I wish I had my sewing machine here.'

'Oh dear, I wasn't thinking clearly. I've got a second-hand one. It's old-fashioned but it works.'

Diana brightened. 'I can be trusted with it, I promise you.'

'I'll find it for you later. About this trap we're setting, I'd better warn you that Mayne doesn't think we women should get involved because it might be dangerous.' Her voice was scornful. 'Your Francis might feel the same.'

'He probably will but I'd still like to help.'

But when Diana was getting ready to go out, trying to smarten up her appearance, Francis came to see her, objecting to her joining in, just as Judith had predicted.

'I'm doing it, whatever you say,' Diana told him. 'She asked me to help and I said I would, and I'm not going back on my word. I have to show her she can depend on me.'

'I forbid you to do it.'

She drew herself up to her full five foot four inches. 'You can't forbid me to do anything.'

'I'm your husband, so I damned well can, and— Oh!'

She realised he'd suddenly remembered that they weren't married. Was that a good sign?

Francis looked at her sadly. '*Please*, Diana. Don't get involved. These people have already murdered one person. They were seen here only a few nights ago with guns. I don't want you getting hurt.'

She shook her head and repeated, 'I'm *not* letting Judith down. She's been kind to me. She bothers to talk to me.

Ros is pleasant enough but she doesn't make the effort to listen to me. I want to fit in, Francis. I *need* them to trust me. Especially Judith. She's a sort of, well, leader of the women.'

He sighed, then said, 'Be careful. I don't want to lose you.'

Which cheered her up.

Leonard Scammell had been furiously angry ever since his daughter ran away. When he tried to find out who had helped her, so that he could teach them not to interfere in his affairs, not to mention forcing them to reveal where she'd gone so that he could fetch her back, he ran into a brick wall.

His prime suspect, Johnson the upstart builder, had to be ruled out because he'd been ill the night of the escape.

His chief clerk brought Johnson's maid to see him by the back entrance to the office. She was happy to be bribed to talk about whether her employer had gone out that night or not, but as she lived in at the Johnsons', she was utterly certain her employer hadn't left the house.

'He was very ill, Mr Scammell, in and out of the bathroom all night, if you know what I mean. I was up half the night, fetching him hot water bottles, and drinks of boiled water, he was so uncomfortable, poor man. And he didn't go to work the next morning, either. Which isn't like him.'

Scammell gave her the promised pound note and dismissed her with a wave of the hand and an order not to tell anyone she'd been talking to him.

She waved the pound note at him and nodded.

'Who else could have helped Diana?' Leonard asked his wife that evening. 'You must know the women she associates with in the village.'

'She doesn't have any real friends here these days. Her two best friends got married and moved away during the war and it's been hard to keep up with people who don't live nearby because of the difficulties of travel.'

'That's what's wrong with this country, too many people moving around, getting ideas above their station,' he raged. 'I was glad when Francis was posted to that special unit and Diana came back on her own. I just wish she'd come to live with us then. I could have kept a better eye on her, started her thinking properly about that oaf she married. Why did he have to buy a house at the other end of the village?'

'It's a nice little house. She and I had a lovely time sorting the furnishings out. It's very hard setting up a home in wartime with hardly any new furniture for sale. You have to hunt the second hand shops and markets.'

'Well, I'm not having *my* daughter disobeying me like this and I *will* find out who helped her.'

'Is it worth it now?'

'Yes, it damned well is.'

A little later he came into the kitchen, where Christine was preparing supper. 'I had a thought. What about that woman from the slums, the one Diana was helping? Could she have helped her escape?'

'I don't see how Diana could have even contacted her. I didn't let our daughter out of my sight, just as you told me, and then we locked her in her bedroom.'

'Well, someone must have contacted her and arranged to help. What's the slum woman's name and where does she live? I'll send my chief clerk to question her first thing tomorrow.'

After running through the conversation with her daughter in her mind, Christine managed to remember the woman's first name. 'Annie!' she said triumphantly. 'And she has an invalid husband. They live on Waterside Brow, but I don't know their surname or their exact address because Diana didn't mention those to me.'

'That'll be enough for my chief clerk to find her.'

When he'd gone, she sighed and sat worrying for a while, but there was nothing she could do to change his mind, she knew from experience.

The next day at work Leonard summoned his chief clerk and told his secretary they were not to be disturbed. Babson was a resourceful man who had helped his employer in many ways over the years and who wasn't too nice to do whatever was necessary, as long as he was well paid for the extra tasks.

Babson came back two hours later and asked to see Mr Scammell.

Leonard closed the office door firmly, not even waiting to sit down at his desk to ask, 'Well? How did you go?'

'I found her.'

'Good man! What could she tell you?'

'Only that Diana had been kind to them. This Annie female said she hadn't seen her for several days and I'm sure she was telling the truth. She's been arranging to put her badly injured husband in hospital and trying to sort out what to do for herself and her children. She's as poor as a church mouse and couldn't have afforded to pay for help. So *she* can't have been involved.'

He looked at his employer questioningly.

'I suppose not.'

'You did mention that Diana didn't have any money, either, Mr Scammell. Am I correct?'

'Just a few shillings. She wouldn't get far on that on her own.'

'I pretended I'd come on Diana's behalf to give Annie a pound and find out how she and her family were. She was pathetically grateful for the money.'

After a short silence, where his anger was almost a visible

thing, Scammell asked, 'Where the hell do we look next, Babson?'

'I have an idea about that, sir. We need to find her husband.'

'But she left him of her own accord. And she knows she's not married to him.'

'Nonetheless, if I may make so bold . . .?' At his employer's nod, he continued, 'Since none of the obvious paths lead anywhere, we should perhaps try the unlikely one. In other words, the husband.'

When the fat old geezer from the law office had left, Annie sat down to recover from the interview, feeling quite shaky.

She'd lied to Mr Babson and if Mr Scammell found out, she'd be in trouble. That lawyer was a powerful sod. She did know who'd helped Mr Scammell's daughter to escape. Well, it was her own cousin, so how could she not know? Wilf had given her a couple of bob out of his earnings from this extra job, because he'd known how bad things were for her.

She wasn't going to give her cousin or anyone else away to that horrible man. He might have been born a gentleman, but he didn't act like one. She'd heard more than one person say how cruel he was.

His daughter, on the other hand, had been kind and had helped Annie when there was no food in the house for the children. Annie had soon realised from their conversation that Mrs Brady wasn't happy staying with her parents. If she'd escaped from them, then good luck to her.

Diana Brady might never know that Annie had helped her in turn by not giving the old sod the information he wanted, but it had made Annie feel good, because she hated taking charity. At least this time she felt she'd earned the money and help she'd received. As for the extra pound, it was a nice little bonus.

She glanced across the room at the pile of rugs where her husband had slept. The new young doctor, just back from the war, had come to look at Terry. How different Dr Smithers was from the old snob who came out of charity, hardly touched Terry and looked down his nose at her.

Dr Smithers had said looking after Terry was too much for her, and had arranged for him to be taken into a special hospital for men who'd lost their minds because of the war.

He really seemed to care about poor people, that doctor did, even when they couldn't afford to pay him. She'd never met anyone like him. He'd come to see Terry, checked her husband out really carefully, and arranged for him to be taken away in an ambulance, because poor Terry couldn't even walk in a straight line now.

And Dr Smithers had also arranged for her to get extra food for her children, said they were malnourished. That had made her cry, but he'd patted her shoulder and told her he could see she did her best to look after them.

He'd stayed to take a cup of tea with her – poor, weak stuff it was, too, because she could only afford to buy the cheapest sort. As he drank it with seeming enjoyment, he'd told her that one day the new government was going to make medical care free for everyone. It'd take a year or two to arrange, he'd said, but the Labour government would show the world how much they cared for ordinary people, so she should vote for them.

He'd been so enthusiastic, he'd made Annie believe things might get better. Not for her husband – the doctor hadn't tried to fool her; it was clear that Terry, the real Terry, was lost for ever – but for her children at least.

She'd thought about it several times afterwards. Even if the new government managed to do only a quarter of what the young doctor had told her about, it'd be a miracle for people like her. Free spectacles (and she could do with a pair of those herself), false teeth, free clinics to check and vaccinate children, all sorts of things that made life easier for people both old and young.

You wouldn't be afraid of seeing a doctor if you didn't have to pay. She knew a lot of women who didn't go for help for themselves, however ill they were, because they had no money to spare. Only the breadwinners were important enough to spend that sort of money on, to keep them fit to work.

During the rest of the day, she thought several times about Mrs Brady and hoped she'd won free of her horrible old father for good, oh, she did hope so!

Maybe now that she didn't have to look after Terry, Annie would have a chance of building a more decent life for her children. She let out a snort of laughter. The pound from Mr Scammell's clerk would be very useful to start things off. She could buy some second-hand clothes, so that she'd look more respectable, then she'd try to find a job as a cleaner. Women with money were finding it hard to get help in the house, so she thought she'd find something.

But she'd not accept a pittance for doing the work. No. She'd hold fast to what she thought was fair. Her neighbour would keep an eye on the kids for a penny or two, and May was a kind woman, wouldn't let them come to harm.

Annie lost herself in dreams of a better future as she cleaned the single room from top to bottom and played with her children.

Leonard Scammell brooded over the situation for a while, but in the end he agreed to Babson's suggestion and sent his chief clerk north to this Rivenshaw place. If anyone could find out where Brady and Diana were, it was Babson.

Leonard was utterly disgusted with his daughter. Talk about ungrateful! He had been doing her a favour, arranging for her to return to the sort of life she'd been raised in. He was even going to find her the sort of husband a young woman like her would be best suited to marrying.

And he was still going to do it, even if she was too stupid to see what was best. He'd bring her to heel and get rid of Brady, if it was the last thing he ever did.

He confided this to his wife.

Christine looked at him in shock. 'You still want to bring Diana back?'

'Of course I do. What if people find out she's not married to Brady? How will that reflect on us, eh? Anyway, no one gets the better of me. *Ever.*'

She lowered her eyes and didn't say anything else. She knew better than to go against him, he thought smugly.

Christine had proved a very satisfactory wife once he'd made one or two things plain to her in the early days of their marriage.

He would now make sure Diana in her turn knew who was master in this family.

As they walked into town, Judith and Diana rehearsed what they were going to say in the shop. When they got there, it was nearly empty, so they walked past it and strolled round Market Square.

'What a pity,' Judith said with a sigh. 'One of the rare times we need a queue and there isn't one. We'll have to wait till there's a shop full of people.'

Fifteen minutes later they returned to the grocer's and found a queue outside.

As they joined the line of women with shopping baskets on their arms, Diana said in her clear, posh voice, 'What did the military police find, then?'

Judith kept her voice slightly lower, but still easily audible to those nearby. 'Mayne said I wasn't supposed to tell anyone, but he won't mean you. You'd find out anyway.'

As they shuffled forward, she spoke only to Diana, but she could see that they'd already got the attention of the women on either side of them in the queue, and that Mrs Wallis had noticed how intently they were listening. That woman would hear a pin drop at fifty paces.

'They found a secret cellar, hidden under the hut,' Judith said in a loud whisper.

'Why would anyone build a cellar under a Nissen hut?'

'Shh! Keep your voice down. The cellar was built hundreds of years ago. The Nissen hut was built on top of it by sheer accident.'

Out of the corners of her eyes she could see that most of the women in the shop were now listening to them, while Mrs Wallis wasn't even pretending to serve her customer.

Diana winked at Judith. 'Goodness me! What was inside the cellar?'

'All sorts of things. Very valuable too, Mayne says: paintings, silver and even some jewellery.'

'Oh, my goodness. I'd love to see it.'

'So would I, but those military policemen locked up the cellar before they left. They said to do nothing about it till they came back. It's so frustrating.'

As they moved near to the counter, Judith consulted her shopping list and Diana pretended to check the contents of her purse. When they didn't continue the conversation, the general chatter gradually resumed. But the other customers kept staring at them and whispering to each other.

When it came their turn to be served, Mrs Wallis said, 'I couldn't help overhearing what you were saying. I'd already heard they'd found some hidden treasures up at the big house. Is that what you were talking about?'

Judith pretended to be flustered and leaned forward, whispering, 'Oh dear. I'm not supposed to say anything.'

'Oh, don't worry. The news didn't come from you. It's been all over town for hours. Whose treasure is it?'

She kept her voice low. 'I can't tell you the details because it's all been locked away again and I didn't see it myself. But they had to break the cellar door down to get inside. It's been a very exciting few days. As soon as the military police come back, Mayne's going to ask if we can all have a look at it.'

'Why was the treasure hidden in a cellar that's not attached to any house? Seems strange to me. I can't figure it out.'

'I don't know either.' Judith hated telling lies, but sometimes you just had to.

'Well, it's too late to keep quiet about it, my dear. People will continue to gossip. I hope there's a lot of really valuable stuff, then maybe Mr Esher won't have to sell the house. There have been Eshers living there for as long as anyone can remember.'

'It'd have to be very valuable to let us stay there. My husband is quite resigned to converting the house into flats.'

Mrs Wallis leaned forward. 'Need an extra loaf, dear?'

'Ooh, yes please. And do you have any bacon?'

'I could spare you a few slices, given there are so many of you now at the big house. It's a good thing you have help with the housework or you'd never be finished clearing up.'

As they left the shop Diana started to speak, but Judith said, 'Shhh!'

She didn't say anything till they'd left the town centre and were walking along the side of Parsons Mead. 'Sorry to shush you like that, but I thought we'd said enough.'

'That's all right. You know the people here better than I do.'

'Well, if you stay, you'll soon know Mrs Wallis. She's going to do our job for us and spread the news about the supposed treasure and the MPs going away for a day or two.'

'You were wonderful. You should have been an actress.'

'I had a lot of practice at making up stories with my first husband.' She gave a wry smile. 'I still think of him that way though he wasn't ever my husband legally. What a shock it was to find out that he was a bigamist! But such a relief to be rid of him.'

Her voice softened and she walked for a few paces, then added, almost as if talking to herself, 'I still can't believe sometimes that Mayne wanted to marry me, after all the scandal.'

Diana nearly confided in her then about her own mock marriage, but couldn't go against Francis's wishes.

Well, at least she had done what Judith wanted and the other woman's confidences made her feel as if she was moving towards acceptance by this important member of the group.

21

Babson took a train north. He always told his employer that he travelled first class when he had to do a job in another town. He took money from the petty cash accordingly and his employer knew better than to protest that this was an extravagance, given the type of job it was sometimes.

But of course the difference in fares went into Babson's own pocket. He wasn't too soft to sit in cheaper seats.

He endured this train journey, as usual, with the help of *The Times* newspaper and was relieved to arrive in Rivenshaw by mid-afternoon.

He summoned the taxi driver across and asked the man's advice about lodgings. He was not impressed by the small, shabby room he was given. Still, it was cheap and clean, and he'd be able to charge Mr Scammell for a better place. It would never occur to his boss to think of counting the pennies because the man had always been comfortably off, but Arthur Babson had grown up poor, so understood the value of a penny saved.

After asking the landlady for directions to the town hall, he strolled there, studying the central district. Mr Scammell's scorn of Rivenshaw wasn't justified, he decided. It was a perfectly pleasant little place, the sort Babson intended to live in once he retired. The most important thing was that his retirement home must be far away from Mr Scammell.

This retirement would, Babson hoped, take place quite soon, but he had to make sure it was what his employer thought he wanted Babson to do, or he'd never get away safely.

The town hall was a neat, square building made of stone. He went inside and asked a bored town hall clerk if he could look through the electoral register. 'I'm looking for someone who has been left a small legacy by one of our clients. It's thought he lives in Rivenshaw.'

'Lucky him!' the clerk said with great feeling, scowling. He looked like a former soldier but limped as he showed Babson where to go, which explained why he had been demobbed early. 'If you wait here, I'll bring the register.'

He dumped it on a scratched wooden table. 'Ask me if you need anything.'

The small room had one wall, all window, overlooked by the clerk, who continued to tend the reception desk and pay little attention to the side room.

Being left alone suited Babson, who was able to look through the registers and find out where the Esher family lived – which was in a house appropriately titled Esherwood. Was that pretentious, or was it really a large house with woods in the grounds? Anyway, since Brady had gone to live there, it seemed fairly certain that Miss Diana would have sought refuge with her so-called husband.

He smiled. His master didn't know that Babson was well aware of Diana Scammell's marital situation. Nor did he understand that his daughter still loved Brady. You had only to see the way she looked at her husband when she thought no one would notice.

If the plan he and Mr Scammell had devised worked as it should – and their plans usually did – she would soon be taken back to her parents' home and Brady would be locked up in prison.

The man must be a fool. Having grown up in the village, he should have known better than to marry Scammell's daughter.

Oh, well. Sorting all this out would be profitable, which was all Babson cared about, and it wasn't his business what happened to people afterwards, or even whether they deserved what happened.

When he handed the heavy register back to the clerk, he asked the man's advice about a local lawyer and was told there were two in town. The man studied him and added, 'People of your sort, sir, usually prefer to deal with Mr Gilliot.'

Babson slipped him a florin for his help, which vanished instantly and the clerk's quiet thank you couldn't have been heard beyond the front counter.

Following directions brought Babson to the lawyer's rooms, but sadly the place was closed. He took out his pocket watch and sighed. Only half past four. Did the fellow always close this early? Pity. He'd have preferred to get things started today.

He'd better stay out of sight when he got back to his lodgings. He didn't want Miss Diana seeing him.

He walked slowly along, so lost in thought about his retirement plans that he took a wrong turn and found himself near a small park. It was most annoying not to know how he'd got here and there was no one around from whom he could ask directions.

He must stop thinking of the pleasures of retirement and concentrate on the job in hand. Turning, he began to retrace his steps.

Diana settled down to some more sewing after she and Judith got back. They'd told their husbands about their visit to the shop and both men had scowled at them, but had said nothing further.

By the time Diana had finished hemming the skirt, her eyes were tired. When Francis popped his head round the door and asked, 'Fancy a stroll before tea?' she was delighted to put the sewing down.

'Won't Judith expect me to help get the meal ready?'

'No, Ros is helping her, and the children usually do the washing up after the evening meal. I thought I'd show you the nearest part of the grounds and then we can walk round Parson's Mead. If we're lucky, there may be one or two old chaps still at work on their allotments. I enjoy chatting to them. One of them served in the Great War and saw a lot of action. He has some interesting tales to tell.'

'I shall enjoy a walk.' She stood up, shaking out the skirt and holding it against herself to show him. 'It's not going to look bad, is it?'

'Anything would look good on you, and you know it.'

He sounded so like his old self, her heart lifted. 'Give me two minutes to visit the bathroom and grab my coat and I'll be with you.' She turned at the door to ask, 'Francis . . . can we leave our troubles behind and let this walk be like when we were courting?'

'Yes, let's. Perhaps I should court you all over again.'

'What a lovely idea. I'd really like that.'

The grounds of Esherwood were overgrown and in great need of attention. Some parts of the ground were flattened where they'd been used for training purposes. The vegetable garden had been tidied up, though, and Diana said wistfully, 'I wish I knew more about growing vegetables. I loved my flower garden, but I'd have preferred to grow food.'

'Why didn't you?'

She sighed. 'My mother said there was no need for people like us to do that. They had suppliers and would give me what I needed. Father made such a nasty remark about it the next time I saw him that I didn't dare go against his wishes.'

'You didn't tell me that.'

'I knew you'd be angry.'

'I thought you were too finicky to get your hands dirty.' He looked down at her beautifully kept hands.

'I don't like getting my hands dirty, but I did plant a row of beans and peas in the back garden where Father couldn't see them. Before I met you, I was going to volunteer for the Land Army and play my part that way, but mother said he'd be furious if I did that. It might have been worth braving his anger, though, because I'm not clever enough for office work. I kept making mistakes.'

'Well, if you ask Jan, he'll teach you about growing vegetables.'

'The displaced person?'

'Yes. He's led an incredible life and has some fascinating stories to tell about his war-time travels round Europe. How he managed to stay out of German hands for years, I don't know.'

'Father says they should send all the displaced persons back where they came from. But some of them don't have anywhere to go back to, from what I've heard on the wireless or seen on the news at the cinema.'

'No. Or any family left there. But Jan loves Helen deeply and I'm sure he'll be a model citizen in his new country. He'll probably make a lot of money one day. He's very clever.'

'I like to hear you talk about people. You always find something good to say about them.'

'Not about your damned father.'

'No. Not about him. Even I can't think about him without getting angry . . . and afraid.'

'I won't let him hurt you.'

'He might hurt both of us. He can be very ruthless.'

'So can I when it comes to protecting my wife.'

She didn't correct that word. She wanted him to think of her as his wife, wanted to *be* his wife again.

They were at the gates of Esherwood now. Francis took her hand and led the way down the central pathway through the allotments on Parsons Mead. As they stopped to talk to an old man, who was sitting on a bench in the fading light, Diana glanced casually across the various plots of land and stiffened.

She tugged Francis's arm. 'Quick! We have to hide.'

The old man they were talking to didn't hesitate. 'Go into the hut, missus.'

She pulled Francis inside and in the darkness whispered, 'I just saw Babson walking along the edge of the park.'

'*Babson?* What the hell is *he* doing here?'

'My father must have sent him after me.'

Francis pulled her into his arms. 'I already promised you that your father wasn't going to take you away from me.'

'You don't understand. He'll play some legal trick and make it happen.'

'How can he do it legally?'

'I don't know exactly what he'll do, but I've heard him boast to my mother that he can nearly always bend the law the way he wants, by choosing his witnesses carefully. Before I left, he threatened to have me locked away in a hospital for lunatics if I didn't do as he said. And he'd have done it, too, to bring me to heel.'

Francis could feel her trembling against him.

'This isn't going to happen in Rivenshaw. He's not even known here.'

'He's a very cunning man, Francis. Don't underestimate him.'

'Well, the first thing to do is find out where Babson is staying and keep an eye on him.'

Her voice was still shaking. 'We should run away to Australia. It's the only way we'll ever escape.'

'I'm not running away from anyone, least of all him. Just let me peep out and see where that man's gone.'

But he had no need to open the door, because they heard Babson's voice outside. He was asking directions to the town centre from the old man.

'Does that drive lead to Esherwood?' Babson asked, as if idly chatting.

'We call it the big house.'

'How big is it?'

'Dozens of rooms, people say.'

'Any visitors staying there?'

'How would I know about that sort of thing, sir? I live in one of the back streets. You'd have to ask rich folk about what goes on inside the big house.'

'But you must see comings and goings while you're working on your allotment.'

'I seen the big Army car coming and going this week. That's all I seen. Couldn't tell who was in it. My eyes aren't so good these days.'

'Well, thank you for giving me directions. Buy yourself a drink.'

'Very kind of you, sir.'

There was the sound of leisurely footsteps going away from them. It seemed a long time before the old man called out, 'He's gone now, turned off Parklea and went towards the town centre.'

Francis peered out to check that Babson really had gone away.

The old man spat on the ground to one side. 'I didn't take to that fellow. Looked at me as if I was a worm, he did.' He grinned. 'I didn't refuse his money, though. It'll buy a pint or two just as easily as anyone else's half-crown.'

'Thanks for not giving us away.'

'I know how to keep my mouth shut and young Mr Esher's a decent sort. If you're friends of his, you're all right.'

They walked quickly back through the twilight to the big house. 'We'd better tell the others what happened,' Francis said. 'And that means telling them about our problem.'

'You didn't want to do that.'

'It was bound to come out sooner or later. I just wanted time to think. Your father is no doubt planning to use it against us.'

'Wait.' She tugged him to a halt. 'Have you decided what you want to do about it yet?'

'I'm thinking . . . of staying together. Do you suppose we stand any chance of happiness, Diana?'

She touched his cheek with her fingertips, a butterfly's caress. 'It won't be my fault if we don't. I want us to be together like we were when I was living away from home. I was much happier then, happier than I've ever been in my life.'

He pulled her towards him to kiss first one cheek, then the other, then said quietly, 'All right. First we have to check that your father was telling the truth, that we weren't married legally. Then . . . Oh, hell, Diana, if you don't put everything you've got into our marriage this time . . .' His voice trailed away and he bent to kiss her properly.

They stayed in a close embrace for a few moments then he stepped back. 'Well then, if your father was telling the truth, we may have to arrange another wedding. But we'll manage this one ourselves.'

He frowned. 'How did you ever persuade your father to let us marry the first time?'

'I threatened to live in sin with you until I got pregnant and he knew I wouldn't be allowed to leave my war work, so he could do nothing about it.'

'Would you really have done that?'

'Yes. I was sorry in some ways when you bought the house and sent me back to the village. Remember how I tried to persuade you not to? Why did you do that? I could have lived near your new posting. You didn't even visit me very often once I'd moved back.'

'I was working on a top secret project. I bought the house because I knew I wouldn't be able to get away for more than the odd day. And I'd signed the Official Secrets Act, so I couldn't tell you what I was doing.'

'Oh. And I thought you were growing cooler towards me. Mummy – I mean, my mother – found out what I was worried about and said it served me right for marrying someone like you.'

'What a mess the war has made of our personal lives.' He frowned and looked at her. 'You never stumble when you're saying "my father" instead of "Daddy" but occasionally you still say "Mummy". You don't seem to feel as bitter against her. Am I right?'

'Yes. The night I was escaping she heard a noise and came into the bedroom to check on me. I had just climbed out of the window and was standing at the top of the ladder. I expected her to shout for my father, but she didn't. I couldn't believe it when there was no pursuit. So she can't have told him. That means she was trying to help me.'

'That does surprise me.'

'Yes. I think, no I *know* that she's frightened of him. Terrified, actually. And she knows him better than anyone else does. So I'm right to be afraid he'll play some nasty trick on us. Francis, please, be very careful.'

'I will. Now, let's go and tell the others. We need them to watch out for you as well. You'd better stay inside the house till Babson leaves Rivenshaw. He won't be able to get to you there.'

'What if he doesn't go? What if he's intending to stay until he gets hold of me?'

'I doubt he'll do anything without your father's say-so. He'll probably report back once he finds out where you are.'

'Don't underestimate how closely the two of them work together. My mother once told me to be nice to Babson but never, ever to tell him anything, because he was hand in glove with my father.'

She shivered and caught hold of Francis's hand. 'He's here to do something to separate us, I know he is.'

When Diana and Francis went into the kitchen, the captain and lieutenant were there and everyone was looking very solemn. 'Something's going on. We may have to wait till tomorrow to tell them about us,' Francis whispered to Diana.

The captain was frowning at them for speaking, so Francis fell silent and put his arm round Diana's shoulders as he prepared to listen.

'We four will spread out around the hut,' the captain was saying. 'I'd like you people to keep watch from inside the house. Only in a dire emergency should any of you come outside. If you see an intruder, use this to contact me.'

He put what looked like a small briefcase on the table. 'It's a rather more elaborate version of the foxhole radios the Yanks made, and you use it by—'

'We've used them before,' Mayne said.

'Are you sure?'

He gave the captain a grim smile and added very quietly, 'Perhaps you ought to know that we three chaps were part of a special unit attached to the SOE.'

The captain looked astonished. 'No one told me that.'

'We don't advertise what we were doing. And we're forbidden to talk about it, even now.'

'That must be why I was told to push on with this fast and not ask too many personal questions.'

'Could be. Let me just check that it's a type of personal radio we've used before.' Mayne beckoned to Francis and Victor. Together the three men studied the apparatus concealed in the briefcase.

'This one's had a couple of amendments,' Francis said. 'But it's basically the same as the one I used.'

'Then I'll leave you to keep watch,' the captain said. 'It's connected to the one I'm carrying, but mine only gives out a faint hissing sound if you contact me. If it's not safe to reply, you may have to wait for an answer but you can hear the hissing sound and it'll prove you got through to me. I'll call you back when I can.'

'The research bods don't tell people about all their little toys, do they?' Francis commented, still fiddling with the radio, fascinated by how small this version was.

The captain cleared his throat to get his attention. 'There were three men who broke into the hut before, you said. Let's hope they don't recruit others this time. I'll get in place now. I doubt the murderers will be here till much later, but you can never be too careful.'

'If they actually turn up tonight,' Mayne said.

'I hope they damned well do. I want to get this job over and done with.'

When the MPs had gone out again, Mayne said quietly, 'I'll make sure all the windows and doors in the house are locked. I'd rather do that myself, because I know the place best, even the new areas the Army added on.'

When he returned to the kitchen, he said, 'I've asked the children to stay out of this, all in one bedroom, and I've put Ben in charge of guarding the girls. That should keep him out of danger.'

He smiled. 'Jan is also on watch outside and I doubt those MPs, however good they are, will so much as notice him. He knows every inch of the grounds by now, and is used to making his way about at night.'

'I suggest we sit round the kitchen table for a while chatting, as we usually do,' Judith said. 'Then we'll have a cup of cocoa and act as if we're going to bed. If we leave the curtains open, anyone watching the house will see us.'

Mayne nodded. 'Yes. Someone is bound to check things out if they're coming tonight. That's what I'd do if I were planning to break in somewhere.'

'Jan said he'd warn us if someone turns up,' Victor said. 'Gravel against my bedroom window at the other side of the house shouldn't be heard by anyone out at the back, we thought.'

Francis took a sip of cocoa. 'Has the irony of all this struck you? Even if these murderers turn up, let alone get through our defences, they still won't be able to open that puzzle lock – not unless they're a good deal smarter than our locksmith chappie, anyway.'

'Those MPs are guarding something that doesn't need it,' Mayne said, 'whereas we are guarding our wives and children.'

'We're not helpless,' Judith said. 'We can guard ourselves, thank you very much. I'm going to find some sort of weapon and if anyone tries to capture me, they'll get a shock, I promise you.'

'Can you find a weapon for me, too?' Diana asked at once.

'And for me,' Ros echoed.

'We'll find something here,' Judith said, and went over to the kitchen drawer near the stove where the various tools were kept. 'How about this, Diana?'

Francis winced as Diana brandished the kitchen steel experimentally and nearly hit the edge of the cupboard door.

The heavy metal bar used for sharpening knives would do a lot of damage if she used it on a person. He couldn't help asking, 'Will you be able to hit someone with it, do you think?'

'Yes, I will.'

Her voice sounded more determined than usual. He felt she really was changing, growing stronger and more independent. That gave him hope.

She looked across the room at him and swung the steel to and fro, as if practising. He couldn't help grinning. From the way she was flapping it around, he doubted she'd manage to hit anyone, let alone hit them good and hard.

It felt as if the two of them were newly acquainted, strangers who were becoming important in each other's lives, rather than people who'd been married for a couple of years.

He watched Judith nudge Diana and heard her quiet remark.

'Stop beaming at your husband. Clearly whatever was wrong between you two has been fixed, and I'm glad to see that. But you need to stay alert. Tonight's encounter could be dangerous. This is a big house to guard and people can get in through all sorts of doors and windows. Glass is easy enough to smash.'

Diana's smile vanished and she cradled the steel against her chest.

It was as if Mayne's wife was leading them all for the moment, he thought. What an admirable woman she was!

Judith drank her cup of cocoa slowly then went to rinse the cup out in the scullery. After pretending to yawn for the benefit of any possible observers outside, she raised her voice a little, 'I'm getting tired now. Are you ready for bed, Mayne?'

'Yes, darling.'

'So am I,' Ros said.

All three couples went upstairs.

'I wish there weren't two staircases,' Mayne worried. 'We'll keep watch from our bedroom windows, since the rooms have different outlooks, but don't hesitate to come and fetch me if I'm needed.'

Inside their bedroom, Francis looked at Diana. 'You'd be best putting those trousers on tonight. Easier to run or fight if you're wearing them.'

'Those men can't win, can they?' she asked as she changed. 'I mean, there are more of us than them, aren't there?'

'Well, we think we outnumber them, but we can't be sure how many will come this time. We don't even know that they *are* coming,' he reminded her.

'I think they will. I don't know why, I just do.' She put on the trousers and a dark sweater. 'There. Will that do?'

'Perfect.' But he doubted she'd need to do anything. Mayne and the captain planned to keep the intruders out of the house itself.

And why should they want to come inside anyway? It was the cellar they'd be interested in.

If they came.

22

Night cloaked the grounds of the house, but the shadows seemed to skitter around, confusing the eyes, as a half moon showed intermittently through the drifting clouds. It was turning chilly now but wasn't cold enough yet for breath to mist the air and give people's presence away.

Jan was in a carefully chosen hiding place, a shallow trough concealed by the branches of a large fallen tree. He knew how to get in and out of the tangle of branches without making any noise that sounded like a human being, but he doubted anyone else would even consider that the tree trunk could conceal a man.

He stiffened as he heard someone moving through the bushes beyond the Nissen hut. That person was good at moving quietly, though not as good as Jan. It wasn't possible to tell yet whether it was a friend or foe.

He lay utterly still as a man passed by dressed in dark clothes with his face blackened. Foe, then. Definitely.

He counted two others, letting them go past him. The rumours his friends had started must have spread, either from the pub or the grocer's, and the murderers had taken the bait.

It was too dark to recognise who they were but the way a tall thin man walked seemed familiar, and after a minute's thought, he remembered where he'd seen someone like that, even though he didn't know the man's name: at the markets.

He waited to see whether they'd have an outlier with the group, as he would have done if he were in charge, and sure enough another man came after them from one side. He was shorter than the others, teeth showing white in his dark face because they were bared in a half-smile. He looked as if he was enjoying this.

Jan felt uneasy, wished there were more men keeping watch outside than the four MPs.

When he was quite sure there were no other outliers, he moved silently from shadow to shadow till he got near the house.

Peeping out from behind the window curtains in his bedroom Mayne saw movement in the bushes. No one came out of them, so it could just have been an animal.

No, there it was again. Was it one of the MPs or one of the murderers moving about?

He reached for his binoculars and focused on the bushes. They thrashed around wildly all of a sudden, then everything became still. Now, what had caused that?

Clearly something was going on out there. Perhaps someone had taken the bait. The two soldiers could have been right to be suspicious of the men at *The Black Horse*. It still seemed like too much good luck to have found them so easily, but there you were; fate was sometimes kind.

From where she was sitting on the bed, Judith whispered, 'Did you see someone?'

'I think so, but I only saw the bushes moving, not the people themselves. It could even be one of the MPs.'

'Hadn't you better use that radio and let them know you've seen movement?'

'Give me a minute or two to be sure.'

★ ★ ★

From his bedroom on the other side of the house, Victor spotted two figures coming from the direction of the Dower House. They slipped round the house and vanished behind the stables. They didn't reappear.

Before he could do anything, there was a faint sound as gravel hit the window. 'Jan's seen someone,' he whispered to Ros. 'I'll go and tell Mayne. You stay here.'

She stood up and took his place by the window. 'I'll continue to keep watch. Did you see those men go by?'

'Yes. But it must have been Jan who threw the gravel. They'd have no reason to do that. I hope he's all right. Our intruders went round the corner of the house and I can't see anything from here now. I'd better tell Mayne.'

He walked along the landing and tapped on his friend's bedroom door, which opened almost immediately.

Mayne listened, then said, 'I saw movement in the bushes as well. Unfortunately I couldn't make out any details. But if you saw two men come up the drive, Victor, we'd better warn the captain. There may be more intruders than we expected if they're coming in from different directions.' Grudgingly he added, 'That's how I'd have organised it, too.'

He went to the wireless set and used it to send a warning that someone was moving about.

There was a faint hiss and a voice whispered, 'What?'

'Two men came up the drive.'

'Damn. There are four others here as well.' The wireless cut out.

'Got through at least,' Mayne said. 'But they're outnumbered, even with Jan out there as backup.'

As Jan slipped through the undergrowth behind the stables, he nearly tripped over a body and dived straight into hiding, doing a circuit of the place to make sure no one was around lying in wait before coming back to the body.

It was one of the soldiers. Alive, thank goodness, but unconscious. Jan checked the back of his head and his hand came away bloody. Someone had hit him good and hard, then tied him up.

No time to help him except for cutting the rope around his wrists and taking the gag out of his mouth. The other MPs might need help. Jan moved back into hiding and listened carefully.

He heard faint sounds of movement in the direction of the Nissen hut. He wasn't stupid enough to investigate until he had a better idea of what was going on. He didn't like the looks of this, not at all. That other sense which had saved his life several times during the war years had kicked in.

The intruders must be good at their job if they'd managed to take down one of the MPs without giving their own presence away. Hell, this whole thing was better organised than anyone had expected, almost like an Army operation.

He moved cautiously forward and saw a man standing in the dark shadows under a tree. Jan stood perfectly still and didn't attempt to help, even when someone knocked out the MP and tied him up. The man was groggy but conscious enough to struggle, in vain.

Two down, Jan guessed. He decided it was time to fetch reinforcements from the house. But first he waited until the intruder had moved on, then he cut the rope, putting one finger to his lips and leaving the soldier free to move.

He bent to whisper, 'I'm a friend of Mayne's. Keep quiet. Get among the bushes and wait there until you hear sounds of fighting.' He was quite sure now that there would be fighting.

The man nodded.

Using every inch of cover, Jan went to look at the Nissen hut. The door was still closed, but the padlock was missing. And where were the captain and lieutenant? Had they been taken out too? If so his friends in the big house were in danger.

He made his way to the laundry door to which he had a key from his time on night duty. Even over that short distance, he stopped several times to listen, making absolutely certain he wasn't being followed.

He let himself in, locking the door behind him, and went to find Mayne, knocking on the bedroom door. 'It's me,' he said quietly.

Two men turned from the window, Judith stepped out from behind the curtains of the second window and another man stepped out from behind the door.

Jan smiled approvingly. 'Glad I didn't surprise you.'

'We were trained not to present one target when we were in special ops. What the hell's happening out there?' Mayne asked.

Jan explained that two of the soldiers had been taken down, one of them badly hurt, the other recovering, and there was no sign of the two officers.

Victor let out a low growl of anger. 'Damnation! It means the murderers are well trained, too.'

'Ex-Army, do you think?' Francis asked.

Mayne shrugged. 'Probably. I think we need to go out and help them. I counted four men near the Nissen hut.'

'Which makes at least six with the two men who came up the drive,' Victor said.

'I don't like this,' Jan said. 'Judith, I think the women should lock themselves in with the children. I doubt those men are interested in what's going on inside the house.'

'I think one of us should stay inside the house as well,' Mayne said. 'Francis, will you do that while we three go outside? We know the grounds better than you do. Yell for help if they come inside, though if they do, we'll probably be following them.'

'I'd rather be out there doing something, but you're probably right that I'd be more use here.'

Judith moved to the door. 'I'll get the others organised. If I'd realised so many men were coming tonight, I'd have put the kids in the secret room in the attic. But it'd make a lot of noise to do it now and, anyway, I doubt Ben would agree to it.'

She moved towards the door, poker in hand. She didn't ask Mayne to take care, but there was enough moonlight coming through the windows for her quick glance in his direction to say it for her.

When the women and children were all in the bedroom, she set Ben to keeping watch at one window, both to keep him occupied and to see what was happening.

She stood by the second window, which was on the side wall of the house, watching for her husband to come outside, praying no one else would be lying in wait for him.

When they got outside the laundry, Jan immediately edged away into the darkest shadows, while Mayne and Victor sought similar concealment. But they stayed together, as they had a few times before when out on ops.

The whole of the garden seemed caught in a breathless hush, as if people were waiting to see what would happen.

Then suddenly they saw the captain run to the door of the hut and press himself flat against the wall, listening to what was going on inside. Mayne put one hand on Victor's arm to stop him joining the other man until there was definite need for their help.

When the captain slipped inside the door, Victor jerked his head towards it as if to ask should they follow.

'Not yet,' Mayne whispered. 'We don't know where the lieutenant is or how they're planning to tackle this.'

Jan appeared to his right and came up to whisper to them.

'I took out the man keeping watch on the hut and tied him up. The lieutenant insisted on following the captain's instructions and staying outside unless needed. I told him about the two men having been attacked, but there was nothing he could do about them, except hope that the second man would be back on the job by now. The first one won't. He'd been hurt too badly.'

Mayne didn't like the sound of this at all. 'It's a good thing we came out to help. I think I'd better have a quick recce inside the hut. I probably know my way about in there better than anyone.'

It was even darker inside than he'd expected, however, and he paused, wondering whether he dare use a torch. Then, as his eyes grew more accustomed to the near darkness, he saw a faint glow ahead. He began to move forward slowly, testing the ground in front of him for obstructions before he took each careful step.

The boards that had been placed over the entrance to the hidden cellar had been removed and the light he'd seen was coming from down there. A man was looking into the hole. Friend or foe?

Victor slipped into the shadows to keep watch on the hut. He thought he had good hearing, but Jan surprised him by appearing suddenly next to him.

'The other intruders are breaking into the house now.'

Victor's heart sank. 'Oh, hell! And if I try to warn Mayne, I might alert the ones in there. I don't know my way around inside the hut.'

'I'll go after the ones in the house. I'm hoping Francis will have noticed them before they notice him.'

Victor hesitated, then said, 'I'll come after you as soon as Mayne leaves the hut.'

If the intruders laid one finger on his wife and daughter,

it'd be the last thing they ever did. Surely these fellows wouldn't attack women and children?

But they'd already killed that unknown soldier. Desperate men could commit acts of mindless violence.

Mayne sighed in relief when he recognised the silhouette by the cellar steps. He made a faint sound to attract attention. 'Psst.'

The captain spun round, gun raised.

'It's me, Mayne.'

The captain beckoned him over. Below them two men were arguing in whispers and gesticulating towards the locked cellar door. Even though they were keeping their voices low, they sounded angry.

Only two of them! If there were six intruders in the grounds and Jan had captured one of them, that still left three others besides these men. Where were they? What were they after?

One of the thieves said clearly, 'We'd better join the others in the house, then, and find out what they've done with the key to this place.'

'It could be a trap.'

'If it is, they won't be expecting six of us. And there are women and children. We can take a couple of hostages, then make our own terms. We'll get them to show us where the rest of the family silver is. It probably won't be as valuable as whatever's in the cellar, but it'll still bring in a tidy sum. My grandmother was a maid at the big house in the old days and she said they had a lot of silver, with a special room to put it in.'

'Come on, then. We're doing no good here. We tried to open that damned lock before and failed. I picked locks of all types before the war, but I never came across anything like this one.'

Mayne tugged the captain backwards from the cellar and they went to re-join Victor outside. As his friend explained quickly what was happening, one of the soldiers came out of the undergrowth, moving unsteadily. He opened his mouth to speak to them, but the captain put one hand across it and tugged him round the side of the hut.

The other two followed them, but Mayne found a tree to one side, from whose shelter he could watch the intruders without being seen. After whispering to the soldier, the captain joined him there.

One of the men from the cellar peered quickly out of the hut then ducked back behind the door.

After a few moments, both men came out.

Something about the way they moved rang a bell with the captain. This wasn't any old group of thieves burgling a house, this was men working together, men with the sort of training provided in the Army for special reconnoitring units, he'd guess.

Someone had trained them too damned well, he thought bitterly. They were very good at it.

Why were they doing this, though? Why had they turned to thieving?

Who knew? He'd heard looting was taking place here and there, and it was difficult to prevent.

Inside the house, Francis moved between the two staircases at the ground floor ends, keeping watch for intruders. On one of his trips into the kitchen, he heard faint footsteps in the laundry, slow cautious steps that you'd not have noticed unless you were expecting something like that. There were pauses between each couple of movements.

Jan would have made no noise at all. Mayne and Victor would have come openly. Damn! Someone must have got in that way while he was checking the front stairs. He crouched under the kitchen table, wishing it had an over-hanging cloth and praying that they wouldn't notice him in the darkness.

A torch played over the kitchen, but didn't linger on the table. He watched three pairs of feet move across the room, following its light.

'Guns at the ready,' a voice ordered quietly. 'We'll go first to the room where I saw the curtains move.'

Francis was unarmed, had vowed never to use a gun again, but at this moment he wished he had broken that vow. If they harmed Diana . . .

He stayed where he was until the men left the kitchen, hearing them go up the servants' staircase in the same cautious manner. The leader seemed to know his way around, but the other two were more hesitant.

Leaving his hiding place, Francis hurried across the entrance hall and ran up the main stairs. He prayed that any sounds he made would be hidden by the old house's creaking and the wind blowing the branches of the trees outside.

He looked round for somewhere to hide and got behind the curtains of the big landing window, crouching on the broad window seat. He watched in dismay through a tiny gap in the dusty velvet as the intruders paused to listen, then moved towards the bedroom where the women had taken shelter.

One of them definitely knew his way around. Why the hell had they come inside?

He risked another move to crouch behind a hanging deco-rating the wall behind a big oak chest. In daylight the bulge he made would have been noticed, but in the darkness he hoped to stay concealed. This had brought him closer to the intruders but he still wasn't armed.

He could just see the door and the three men. He jumped in shock as one started hammering on the door.

'We know you're in there,' the man yelled. 'If you come out with your hands up, we'll not hurt you. We don't want to have to shoot the lock off the door. And you don't want to make us angry, believe me.'

Inside the bedroom the women and children gasped as the noise started then froze as a man yelled instructions.

'They must have caught Francis,' Judith muttered.

'Oh, no!' Diana stared at her in terror.

The man yelled again. 'We've caught one of your menfolk, and if you don't come out, I'll shoot him in the leg, then higher up his body.'

'And if we do come out, you'll kill us as well,' Judith yelled back.

'If you do as you're told, no one will get hurt. We want you – and him – to help us find the valuables and then help us get away. A few hostages can work wonders on the author-ities.' He laughed, but his laughter had a sharp, unpleasant edge to it.

'We can't defy them or they may start shooting indis-criminately,' Judith said. 'Bullets can pass through doors.'

'I can hide from them when the rest of you go with them,' Ben said.

'And do what? These are armed men.'

'I can get out of the house after they've left the bedroom and warn Mayne.'

'It can't hurt to try,' Diana pleaded. 'I'll hide as well. They can't know how many of us there are. Judith, if they seem about to discover Ben, I'll give myself up. There's a chance that one of us can get away and give warning.'

Judith hesitated, then nodded.

'I know where you can hide. I can't fit in, but I bet you can.' Ben took Diana into the dressing room, showing her an extremely narrow cupboard in a corner of the wall. He'd only found it by chance and it wasn't at all obvious. 'I'll go on top of the wardrobe.'

She squeezed herself into the narrow cupboard, looking up at the huge wardrobe next to her hiding place. It had a triangular pediment decorating the top edge at the front. 'How on earth will you get up there?' she asked as he started to close the door on her.

'I can use that chest of drawers to climb up then lie down behind the carved part.'

As he shut her in the cupboard, she kept hold of her makeshift weapon. If they hurt Francis, she'd use it on them. She'd do anything to help him.

She listened intently and after a few moments heard the sound of bolts being drawn back and men's voices in the other room. Lights were switched on, casting a thin line of light into her narrow cupboard. To her relief, the intruders didn't sound to be hurting the others, simply ordering them about.

'Where's the boy?' one asked suddenly.

'Ben disobeyed his father and followed the men outside.'

'We saw no sign of him there. You're lying.'

Diana heard the footsteps come into the dressing room and a man said loudly, 'We know you're in here, lad. Either you come out or we'll hurt your mother.'

She knew it was no use her trying to distract them, so stayed where she was. Could she do it? Stay hidden, then get outside and warn Mayne and the others what was happening? She could try.

There was dead silence, then the man opened and shut the wardrobe doors with loud bangs. After that he began laughing. 'Your foot is showing on the top of the wardrobe, lad. Now come down or your mother will face the consequences.'

There was the sound of movement. 'If you hurt her, I'll—'

'You'll do what? Anyway, if you all obey orders, no one will get hurt. We're *not* murderers. It's valuables we're after. Why should rich sods like Esher have so much and our families so little?'

'Mayne isn't rich. He has to sell this house.'

'That'll still leave him rich in my books. But he'll be less rich by the end of this night, he most definitely will. I'm going to make up for all the years they paid my mother a pittance and *his* mother treated her like a slave.' His voice changed. 'Now, have we got them all, lads?'

The other man started counting.

Judith waited for him to realise there was another person missing, but Gillian suddenly began to cry and flung herself in her mother's arms, wailing to be saved from the men. This wasn't like her, so Judith held her breath, guessing it was a distraction to stop the men counting heads.

The first man said, 'Shut up, you stupid kid. No one's touched you. Come on, lads. Let's get going. We'll pick up as much of the silverware as we can carry. I'm sure Esher will be happy to let us get away with that if we release his precious new family.'

Ben took a step forward, opening his mouth, but Judith dragged him back by his sweater and said in an undertone, 'Shut up.'

The men laughed.

'You've got more sense than your son, missus. Come on. Down the stairs with you. We'll go out the front way eventually, but we'll collect the silver before we do that. You'll know where the valuables are kept, Mrs Bloody Esher, so lead us to them.' His voice grew softly menacing. 'I'm sure you value your children's lives more than a few lumps of silver.

'Yes, I do. Much more.'

Diana heard them leave the room, astonished that she

seemed to have got away with hiding, thanks to Gillian's quick thinking. No more than Judith did she believe Gillian would have cried out of fear, even though she'd not known the family for long.

But would the men really release the others if they got what they wanted?

They seemed ruthless.

She didn't dare risk them not keeping their word; she had to get help.

Francis watched helplessly from his hiding place on the landing as the women and children made their way down the front stairs, covered by two men with guns. It took him a minute to realise his wife wasn't with them.

Where was Diana? Had she managed to hide? Or had they hurt her?

He didn't dare go looking for her now. He had to stay near this group in case he could do something to help them.

When the second man had started down the stairs, Francis risked creeping across the landing behind him and made it to the servants' stairs without being caught.

He nearly cried out in shock as Jan met him at the bottom. He put one finger to his lips and held his gun at the ready.

Quickly Francis explained what was happening.

'I've already seen that these men know how to fight. I can deal with one of them at a time, but not all three at once,' Jan said. 'We must wait for a time when you can distract them, so that I can put one out of action. Perhaps you could throw something at one of them?'

'I'm a good bowler at cricket, so I'll have a damned good try at hitting him on the head.'

'Shh!'

They waited but there was an argument going on in the hall.

'We have a moment or two,' Jan said. 'Find something to throw, something heavy. When I shoot the leader, you try to hit the last man.' He moved across to hide at the other side of the room, nearer to the outer door.

Francis collected three of the heavier weights from the big kitchen scales, putting two in his trouser pockets and holding the other one. He went to peep through the hall door, grimly determined to stop the men taking the women and children away.

'You lot can sit on the stairs while Mrs Esher takes me to the silver,' the leader said. 'Do it quickly and then stay very still. Remember, the man above you on the stairs will be holding a gun on you the whole time.'

A shot rang out and the leader staggered. Francis hurled his weight at the other man in the hall, hitting him squarely in the head.

The leader was injured but not out of action. And he still had a gun.

To Francis's horror he saw Diana creeping along the landing, holding the heavy bar of sharpening steel. He didn't yell to her to get back, didn't want to draw anyone's attention to her.

But the third man had seen her.

Francis yelled, 'Stop! Don't fire.'

'You first, her second.' The intruder raised his gun and took aim.

Francis knew he couldn't get away in time. If the first shot didn't kill him, the next one would. He could only hope Jan would stop the leader from shooting at him as well.

All he could do was throw himself to one side. Before he could throw another weight, a shot rang out and he felt a burning sensation in his upper arm.

But Diana had leaped down the stairs from the landing far more quickly than anyone could have expected and her steel bar connected with the man's arm just as he was about to fire again.

Another shot rang out and the leader fell to the floor, gun clattering on the tiles. Ben pounced on it and the group on the stairs took the opportunity to scatter.

There was the usual feeling of chaos being unleashed that you got in minor skirmishes, so Francis concentrated on what was happening in the hall. He dived for the gun, which Diana's blow had knocked out of the hand of the man on the stairs, seeing out of the corner of his eyes that she'd managed to hit the man again with the steel. But she'd missed his head and hit only a glancing blow on his shoulder. He was cursing her and trying to grab the steel from her when Francis hit him over the head with the butt of the gun.

'Quick! Find something to tie him up!'

She looked round desperately and ran to pull the tie-back cord off a curtain.

'Good girl! Is there another for his feet?' The man had started to regain consciousness but Francis had his hands and feet secured before he gathered his wits together.

To his relief, one man was lying on the floor of the hall below, moaning and bleeding from two wounds, while the other was sitting with his hands on his head, under the cover of a gun held steadily by the captain, who had now joined them.

In fact suddenly the hall seemed full of men, more intruders having been brought in.

Mayne was holding two of them at gunpoint.

'I think that's all of them!' he said. 'Captain if we can hand these men over to you, Jan can you go out and check that we have them all. He's far better than anyone I know at reconnoitring.'

'My pleasure.'

Jan came back a few minutes later, by which time the

three men who weren't wounded were secured by handcuffs. 'If there were any others, they've left, but I don't think there were.'

He stared across at the tallest of the men. 'I'm trying to think where I've seen you.'

'At the markets,' Judith said. 'Newton's. The café there. Your father was so happy that you'd come out of the war safely, Sam Newton.'

'My family don't know about this,' Newton said at once.

'You come from an honest family. They'll be horrified at what you've done.'

'Yes, and what have they got for behaving themselves? My mother's nearly killed herself working every hour she can stay upright, and my sister's got TB, while you rich sods live in luxury you didn't earn.'

'Quiet, you.' The captain formally arrested the men. While he was doing that, the lieutenant had been phoning for other officers and vehicles.

'Just out of curiosity,' the captain asked. 'How did the man in the hut die?'

'He got into a fight and we had to stop him or he'd have given us away,' Newton said sourly. 'Stupid bugger, he was. It was an accident that he died, but he deserved a good thumping.'

'Couldn't you have found somewhere better to hide his body?' the captain asked scornfully. 'That was stupid.'

'We were leaving the next morning and it was all we could think of. We put some cupboards over the place, only they must have moved them about.'

He stared at the captain and mockingly echoed what he'd said. '*Just out of curiosity*, Captain, had you managed to open the door of that damned cellar?'

'No. It's a thing called a puzzle lock and if you do the wrong thing, it will lock the whole thing with steel bars. We need to find the actual key and then let an expert do the opening.'

'That's typical,' Newton said sourly. 'I never was lucky. I bet there's treasure in there, too.'

'Who knows? It'll belong to Esher if there is.'

23

The Army was sending a truck to take away the intruders, because no one was certain whether the men's claim that the soldier's death had been an accident was true. And anyway, the men had learned their skills in the Army, so it behoved the Army to make sure they didn't use them again to steal and threaten violence.

'Let the legal wallahs sort it all out,' the captain said to Mayne. 'After all, your local police officer doesn't have the facilities to deal with these men.'

'As a courtesy, I'd like to inform Sergeant Deemer of what has happened,' Mayne said. 'It's always good to keep the local police on side.'

The captain shrugged. 'As you please. He seems a nice old chap. I have a lot of respect for these older people who came out of retirement to keep the country running during the war.'

'I'll walk into town to see Deemer myself,' Mayne decided. 'I could do with some fresh air. You don't need me here, do you?'

'Not at all.'

'I'll come with you, Mayne,' Judith said. 'There is, as always, the question of shopping for food, and we need some more bread.'

Mayne left her at the grocer's shop and went into the police station, to find an older man sitting waiting to see the sergeant.

He was very well dressed and looked as if he belonged in a big city rather than Rivenshaw. He nodded politely but didn't speak.

'I have an emergency to report. I do apologise but I'm afraid I'll have to go before you,' Mayne said to the stranger.

The man waved one hand. 'Be my guest. I do hope it's nothing serious.'

'Not now.'

Deemer came out of his room, was about to speak to the stranger, but stopped when he saw Mayne. 'Mr Esher! How can I help you?'

'I have an incident to report.'

'Ah.'

'It's all right. I can wait,' the stranger said.

When the sergeant had taken Mayne into his office, Babson whistled softly. Esher, eh. What had been going on at this Esherwood place? Whatever it was, it might affect Diana Scammell. He moved to a chair as close as possible to the little office and was pleased to see that the door was slightly ajar.

He was amazed at what he heard about the goings-on of the previous night, but when he heard that Diana had been quite the heroine and had saved her supposed husband's life, he began to think furiously about his task here.

No, he couldn't possibly do as planned now, because they'd all be congratulating her and fussing over her. He'd have to tell that local lawyer not to do anything. Damnation! This meant a major part of Mr Scammell's plan couldn't be implemented.

He continued to listen, then as the conversation in the office began to wind down he got up quietly and left the police station. If there was one thing he was good at, it was spotting when it was time to change one's plans. And this was undoubtedly one of those times.

His employer would be furious, but you couldn't accuse

a heroine of not having her wits about her, let alone lock her away in a quiet little private hospital. She'd just proved the contrary.

In any case, he'd always thought this was unnecessary, another example of Scammell's sheer spite when his wishes were crossed. Miss Diana could count herself lucky – well, she could if she ever found out what had nearly happened.

He left the police station quietly and walked across to the railway station to find out the time of the next train south. Sadly, with connections being what they were, it'd be better to leave first thing in the morning if he wanted to travel straight through to Hertfordshire, which meant spending another night in that dreary lodging house.

Or else spending the night in Manchester, and travelling on from there. Yes, that'd be better.

He had learned a lot about Diana and Francis's situation here by chatting to the lawyer and then to his landlady. He would report that back to Mr Scammell and leave his employer to decide what to do next.

Babson smiled suddenly as he realised that if he played his cards right, this might offer him a path to retirement. If he made it seem as though he was losing his touch, Scammell might start looking round for someone to replace him. He smiled. Yes. He could do that. Scammell always found it easy to assume others were stupid.

He went to collect his luggage and was sitting on a train within the hour.

Strange how those intruders had saved Diana from her father's grasp – who'd have thought she'd have the courage to confront anyone?

Would Scammell go after her again? He'd be a fool to do that. But Babson didn't intend to get involved.

★　★　★

It wasn't until the six men had been taken away and the flesh wound in his own arm dressed that Francis managed to get Diana on her own.

'You look tired,' he said to her.

'I am.'

'Too tired to discuss our situation?'

'No, never that.'

'Let's go up to our bedroom. I'll tell Mayne we have something important to discuss.'

In the bedroom, he took her into his arms, taking care not to jar the wound in his arm. 'You saved my life tonight.'

She shuddered.

'Thank you.' He kissed her gently on the lips and stared at her. 'You're changing.'

'For the better, I hope.'

'Definitely for the better. Diana . . . do you really, truly want to be married to me?'

'Yes. Oh, yes, Francis. I really do.'

'Then we'd better go into Manchester tomorrow and make enquiries about our marriage.'

She looked at him with tears in her eyes. 'Oh, Francis, are *you* sure? This isn't because I helped you? I don't want you marrying me again out of gratitude, even though I do want us to stay together.'

'No, it isn't out of gratitude. It's because I never stopped loving you, even when you and your parents annoyed me, even when I wasn't even sure you really cared about me. But since you've come to Rivenshaw, you've seemed different, more my wife than your father's daughter.' He brushed away a tear with one fingertip. 'Don't cry.'

'Not even tears of joy? I can't help those.' She raised her face for his kiss.

★　★　★

By midday all the outsiders had gone away, and all the occupants of Esherwood were exhausted.

'Let's go and sit quietly in the kitchen,' Judith said. 'We need to discuss what to do now.'

'Get into that concealed cellar somehow, I suppose,' Victor said. 'We can't just leave it like that.'

Mayne frowned. 'I don't think we should do anything until I find the key. Though where my parents could have hidden a key so big, I can't think.'

Diana frowned across the table at him. 'A big key? So big it doesn't look like a real one?'

'Yes. Why?'

'There's one hanging up in that strange little cupboard behind the big wardrobe in your bedroom.'

'What cupboard?'

'It hardly shows,' Ben said. 'I only found it a few days ago. It's very narrow and I couldn't get inside. But I didn't see any keys.'

Diana blushed. 'I was so frightened I pressed myself against the back wall. I felt a bump in the wall against the back of my head and found another little cupboard. It was just a small one about a foot square. I felt around in it, in case there was a gun or something hidden there, but all I found was a stupid key.'

Mayne threw back his head and laughed. 'Stupid key. Diana, dear Diana, you've solved a big problem for us, the first part of the puzzle.'

'I have?'

They explained about the strange lock.

'The locksmith forbade us to try to open the cupboard. He's going to do it for us. But he wants us to look for the key *and* some instructions.'

'There wasn't anything else in the cupboard,' she said regretfully.

'But finding the key is an excellent start.' He stretched and yawned. 'I don't know about you others, but I need a nap now and an easy day tomorrow.'

'Diana and I are going into Manchester tomorrow.' Francis looked at her for permission to explain why and when she nodded, he told them about her father's nasty trick, which might have made their marriage invalid.

'He's as bad as our father!' Ben exclaimed. 'Worse! Because yours has a lot of money and he doesn't *need* to behave like that.'

'Ben!' Judith said in a warning tone.'

'Well, he is worse.'

Francis grinned. 'I agree. If we find we have to get married again, Diana and I will buy a special licence and stay in Manchester till we can tie the knot again.'

'I'll have to finish my new skirt before we do that, at least,' Diana said.

'You should probably wash your hair as well.' Judith leaned forward and pulled a cobweb from her hair.

Diana shuddered and jumped up to stare at herself in the mirror, exclaiming in dismay.

Francis smiled. A minute ago, his wife had been slumped beside him in exhaustion. But as usual, a problem with her appearance had got her moving. 'You look beautiful, even with cobwebs,' he said.

'Awww! What a nice thing to say.' Gillian beamed at them both.

Ben opened his mouth to make a sound of disgust, caught his mother's eye, and changed his mind.

'Poor old Daniel,' Victor said. 'He's missed all the fun.'

Mayne shook his head. 'It's probably as well. He's not in a state to be fighting anyone. I'm worried about him.'

'We'll look after him once he joins us,' Judith said quietly.

'I think it's lovely that you all look after one another,'

Diana said thoughtfully. 'My family aren't at all like that. Though my brother's not too bad.'

After a lazy few hours, they all went to bed early, leaving Al and his friends to patrol the grounds, just in case.

'We'll leave early,' Francis said. 'Victor's told me where to go.'

Diana snuggled against him in bed. 'I'm so glad we're getting married again.'

'You'll miss the fancy dress and all the fuss we had last time.'

'No, I won't. I'll have you, and that's what matters most. I *am* growing up, darling. I know I'll never be perfect. I'm not like Judith. But I will do my best to be a good wife.'

'You're the only wife I want. And it'd be tedious to live with someone who was perfect.'

The registry office in Manchester was crowded and they had to queue for over an hour to see someone. When they explained their situation, the woman stared at them in shock, then frowned.

'We'll have to check, of course, but I'm sure it wouldn't have been allowed.'

'What wouldn't?'

'Not doing the paperwork properly.' She leaned forward and said in an undertone, 'I'll deny this if you tell anyone, but during the war, things were a bit chaotic, with people rushing in to get married, then rushing out again. If they forgot to sign something or filled in a form wrongly, well, we did it for them. And though no one told the managers what we were doing, I think they knew.'

Francis was surprised. 'Why would you do that?'

'A lot of these people were fighting for us, so we did

whatever we could for them. We *all* tried to do our bit, you know.' She looked at them warily.

'How do we find out whether we're married, then?'

'I'll have to make a phone call.' She glanced at the clock. 'Could you come back later? Give me two hours, because they'll have to check the paperwork. Where did you say you got married?'

They gave her the details then went outside into the sunshine and stood looking at one another.

'What next?' he asked at last.

'I hope we *are* married,' she said fiercely. 'And if we are, I'm going to write to my father and tell him.'

'Tempting, but you can't give the people at the registry office away.'

'Oh, rats!'

'So . . . what do you want to do for the next two hours?'
She hesitated.

'Go on. Tell me.'

'I desperately need some underwear. I don't think my father will allow Mummy to send my things on. Could we afford a few bits and pieces, do you think?' She blushed. 'I particularly need knickers.'

'Yes, darling. I can definitely afford to buy you some knickers. I made nearly two hundred pounds from the bits and pieces I salvaged at my parents' place, you know.'

She gaped at him in shock, then smiled. 'So my father was wrong about that too. I shouldn't have believed him so easily, should I? You did tell me you were making money out of it.'

Two hours later, having told the shop assistant Diana had had nearly everything she owned stolen, they were allowed to buy her two of everything without coupons.

'It's not enough, is it?' Francis asked.

'I'll manage. There are things in the attic at Esherwood I can alter.'

'Good girl. Now, are you ready to face the registry office again?'

'Yes.'

The train pulled into Rivenshaw in the early evening and they smiled at one another as they got out.

Diana couldn't hold back a weary sigh as she checked that she had all the parcels and joined Francis on the platform.

'I'm tired. We'll splurge on a taxi, eh?' he said.

'Yes, please. I'm absolutely exhausted now.'

They didn't say much on the short journey to Esherwood, but they held hands the whole way.

When the taxi drew up behind the house, there was just a low light in the kitchen. Ben must have heard the taxi because he opened the back door and took the parcels from Diana.

'Everyone's in the small sitting room.'

'All right.'

'I'll take your parcels up and put them on your bed, shall I?'

'Just put them on the stairs. I'll take them up myself once we've said hello,' Diana replied. 'I'm too tired to stand upright.'

But when they opened the door to the sitting room, they found it brightly lit, with bottles of wine on the table, and a neat row of glasses. Someone had baked a cake, and Jan and Helen were there, together with Miss Peters.

Everyone yelled, 'Congratulations!'

Diana stared open-mouthed. 'How did you know?'

'Someone phoned us from the registry office, a very nice woman who said Mr Brady wanted to surprise his wife.'

Tears were trickling down Diana's cheeks, but they were

tears of happiness. She kept repeating, 'Oh, how wonderful. Oh, you are so kind.'

'Here.' Mayne thrust a glass of wine into her hand and Victor continued to fill the other glasses.

Then someone yelled, 'Speech!' and there was a great deal of shushing.

'Tell us exactly what you found out,' Judith urged.

'It turned out that someone had "corrected" the error my father had deliberately made and we really are married.'

'I have written a small speech,' Mayne began.

The hooting and yelling for a toast stopped the speech in its tracks.

'Very well, we'll just offer a toast to the bride and groom,' Mayne said. 'Here's to long life and happiness for you both!'

They all raised their glasses.

'Now can we cut the cake?' Betty begged.

'Indeed we can. Mrs Brady, will you and your husband do your duty to this cake?'

Together they thrust a knife into it, then let Judith take over dividing it up.

After they'd eaten, Gillian put on a record and as they had before, the whole group got up to dance. Somehow Betty persuaded them into a conga, and the line of people wound round the kitchen and out into the hall.

'Are you still tired?' Francis yelled into his wife's ear.

'Not at all.'

Later that night, Mayne and Judith lay talking in bed. 'We've got a lot to sort out still,' he worried.

'We can't kill all the dragons at once. I think things are going well and I'm sure we'll find the instructions for that lock.'

'I dare say we shall.'

'There's only Daniel to come back now, then you four will all be together again,' she said softly.

'He'll come when he's ready.'

'Didn't Diana look pretty? Even if she didn't have a fancy dress to wear for her second wedding celebration.'

'That woman would look pretty in a sack. But not as beautiful as you do in the moonlight tonight.'

Which put an end to the conversation.

ABOUT THE AUTHOR

Anna Jacobs grew up in Lancashire and emigrated to Australia, but she returns each year to the UK to see her family and do research, something she loves. She is addicted to writing and she figures she'll have to live to be 120 at least to tell all the stories that keep popping up in her imagination and nagging her to write them down. She's also addicted to her own hero, to whom she's been happily married for many years.

CONTACT ANNA

Anna is always delighted to hear from readers and can be contacted via the internet.

Anna has her own web page, with details of her books, some behind-the-scenes information that is available nowhere else and the first chapters of her books to try out, as well as a picture gallery. You can also buy some of her ebooks from the 'shop' on the web page. Go to:
www.annajacobs.com

Anna can be contacted by email at
anna@annajacobs.com

You can also find Anna on Facebook at
www.facebook.com/AnnaJacobsBooks

If you'd like to receive an email newsletter about Anna and her books every month or two, you are cordially invited to join her announcements list. Just email her and ask to be added to the list, or follow the link from her web page.

RY 06/16.